Praise for
False Positi[ve]

"With futuristic technology, front-page ethica[l ...] ing view inside of today's medicine, *False Positive* grabs your imagi[na]tion and won't let go. You won't be able to put it down."

— DAVID STEVENS, M.D., *executive director,*
Christian Medical Association

"The authors boldly address some of the ethical issues facing those who embrace the sanctity of human life. Their intimate knowledge of science and the redemption of Jesus Christ intertwine to create a captivating novel. This is truly a fascinating and challenging read!"

— DARLENE NORBERG, *executive director,*
Dallas Pregnancy Resource Center

"This is a valuable book that takes the reader to the heart of ethical issues that are too often hidden in euphemism. The excitement and intensity of the medical situations are true to life, and the emotional consequences are played out poignantly and accurately. Bill Cutrer and Sandra Glahn are writers of integrity and faith who have firsthand experience on the front line in the fight for life."

— STEVEN A. HARRIS, M.D., *obstetrician and gynecologist,*
Dallas, Texas

"This book brings the struggle between life and death into vivid reality. Dr. Cutrer and Ms. Glahn accurately portray the struggles and triumphs of working in a crisis-pregnancy center."

— *the staff at A Woman's Choice Resource Center,*
Louisville, Kentucky

ALSO BY THE AUTHORS:

FICTION

Lethal Harvest

Deadly Cure

NONFICTION

*When Empty Arms Become a Heavy Burden:
Encouragement for Couples Facing Infertility*

Sexual Intimacy in Marriage

FALSE
POSITIVE

WILLIAM CUTRER, M.D.
SANDRA GLAHN

WATERBROOK
PRESS

FALSE POSITIVE
PUBLISHED BY WATERBROOK PRESS
2375 Telstar Drive, Suite 160
Colorado Springs, Colorado 80920
A division of Random House, Inc.

ISBN 1-57856-567-7

Library of Congress Cataloging-in-Publication Data
Cutrer, William, 1951-
    False positive / William Cutrer.
        p. cm.
    ISBN 1-57856-567-7
    1. Pro-life movement—Fiction. 2. Medical students—Fiction. 3. Dallas (Tex.)—
Fiction. 4. Abortion—Fiction. I. Title.
    PS3553.U848 F35 2002
    813'.54—dc21

                                                                2002003718

Printed in the United States of America
2002—First Edition

10 9 8 7 6 5 4 3 2 1

To all who have stood at the crossroads

*And for the clinics, physicians, and counselors on the front lines,
defending life at its earliest stages*

————————

Speak up for those who cannot speak for themselves.

PROVERBS 31:8

Acknowledgments

In this our fifth collaborative work—and our third work of fiction—we have endeavored to write an engaging drama set in the context of real-life ethical dilemmas. The rapid advance of scientific knowledge and the legalities of research relating to life and death, love and loss, have enormous ramifications that require our careful consideration.

We are grateful to our families, who have once again given generously of their time and support. Thanks to Jane Cutrer and Jennie Snow for careful editing. Also, thanks to Gary Glahn, Dan Clements, and Kelly North, who have freely provided invaluable advice on legal aspects of the story. Any procedural weaknesses in this work are ours, not theirs. Our special gratitude and admiration go to the staff at A Woman's Choice Resource Center of Louisville and the Dallas Pregnancy Resource Center. We're thankful too for Erin Healy, who has encouraged us in this project from the start, and for our excellent editor, Karen Ball. We also appreciate Kelley Mathews's, Alison Mullins's, and Kathy Rhine's attention to detail on our behalf.

While we have created a fictional plot and characters in *False Positive,* we have based most of the medical cases in this work on real-life events that we have either seen firsthand or heard about from the very patients who experienced them. With their permission, we have drawn from their stories.

While we've patterned most of the techniques portrayed in this story after existing medical technology, some of the more dramatic procedures exist only in the imaginations of those who long for better capabilities to support tiny human lives. The medical information in this work is not intended to substitute for qualified, individualized medical advice.

PROLOGUE

Early December

"It hurts! Gimme somethin' for the pain! I got to have somethin'—*Ow!*"

Red Richison clutched his stethoscope and trotted toward the sound of yelling. Wheeling into the room, he found a patient writhing on the bed.

"Oh, Doc!" She clawed at the pillow, then let out a scream.

Red turned to the nurse. "Get her some Stadol, two milligrams IV push."

The patient cried out again, then spit out several expletives. "Oh, Mama! *Mama!* It hurts bad!"

Red looked around for the girl's mother, but the nurse shook her head.

"She came alone."

Red nodded. *Just like most teen mothers I've seen here in the past year—crying for Mom, not for her man. So sad.* He stood over the laboring girl.

"Are you the one who called to tell me your water broke?"

She groaned and nodded. "Uh-huh, that was me." When she groaned again, the nurse gave her the IV medication.

Red sat on the side of the bed and laid his hand on her abdomen to assess the uterine size. Then he spoke in a soothing voice. "Why'd you wait so long to come in? What was that—three, four hours ago?"

"Yeah. And I kept calling the clinic, but nobody answered. I didn't have a ride."

What clinic? Wish I'd known. I could've suggested a cab.

"Doc, it *hurts!*"

"Hang on. You'll feel better real soon. Now I need to ask you some questions and take a look, okay?"

She screamed again and gripped the sheets.

"All right. Give it another minute or two and the medicine will kick in. I promise."

Red rested a hand on her shoulder. She nodded and wiped sweat from her brow.

"That doctor put in the seaweed yesterday." She panted. "Then I started leaking. It wasn't supposed to happen this fast. He said to come back Monday or Tuesday."

Red stared into her eyes. "What? What doctor?"

"The one at the clinic."

"The hospital clinic?"

"No! The abortion clinic. It was, like, Dr. Orion or something."

"Oh." *No way! Not the VIP clinic!* Red turned to the nurse. "Call Dr. Ophion. And up the dosage of Stadol. Let's get her comfortable." There was nothing they could do for the baby anyway.

Red did an exam and found a lone foot dangling at the vaginal opening. The patient was dilated to about four centimeters with a footling breech, and he guessed she was about fourteen weeks pregnant— months from viability. *Not even big enough to call a stillbirth.*

"I can feel it!" The patient screamed again. "It's comin'! Oòooh! It wasn't…supposed…to be like this." She panted, then pushed. *"Ugh!* He said…it wouldn't hurt."

"Doctor, the other leg has come through," the nurse said.

"Let's take her to delivery." Red wanted good lighting in case he ran into trouble with the placenta. They wouldn't need the fetal monitors— no need for heroics.

By the time everything was set up, the sedation had taken over and the patient lay mumbling. She pushed a time or two, and Red delivered the body out to the head. He detected no pulse at the umbilical cord. A moment later, he guided the tiny head out of the birth canal.

Red gazed at the Barbie doll–size child, another tiny victim of abortion, and suddenly his throat constricted. *She's perfect.* He glanced at the mother's eyes, expecting to find some acknowledgment of her child's beauty, but she didn't seem to care. "The baby is here, and it's a girl." He cleared his throat. "I'm so sorry that she didn't make it. Would you like to hold her?"

The girl grunted and managed an emphatic no.

Red wrapped the baby in a blanket and handed her to the nurse. She set the child in the warmer, then turned to do paperwork while Red handled the placental delivery, cleaned up the patient, and took her to recovery. As he worked, one persistent thought kept bothering him like a paper cut. *How can people so devalue life?*

Red was working to make the patient comfortable when he heard a voice behind him. "Dr. Richison?" Looking up, he saw the nurse standing in the doorway, motioning for him to return to the delivery room.

"What is it?" He followed her as she walked over to the warmer and pulled back the blanket. Red was taken aback. The baby lay gasping for air.

She's alive! Red stared. *I was sure she wasn't breathing—probably depressed by the narcotic.* He shook his head at the futility of the child's desperate effort to get oxygen. *I have nothing to offer her. She's too small. She'll die in minutes.*

He turned to the nurse, a woman with many years' experience compared to his one year of OB residency and mere months of hands-on training. "What do you usually do in these situations?"

"We just leave them for a while or put them in formalin and take them to the lab once they quit."

Red nodded.

The nurse shrugged, got a small basin of formalin—the liquid used to transport tissue specimens to the lab—and submerged the gasping baby. Then she returned to her charting duties.

Red stood frozen, staring at the tiny infant under the fluid, watching as she struggled to breathe. *I can't believe this.* A wave of nausea washed over him. Of course the infant would die in minutes, even without the fluid. But still…

I can't believe I just let the nurse do that! He turned out the lights so the only illumination came from the hallway. After reaching a trembling hand toward the nearest chair, he pulled it up and sat down. Resting his chin in his hands, he stared at the child in the small plastic basin. The infant's chest heaved as she struggled. *What's taking so long? What have I done?*

"Well, I see I'm too late for the delivery."

The words jarred Red out of his thoughts. He looked up to see Dr. Ophion leaning against the doorway. Red glanced at the child, then back at Dr. Ophion, and his heart pounded. Now Ophion knew what he had done!

"Where's Dr. Damon? The nurse told me he's the chief OB resident tonight."

"He's here—sleeping. Said not to bother him." He'd told Red that calling for help was a sign of weakness, and Red fought to keep the anger he felt from showing. *Truth is, he just wants a decent night's sleep, probably so he can moonlight at your abortion clinic.*

Dr. Ophion nodded, turned, and headed for the recovery room.

When Red looked back at the infant, she had stopped struggling. Relieved, he rose and stood over her, then whispered a prayer for the infant, grateful that her struggle was over. After lingering a moment, he went and found the nurse and asked her to take the baby down to the lab. Staring at his paper boots as he walked, he headed to recovery to finish the paperwork.

He found Dr. Ophion checking on the patient. When Red took out the girl's chart, he clenched his teeth when he noticed that Dr. Ophion had already made some notations. Not only had he signed off as the attending physician, but he had also changed the age of the baby from fourteen weeks to twenty.

When Dr. Ophion exited, Red followed and caught up with him. "Excuse me!"

The doctor stopped and turned. "Yes? You need something?"

"I'm sorry, Dr. Ophion, but that child was barely fifteen weeks, if that."

The senior physician smiled. "Eighteen weeks is the Medicaid cut-off. If the baby's older than that, we get better reimbursement."

"But…" Red hesitated. *You just falsified the record.* On the heels of that thought came another: *But could I prove it?*

"Don't worry. The reimbursements are so low, we all have to stretch it to make ends meet, or these patients couldn't even *get* medical care." He smiled, looking for all the world as though they were discussing their holiday plans or where to have lunch. "Hey, are you one of the residents who'll be helping at our clinic?" His expression was open and friendly, and it took all of Red's control not to curl his lip at the suggestion that he might perform elective abortions.

Red swallowed hard. "Uh, no. Actually, I'm opposed to abortion."

Dr. Ophion smirked. "Really?"

Red nodded, though the movement felt stiff. "I'm generally pro-life."

"I see." Dr. Ophion glanced toward the room where Red had watched that futile struggle for life, then back to him. The mockery in the older doctor's eyes matched the sarcasm in his words: "Yes, and it certainly looked that way."

With that, Ophion turned and strutted out the door.

ONE

"Heaney clamp!" Dr. Dalmuth Kedar reached toward the scrub nurse.

She whirled around and barked an order to the circulating nurse. "Open a hyst set! I don't have the Heaney's up."

"We're doing a hysterectomy?" Red stared at the surgeon, who stood hunched over the patient. *But she's so young.*

Dr. Kedar nodded and turned toward the circulating nurse. "Blot me, please."

The nurse came over and wiped the perspiration from his forehead and around his eyes. Then the surgeon turned his attention back to Red and lowered his voice. "We can't save the uterus; the damage is too extensive. I can't believe this." His eyes burned from behind his face mask. "They not only perforated it, they also destroyed all the blood vessels on this side. No wonder she was in shock when she hit the ER. Have you ever first-assisted a hyst?"

"No. But I scrubbed in on a bunch last year as an intern, and I'm ready to learn." Red had stood by for the past twenty minutes, sweating from the stress as the patient in shock seemed intent on bleeding to death. *Training on an emergency hyst with the head of MFM and chief of residents… How lucky can I get? Hope I don't blow it.*

Their eyes met, and Dr. Kedar nodded. "All right then. We can do it. No need for another resident, right, Dr. Richison?"

Red gave the thumbs-up and Dr. Kedar nodded again.

"It *is* Richison, is it not?"

"Yes. Red Richison. Red's a nickname." *Seems like this has already taken hours.* Red glanced at the clock. *11:43.*

The circulating nurse came through the OR door carrying the

wrapped instrument set, which she proceeded to open and slide onto the OR table using sterile technique.

"You saw the patient in the ER, correct?" Dr. Kedar asked Red.

"Yes sir."

"And you say she was already in shock when she got here?"

"Yes sir. We'd had a call from the megavolume abortion center—the one everyone calls VIP—alerting the ER that a *complication* was on the way. The patient came in around eleven, shocky and bleeding profusely per vaginum. She already had one IV running, and we started a second one—large bore, full throttle. Then I set up for the laparotomy and had you paged. I assumed we'd need at least an exam under anesthesia. Blood was pouring out fast. Bright red, so it was arterial. And I knew we didn't have much time." *Glad we got some of the bleeding stopped. I thought she was going to die—and she still might.*

"H'm. Good call. How old is she?"

"Seventeen."

Dr. Kedar shook his head. "Tragic." He leaned over the anesthesiologist's screen to glance at the patient's face. Then he shook his head again and looked back at Red. "She has a pool of blood collecting just under the surface and to the side of the uterus. I have isolated the blood supply and clamped off the bleeders, but I found enormous damage to both the uterine artery and vein."

Red noticed Dr. Kedar's somewhat formal speech patterns and wondered how many years it had been since he'd left India.

"It must have been done with the suction curette or uterine sound." Dr. Kedar pointed to a specific spot with his tissue forceps. "I have clamped off these traumatic injuries to the side of the uterus, and we can probably get her stabilized. But there is no way to prevent infection; we have to remove the uterus."

Red stared at the doctor, noticing how he exuded calm while blood spilled everywhere.

"She's only seventeen, sir."

Dr. Kedar nodded and set back to work. "Yes, but the ovaries are undamaged, so she will still have some opportunity with the reproductive technologies available. She will need a surrogate though."

Red turned to mimic Dr. Kedar's surgical steps as he himself worked on the undamaged side of the uterus. They methodically made their way down the uterine supporting ligaments—clamping, cutting, tying, and double tying—until they reached the top of the vagina. Red looked at the clock again. *12:14.* They made an incision and removed the damaged organ.

Dr. Kedar sighed. "She was probably only twelve weeks along."

"Yes sir. The chart they sent from the clinic said 'voluntary interruption of pregnancy, ten to twelve weeks.'"

"Another VIP from VIP," Dr. Kedar muttered. "It seems as though every time I am on ER walk-in call, we get some catastrophe from that place. I thought our own residents helped staff it."

"They do. Along with several other ob-gyn programs in the city." Red tensed his jaw. *And I'd love to see it shut down.*

"Well, you need to call the guy who did this and tell him—or her— how it all turned out. I am certain they will be hearing more about this, probably from the friendly legal eagles."

"Okay. You think whoever did it will get sued?"

Dr. Kedar stopped in the middle of a stitch and looked up. "A seventeen-year-old woman goes for an abortion and winds up nearly bleeding to death. Then she leaves the hospital without a uterus." He lowered his voice. "We'll all get sued."

Bethany Fabrizio pulled her silver Mercedes SLK into the space that bore her name in the parking lot of Women's Choice Clinic. She clicked off the Chopin CD, turned off the car, and then slid on her new two-tone pumps. Her flight from Reno to Dallas had been late. Bethany took a deep breath. *No problem.*

After applying fresh lipstick, she blotted her lips and smiled at her reflection. Then she tucked a shoulder-length strand of dark hair behind her ear and stepped out of the car. Smoothing the wrinkles in her skirt as she walked, she hustled her petite frame up the walk into the one-story building.

Once past the children's play area and the waiting room decorated with floral prints, she went behind the front desk and pulled the contents out of her in-box.

"Afternoon, Bethany." Her assistant, Margaret, smiled. "Welcome home."

"Hey! Thanks."

"Got a client waiting for you."

Bethany looked around at the empty reception area.

"She's in the rest room. How was the trip?"

"Great, other than the flight making me late."

Margaret waved it off and handed her a chart. "No problem. We've got you covered. Was it a receptive crowd?"

Bethany nodded. "We managed to raise enough funds to get the clinic there started, at least."

"Great!"

Bethany fell silent as she studied the chart. *Oh no.* Her happiness of just a moment ago faded to concern.

Margaret lowered her voice. "Yeah, she's abortion minded."

Having concluded the operation, Dr. Kedar and Red steered their patient's bed toward the recovery room. Red exhaled his relief at having done his part without embarrassing himself, but he couldn't stop thinking about getting sued. He looked up to see the senior physician's eyes fixed on him, and he realized Dr. Kedar had asked him a question. "Excuse me?"

"Does she have any friends or family?" Dr. Kedar motioned his head toward the patient. "Who brought her?"

"They buzzed her over here from the clinic by ambulance, but I'm pretty sure I saw someone with her. Maybe a sister or a friend."

Dr. Kedar pursed his lips. "We need to notify her family and see if we can obtain some additional medical history."

Red hesitated. "Should we have done that when she got here, since she's a minor?"

"No. Since she was pregnant, the law considers her able to give consent both for the abortion and for treatment of complications."

"I see." Red hesitated. "Doctor, is the hospital at less legal risk if she recovers well?"

Dr. Kedar shook his head. "Actually, when the patient dies, the malpractice exposure is limited—less than if she lives and has long-term problems."

"But we did everything right. We saved her life!"

"Unfortunately, malpractice is rarely about right and wrong. It is mostly about money, and in whose pockets most of it ends up. And, just so you know, ob-gyn is a popular target for malpractice lawyers."

Red swallowed hard. After they got to the recovery room, Red wrote the orders and overheard Dr. Kedar calling his office.

"How many waiting patients? No emergencies? I see. Thank you. I appreciate your work to reschedule everyone. No doubt that was a challenging task."

Red continued to listen as Dr. Kedar spoke to his office assistant. *Nice guy. Treats the staff with respect. No wonder everybody wants to work with him.*

Dr. Kedar hung up and turned to face Red, then smiled broadly. "It looks like they have cleared my schedule. I have no patients until two this afternoon. Would you care to join me for lunch in the doctors' café?"

"Sure! But shall I first dictate the operative note?"

"Certainly, if you wish."

Red fumbled. "I…uh…I've never dictated that type of procedure, and I'll need to get help from one of the upper-class residents to—"

Dr. Kedar shook his head. "Unnecessary." He leaned toward Red. "As I told you, there is a good chance this case will end up in court. Let me do it, and you can just listen in, okay?"

More than okay. "If you don't mind…yeah…that would be great."

Dr. Kedar picked up the phone and called in his name and physician code number followed by, "Ms. DeVeer, seventeen-year-old, African-American female, twelve weeks' gestation, elective abortion…"

Red listened as Dr. Kedar rattled off the vital information about the procedure they'd just performed.

"Vitals are stable," the recovery-room nurse assigned to the patient told the doctors. "Pulse 90; BP 110 over 70; sixth unit of blood infusing.

We sent a crit to check the blood count, urine output looks good, dressing is dry and intact, minimal bleeding from the vagina."

"Thank you, Cynthia," Dr. Kedar said. "Do not hesitate to page me if you need me. And when the patient is more lucid, will you please let her know that Dr. Richison here will be back to see her later?"

The patient stirred, and Red caught a whiff of her honeysuckle fragrance—the same stuff his sister used for dress-up when she was a kid. *How am I going to tell this girl that her uterus is gone?*

Whoever had done this to her needed to be held responsible.

"Good morning, Ms. Spencer." Bethany extended her hand to greet the teenager as she emerged from the rest room.

"It's Dawn—my name's Dawn." She stood.

"Hi, Dawn. I'm Bethany Fabrizio. Pleased to meet you. Would you like to come back to my office?"

Dawn shrugged and shuffled down the hall. Upon entering the office, she plopped down on the sofa, tucking a blue-jeaned leg under her. She wore high-top tennis shoes and a wrinkled white T-shirt with a juice stain on it. A plain girl, she was a little overweight, and her chin-length brown hair needed attention. Her nails sparkled with blue glitter paint.

"Would you like something to drink? We've got decaffeinated stuff so you don't have to worry about harming the baby."

Dawn spoke just above a whisper. "Sure."

"Ginger ale? Sprite? Caffeine-free Coke?"

"Coke."

"Okay, just a sec." Bethany stepped out. *Lord, make me an instrument of your peace.* She walked down to the boardroom, took a Coke from the refrigerator, and returned with the drink. She handed it to Dawn and sat in a high-backed chair facing her. "So how far along do you think you are in this pregnancy?"

Dawn took a sip and shifted her weight. "I'm three weeks late."

"Have you already had a pregnancy test? If not, we can do one for you."

"No. I just told my boyfriend I was late, and he said to take care of it." She turned her face away. "He said…said that it probably wasn't his *anyway.*" She wiped a tear with the back of a dirty hand.

Bethany moved forward. As she gently touched Dawn's arm, she smelled cigarettes. "I'm sorry he isn't being more help. Maybe he's just scared and he'll come around later. Have you been dating long?"

Dawn nodded. "Yeah. We've been together almost three months now."

"Ah, I see."

"He had been so…so good to me." Suddenly the tears erupted into a sob. "Well, he was just *mean* about this."

"I'm sorry. Young men often don't know what to say or how to react in situations like this."

Dawn cursed and looked out the window, then back at Bethany. "Did you say your last name's Fabrizio?"

Bethany blinked, momentarily taken aback at this departure. "Yes. Why?"

"My boyfriend's next-door neighbor has the same last name."

"Interesting. H'm. Well, may I—"

"Think you might be related?"

Bethany shook her head. "I don't have any relatives in the Dallas area."

"Oh." Dawn fell quiet again.

She's stalling. Bethany sat on the edge of her seat, her heart already moved by the poor girl's plight. "May I ask you a few questions? They're sort of medical. They'll help us to figure this out."

Dawn nodded and grabbed a tissue from the box on the coffee table. She dabbed her eyes and blew her nose hard.

Bethany reached over for her clipboard, which already had a Client Intake Sheet fastened to it. She looked down at the form and then began. "All right, may I have your full name?"

"April Dawn Spencer."

"And your age?"

"Eighteen…and three months. My birthday was in April, on the ninth."

Bethany nodded as she wrote, mentally subtracting eighteen from the current year to get the year of birth. "And your address?"

Dawn's eyes grew wide. "You're not gonna tell my family, are you?"

Bethany shook her head. "We'll tell your family only if you ask us to. And we don't need your address if you'd prefer not to give it."

"I'd rather not. My mom and stepdad would kill me if they was to find out."

"No problem. All right then, when was your last period?"

"I think it was in the middle of May. It was a little lighter than usual, but it was pretty normal."

"Are your periods regular?"

Dawn nodded. "Oh yeah. Usually, about thirty days apart." She relaxed the death grip on her Kleenex. "It flows for three or four days."

"Are you using any birth control?"

"We used condoms…uh…*most* of the time…"

"Okay. And are you having any pregnancy symptoms—like nausea or vomiting? Tender breasts? Getting up at night to go to the bathroom?"

"Yeah, all those." Dawn rubbed her stomach. "I'm queasy, but not just in the mornings. And lately my bra don't fit so good."

"Okay, let me ask you some medical history questions, if I may."

Dawn nodded.

"Are you on any medicines?"

She shook her head.

"Any history of problems with blood pressure or diabetes?"

"No."

Bethany knew it was unlikely that an eighteen-year-old would answer yes to any of these, but she asked as much to keep conversation flowing and build rapport as she did to gain needed information.

"Have you ever had a sexually transmitted disease?"

Dawn cast her gaze upward. "No way! Brad is the only one I've ever…you know, been with. He loves me and I love him…though we're not talking right now."

"Okay." *I wonder how* he'd *answer that question.* "All right. So this is the first time you've been pregnant?"

"Of course. I am…I've only been…him and me, we've been together three months, and, like I said, he's the first."

Bethany picked up an obstetrics wheel and subtracted from July to Dawn's last period. *Looks like she's about seven weeks along.* She looked up at Dawn and smiled. "Let's find out for sure what we've got. We'll need a urine specimen so we can run a pregnancy test. And then if you'd like, we can do a sonogram and show you your baby. It's still pretty early, but we have this special machine that lets us see right into your belly using sound waves."

Dawn smiled and pulled the locket on her necklace back and forth. "Yeah, my cousin had a baby, and she had the sono pictures. They were cool!" She stopped and leaned in toward Bethany. "But I don't have much money. How much does it cost?"

"Nothing. Our services are free. We just want to help you—to find out what's going on and get you the best care we can."

"And abortion. I've heard there are some pills I can take…"

"We don't prescribe those. So right now let's get all the information we can, and then we can help you decide what's best for you and your baby."

"Okay."

"C'mon. Let's get you a pregnancy test." Bethany guided the girl back to the rest room, where she handed her a specimen cup.

"I just went," Dawn complained.

"We don't need much."

Afterward, while Dawn and Bethany waited for the test results, they went into a conference room. Bethany picked up a videotape, slid it into the VCR, and hit Play. "This will give you some information about the process and procedures. And it'll help you understand what you see on the sonogram if you decide you want us to do one."

"Okay." Dawn sat back and clicked her nails together while Bethany cued up the tape.

While Dawn watched the video, Bethany left to check on her test results. They were as Bethany suspected. She waited until she heard the tape stop and then entered the room again. Sitting down across from Dawn, she touched her arm.

"Your test is positive."

TWO

Red and Dr. Kedar walked in comfortable silence to the doctors' café. They made their way through the food line, and Red ordered a burger and fries, while Dr. Kedar opted for a more healthy pita sandwich with tabbouleh.

When Red reached for his wallet, Dr. Kedar shook his head.

"Please. Allow me." He handed the cashier his dining card, which she scanned and returned to him. Then he led the way out of the busy dining room to an adjacent, smaller, carpeted room with a few round tables. The only noise was the television news, which the few doctors present ignored.

Red and Dr. Kedar took their seats, and the senior surgeon was the first to speak. "You have good hands. Steady. Unshakable. You did a nice job under duress."

Red smiled. "Thank you, Doctor. It was an honor to assist you— you were amazing." Red had worked with Dr. Kedar a few times the previous year as an intern in high-risk obstetrics, but this was their first time to operate together under emergency conditions. "Is this common? To have to remove the uterus on such a young patient?"

"Fortunately, no, but complicated abortions can sometimes go this way."

Red leaned closer and focused intently on Dr. Kedar. "May I ask you something else?"

"Certainly."

"When you got control of the bleeding on the damaged side, why couldn't we leave in the uterus?

"Ah, good question, and I appreciate your waiting until now, when we have privacy, to ask it."

Red looked down at his tray, realizing this inquiry might be taken as questioning the judgment of one of the top staff physicians. "N-no,

I know you had good reason. I just want to know how you made the decision, if you don't mind."

Dr. Kedar put his elbows on the table and clasped his hands together. "I do not mind at all. I meant it when I said it was a good question. And you are correct. When I was able to stop the bleeding, it became clear that the blood supply to the uterus was reasonable, but I could see through the perforation that they had not completed the abortion procedure." Dr. Kedar took a bite of his sandwich, and then glanced up at Red before continuing. "The tissue was most assuredly infected, having been instrumented at the clinic, and then probably contaminated by your exam in the ER."

Red gulped. "You mean I made things worse?"

"Oh no. Do not worry. The situation was grave when you took the case. You had to make a proper diagnosis. But to leave the uterus in along with the gestational tissue…well, she would have continued to bleed and get infected. As you know, there is no way to treat that kind of infection. And it would have spread."

"Pelvic inflammatory disease?" Red shook his head.

"Right. She would have gotten septic, in my opinion, requiring reoperation. It is impossible to do a D and C after the repair in the uterine sidewall, so she probably would have lost her ovaries as well. Then we would have had a seventeen-year-old who was not only sterile, but requiring total hormonal replacement all her life."

Red shook his head.

"Yes, at times we must make difficult decisions. At least this way, she will make her own hormones and still produce her own eggs. It was the best solution in a bad situation."

Red nodded, struck by all the young woman had lost. If only she hadn't gone to the clinic…

"You did a good job assisting. Where did you get your training?"

"Premed?"

"All of it."

"Undergrad, I went to Hardin-Simmons. A private school in Abilene—Texas, not Kansas." Red wondered where Dr. Kedar got his training, then remembered it was at USC. *The guy's a regular Einstein, even if he never gets Aggie jokes.*

"And after that?"

"I worked five years in biomedical engineering."

"Really?" Dr. Kedar put his fork down, folded his hands, and leaned forward. "Tell me what you did."

"We designed equipment for rapid analysis of blood chemistry."

Dr. Kedar grinned. "Then I *have* to show you my lab sometime! I will put those skills to work. But how did you go from engineering to med school?"

"Loved the lab work, but I wanted the people contact. So I went to Baylor-Houston."

"Very good. A fine program there. I have consulted with some of their staff at our specialty meetings. And in your free time—as if you had any—any hobbies?"

Red laughed. "Here and there I manage to grab a second or two. I can usually be found polishing my MGB roadster and playing golf."

"Oh yes, I believe I heard that about you." Dr. Kedar's face lit up again, and when he leaned back, Red had the impression he was being reassessed through new, more positive eyes. After Kedar grilled Red for a few minutes about his golf handicap, he pressed his fingertips together. "We should play sometime. Golf is my permissible vice. It is a humbling game but my favorite escape."

"I'd love that." Red tried not to sound overly enthusiastic. "But I'd heard chess was your deal, not golf."

Dr. Kedar beamed. He lowered his eyes, then looked back up. "I do love a good chess match. But golf is…my obsession."

"Dr. Kedar!"

Red looked to find another physician approaching their table, and Dr. Kedar stood to greet him, grabbing both of his hands and giving a slight bow.

"Dr. Josephson, meet Dr. Richison." Dr. Kedar gestured as he made the introductions. "Red, Dr. Josephson is a specialist in infertility."

Red started to stand, but Dr. Josephson said, "That's okay. Keep your seat. Nice to meet you." Then he turned back to Dr. Kedar. "I saw that endo story your wife did. Tell her she did a great job."

"Certainly, I will do that. She will be so pleased that you liked it."

Red watched Dr. Kedar as the two physicians talked. He gauged the man's age to be somewhere between forty-five and fifty. A tall, prim man, Dr. Kedar spoke flawless English.

When Dr. Josephson departed, Dr. Kedar sat back down. "My wife is an anchor for the ABC local news affiliate. She just did a story on endometriosis."

"Yeah?" Red suddenly made the connection. "Your wife's Yvonne Kedar, on the news?"

"Yes."

"Hey, she's great. And beautiful!" Red caught himself. "I'm sorry, but she really is stunning."

Dr. Kedar chuckled. "There is no need to apologize. She is also a wonderful person—a great wit and a captivating speaker. But your vision is clear." He took another bite and then looked at Red. "You did well today. You can operate with me anytime. And if you ever get a free moment, come on over to my office, and we will let you test your skills on our sonogram equipment."

Red welcomed this opportunity. After all, what could be better? Not only would he have the chance to hobnob with the OB chief of service, but he'd get to try out *the* state-of-the-art equipment.

As Dr. Kedar headed back to his office, Red made his way back to recovery to check on their patient. As his mind returned to her, his stomach knotted at the prospect of a lawsuit.

He drew a calming breath. *I need to call the VIP Clinic...and I sure hope Dr. Kedar was wrong about getting sued.*

After the sonogram Bethany led Dawn back to her office and sat across from her.

Dawn's hands shook as she stared at the pictures she held. Then she looked up at Bethany. "I didn't expect it to look so much like a baby."

"We want to assist you in any way we can."

"And I didn't expect to see a beating heart." Dawn's voice trembled. "I thought it would be just a black blob."

Bethany nodded and reached out to squeeze Dawn's hand.

"I don't know what to do. I'm only seven weeks pregnant, and there's already a heartbeat..."

"We can help you with medical care for your baby, give you maternity clothes as you need them. We've got a job assistance program and financial aid; we can help you tell your parents…"

"What about abortion?"

"We don't do abortions here, but we'll stand by you throughout the pregnancy."

Dawn sighed. She looked back at the sono pictures. "Maybe…maybe if I show these to Brad, he'll change his mind. But probably if I have this baby, he'd take off. And I don't think I could give up my baby."

"That would be hard. But no matter what he does, Dawn, we're here. *I'm* here for you and your baby." *It's sad how many clients think abortion is less painful than adoption. If they only knew what I do about the lifetime of regret.* Bethany handed Dawn a business card. "Here's my name and number. Call me with questions anytime. My home number is on there too. Can we plan to talk again next week?"

Dawn looked up at Bethany. "I thought this was an abortion place. When I called, they said it was on this street."

"There's an abortion clinic down the street a ways." Bethany pointed toward the window in her office that overlooked the sidewalk.

Dawn studied her in silence, and her eyes welled with tears. "I didn't expect it to be like this." Her fingers tightened on the sono pictures. "I'm gonna have to talk to Brad again."

Each year, during the last week of June, the first-year residents arrived from medical school—and pity the poor patient admitted July 1! With the promotion of each level of resident, a new chief took the reins, and this year Dorie Chambers was the obstetrical chief resident. One of her perks was arranging all the residents' night-call schedules. By controlling the duty calendar, she could choose for herself the hours that best fit her schedule and which weekends she wanted off. The residents—who knew little but were anxious to please—received relatively low wages and generally had huge debts, so most moonlighted in ERs or assisted in surgery, scrubbing in as paid assistants.

At the Center for Reproductive Choice, a nearby clinic, the job of administrative physician had traditionally passed from one OB chief to the next when the presiding chief graduated. Now it was Dorie's turn to take charge of this lucrative opportunity.

Dorie sped around behind the Center to the doctors' reserved parking places. She pulled her car into her newly assigned space. Even though only two other cars sat in the parking lot, she loved the status that came with her new position.

Her normally steady hands quivered as she turned off an old Beatles number blaring in the car. Though she had seen the clinic's director, Dr. Ophion, many times while working shifts at the clinic, she'd never sat down with him to discuss the business. Today they would talk about her new job responsibilities.

Of all the days to have to bring up a perforated uterus.

She had generated about forty thousand dollars in gross income from the clinic the prior year by working two evenings a week and alternate Saturdays. Though uncertain as to the new administrative demands she'd face, she knew the income benefits would more than offset the tougher hours.

She grabbed her briefcase and headed for the back door. After punching in the security code, she walked in. Normally the place bustled—women in the recovery room, more patients in the four operating rooms, and many more in the waiting room. Even with all the activity, patients didn't ordinarily visit with or even glance at each other. Loud background music usually covered the sounds of the machines or what little noise the patients made.

It was too early for patients though. The sun had just begun to rise, casting a golden glow through the tinted windows. Dorie tiptoed down the hall to deaden the sound of her heel clicks reverberating on the linoleum floors. Reaching the side window, she greeted the receptionist at the main desk.

"Hey, Mary Sue. Is Dr. Ophion here?"

"Good morning, Dr. Chambers. Yes, he's here. I'll let him know *you* are." She picked up the phone.

Dorie turned and looked through the large, elegant waiting room toward the operating suites where she had spent many hours. She strained to hear a phone ringing in one of the offices as Mary Sue paged the boss, but the doors and insulation made the place soundproof. She'd hoped for some hint of Dr. Ophion's mood, but no such luck.

Moments later he strode down the hall, a grin on his face, dressed, as always, in a tailored suit and silk tie.

"Dr. Chambers, so good to see you again. You're a bit early."

"Sorry. No traffic, and I came straight from the hospital. I had call last night. It's a little tougher this time of year with the new crop of residents."

"No reason to apologize. I like your efficiency. And you look terrific, not even a little tired. Please join me in my office." Dr. Ophion waved his hand toward the door.

Dorie walked down the familiar hallway to a huge corner room. She'd never actually been inside Ophion's office before. As she entered, she smelled leather and varnish. "Lovely office." She eyed the new paneling, the paintings, and a collection of Dallas Stars hockey memorabilia. Her eyes stopped on a photo of Dr. Ophion in a tuxedo handing a check to a woman in a gown.

"That shot was taken at the Crystal Charity Ball. We try to give back to the community."

Dorie nodded. "And you're a big sports fan?"

"Oh yes. Hockey. I rarely miss a Stars game." He smiled. "We've got season tickets. Someday I hope to be a part owner. Please, sit down."

She sank into the leather couch behind a glass-topped coffee table, and Dr. Ophion pulled up a large wing chair opposite her. "Have you checked with the new second-year residents to see if any of them have any interest in working some shifts here?" He sounded optimistic.

Dorie shook her head. "Not yet. I thought perhaps we should talk more officially about my position and duties before I start recruiting new talent. Besides, I think my entire group will be game. The new third-years who worked last year have already begun hitting me with their shift preferences."

"Good, good. I'm glad to know there's interest."

"Oh yes, plenty of that. You've always taken good care of the residents who work here."

Dr. Ophion studied Dorie, then grinned and pulled a contract off the table. "I need at least two residents every evening, four to eight o'clock, and two or three on Saturdays. Nine to five. Those are the busy times."

"Yes. Some Saturdays I've been here until almost nine o'clock."

Dr. Ophion nodded. "It's good for business. I'll mostly handle administrative details and counsel the patients asking for RU-486."

He seemed to be watching her for a reaction, so Dorie measured her words. "RU-486 hasn't been as popular as we thought it might, has it? How are you expecting that to affect the numbers overall?"

"My thinking is this, get the patients here to the clinic. Some will decide to go the RU-486 route; some won't be good candidates. Some will want to go ahead and do the D and C to get it over with. In any case, more exposure means more numbers. Eventually, I think it'll work to our advantage. In fact we've just worked out an agreement with a nearby pharmacy to provide RU-486 essentially at cost by using them to provide the bulk of our other medications. That way we'll generate good PR, and patients should come see us for the more lucrative problems, such as complications, and they'll refer their friends."

Dorie nodded and smiled. *Remarkable. The stuff could hurt his business, but he's figuring a way for it to actually boost the numbers.*

Dr. Ophion crossed his legs and folded his hands on his knees, an expensive watch peeking out from under his sleeve. "My partner and I do most of the second trimester procedures until the fourth-year residents are up to speed. They're a little riskier, so we like a high level of skill. We usually do them Monday or Tuesday, the lightest clinic days. We can put in the laminaria on Fridays, give the patient a little Prostin gel, and the cervix is usually ready in forty-eight hours or so. Have you had much experience with those?"

"With second-trimester abortions?"

"Right."

Dorie felt most comfortable doing abortions in the first trimester. "No, not much at all. I've seen a few. And a couple of stillbirth deliveries. I have reservations about the partial-birth technique. You do many of those?"

"More and more. The specimens are really in good shape to sell for research. In fact, we sell some of them to Taylor Hospital. Some to the embryology folks, some to Maternal-Fetal Medicine. Pretty much a win-win-win. The mother gets the abortion she needs, docs get good fetal specimens for research, and, of course, it adds to the clinic's bottom line."

"I see."

"Don't worry. I'll walk you through the first couple of procedures. It's a good technique; you'll pick it up in no time."

Dorie shifted her weight.

"And speaking of training, I guess at some point we'll need to discuss the protocol for handling errors," Dr. Ophion told her.

I'm barely on board, and we've already got a disaster. What's he going to think?

She took a deep breath. "Yes, Doctor, and that reminds me. I'm afraid we've already had one."

THREE

Dr. Ophion raised his eyebrows. "Oh? A problem?"

She nodded. "I got a call yesterday from one of my OB residents over at the hospital…uh…"

Dr. Ophion waved his hands, clearly eager for her to get to the point. "Yes?"

"It was about a perforated uterus we sent to them. They had to remove the uterus on a seventeen-year-old. I didn't do the case myself, but it was Denny Damon, one of our fourth-year guys." She held her breath for a response.

Dr. Ophion shrugged. "Oh, that. Yes, I already knew; these things happen. That's why we have good insurance coverage. Listen, I'm sure it makes you nervous, but you can't get too worried about it. Just do your work well, keep good records, and recognize that malpractice premiums are a part of medical practice. We've never yet had to go to court. We have good legal advisors and we settle when appropriate. It's a complicated system, but it works. Besides, many of the women who come here don't have the resources to sue." He handed her the contract he'd been holding. "Here's the deal. You'll get two thousand dollars per month on top of your usual pay scale for actual operating, and you have an office. Let me show you."

Dorie had known the financial remuneration would be good—the outgoing chief had told her not to worry about it—but she had no idea it would be so much.

She followed Dr. Ophion out the door.

He gestured toward an office and motioned for her to enter. "You're next to me. I've had Mary Sue set up your computer with all the appropriate flow charts, dates, and times. You'll need to make out the work schedules, cover all the time slots, and log in all the resident physicians who will be helping us here. The contact numbers for people at the other hospitals in town are there too. Mary Sue or Shelley can take the OR slips daily and keep track of the flow of patients and how many procedures our docs are doing. The main thing for you is to keep people moving through; keep it all running smoothly so we can do high volumes with few hassles."

"All right." Administration was Dorie's strong suit.

"You can use your own password and have a private copy of all these documents. Feel free to use this computer and the Internet connection all you like. Just patch each patient's file into the database so the nurses and secretaries can keep it up to date. I can follow all the cases, numbers, complications, weeks' gestation. I track it all."

The man certainly knows how to make money.

"Please sit down." He gestured toward the high-backed leather chair behind her cherry desk. "I'll leave you here with the contract to read. Just let me know if there's anything you need. Oh! And there's a stocked refrigerator in the right side of the credenza. We will certainly try to make you comfortable—and efficient!"

After Dr. Ophion departed, Dorie sat reading through the contract. *Yes! An extra two grand per month.* She scanned her responsibilities: scheduling shifts, arranging coverage, choosing residents, interviewing, hiring, firing, though Dr. Ophion had the final word. And she had to carry her own malpractice coverage.

All in all, it seemed pretty standard.

She leaned back and drank in the whole atmosphere. *The nicest, busiest abortion clinic in town.* Though advertised as the Center for Reproductive Choice, the residents called it the VIP Clinic: *voluntary interruption of pregnancy*—doctorspeak for *abortion.* The residents who worked there used the acronym to imply the special status they gave to the patients they served. Detractors, on the other hand, made jokes using various interpretations, which ranged from "vastly inferior procedures" to, when referring to Dr. Ophion, "very inflated personality."

None of which mattered. Not any longer. Because Dorie was determined to establish VIP as the premiere facility for women's health services.

Red went to his locker and took out his contacts. They drove him nuts when he'd been up all night. He put on his glasses, and after leaving instructions for the staff to page him if necessary, he headed for the doctors' café for breakfast. When he arrived, he looked across the crowd of residents and early-bird surgeons, most of whom were an hour early for their 7:30 start times. The only faces he recognized were the usual single physicians who came daily for breakfast, none of whose company particularly interested him. He carried his tray to the food counter, ordered scrambled eggs and biscuits with gravy, and then stood waiting.

"Greetings, Red." Dr. Kedar joined him in line. "How is our patient—the hyst?"

"No calls from her nurse through the night, so I guess she's all right. Just the usual assortment of fevers and pains. Gonna go make rounds after breakfast."

"Excellent. Would you mind if I joined you for a bite?"

"That'd be great. I'll grab a table near the band."

Dr. Kedar laughed.

The men got their orders, added some juice to their trays, and proceeded to the checkout line.

"Let me get that." Dr. Kedar reached for his wallet. "I got more sleep than you did. Besides, I have a dining card with an allowance I never use up."

"Okay. Thanks. Makes the food taste better when it's gratis."

They found a corner table, and sat and talked shop, beginning with the case they'd done together. Then Dr. Kedar asked Red about the other patients he'd handled through the night.

When Red had finished, Dr. Kedar tapped his lip with his forefinger. "Listen, just so you know, on that case we had from VIP... I just spoke with Lexie Winters."

Red frowned. He'd heard the name before, but couldn't place it. "Winters?"

"The hospital's lead attorney. Lexie detests surprises, so I filled her in on the case, and she had some advice."

"What's that?" Red leaned forward, putting his weight on his elbows.

"She said, 'Write nothing extraneous in the chart, nothing that you would not like to read aloud to a jury. Take excellent care of the patient…and wait.' Hopefully, the patient will do well and understand that her life was at risk."

"Okay." Red swallowed hard.

Dr. Kedar cocked his head. "Listen, Red, do you have anything on the schedule this morning?"

"No. Since I had call, they didn't assign me any morning cases."

"I have a complicated case scheduled for 7:30." Dr. Kedar described the procedure he'd be doing to stitch a patient's cervix to prevent another premature pregnancy loss. "If you would like, you may observe and assist, though there may be little for you to do."

"Thanks, Dr. Kedar. I'd love to." *I can't believe he's asking me instead of one of the fourth-years.* "You only get the tough ones, don't you?"

"It certainly seems that way. I also have a repeat C-section booked at 11:30, which is the third time in for a brittle diabetic. I am assuming the lab will come back okay. I just scheduled it, so no resident has been assigned yet. Would you like to scrub in?"

"Yes, of course." Red grinned.

"You are not too tired?"

"I'm never too tired for an experience like this. Let me go check on our hyst, put my contacts back in, and I'll come find you in the OR."

Dr. Kedar raised his eyebrows. "And afterward, if you have time, I would like your opinion about something I am working on down in the lab."

After they had finished the second case, Red's stomach growled. As he and Dr. Kedar peeled off their gowns, the senior physician looked over at him.

"Would you like to see my Frankenstein's secret lab?"

"Sure."

When they'd finished their duties, Red followed him to the elevator, and Dr. Kedar punched the button for the basement.

"I've heard you do amazing stuff downstairs."

"You will have to decide that for yourself."

The lift stopped, and Dr. Kedar held the door open so Red could depart first. They wound through the corridors past Central Supply, their footsteps echoing as they walked. After passing the pharmacy and the morgue, they entered a wing where Red had never been. They approached the door that said RESEARCH LAB.

Dr. Kedar reached to the keypad next to the door and punched in the code, and they entered the room. The faint, sweet smell of an anesthetic agent filled Red's nostrils. The large room with cement walls and tile floors had lab tables and equipment all around. In the center, operating room lights hung from the ceiling, and a draped operating microscope was set near a small table.

Red looked from the equipment to the man beside him. "What kind of stuff do you do down here?"

"As you know, we get all the high-risk referral patients from North Texas, all the premature labors and multiple pregnancies. Down here we work out some of the new techniques for treating preemies. We already have intact survival at twenty-five weeks of age, and we are having some success in even younger babies. We also do a lot of training for infertility work." Dr. Kedar pointed through an observation window to some cages. "We keep our animal specimens there. Rabbits have a uterus that approximates the size of the human fallopian tube, so they are great for learning the dexterity you need."

"Rabbits? You did infertility surgery on rabbits? Isn't that like trying to make water more wet?"

Dr. Kedar chuckled. "Yes, I suppose it is. But you can develop good hand-eye skills under the microscope before you ever scrub in with the microsurgery pros."

"So what are you working on now?" Red's eyes scanned the equipment.

Dr. Kedar beamed as he pointed to an overhead warmer. "There. Beside the ventilator. The one that looks like a sawed-off fishtank. That is my favorite project. I call it the Artificial Placental Platform; APP for short. I hope someday to use it to push back viability even earlier than twenty-four weeks." He motioned Red toward the contraption.

"How does it work?"

"It does not work—yet. I am still working through some ideas on it. I have been working with fetal pigs and human umbilical cords with placentas." He walked over to a storage cabinet and pointed. "See these plastic tubes?"

Red nodded.

"I can slide these into the umbilical vessels of fetal pigs and human umbilical cords so I can connect them to my machines."

Red frowned, trying to follow. "And from there?"

"From there I connect them to machinery that can duplicate the functions of the placenta. I should be able to sustain life right here in the tank until the fetal pig matures enough to survive. At least, that is my theory."

Amazing! An artificial womb. "How's it going?"

"Not too well yet. I am amazed at the diversity and complexity of the human placenta."

"'Fearfully and wonderfully made,'" Red muttered.

"Excuse me?"

"Hebrew poetry." He shook his head. "Never mind. You were saying?"

"Fetal pigs are fairly easy to oxygenate. But getting the fluid balance right, maintaining the proper blood pressure for the developing fetus, handling the nutrition issues, and all..." He sighed. "I am hoping that perhaps with your engineering background, you can help me."

"You know, I just might be able to." Pleasure warmed Red. He had not expected the MFM chief to be willing to accept suggestions from a second-year resident. He leaned forward to get a closer look at the instrumentation.

Dr. Kedar continued. "This machine works much like the heart-lung machine in that the blood circulates through it. I can pull off the carbon dioxide and make sure the oxygen content of the blood is correct." He pointed. "This second machine has a membrane like a dialysis machine. I am still trying to work out how to maintain proper blood chemistry, but with all this equipment, I have kept a fetal pig alive for almost two days so far."

Red studied the setup. "You submerged the pig in the tank?"

Dr. Kedar nodded. "Yes. The saline solution is just like pig amniotic fluid."

"That must be something! A pig submarine? A pigmarine?" Red knelt to get a closer look. "I just love the instrumentation. I spent five years working on projects related to medical equipment. Do you have any of your flow diagrams—how you hooked it up, the specs and all?"

"Why, yes, I do. I have some of my drawings, from the early stages up until now, including the current working prototype."

Red examined the connections, tracing the course of the tubing. "This is awesome. Any chance you also have the technical manuals on these machines?"

Dr. Kedar turned to the laboratory assistant, whom Red hadn't even noticed until that moment. The man nodded at Dr. Kedar.

"Would you please get them and let Dr. Richison take a look?"

The assistant went to the filing cabinet and pulled out a set of manuals. He handed them to Dr. Kedar, who gave them to Red.

"Thanks. Most docs love to read their specialty journals, but I still love a good technical piece." Red grinned. "With these and your diagram, I can bring myself up to speed on what you're trying to do."

"Wonderful! All of this is still in the early stages, though. I have not been able to get one past the second day…so many variables. Perhaps a fresh perspective from someone with your technical experience can advance our progress."

Hanging on the wall behind the nurses' station in L and D was a marker board that provided up-to-date information on each patient in labor. A color-coded list included name, number of pregnancies, the doctor's name, and any complications. It also included three pieces of information obtained by vaginal exam: dilation, effacement, and station.

At 6:25 A.M., Red scanned the board as he waited for the crew that had been working all night: a fourth-year resident and several med students rotating on the service. He'd worked an extra shift to cover someone on vacation, so Red had been at the hospital virtually nonstop in the two days since he'd been invited to assist in the surgery. Now he turned to see Dr. Denny Damon, the short, fourth-year resident from

New Jersey, as he swaggered up to join the "changing of the guard" for the new shift.

Red observed the OB chief resident, Dorie Chambers, as she led the medical students. While waiting for the residents to arrive, she quizzed the students. "Tell us, Dr. Jones, what is *effacement?*"

Red grinned. Calling a medical student *doctor* was like calling a math student a CPA, and it couldn't help but endear Dorie to the students. A young man, clearly unintimidated by the question, answered, "It's the percentage that the cervix has thinned in preparation for delivery. Ordinarily by four centimeters' dilation, effacement has reached 100 percent."

"Good. And you, Dr. Chatham. What is *station?*"

"Station is how far into the pelvis the baby's head is."

"Yes, go on."

"I think…at zero station, the presenting part is at the level of the ischial spines. At plus-three, the head is visible at the vaginal opening."

"So that's what you think, Dr. Chatham? Dr. Brazell, can you give us a more definitive answer?"

"He is correct about zero station. Each plus is one centimeter. So plus-three is three centimeters down from the midpelvis."

"Good. And what do the different marker colors stand for?" She had a deadpan expression, but then broke into a laugh. Red knew such a nontechnical question was intended to loosen them up and was not part of the normal line of questions he'd heard her ask numerous times. *She's so good at what she does. How can she do such a good job caring for pregnant moms by day and aborting babies by night?*

Chatham worked to rally to the occasion. "Black for normal, red for abnormal, green for unusual findings."

"Nice comeback, Doctor." Dr. Chambers nodded for the resident covering the board to take over and address the group of ten. He stepped forward and reviewed each patient's status, discussing briefly a few problems on the wards.

Red's eye wandered over to Damon, whose attention seemed more focused on one of the female med students than on the information, but this was nothing new. *He hasn't even been by to see the patient whose uterus he perforated.*

Though a skilled physician, Damon seemed to take his greatest pride in his reputation as a party animal and a ladies' man—a reputation he did his best to encourage by sporting an unconventional appearance, complete with a ponytail. Even now, the man was engaged in playful banter about his "wavy locks."

After the briefing, Red stood waiting in the hall near the outgoing team. Dr. Damon stayed back with the group in L and D, but when he came near where Red stood to get a drink, Red saw his opportunity. He made sure no one was within earshot, then he addressed Damon. "Looks like Ms. DeVeer's healing well."

Damon gave him a blank stare. "Who?"

"Ms. DeVeer."

"Don't give me a name, gimme a case. What case was it?"

"The seventeen-year-old postabortal hyst."

"And your point is…?"

"She's the lady you perforated."

"So?"

Red couldn't believe the man could be so callous. "Dr. Kedar and I had to hyst her. Multiple units of transfusion. And we tried to keep her settled, you know, out of *lawsuit* mode."

At this Damon looked around, then lowered his voice. "Perfs happen, man—especially when the patients are too stupid to stay still. She was bucking around like a bronco. Nobody coulda done that case. Besides, what's it to you? You got to do an emergency hyst with Radar-Kedar. You should be *thanking* me. That shoulda been an upper-level case, but you got the experience."

Red stood dumbfounded by Damon's arrogance. For a moment he couldn't find any words, but then he regained his composure. "I'm just surprised you haven't stopped by to *see* her, to…you know…"

"To what? She's a patient that had a complication. I transferred her here for appropriate care, and she received it." Damon narrowed his eyes. "You got a lot of nerve questioning a fourth-year, Red. So don't get all white knight on me. You're not some hero here. Kedar pulled the save; he just brought you along for the ride."

Red held up his palms. "Right. Just thought you might want to smooth things over and maybe avoid legal problems." *Must be true what they say, that he only makes social calls with the nurses.*

"Man, rookie, you never had a complication? You think you're such a hot surgeon you'll never get a perforation?"

At that moment Dr. Tsai, one of the residents, emerged from the ladies' room. She looked at both of them, and Red wondered how much she'd heard. Damon waited for her to pass out of earshot, then he squinted at Red.

"Give it a rest. My work at the clinic is my private business, and I keep it separate from residency. So how's about you do your job and I'll do mine?"

Damon spun on his heel and stormed off. Red watched him, not sure what bothered him more, the fact that Damon had been so defensive or that he had such cold disregard for his own patient.

Red leaned back against the wall. Damon had sure seemed unusually touchy.

He crossed his arms, wondering.

Should people trust this guy with their lives?

FOUR

Red's day off came not a moment too soon. He needed the rest.

After a morning of sleeping in, Red met Dr. Kedar in the locker room of the Preston Woods Country Club. He eyed Dr. Kedar's impeccable attire, which included a brand-name polo shirt bearing the club's logo.

"Red, I want you to meet my brother-in-law, Phil Hartwell." Dr. Kedar motioned for a man with a medium build to join them.

Red extended his hand; Phil smiled and nodded as they shook.

"He is married to my sister, Regan," Dr. Kedar added.

"And I'm certain Dalmuth can't, for the life of him, see what she sees in me." Phil grinned. "But he's too dignified to say so."

Dr. Kedar shook his head and chuckled. "Phil, this is one of the residents from the hospital. We call him Red."

"Last name's Richison." Red pointed to his red hair. "And the reason I go by Red should be obvious."

"So you're a doc, eh? I'm in real estate to support my golf habit. Can you play?"

"Ah, well, I did a good bit in college and some in med school, but not much since. So it's been a while."

Phil looked to his brother-in-law. "Sandbagger?"

Dr. Kedar gave Phil a thin smile, and his eyes widened. "It is hard to say. I have never seen him play, but he has other qualities I respect."

By the fifteenth hole, Red had learned a lot about the rather quiet, self-effacing doctor from his talkative brother-in-law. Dr. Kedar's parents were from Delhi, India, and had immigrated to the States. Dr. Kedar and his nine siblings had lived in San Diego, where their father sold insurance. Only Dr. Kedar and his younger sister, Phil's wife, Regan, lived outside of California.

Dr. Kedar had been married to Yvonne for nearly twenty years. Back in Los Angeles she had been a reporter when he was in the M.D./Ph.D. program at USC. Due to a family history of endometriosis, the then unmarried Yvonne came to do a story on Dr. Kedar's research. He took a personal interest in her case, and they ended up getting married. Much to their regret, they had never been able to have children.

With Yvonne itching to change markets for a variety of reasons, Dr. Kedar had accepted the opportunity to move to Dallas to head the Maternal-Fetal Medicine, or MFM, department, thanks to a retirement that left the job vacant.

Knowing of Red's interest in ob-gyn, Phil shared how he and his wife, both in their midthirties, had been trying to have a baby for some years.

While they waited for Dr. Kedar to tee off on the sixteenth hole, Phil took the cell phone from his back pocket. He punched in some numbers, then looked up at Red. "You'll get to meet my wife. She said she'd meet us at the nineteenth hole, if I'd remember to call."

When he had finished, Dr. Kedar looked at Phil. "So how have things been going?"

"Trying to distract me, eh? I'm up two holes with three to play, and you want to mess with my mind, throw me off track?" Although Phil was grinning, he sounded serious.

"Phil, you have been doing that special scorekeeping again. Take six, put down a five." Dr. Kedar chuckled.

"Don't talk to me about scoring. This ringer redhead you brought is kicking both our tails. Fortunately, I've added those strokes of mine to his score, so we're pretty even."

Red smiled, stepped up, and lofted a perfect six iron to within five feet of the pin on the par-three sixteenth hole.

Dr. Kedar raised an eyebrow and nodded.

Phil stood slack-jawed. "You're killing me!"

Red headed to the golf cart.

After their round of golf, the three men left their clubs for the caddy master to clean. "We will pick up Dr. Richison's clubs in the parking lot," Dr. Kedar said. He slipped the man a tip and motioned for Red and Phil to follow him to the restaurant.

Entering the walnut-lined room, Red breathed in the aroma of Reuben sandwiches and frying bacon. A dark-complexioned woman waved in their direction.

"That's Regan." Phil beamed as he made his way to her and kissed her cheek. She greeted her husband warmly, gave her brother a hug, and then turned her attention to Red. Phil introduced him saying, "This is Red—a gen-u-ine golf hustler. He's also an OB doc-in-training, so I guess that means he knows a thing or two about babies."

"How appropriate." She and Phil exchanged glances, and she motioned for them to join her at the table.

Dr. Kedar looked at his sister and then at Phil. "Appropriate, you say? Why is that?"

"Very appropriate," Regan insisted. "Because our doctor says we are going to have one!"

Dr. Kedar reached out to clasp her hands in his. "It worked?"

"Yes!"

He sat back, his face wreathed in a smile. "This is such wonderful news. You know I am thrilled for you both. So…that means you must be due around…"

"March 11."

"No wonder you played such fine golf today," Dr. Kedar said to Phil. Turning to Red, he explained, "He never wins, but to come so close… " He looked back at the happy couple. "So the cycle worked."

Phil nodded and looked over at his wife to signal that he wanted her to tell the details.

"We did the in vitro cycle with Dr. Josephson a few weeks ago."

"Remember, Red? I introduced you to Dr. Josephson in the cafeteria," Dr. Kedar said.

Red nodded, making the connection.

"We had four embryos transferred, followed by a positive test… good HCG levels and climbing fast. I am scheduled for a sono next week to evaluate the pregnancy—or pregnan*cies*."

Dr. Kedar offered congratulations again, as did Red. *I wonder where they stand on the ethics of freezing embryos…if they cryopreserved more, or if four's all they had,* Red thought.

"Yeah!" Phil said. "Dr. Josephson had ten harvested, nine fertilized, five frozen, four implanted, and a partridge in a pear tree."

"*Transferred* four, not *implanted,* honey." Regan patted him on the arm.

He grinned. "Yeah, okay, whatever."

Guess that answers my question.

"And my infertility buddy, Teresa," Regan added. "Remember her, Dalmuth?"

Dr. Kedar hesitated. "She is the one who told you it was unethical to fertilize more than you planned to implant, right?"

Regan slanted a look at Red. "Teresa's a little assertive, but she's a good friend. Anyway, our IVF cycles were a week apart, and Teresa and her husband had a positive test too!"

When the phone rang on Sunday night after ten, Regan hit Pause on the VCR. She glanced at the caller ID and recognized Teresa Murdock's mobile number. She answered, but her friend's greeting was barely above a whisper.

"Teresa, what's wrong?"

"Oh, Regan…"

"What happened? Tell me—is it the baby?"

"I'm still pregnant, but I was so scared…" With that, her friend's shaking voice trailed off into a quiet wail.

While Regan waited for Teresa to gain composure, she motioned to her husband to resume watching the video without her. Then, pressing the phone against her ear, she walked into the next room.

"We're on our way back from the emergency room. I started spotting," Teresa told her.

"Oh my gosh!"

"We called Dr. J's office. They paged him, and he called back and sent us to the hospital."

"What did you find out?"

"One of the OB residents did a sono. Still too early for a heartbeat, but he said I had a mildly retroverted uterus. He also said something about an intrauterine collection of fluid. He thinks I'm carrying a singleton, not twins. Too early to be sure. But he suspects the flow was caused by implantational bleeding related to the IVF procedure and all the hormones. I've got to stay on bed rest for a while. Dr. J postponed my next appointment with him for another week, so we should be able to see the heartbeat when we go in. Only problem is John's going to be out of town. Do you think you could go with me?"

"Sure, Teresa. But, well, it all sounds like a pretty good report."

"It *is* good news, Regan. But I was so *terrified.* I thought I was losing the baby, the child we've longed for. Here we'd had this great news, and I thought it was all being ripped away. It just seems so unfair that after all those years of hoping and praying I can't just sit back knowing I'm going to have a baby in nine months. Instead I have to go through all this terror."

"I know what you mean."

"Oh, *man.* See, now I've scared you, too! Oh, Regan, I'm so sorry. That's why I didn't call you from the hospital. I wanted to wait until I knew something."

"No, Teresa, that's not what I meant. I was just agreeing that it's scary being pregnant after infertility. I always dreamed it would be so exciting, and in one sense it is. But I find myself saying 'I'm pregnant' instead of 'We're going to have a baby.' The latter seems so presumptuous."

"Yes. That's why I don't want to go alone to see the doc. I'm always afraid the news is going to be bad. And if it is, well, I don't want to be alone."

Dr. Josephson stood outside the exam room, pausing to give Teresa Murdock's chart a quick review. *Spotting last week, went to ER. Okay since then.*

"Regan Hartwell came with her, since her husband's out of town," the nurse told him. "Guess they became fast friends in the IVF prep class."

The doctor nodded, then tapped on the door. When he entered, he found Teresa lying on the exam table, while Regan sat out of the way on a stool. He greeted both patients, then focused his attention on Teresa. "Let's see. You're now four weeks after embryo transfer, so we can figure six weeks' gestation. Maybe we'll see a heartbeat today, huh?"

He flipped a switch, and the ultrasound machine whirred. After preparing the probe, he gently inserted it while Teresa, Regan, and the nurse focused on the screen.

A sac—a dark black spot with a bright halo around it—drew his attention. He searched for the white streak that represented the embryo. *Yes! Very early fetal heart…* "There it is!" He pointed it out on the big screen, and then moved the transducer a bit. *Oh my…* He grinned and then angled the transducer so both sacs were in view.

"Whatcha got there?" Teresa asked.

"Whatcha see?" He couldn't hold back the smile.

"Not…" Her eyes widened. "*Two* sacs?"

"Yes! Right you are! And notice the two separate heart motions."

"We're, we're going to have… It's *twins!*" Teresa covered her mouth.

"So far. I'll just look around a bit."

"Two is plenty!"

The doc said nothing as he scanned, noticing that the twins appeared to be in a single gestational sac. *Oh no.*

He focused in, studying the new collection of fluid he'd found in the uterus. He increased the magnification and gain on the sonogram machine, carefully exploring the inside of the womb.

His heart sank. *The pregnancies won't make it. They aren't growing in the uterus…they're in the tube directly behind it.*

"You didn't find more than two, did you?"

Teresa sounded worried, so he schooled his voice to its most neutral. "No. Let me take a few pictures, and I'll meet you in the office." He felt the tightening in his shoulders. It always happened when he had to deliver bad news. *And after IVF, this is especially crushing.*

He knew he hadn't been subtle enough with his expression when Teresa cursed under her breath. "What's wrong? Is something wrong with the babies?"

Regan bit her lip. "It *is* twins, right?"

"Yes, twins." The doctor looked at Teresa. "Please, just let me review these pictures and measurements while you dress, and I'll have the nurse bring you to my office."

He shot his nurse a look, then stepped outside, easing the door shut behind him, and leaned against the wall.

FIVE

Regan didn't know what was coming, but from the look on the doctor's face, she had no doubt that it was bad news. At Teresa's request and with the doctor's permission, she slipped into the chair next to Teresa in Dr. Josephson's office.

As the doctor glanced at the women, Teresa's hand shifted to grip Regan's. She gave her friend a reassuring squeeze.

Dr. Josephson leaned toward Teresa. "I'm afraid the twins have picked the wrong place to grow. They aren't in the uterus; they're in the right tube."

"How can that be?" Teresa's eyes welled up. "Everything was okay in the hospital. What happened? How could they move to the wrong place?"

Dr. Josephson's tone became more formal. "They didn't move, Mrs. Murdock. The resident was in error. What he saw is called a *pseudosac*, a false sign inside the uterus. He didn't pick up the pregnancies or notice that they were outside the uterus. I'm so sorry, but actually, it's an all too common mistake. I'm afraid the equipment in the ER is nowhere near as precise as what I'm using here."

"You're telling me this is a tubal pregnancy?" Teresa reached in her purse for a tissue and then wiped her nose and eyes.

The doctor bowed his head. "I'm afraid so." He looked back at her. "The babies can't survive. They will grow until they rupture the tube, and that can cause internal bleeding."

"Yeah, I know tubals are bad—" Teresa choked on the words.

The doctor nodded. "I'm so sorry. There's nothing we can do to save the babies, but we can do our best to protect you."

When Teresa's sniffles turned into out-and-out crying, Regan patted her knee.

"But we've waited so long! Tried so hard. I knew this would happen, that our positive pregnancy test was too good to be true. Now you want to kill my babies?"

"Mrs. Murdock, I'm very sorry, but there's nothing we can do. We just have to take the best care of you that we can."

Regan marveled that the doctor didn't grow defensive in the face of Teresa's anger. But then, he'd been at this a long time. He'd probably learned to stay calm when patients railed at him, especially in the midst of their initial shock at bad news.

"How could they get into the tube? Didn't you put them back into the uterus?"

"Yes, we did. But in rare instances, before they get a chance to implant in the uterus, they migrate out into the tube and implant there. I suspect in your case one embryo did this and then divided into identical twins. It would be most unusual for two separate embryos to do this."

Teresa cradled her cheeks in her hands. "What do I do now?"

"The pregnancy is still very small, so we have a couple of possibilities. We've had some success treating tubal pregnancies with a medication called Methotrexate, though I'm not sure about the twin situation. Of course, the safest and quickest solution is to operate, remove the pregnancies, and save as much of your fallopian tube as possible."

"Do you have to take the babies?" The desperation in Teresa's voice made Regan blink back her own tears. "Isn't there *anything* else? No other options? Could the sono be wrong again?"

The doctor shook his head and spoke in a soothing tone. "I'm so sorry. I'd be happy to repeat the sono in a couple of days. And I'll refer you to the hospital for another opinion if you'd like. *But* we don't have too much time." He pressed his lips together. "Again, I'm sorry."

Teresa nodded, then dissolved into tears again. Regan got up and wrapped an arm around her. Then she looked up at the doctor. "Since you mentioned a second opinion…"

"Yes?"

"I'm sure you know my brother—Dalmuth Kedar—the chief of OB staff, who also heads the Maternal-Fetal Medicine department. I'm wondering what you would think if we asked him to examine Teresa?"

Doctor Josephson looked at Teresa. "It's up to you."

She stared at her hands and nodded. "I'd feel better."

"I will send him your file. Just remember—you don't have a lot of time."

Dorie pulled off her latex gloves and tossed them into the kick basin below the patient. *Another routine abortion. How many more till I can go home?* She walked to the sink and washed the powder off her hands. The patient was still mentally fuzzy from the IV injection of Versed.

Dorie pulled the microcassette player from her pocket and dictated an operative note: "Ms. Pattel, eighteen years old, white, female, ten weeks' gestation for elective abortion. Patient positioned in dorsal lithotomy, prepped, draped, given IV sedation, and Pitocin. Pelvic exam under analgesia confirmed appropriate for—"

The patient groaned.

Dorie looked up, then finished. Replacing the recorder in her pocket, she looked for other signs that the patient was becoming more alert. "You did fine, Jeri. Everything went smoothly. No problems at all." Dorie had found that if she used a first name, it often helped patients wake up.

The patient strained to speak. "I-I'm cramping."

"That's normal. We have medication for that and some medicine for you to take when you get home. We're going to sit you up now and move you to the recovery room in this wheelchair."

A nurse entered the room. "Dr. Chambers, we're ready for you in Room B."

Dorie nodded. "Okay. I'll step over there and take the history while you help get Jeri to recovery."

"Yes, Doctor."

As Dorie walked to the operating suite next door, she glanced at her watch. *Almost two o'clock. What a Saturday this had been! Three doctors in almost constant motion.* Dorie had lost track of the number of procedures she had performed, but her feet and shoulders hurt. She pulled the chart off the rack outside the room and walked in to find her patient, a woman in her thirties with thick, long, brown hair. Dorie glanced back and forth between chart and patient. "Has everything been explained fully to you?"

Tears filled the woman's eyes, and her voice shook as she spoke. "I don't want to be here. I don't want to do this."

"Well, you certainly don't have to."

"I know. But I have four kids already, and my husband… He said he's leaving if we have another baby. He says we can't afford the ones we've got. We both work, and, well, I was gonna get my tubes tied, but…"

Dorie lowered herself onto the stool beside the table and rolled closer to the client. "Tell me more. Are you sure you've thought this through?"

"Oh yeah. For weeks. Actually, he left last night. He said he isn't coming back unless I *take care* of it."

How very sad. "You're almost three months along according to your chart." Dorie glanced at her. "Does that sound about right?"

She nodded. "I don't want another baby. We can't afford it. It wouldn't work out. But this is…so…hard." She took a deep breath, and her face showed her resolve. "I need to do this…for my family. My kids need their dad. Let's go ahead. I really don't have a choice."

"I see you've signed all your consent forms, but I don't want to proceed unless you're absolutely sure."

The nurse returned from taking the last patient to the recovery room. "Any problems, Dr. Chambers?"

Dorie shook her head, wishing the nurse had allowed just one more minute of privacy. "Just taking the full history."

"I trust you, Doctor." The patient spoke barely above a whisper, and then closed her eyes tightly. "Let's go ahead."

"Okay then." Dorie squeezed the woman's hand and turned to the nurse. "Let's give her the Versed. Is the Pitocin in the IV already?"

"Yes, Doctor."

Dalmuth entered the room where Teresa Murdock sat with her husband, John. According to the chart, Teresa was an attorney and John was an international sales rep for an oil and gas company. John was wearing a suit and had his briefcase beside his chair. Teresa was next to him, dabbing puffy eyes. When Dalmuth introduced himself, the couple stood to shake his hand.

"Thank you so much for agreeing to see us." Teresa sat back down on the edge of the wing chair.

"Certainly." Dalmuth took his place behind the desk and studied the sonogram pictures, the tips of his fingers tented together. After looking first at Teresa, then John, he took a deep breath and launched in. "As I told you on the phone, your doctor—Dr. Josephson—he is a fine physician, as good as anyone in his field. And these are clear sono images." He paused to form his words. "I am afraid I agree with his findings."

At this Teresa reached for John's hand and squeezed her eyes shut.

Dalmuth continued. "We have twins outside the uterus. It is an ectopic—or tubal—pregnancy. No doubt Dr. Josephson advised you that we have no techniques to save the babies, not even anything on the horizon. And not only that, the mother's very life"—he looked at Teresa solemnly—"*your* life, Mrs. Murdock, is at risk if we don't act quickly."

John leaned forward. "Doc, could you take another look? We have to know for sure. You have a good sono machine, right?"

"Yes, of course I can do that. It would be good to reevaluate. It has been three days, correct?"

They nodded.

Dalmuth stood and gestured toward the hallway. He called his nurse and showed the couple to the sono room.

Minutes later in the quiet darkness the ultrasound machine made the only sound. Dalmuth surveyed the entire pelvic region. First he visualized the uterine cavity, still with a bit of fluid in it. "Yes, I see how the resident could have made a mistake last week using abdominal sonography. We can see much more here by transvaginal sono." He continued scanning carefully.

There it is. A twin pregnancy, clearly outside the uterus, but right behind it. No wonder it took awhile to determine it was ectopic.

He leaned back and looked at the couple. "Mr. and Mrs. Murdock, I am very sorry, but your doctor is right. The twins are not in the uterus, but in the tube that wraps around behind the uterus. And they are still growing."

"Are their hearts still beating?" Teresa bit her lip.

Dalmuth looked at the screen and then back to her. "Yes. The embryos are still alive." Usually he referred to them as *babies,* especially when his patients did so. But he wanted to help prepare the Murdocks for the loss. Better to call them *embryos.*

Teresa began to cry.

"Surgery, then?" John's voice was hoarse.

Dalmuth nodded. "I think surgery is the only option. Your doctor can remove the pregnancy and save as much tube as possible."

"Tubes! Mine didn't work right, anyway," Teresa wailed. "That's why we did in vitro. Is that what caused this?"

If only he had a good answer for her. But he didn't. All he had was the truth. "It is hard to say, Mrs. Murdock. These things just happen. Sometimes it can be related to endometriosis or tubal disease. Some women are even born with imperfect tubes."

Teresa's voice became elevated, and her speech grew more rapid. "You want to take out my babies? While they're still *alive?* With their hearts beating?"

Dalmuth blinked and searched for the right words in the face of her anguish. "I am so sorry, Mrs. Murdock. There is no other procedure developed. We have nothing that will work, nothing to offer you."

"Why can't you just take the babies from the tube and put them back where they belong?" John blurted out.

Dalmuth shook his head.

"But they transferred them in there, right?"

"I am sorry, Mr. Murdock. But once you move the pregnancies, you cut off their blood supply. They cannot survive that."

Mrs. Murdock, her eyes ablaze, slapped her hand against the table. "No! I won't let you do it. You can't kill my babies! How did they get 'planted' in the wrong place, anyway? You can't just kill them. Not with drugs, not with surgery. You just can't. I won't let you!"

Dalmuth stared at the floor, stunned by the force of the word *kill.*

John reached for his wife's hand, which was still pressed stiffly against the table. "Teresa, honey, I'm losing my two children, but I'm not about to lose my wife, too. We can't have this thing rupturing on you and there you are, bleeding to death." He turned back to Dalmuth. "That can happen, right?"

Dalmuth looked up. "Yes, I am afraid that is a very real risk." He wiped sweaty palms on the insides of his pockets.

"No!" Teresa stared at him. "Are you pro-life? Would a pro-life doctor tell me something different?"

He took a deep breath. *Oh my.* Regan had warned him that Teresa Murdock was rather militant. He hesitated. He needed to be careful not to make the woman even more upset by stating his personal views. Besides, this case wasn't about abortion.

"In this case any doctor would be pro-life, Mrs. Murdock. You want to keep the children, and I want you to be able to do that. Anyone would. But you have to choose between losing the children or losing possibly both mother *and* children, between two lives or three."

John drew close to his wife. "Would you let Dr. Kedar do the surgery?"

She stifled a sob. "Not if he's going to take my babies."

Dalmuth exhaled his frustration. This was getting them nowhere. He looked from Teresa to her husband and shook his head. "Please get dressed and meet me in the office." He motioned for the nurse to join him in the hall, and the two of them left the room.

Once outside the door, the nurse turned to him. "Looks like you've got a stalemate in there."

He nodded and headed to his office. "Bring them to me when they are ready."

"What are you going to do?"

He paused, turning back to face her. What *was* he going to do? He shook his head "There is not much I can do. We cannot operate without permission. We will have to get consent somehow."

Exactly how he was going to do that, he didn't know, and he had only about three minutes to figure it out. He knew the rules of patient autonomy only too well—he couldn't force a patient to have a procedure, even if it was to save her own life.

SIX

A few minutes later the nurse guided the Murdocks into Dalmuth's office, and they seated themselves across from his desk again.

Dalmuth spread out the sonogram pictures before them. He pointed to the tiny sacs, keeping his expression and tone solemn. "Mrs. Murdock, your life is in danger. You need an operation immediately. I am sure Dr. Josephson will be available to schedule you as soon as possible, probably tonight."

Teresa dug in hard and sobbed. "I'd rather die than kill my own babies."

"Teresa, don't say that!" John looked at Dalmuth, his eyes pleading for help.

Clearly, Teresa Murdock was committed to saving her babies, even to the point of risking her own life.

As Dalmuth turned back to the sono pictures, an idea came to him. Maybe it was time to give his theory a shot. Teresa Murdock might be a good candidate. And if his idea worked, there was a slim chance for a happy ending. *We can break this impasse and protect her life.*

He stared at the pictures, then at John, then back at the pictures. His pulse quickened. He reached into his desk and pulled out a simple diagram of the female pelvis, complete with uterus, tubes, and ovaries. During lighter conversations he often described it as a longhorn steer with earrings. But not now. Now he needed to be serious—deadly serious.

"I have an idea."

Teresa grew quiet and looked up. "What? What did you say?"

"I have an idea."

Teresa studied his face. "What is it?"

"You would have to trust me."

"What, Doctor? What are you thinking?" The hope in John Murdock's face made Dalmuth shiver.

"Listen carefully," he began. "What I have in mind—it has never been done before. I do not know if it has even been tried, but I doubt it. I have been giving it thought for some years. As the technology has advanced…"

When he paused, Teresa leaned forward, hope replacing despair on her face. Dalmuth pointed to the sono photos.

"As you can see from the pictures, the babies are out toward the end of the tube."

The couple nodded.

"And the tube is folded around behind the uterus."

"Right, but I thought you couldn't move them—couldn't take them out of the tube," Teresa said.

"Yes, that is true. But my idea involves leaving them in the tube. Imagine if I made an incision in the uterus and surgically put the tube—where they are implanted—into the uterus through the incision…"

Teresa gaped at him. "Can you *do* that?"

"As I said, it has never been tried. The idea is to keep the babies' blood supply intact and get them to grow into the uterine wall."

John frowned. "But won't the tube eventually explode from the pressure growing inside? Isn't that what makes women with tubal pregnancies bleed to death? I mean, how would twisting it around so it goes inside the uterus keep the tube from blowing?"

"Maybe I could cut the tube open without harming the pregnancy. Still, we have plenty of risk, many unknowns. But theoretically, it might work." Dalmuth looked at the couple and took in the growing hope on their faces. *Am I really ready to do this?* The answer was swift: Yes. He'd said too much to back out now. Besides, he'd wanted to try it for a long time, and this woman was the perfect candidate.

Of course, in reality, we have such a slight chance of success.

He sat back and rubbed his chin. "You would have to sign a stack of legal releases. And I must advise you that the safest option is to have that portion of the tube removed. Your risk in that would be minimal."

Teresa set her jaw. "The babies wouldn't have any chance that way though."

"Correct."

She cocked her head. "You aren't just trying to get me to sign up for surgery with no intention of trying to save my babies, are you? Tell me you wouldn't lie to me."

The words stung, but Dalmuth kept his voice steady. "No, of course not. But there is at least a fifty-fifty chance that the location of the pregnancy and the blood supply will not even allow me to try this. In that case I must have your permission to do the best thing, which might be to remove the pregnancy. I am willing to try to honor your wishes, but you must know how dangerous all of this is."

Teresa raised her palms. "I'll sign whatever I need to if you'll promise to try to save our babies."

"All I can promise is to try."

"You promise me"—Teresa looked him right in the eye—"*promise* you will do everything you can to save them."

Dalmuth felt his chest tighten. Then, as if making a solemn oath, he held Teresa's gaze. "I will."

John jumped in. "When should we give this a go?"

Dalmuth's heart raced. "As soon as possible. Our chances will not get any better. When did you last eat, Mrs. Murdock?"

"Eat? Um, lunch. I'd say about four hours ago. Why?"

"For elective surgery, we need an empty stomach."

"You operate at night?" John asked.

"Not normally." Dr. Kedar's excitement matched his anxiety. "But this is hardly a normal situation." He stood and shook their hands. "Please wait here. I need to go make the arrangements."

Red stood at the sink feeling honored that Dr. Kedar had specifically requested him. The distinctive smell of Betadine permeated the air as he lathered up with the iodine-colored scrub soap.

"Red! Good to see you." Dr. Kedar came up from behind him. "I am glad you were on call tonight."

"Thanks. Me, too." Red glanced at his companion. "What've we got? They told me it's an ectopic. Is that right?"

Dr. Kedar nodded, his expression somber. "Yes. You remember my sister from the Country Club?"

"Oh no."

"Do not worry. She is not our patient. But her friend is—the one she told us about, who went through IVF the week before she did."

"The in vitro turned out ectopic? Bummer."

"That is not the half of it. Literally. She is carrying twins."

Twins! Red shook his head. "Doubly sad. How's she taking it?"

"Not too well." Dr. Kedar stared over at the wall.

"You planning to do a linear salpingostomy?"

Dr. Kedar didn't seem to hear the question, and Red hesitated to press the issue with such a senior member of staff.

They backed into the room, keeping their scrubbed hands elevated in front of them. After taking the sterile towels from the scrub nurse, they methodically gowned and gloved. Red eyed the CO_2 laser draped for use.

"Laser? For an ectopic?" He angled a look at Dr. Kedar. "What have you got planned?"

It was hard for Red to know for sure with the mask hiding Dr. Kedar's face, but it seemed that he was more tense than usual. "Just follow my lead. I have to see inside first, before I know for sure. We may need it, and if we do, we are either making history or setting ourselves up for a catastrophe."

Catastrophe? I don't need another catastrophe! Red approached the table. "Making history…?"

They draped off the scrubbed abdomen, which was now yellow from the Betadine wash, and Dr. Kedar proceeded to make an incision. Red worked alongside him, keeping the field clear of blood.

Before long, Dr. Kedar inserted his left hand into the incision, cupping the uterus from behind and lifting it forward. "Hold this in place, will you?"

Red complied.

Dr. Kedar slipped his fingers behind the swollen uterus and flipped the ovary and tube from the patient's right side so they could see it. "There it is," he whispered. The tube with the pregnancy was in plain view.

Red got goose bumps as he gazed at the tube. *So small, maybe an inch in diameter. Yet containing two tiny lives.*

Dr. Kedar looked at it from all angles, tracing the blood supply. "Cautery, with a clean blade please."

Next he asked for the saline-soaked cloth that he used to pack the ovary and tubal pregnancy out of the way. Then he made an incision in the back wall of the uterus.

Red glanced at the scrub nurse, then back to the senior physician. "Dr. Kedar, what are you *doing?*"

"I made a promise to try to save these babies if at all possible."

"But"—Red stared at him—"that's impossible!"

"Hey, I thought the nurses told me you were the big faith guy around here. Follow me with this."

Speechless, Red assisted as Dr. Kedar proceeded with the incision. Due to the hormones of pregnancy, Teresa bled profusely. Dr. Kedar targeted the area with the least blood supply. Having done so, he got to the uterine cavity without much trouble. He took the tube with the pregnancy inside and brought it over to the incision they had just made.

"But won't it just rupture inside the uterus and die when we tie off the blood supply?" Red asked.

"Laser, please."

Using a wet gauze pack, the doctors covered the patient's uterus and the fallopian tube that contained the pregnancy. Then they stepped back from the operating table so the nurse could move the operating microscope—complete with an attached carbon dioxide laser—into place. Once the teaching microscope, which had eyepieces for both surgeons, was ready, the surgeons resumed their positions.

Dr. Kedar removed the gauze and focused the scope on the compromised tube.

Red gave out a little gasp when he saw it. "Amazing."

His hands steady on the instruments, Dr. Kedar examined the tube and found the implantation site. He then rotated it and, aided by the microscope, made a small, linear incision with the laser. It cut precisely and cauterized the bleeding. In a matter of minutes, the tube lay flat open. Looking through their microscopes, both doctors could visualize the glistening gray of the single sac that indicated an identical twin pregnancy.

"Wow." Red's voice was little more than a whisper. "So now the pregnancies can expand through. But I still don't see how the implantation can support them."

Dr. Kedar rotated the tube again until they could both see the place in the tubal wall where the pregnancies had implanted. He moved the red helium-and-neon sitting beam for the laser onto this position.

Red started. "You're going to fire *at* the pregnancies?"

"Patience, Doctor. Watch." With pinpoint accuracy, Dr. Kedar made tiny holes in the tubal wall, using brief pulses of the laser energy and stopping precisely at the implantation site. Methodically he worked to make a Wiffle ball pattern of burns beneath the pregnancy.

Red felt his mouth drop open. "So the placenta can grow through and attach to the uterus!"

Dr. Kedar looked up. "I certainly hope so." With gentle movements, he pushed the tube through the incision in the back of the uterus as Red retracted it open.

"Ah, so you aren't *planning* to cut off the blood supply, are you?"

Dr. Kedar looked at Red and nodded. "We will leave the blood supply to the tube so the pregnancy will continue to grow. I have made an incision and several smaller holes so, hopefully, as the placenta grows, it can split out of the tube and grow to the sidewall of the uterus. Now if only the tubal blood supply will hold out long enough for the babies to implant and draw their nourishment from the uterus…"

What an amazing concept. Red realized he might be watching Dr. Kedar make medical history. "Has that ever worked before?"

"I have never heard of anyone trying it, but I have thought about it for years. To do so, we had to have a pregnancy out at the end of the tube with enough mobility to swing it this distance and not impinge on the ovary."

"But this tube will be shot forever."

"Correct. But the patient had tubal problems anyway. That is why they did IVF in the first place."

With the pregnancy now safely inside the womb, they began to stitch the uterine wall closed. "Not too many stitches, not too tight. Keep the blood flow going for a while," Dr. Kedar coached. It was a most unusual sight to see the fallopian tube traversing behind the uterus and then diving into it.

"What about delivery, assuming this all works?" Red asked.

Dr. Kedar chuckled. "I think we can pretty well anticipate a C-section."

"No kidding! Wouldn't want this uterus to contract much. Man, you've got guts! I mean, uh…" Red fumbled. "I mean, you're amazing."

Dr. Kedar didn't seem to mind Red's words.

"Did you tell me Dr. Josephson did her IVF procedure?"

"Yes."

"Does he know about this?"

Dr. Kedar nodded. "I called and invited him to assist, but he was unable to make it."

"Did you tell him what you planned to do?"

"Yes. He commended me on trying to save the twins and said he would stop by to see our patient in the morning, and…"

"And what?"

"And he said, 'You're crazy!' He is probably right."

The microscope and its drapes obscured the operative field to anyone except the surgeons looking through the eyepieces, so the anesthesiologist had read a novel throughout the procedure, unaware of the marvel that had just unfolded. Now as Red and Dr. Kedar finished closing the abdomen, the nurse affirmed that the patient had remained stable. She completed the charting and called for transport to the recovery room.

After dressing the wound, Dr. Kedar tossed his gloves in a big hamper for disposables. Then he turned toward Red. "Simple courtesy—throw your used gloves in here instead of in the kick basin. It keeps the nurses from having to fish them out."

Red nodded. *No wonder the nurses like him.*

After disposing of mask and gown, Dr. Kedar seated himself on a stainless steel stool for long enough to make notations on the patient's chart. Then a uniformed transport aide wheeled into the operating room with a gurney, and Red followed as Dr. Kedar accompanied the aide and Teresa into recovery.

Red shook his head. "Amazing! You've got twins living in a tube in the uterus."

Dr. Kedar nodded. "Yes. And hopefully the placenta will contact the uterus. If that happens, the rest has a shot. She will lose the tube, but then, that was already gone. Still, for a chance at having these twins…" He looked down at their patient. "She is definitely going to need a C-section though. And we do risk uterine rupture."

Red's amazement dissolved into dread. "Uterine rupture…?" He thought of the high-risk hysterectomy that he and Dr. Kedar had done together. "Do you think that's likely?"

Dr. Kedar pressed his fingertips together. "I have no way of knowing. But this much I do know—right now, three lives are hanging in the balance."

SEVEN

Red looked on as Dr. Kedar stood in the recovery room writing orders following the procedure on Teresa Murdock. When the doctor had finished writing, Red scanned the notes. Dr. Kedar had described the procedure as a "transuterine transposition of ectopic gestation."

"Hereafter known as the Kedar procedure," Red said.

Dr. Kedar smiled. "Shall we go talk to the husband?" He motioned toward the general direction of the waiting area. They passed through the doctors' dressing room on their way out to the waiting area, and Dr. Kedar stopped long enough to reach for his lab coat. He checked to be sure he had a pad in the pocket, then proceeded through the double doors to the waiting room.

Looking around, Red spotted a tall, professional looking man who was sitting by himself reading *Business Week*. Red took in the clear signs of strain on the man's features.

Must be the husband.

Dr. Kedar's next words confirmed the fact:

"Excuse me, Mr. Murdock."

Red followed Dr. Kedar as he approached the man, who jumped to his feet. "Doctor Kedar! My wife? How is she…and the babies?"

Dr. Kedar motioned to the chairs and introduced Red as they sat. Then Dr. Kedar rested his elbows on his knees as he spoke. "Your wife came through fine; she is in recovery. I have done what I can to save the babies. It was a risky procedure, and the twins are not out of the woods yet. Not by a long shot. But I believe it was worth the try. The first few days will be critical. I cannot be sure yet if the babies have even survived. Beyond that, we have to hope they will implant. I made some tiny incisions with the laser through the tubes for their placentas to grow through and, if all goes well, attach to the uterine wall. We have many unknowns at this juncture. Now let me show you what we did." He reached into his lab coat pocket and pulled out his prescription pad and pen, then sketched a diagram of the procedure.

John Murdock watched, clearly fascinated. When Dr. Kedar was finished, Murdock turned wide eyes to the surgeon. "That's amazing! Thank you, Doctor. Teresa will be so thrilled. Listen, I know you went skating on thin ice—maybe even walking on water." The man's laugh seemed to dispel his own tension, but he grew serious again. "Even if it doesn't work out, we will know, Teresa and I, that we did everything possible to save these little guys." He put his hand out. "We can live with that."

Dr. Kedar shook his hand. "Thank you for your kind words. I am so glad you feel that way." He then excused himself. Red nodded, then followed Dr. Kedar back to recovery, where the nurse was tending to Teresa.

The nurse glanced at them as they came in. "I think she's asking for her husband. Is his name *Bubba?*"

Dr. Kedar shook his head.

In a few minutes Teresa's speech became clearer. "Babies? Did you...save my babies?"

Dr. Kedar took her hand. "We did everything we could. We will have to wait and see now."

The anesthesia was still affecting Teresa's short-term memory, so she kept repeating her questions as she drifted in and out of consciousness. Red watched with amusement as Dr. Kedar waited by her bed and gave the same answers three times. When she finally opened her eyes, she gave Dr. Kedar a dreamy look.

"You're so wonderful, Doctor. How can I thank you?"

The nurse brought ice chips for her to suck on.

"You're wonderful too," Teresa told her. In fact everyone who came near Teresa within the next ten minutes was *simply wonderful.*

Dr. Kedar smiled at his patient's enthusiasm. Then he turned to Red. "While she is in recovery, I need to go check on a patient in the unit. Would you care to join me?"

"Sure."

Dr. Kedar led the way to neonatal ICU. He stopped at the nurses' station there and searched for a chart.

"Good evening, Doctor." As the nurse approached, Red thought she looked pale. As she grew even closer, he could tell she had been crying.

"Good evening. I am here to check on the Patrick baby," Dr. Kedar said.

The nurse's lower lip trembled. "I'm sorry, Doctor. The baby expired about three minutes ago."

"Oh my. I am so sorry." He wrapped his arm around the nurse's shoulders, aware she had most likely cared for the baby for much of his time in the nursery. "Thank you for your excellent care."

The nurse, growing misty eyed, excused herself and stepped outside the unit.

Dr. Kedar motioned for Red to follow. They entered the isolation room where the two-pound infant lay still connected to numerous wires. The drape had been pulled around the work station to keep the child out of view. Dr. Kedar laid a hand on the baby's back and stroked his index finger against his tiny neck. "So beautiful…just too small." He gently removed the wires.

Red noticed that he started to speak, but hesitated. "What?"

"The nurses hate to do this part," he whispered.

So you do it yourself. And you've shown more respect for a dead child than I showed for a live one. Red stared back at the baby. "O Lord…" He hadn't meant to say it aloud.

"Excuse me?" Dr. Kedar turned.

"Sorry. I was just praying, I guess."

"Feel free to…"

"What? Pray?"

"Yes, if you like."

"Uh, sure. All right." Red cleared his throat, closed his eyes, and bowed his head. "Heavenly Father, thank You for this precious life that You created and for the knowledge that each tiny life has eternal significance. We commit his soul to You and ask that You comfort his family and the staff who cared for him. Thank You for Jesus, who conquered death, and for the coming day when those who know Him will cry no more. Amen."

"Thank you," Dr. Kedar whispered. He wiped a tear, then motioned for Red to sit beside him. "May I ask you a question?"

"Yes sir."

"At what point do you think a person has a soul?"

Red hesitated, forming the words carefully. "When a unique human being is formed."

"So, at fertilization?"

"Yes. At the moment when the sperm penetrates the egg and the DNA lines up."

"What about all the cryopreserved embryos? Do they have frozen souls?"

"I presume so, though honestly I'm not sure what it means to be human and frozen; it's a mystery."

"In your ethical construct, even at the one cell—the zygote—it is fully human?"

"Yes."

"Do you think it has the same moral significance as a full-grown person?"

"As far as I understand it, yes."

"But it is only microscopic."

"True. But we humans have dignity simply by being created and existing, regardless of size. How can we judge a person's value by relative size, age, or ability to perform? The zygote is human at the smallest and youngest stage. Both you and I were once one celled, right?"

Dr. Kedar inclined his head. "True. But this is different, is it not? A person is someone who can think and feel and even *know* that he or she is a person."

"Lots of intelligent people hold that view. But if we define person-hood as having self-consciousness or function, then what happens when we lose consciousness or function? A person in a coma isn't thinking or feeling, yet he or she still hasn't lost personhood, right?"

"True." Dr. Kedar sat thinking.

"May I ask you a question, Dr. Kedar?"

"Certainly."

"What do you believe? Do you practice any religion?"

He shook his head. "I am not sure about God. My wife reads the Bible sometimes, and my grandparents were Hindu. My parents did not practice any religion, so I was not raised to either. I have never believed in a personal God, but lately I have been wondering."

Red didn't know exactly what he'd been wondering, but it felt too personal to probe. So they sat in silence until Dr. Kedar said it was time to go.

Dawn stood with the nurse as she tapped on the doctor's door. *I've only got seventy-five bucks, and now I have to see the doctor.*

"Yes?"

The nurse nudged it open. "I brought a new patient, Dawn Spencer, to see you."

The doctor stood and smiled. "Come in."

Dawn shuffled into the room, then eyed the palatial office. The doctor motioned to one of the leather chairs and took the chart from the nurse. "Please sit here. Make yourself comfortable."

The nurse backed out, pulling the door shut behind her as Dawn sat down.

"I'm Dr. Ophion, the director of this clinic. The nurse called and said you were having some difficulties with your decision. So I thought, perhaps I could help"—he glanced at the chart—"Ms. Spencer."

"Well…um…I'm pregnant and…and I can't be. So I came for an abortion, but…" *This is embarrassing!* She fought to keep from crying, but her voice cracked anyway. "I don't have enough money, so I don't know what I'm…what I'm gonna do…"

Dr. Ophion took his seat behind the desk and studied her chart. "I understand this can be overwhelming news. You've had a positive pregnancy test?"

"Yeah, they ran one at another clinic. But I already knew I was pregnant. I got the symptoms. One of my friends who…uh…came here said everything was taken care of."

"Of course. We offer the finest in women's healthcare."

"But the money…"

"I see you've listed an insurance card, and this is a fine company. I'm certain they'll cover any difference between what you have available and the cost of the pro—"

"No! I gave that because the lady at the desk said they needed all the information before I could see anyone. It's my mom's insurance through her work. But she *can't* know. She can't!" Dawn broke into a sob. "They told me up front that nobody has to know, that I can decide for myself."

"It's okay, no one has to know." He thought a moment, then nodded. "I see the problem."

Dawn wiped a tear, then stared down at her hands. As she waited for the doctor to speak again, she chipped away at the paint on one of her thumbnails.

"You have made up your mind to terminate this pregnancy?"

"Yeah, but I don't know what to do."

"Let me make a suggestion that should help you with your difficulty and also keep things confidential. Some women choose this approach—"

Wasn't he listening? "What? I don't have much money. Seventy-five dollars is all my boyfriend and me could get together. And my mother would *kill* me—"

He shook his head and held up a hand. "It's all right. It's a medicine; pills that you take by mouth. Then in a few days, you miscarry at home. But we must be sure of your dates, of how far along you are. I'll do a sonogram to be sure."

"But I already had one at the other place, and they told me when I called that sonos cost hundreds of dollars here." Dawn's sniffled. "And I only have seventy-five bucks."

"Please, don't worry. I'll charge this visit and the sonogram to the insurance comp—"

Dawn stopped crying and put a fisted hand on the doctor's desk. "No way! I *told* you, if Mom finds out, she'll kill me. And she'll kill Brad, too!"

"No, that's not really a problem, Ms. Spencer. We'll code this as *amenorrhea,* the absence of menstrual bleeding. You haven't had a period for a while, correct?"

She squinted at him. *Where is this leading?* "Uh...right."

"I won't even charge the usual copay for this visit. Just let me write a prescription for mefipristone. You may have heard it called RU-486.

You'll need to go to the pharmacy next door; they give my patients a special price on this medication. You should start bleeding a few days after you take it. And I'll give you a few samples of a medicine that you can take when the bleeding starts, to ease the cramping. Do you understand?"

"It's not gonna cost more than seventy-five dollars, and nobody will know about it?"

"Right. And most women have no problem at all."

For the first time in days, Dawn smiled. "Awesome! That is so nice!"

Dr. Ophion smiled as well. "Occasionally a woman might have some complications. Let me give you my card and the clinic's hot-line number, in case you have any difficulties."

Difficulties? Dawn frowned. "What kind of difficulties?"

"Sometimes, not too often, a patient will not miscarry completely, and then we need to do a minor surgical procedure that's similar to the abortion procedure. It takes care of any complications."

Here we go again! "But how much does that cost?"

"Like I told you, we have an insurance code for abnormal bleeding, and the actual cause of the bleeding can remain confidential."

Dawn heaved a sigh of relief and sat back. *Yes!* "So, I get this sono test, take a pill, and all my problems are solved?"

Dr. Ophion scribbled the prescription. "That's correct." He handed it to her and smiled. "Just get this filled at the big pharmacy down the street and take it as directed. Call me if you have any problems. Now let's do a quick sonogram to be sure you are pregnant and at the correct stage for using this special medication. Then we'll have you on your way."

"That's all? Just take a pill? Why doesn't everyone just do this?"

The smile faded. "Most pharmacies charge much more than you will be paying. And it takes several days, even a week, to be completed; many women don't want to wait that long. In fact, since it's Friday, you might want to wait until after the weekend to take it. The bleeding can be a little heavy, and as I mentioned, the cramping can occasionally get pretty rough. So, let's go get you a sono, and then I'll give you some samples for the cramp medicine so you won't have to pay for it."

———

"Did you have a good weekend?"

Bethany looked up from her paperwork and nodded at her assistant, who stood holding a file. "What've you got, Margaret?

"Dawn Spencer is back, and she's asking to see you."

"Great."

"She pretty much avoided eye contact with me. She seems really nervous."

"Thanks, I'll take it from here." Bethany took the file and glanced through it, then placed it on her desk and walked out to greet Dawn. Margaret followed.

"Dawn!" Bethany extended her hand. "I'm so glad to see you. Would you like to come back to my office?"

The young woman nodded as she stood, and her eyes met Bethany's. Though she was dressed just as before, this time her T-shirt had fewer wrinkles. "I just wanted to tell you… I talked to my boyfriend about what you said, and it didn't go so good."

"Okay. Why don't you come on back?" Bethany led Dawn to the sono room, where they sat down. "What did he say?"

Dawn cursed and shook her head. "Brad is all mad that I haven't taken care of it yet. He said he ain't speakin' to me again until I do. I'm having a bad time trying to make up my mind about it."

"I'm so sorry."

Dawn's eyes clouded over, and when she blinked the tears spilled out. For the next fifteen minutes Dawn talked and cried. When she was finished, Bethany stood.

"Let's do another sono to see how the baby's progressing; the more facts we have, the better. Afterward we can talk about it some more. Okay?"

Dawn shrugged. "You said it's free, right?"

"Right. I'll go get the doctor."

Dawn started. "I thought you *were* a doctor!"

Bethany shook her head. "I'm the clinic administrator." She handed Dawn the drape. "Just put this on—"

"I know what to do." Dawn gave her a half-smile. "I'm getting experienced at this."

Minutes later Bethany returned with the physician volunteer, and they proceeded with the sonogram.

"There it is." The doctor pointed to the pregnancy sac on the screen.

"I see it! See the heart beating?" Dawn looked over at Bethany, and her face broke into a grin. "That is *so* cool! It's like it's galloping or something."

"It *is* amazing." *I never stop being amazed.*

The doctor took a series of measurements. Then, at Dawn's request, she pointed out the eyes, the nose, the fingers, the spine, and the toes.

"That ain't no blob!"

Bethany cocked her head and frowned. "What? What do you mean?"

"Brad tried to tell me that the baby's just a blob, just a bunch of tissue. But that ain't no blob right there."

Bethany looked her in the eyes. "No, you're absolutely right. It's more than that—far more."

After the sono, Dawn followed Bethany back to her office. With a deep sigh, she plopped down on the couch. "I just don't know what to do." She sat staring down at the new sono pictures. "I can't raise a kid alone. My parents would kill me. Brad would break up with me."

"That's why we're here," Bethany assured her. "We'll do all we can. We'll even help you find a place to live, if you need it."

Dawn looked up at her. "You know, when I came here last time, I thought this was an abortion clinic. I guess I went to the wrong place by mistake."

Or by divine appointment. Bethany restrained her smile.

"But when I got home, I called that clinic. They said it would cost me five hundred dollars for an abortion, including the sonogram. And then if I changed my mind and kept the baby, they'd still keep the two hundred bucks they charged the insurance company for a sono."

"Yes, I'd heard that was the rate."

"Well, thanks for letting me do these free."

"Sure."

Dawn fell silent, and Bethany waited, giving the girl time to think. Finally Dawn spoke.

"I...I believe it's a baby, like you said. I mean, I saw it! But I just can't see how it would work with Brad and with my mom." She looked up at Bethany, her desperation clear in her eyes. "My mom...ain't no way I can tell her!"

Bethany remembered how that felt. She reached over and squeezed Dawn's hand. "I'll go with you when you tell her if you like."

Dawn shook her head, but Bethany's words seemed to have infused her with new confidence. "Wow, that's real nice of you. But naw, I'll figure it out somehow." She looked up at Bethany. "Still, thanks for offering. I appreciate it—a lot."

EIGHT

I can't believe I'm still pregnant. O Lord, I know I don't deserve it, but please let these babies make it.

Teresa Murdock rubbed her stomach. She was having trouble sitting still at her first major outing since the surgery, a Saturday night fund-raiser for Women's Choice Clinic. She glanced around the Omni Hotel ballroom, wishing she had stayed home but reminding herself that the four walls there drove her crazy too. Besides, they needed her here tonight. After all, she was chair of the clinic's board. Teresa refocused her thoughts to business concerns as everyone around her ate chocolate mousse. After a few moments, she mounted the steps to the stage and introduced the clinic's executive director. Bethany Fabrizio stood and walked to the platform.

Teresa took in the clean lines of Bethany's outfit compared to her own growing shape. *She looks downright regal in that suit.*

Bethany shook Teresa's hand, then stepped up to the podium. "Thank you, Teresa, for that kind introduction and for all you do chairing our board and handling all the legalities of running a clinic such as ours."

Teresa returned to her seat as Bethany continued. "A lot of people ask if it scares me to work in the Deep Ellum district of downtown Dallas. They ask about our clientele, if they ever get violent. And while I'll admit that some may look rough, every one of our clients has been respectful with the staff—even those clients you might not expect, including motorcycle gang women covered with tattoos."

Teresa watched as Bethany's hands grasped the sides of the podium and she leaned forward to emphasize her point. *Her eyes always sparkle when she talks about her work at the clinic. She's perfect for the job.*

"And I have a theory," Bethany said. "I believe women respond respectfully when treated with respect, as, sadly, so few of our clients have been. And tonight I want you to hear for yourselves from one of these women."

Bethany nodded to someone in the crowd, and a short Latina woman stood and began to make her way to the front. She walked up to the microphone and adjusted it for her height. Then she cleared her throat. "Hello. I'm Carissa. And, well, my boyfriend, Chuy, and me, we went to the center to get an abortion. We were not married, and it was my third pregnancy. I wanted to keep my baby, but I did not have no money. We had talked about marriage, but we couldn't afford it. At the center, I got an ultrasound, and we saw the baby. It surprised us to see it was big enough to suck its thumb. So Chuy and me took a walk in the park, and we talked about marriage again. Just then a justice of the peace came to us and asked if we could witness a wedding he was doing. We said okay. And it turned out the people getting married had a situation just like ours."

She took a deep breath. "So Chuy and me went back to the center and told them, 'God must want us together.' The next day, they gave us money for a marriage license and helped us catch up on bills."

The audience applauded.

"Today I volunteer at the clinic. My husband and me, we have a seven-month-old child. And we love him so much. So all you who give to help the clinic, I just wanted to say thank you." She looked back to Bethany for support.

Teresa watched as Bethany hugged her, the crowd clapped, and Carissa returned to her seat. She fought the tightening sensation in her throat. Why was it that she and John, who longed for children, had so much trouble conceiving, while others who didn't even want children got pregnant without trying?

She lowered her head. *After all, I have no right to complain. I brought it on myself.*

Early Sunday evening Red had just sat down in L and D when he received a phone call.

It was a nurse from the ER. "Are you covering OB down here?"

"I'm the one." He sighed, wishing for just five minutes' rest. "Whatcha got?"

"Eighteen-year-old, white female. First trimester. Vag bleeding. Failed chemical abortion."

"Vitals stable?"

"Yes, Doctor. She's a bit pale, but not volume depleted. Got an IV of half-normal saline. Large bore IV catheter. Labs sent."

"Great job. I'm on my way." Red turned to the administrative assistant in L and D. "Who's today's doc-in-the-box?"

"Dr. Lanier," came the reply.

"That'll work. I'm heading down to the ER to work up a patient. I'll give Lanier a call from down there."

Red trotted through the bowels of the hospital, making his way from one end of the campus to the other. He was winded when he walked into ER, and as he approached the desk, he caught the nurse's eye. "I need the OB case."

She handed him the chart, which he scanned. "Who's the nurse taking care of the patient in twenty-one?"

"Joan. You need her?"

Red nodded. "If you'll just send her down to the room, I'll take the history, and she can join me for the exam."

"Okay."

As Red walked toward room twenty-one, he heard Joan being paged on the overhead speaker. He paused for a moment outside the door when he heard voices inside. He tapped on it and entered. Sitting by the patient's bed was a dark-haired woman with deep brown eyes. She looked to be in her late twenties. A warm feeling came over him, and he smiled and nodded at her. She smiled back. *What a stone fox.* With effort he directed his attention to the patient, who lay with her back to him.

"Hello, Ms. Spencer. I'm Doctor Richison, one of the OB residents. I understand you're having some bleeding problems."

"Yes," came the timid reply. She kept facing the wall.

"Are you having much pain?"

"No, just cramping a little," came the small voice.

"When did the bleeding start?"

"About noon."

"Okay. That's been about six hours. Was it real heavy, bright red, clotty?"

"It got real heavy. I got scared, and my mom made me come in."

Red looked at the woman sitting by the bed. "Are you her... mother?"

She coughed. "Excuse me? Her *mother*? No way! Not unless I gave birth at age ten. I'm a friend, Bethany Fabrizio." She extended her hand to shake Red's.

"I, uh, gee, I'm sorry." he stammered. If the heat surging into his face was any indication, his cheeks must have matched his hair color. Clearing his throat, he moved closer to shake her hand. It felt tiny in his—and what was that fragrance? Oh yes. Fantasy. That was what Sharon used to wear.

When he didn't immediately return his focus to the patient, Bethany added, "I direct Women's Choice Clinic in Deep Ellum." She motioned to the patient. "Dawn called and asked me to accompany her, so I met her here. We know each other through the clinic."

"My mom said I got myself into this mess, so I was on my own." The girl's muffled voice came from the bed.

Bethany reached over and placed a hand on the girl's shoulder. Red followed by turning back toward her.

"Since you don't have any family here, we'll need your signature on a few forms."

"I'm on my mom's insurance," she insisted.

"Okay. Well, can you tell me when your last period was?"

"The doctor said I was only six or seven weeks pregnant. But the way I figured it with Bethany here at her clinic, it had been about nine weeks."

"A doctor gave you some medicine?"

The patient nodded, still facing the wall.

"Do you know what it was and how much you took?"

"No. I just did what he said. And he told me it would help me to miscarry...so I wouldn't be pregnant anymore."

At this, Bethany turned and stared out the window.

Red considered this. "I understand. And when did you take this medicine?"

"About a week ago."

He asked a series of additional questions, and about the time he finished, the nurse entered carrying a tray of instruments.

"Okay, Ms. Spencer, the nurse is here to help with a pelvic examination. I'll need you to put your feet in the stirrups." The young woman turned to see what he was referring to, and Red patted the metal gadgets. "We need to find out how much bleeding you've got."

Dawn clutched her hospital gown, rolled over on her back, and rested her feet on the metal loops. As the nurse draped her with a sheet bearing the hospital logo, she covered her face and stifled a sob.

Bethany patted Dawn's shoulder.

She's so young and frightened. "Good job," he said, hoping to calm her. "Now I need you to slide down a little so your bottom is right here, at the end of the table."

Again she complied.

"Super. Now I'm going to touch you with these gauze sponges to clean away some of the blood." He pulled on sterile gloves and wiped the blood, then ran warm water over the cold speculum, put a dollop of lubricating gel on it, and returned to the table. Careful to avoid the word *pain,* he said, "You let me know if it's too uncomfortable."

It didn't take long to see she was bleeding profusely.

"Is the sono machine being used down here?" he asked.

Joan shook her head. "It's at the shop. Sorry."

"Okay. Could you reposition the light for me, please?"

When Joan had adjusted the light for optimum viewing, Red surveyed the dilated cervix. *Placental tissue at the cervical opening.* "Let's put an amp of Pitocin in the IV."

Joan nodded and set to work.

"Ms. Spencer, how long ago did you eat?"

"I had a little for lunch a few hours ago."

"Okay. Then let me do an examination now. I'll be checking the size of the uterus just to make sure everything is doing well."

Again she nodded.

Red conducted the exam, feeling an enlarged uterus but noting it was not unusually tender. When he had finished, he sat next to the patient. "You've had what we call an incomplete abortion."

"What does that mean?"

"Your body was unable to finish miscarrying. That means you're at risk for bleeding and infection. We'll need to do a D and C, which is—"

"That's what they said at the clinic when they gave me the pills." Dawn was looking at him now.

"What?"

Her lips trembled as she spoke. "The doctor at the clinic. He said if it didn't work, they'd do a little operation. But they aren't open on Sundays, so I came here."

"I see. All right then, I'll page Dr. Lanier, the attending physician on call tonight, and we'll make all the arrangements to get you taken care of."

"Am I gonna be okay?"

"Sure. We'll even have you home late tonight or early in the morning." He looked at the nurse. "I'll need a consent form for D and C."

Joan turned to go for the paperwork. As Red watched her walk away, he sighed. It seemed wrong that such a young patient was under-age to give consent for an appendectomy, and yet the law considered her adult enough for surgery related to pregnancy.

Red looked back at the patient. "Do you know your blood type, Ms. Spencer?"

She shook her head.

"Nurse, check a type and Rh as well, please."

"Already ordered, Doctor. Should be back with the CBC shortly."

"Good job. Thanks." Red turned his attention back to Bethany. He glanced at her left hand. No wedding ring. The observation brought him an inordinate amount of pleasure. "If you'd like to stay in the wait-ing area, I'll be happy to let you know how everything went once we're finished."

Three hours later Red spotted Bethany in the nearby empty waiting room. As he approached, she stood to meet him.

"Ms. Fabergo." *Such expressive eyes.*

She smiled. "It's Fabrizio, but that's okay."

Heat flooded his face again, and he grimaced. "Oh. Sorry. I'm really blowing it here, aren't I? And it's not that I thought you were old enough to be her mother either…"

"Actually, you've been great, Dr. Richardson. It was kind of you to offer to keep me posted."

"Thanks." Choosing not to correct her mispronunciation of his name, he motioned for her to sit down, and he took the adjacent seat. "Sorry it took so long. First we had to wait for her doctor to get here, and then we had to wait for an operating room. But Ms. Spencer's doing just fine. She's in recovery now."

"Thank you. I appreciate it."

Red nodded. "It's late enough now that we'll probably keep her for the night." Red had nothing more to say, but he didn't want the conversation to end. "It's going way beyond the call of duty for you to come up here with a client. She told me she'd met you only twice."

"Yeah. Sadly, this sort of mess is the very thing we'd hoped to prevent. And it's only the beginning of the pain for her, I'm afraid." She looked away.

"Actually, recovery from a D and C isn't so bad."

"That's not the kind of pain I meant."

"You mean the abortion then."

She looked back at him and nodded.

"Yeah, it's a bad deal. And you'd be amazed at how many cases we get from VIP, which is especially sad since some of our own residents help to staff the place."

"Do *you* work there?"

His beeper went off. "At VIP?" He reached down and checked it, then looked back at her. "No way." He reached out to shake her hand. "I'm so glad to have met you. I appreciate the fine work you're doing, and maybe someday when I have some time, I can drop in and lend some aid at *your* clinic."

Bethany's eyes lit up.

What he wouldn't give to stay there and talk with her. He sighed. "Excuse me. I have to go now."

Later, when he visited Dawn Spencer in postop to tell her they'd be taking her to a room, he asked a few more questions about her friend.

By the fourth question, Ms. Spencer told him, "I have her business card in my purse."

A smile sneaked out before Red could stop it, and he gave her a casual nod at this news. "I'll stop by your room in the morning and get her number from you then." Red tried to take good care of all his patients, but he planned to hover a bit around this one.

Perhaps she would have a visitor.

NINE

Red dreaded the nights when the call schedule assigned him to labor and delivery under the supervision of Denny Damon, the fourth-year resident. Unfortunately, tonight was one of those nights. When Dorie had taken over as chief OB resident, she'd instructed all the first- and second-years to clear all clinic cases—patients with no physicians other than the residents—with the upper-class residents. If there was still uncertainty, she told them they could call her. She had warned them by saying, "I don't like surprises."

I wish Damon was half as conscientious as Dorie.

Red was supposed to call Damon if he needed help, but the senior resident had made it clear that he wanted sleep when he was on hospital call.

Red hated to phone him, but he also knew that if he got into trouble and didn't call Damon, Dorie would get riled.

At the moment one of the clinic patients was in labor, and Red was doing his best to manage it. This was her second child, and she was dilated to six centimeters, but she had stayed there for three hours. Red had aggressively managed the labor using Pitocin to augment the contractions, but nothing seemed to help.

"Got a deep transverse arrest," he told the L and D nurse assisting him as he headed back from the phones. "Kind of tricky. Contraction pattern looks good, but it's a big baby."

"You gonna call Dr. Damon?"

"I just did."

The nurse grimaced. "And what did Sleeping Beauty say?"

"He told me to increase the Pitocin and slammed down the phone." Red had censored the wording.

"Nice guy."

"So I guess we advance the Pitocin." Maybe he should go over

Damon's head to call Dorie. That could kill his chances of surviving residency, but he didn't want the patient to suffer for his mess either. He headed back in to see the patient, the nurse trailing behind him.

"How're you doing, Mrs. Byers?" he asked.

"Okay…pretty comfy since you put in the epidural. But my first labor didn't go this slow, and I figured the second would be faster, if anything."

"The size of your baby and its position are making it a bit tough to fit through the birth canal. I checked with my superiors, and they've advised a bit more time and a little more Pitocin."

As the night wore on, the patient progressed to about nine centimeters, but she was still at zero station, and the baby's head was still transverse. To help her along, Red tried a few tricks. First he had the patient turn from side to side. Then he tried to rotate the baby with his fingertips, but its head had begun to form to the pelvis, becoming cone-like, and stuck.

It took Red awhile to work up the nerve to phone Damon again. When he did, Damon answered with the charm of a disturbed rhino.

"This better be good!"

Red plunged in. "Patient's dilating, but the baby's not descending. I'm afraid a C-section's likely."

" 'Pit her and don't wake me again!"

Red heard the receiver slam down. *He's gonna sleep all night and expect me to cover for him.* He gritted his teeth and returned to the laboring patient.

"You're making decent progress," he assured her. "You should be fully dilated soon, and then you can begin to push. The baby should turn then."

By 1 A.M., the patient was completely dilated and began to push. But after two hours, she was still where she'd started: zero to plus-one station, with the head getting more pointed and failing to turn. Having waited until almost 4 A.M., Red went to the phone one more time.

"Dr. Damon, it's Dr. Richison again."

Damon yelled expletives at him. "Can't you handle it, man?"

"Mrs. Byers is complete, but after three hours of pushing, she's still stuck at zero to plus-one station. Deep transverse arrest. I think we'll need to do a section. If you don't want to help, I'll have to call Dr. Chambers."

"Take her to the back. Do a double setup. Get me the Kieland's, but have the nurses scrubbed for a section."

"Don't you want to *check* her first?" Red couldn't believe the man's audacity.

"Call me when she's ready." Damon hung up.

Feeling the wear of stress and hours without sleep, Red went to the rest room and splashed cold water on his face. Then he returned to attend to Mrs. Byers. "We're going to the delivery room, where we can do a good exam." He tried to calm her by his tone. "You probably need a C-section, but one of the more experienced residents is going to take a look and perhaps try to maneuver the baby with forceps."

Her eyes grew wide, and she swallowed hard. "You really think so? A C-section?"

Red nodded.

"I didn't have any trouble the first time. I just never imagined…"

The medical team moved Mrs. Byers to the OR, got her prepped and draped, and prepared all the equipment in the room.

The nurse, having worked with Red for most of the night, seemed to understand his dilemma. She pointed out to him one of the other nurses. "Damon likes her, if you catch my drift. Want me to have her call and let him know we're ready for the trial of forceps?"

Red nodded. Seconds later he listened as the young nurse cooed on the phone to Damon that the patient was ready for him. Another five minutes passed and then, with all the cockiness that gives doctors a bad name, Dr. Damon sauntered into the room, adjusting his mask. He approached Mrs. Byers, took her hand, and introduced himself. Then he told her, "I'm supervising Dr. Richison here tonight. Ready for some VIP treatment? How's about I take a look at the situation here?"

She nodded.

Damon muttered to Red, "We try to treat *all* our patients like VIPs, even if you have a *problem* with VIPs." Then he looked more closely at the mask that covered Red's eyes. "You're wearing glasses tonight. I didn't know you wore glasses."

"I don't usually, but when I've been up all night, sometimes my contacts hurt my eyes."

"Haven't you heard of the new laser eye surgery? Get it, and fast." He lowered his voice so only Red could hear. "With those glasses you look even *more* like a pinhead." He pulled on gloves and examined the patient. Then, ignoring Red, he looked at the nurse. "You have the Kieland's?"

"Yes, Doctor."

He turned his attention back to the patient. "Ma'am, Dr. Richison here has correctly diagnosed your situation. The baby is lodged transversely, looking sideways. But I think there's enough room to get this baby turned and out."

Mrs. Byers motioned with her head toward Red. "I think he already tried that."

"I'm sure he did. Let me scrub in a minute. I'll be right back." Damon left everyone standing while he went out to the sink.

Mrs. Byers looked at Red. "Can he turn the baby, Dr. Richison?"

Red did his best to exude confidence and not choke on his words. "Dr. Damon has considerable experience, and we can do a C-section if we need to. Your baby is just fine."

Damon strutted back into the room, dried off his hands, and pulled on his gown and gloves. He unwrapped the forceps.

The patient eyed them. "They look like salad spoons."

Damon ignored her. He reached his left hand into the vagina and guided the top blade of the forceps into place. Then he evaluated what he'd just done. Apparently happy with the position, he slid in the lower blade and locked the two together. Then he checked the position again.

Almost against his will, Red had to admit that the guy was fast and skilled, even if he was totally callous.

"Ever seen one of these before?" Damon asked him over his shoulder.

Of course he had seen one. *Thanks for making me feel like a total zero.* "I've seen a few. But they don't let first-years do forceps rotations. And this is my first transverse arrest as a second-year."

"Watch and learn, watch and learn," Damon said, showing off and teaching nothing. Damon grasped the forceps, now locked together, and rotated the baby's head.

Red frowned when he saw Damon's hands shaking. He had to be using too much force. When the baby's head rotated, Red felt a surge of relief—until Damon started to pull the infant down and out. Kieland forceps were meant only to rotate, not to deliver.

But Damon gave the forceps a firm, steady pull, and the head came into the pelvis. Then he deftly slipped off one of the blades and slid on the first of the Simpson's delivery forceps. Once he had it positioned, he removed the remaining Kieland's blade and replaced it with the opposite Simpson's.

Damon, his eyes gleaming, looked over to Red, then back to his work.

Well, he obviously knows what he's doing. Red sighed with relief, but he was also annoyed.

Damon pulled down with the forceps, bringing the baby's head to the vaginal opening. Then he cut an enormous episiotomy and pulled the baby through, ripping the patient's anus and rectum.

Good thing she had an effective epidural. She didn't feel a thing—yet, Red thought.

"It's a boy!" Dr. Damon told the thrilled mother.

The nurse applied a bit of suction to clear the baby's nose and mouth of secretions, and the baby cried. After clamping the cord and putting the baby up on the mother's abdomen, Damon turned to Red. "You can close."

Red nodded, knowing he'd spend the next hour—at least—stitching.

The young mother looked at Damon with grateful eyes. "Thank you so much, Doctor!"

"No problem, ma'am. And congratulations! You have a beautiful baby." He pulled off his gloves and scrubs and swaggered out the door.

"You were wonderful," she continued.

"Thank you so much, Dr. Damon!" The nurse was all but gushing.

Red choked out a thank-you as well.

————

At half past eight Monday morning, Bethany tapped on Dawn Spencer's door. She strained to hear an answer.

"Come in."

Bethany peeked around the door to find Dawn in a double room, sitting up and blowing her nose. She had swollen eyes.

"You okay?" Bethany walked in.

Dawn shook her head. "I had a sad night."

Bethany grabbed the chair by the window and scooted it next to the bed. "Want to tell me about it?"

"I woke up, I guess around eight o'clock last night. And that doctor guy said I needed to stay over. So I called my mom and told her. She said I'd have to stay up here alone because she wasn't going to miss her favorite television show. And Brad don't want to talk to me right now."

"I'm sorry."

"He said he would talk to me after…" Dawn put her elbows on her knees and laid her face in her hands. "When Brad and me started going out, I was so happy. I thought someday we might even get married. But then I found out I was pregnant. I knew we'd never get married if I had a baby. But now even with the baby gone, he don't want to talk to me."

"I'm sorry."

They sat in silence for a few minutes. Finally Dawn looked over at Bethany with a sly smile.

"That cute doctor came by twice this morning. I guess he called you?"

"What?" Bethany shook her head. "No, he doesn't have my number."

"Yes he does. I gave him your card. Is that okay? I mean, I hope you don't mind. I had him get it out of my purse for me."

"Sure, no problem, but—"

"He said he'd call and tell you how I am. This morning they said I have an infection, so I have to stay here for at least another day. I figured you came up here because he called you."

"No." Bethany stood and put a hand on Dawn's arm. "I'm just here because I thought you might need a friend through all this."

She sighed. "Thanks. I was so confused. I finally showed two of my friends those sono pictures you gave me. They said, 'Just try the abortion pill.' They said it would be easy. Just pop a pill and…all gone.

After I met you, I went to that other clinic. The doctor there told me the same thing my friends said—just swallow the pill. But I saw a *heartbeat*." Dawn's grip tightened on the blanket. "I didn't know what to do. I figured I could just take the pill and it would be over. The doctor said if I had any problems, I could come back and maybe have an operation."

"An operation?"

"Yeah. He asked if I had insurance in case I needed a surgery abortion. I said I didn't want no operation if I could have the pill. But they said sometimes you have to have both."

"Are you sure?" Wasn't that the whole point of RU-486? *Not* having a D and C?

"Oh yeah."

"Do you know which doctor you saw?"

"His name sounded like 'opium' or something. That's when I came back to see you. I just couldn't decide what to do."

"When did you take the second prescription?"

Dawn shook her head. "There wasn't no second one. The doctor gave me some free pills to take when I started cramping. So I took some yesterday, but they didn't help, so I came here."

"You got only one prescription?"

"Right. The doctor gave me one prescription."

Bethany fell silent. *Either Dawn was confused or… or the doctor didn't follow protocol.*

"Then Brad and me had another fight," Dawn continued. "He said if I didn't do it, I'd be raising a baby on my own. He'd already told me that, but I kept hoping when I showed him the pictures, he would change his mind. So I finally told my mom, thinking she'd help me. But she called me a little slut and said if I had a baby, she'd kick me out. So"—she shrugged—"I went and got the prescription filled."

"At the pharmacy by the clinic?"

"Uh-huh. But it was harder than I thought. I had to work up the guts to stop the pregnancy instead of letting somebody else do it. I just sat there crying alone in the bathroom, knowing it was me or nobody. So I choked down the pill." Dawn burst into tears. "It was so awful."

"I'm sorry." Bethany reached over and squeezed her hand, and Dawn didn't let go.

"I waited and waited and nothing happened. But then all of a sudden yesterday at lunch I started bleeding real bad and had to come here. And it really started to hurt, too. At first I thought it was good I could keep it secret with that pill, but then it scared me when I started bleeding with no doctor around."

Bethany sighed. She had heard stories like Dawn's at least a hundred times, and she wished she could stop the pain instead of always trying to repair it after the damage had been done.

Perhaps if she could find a way to shut down that clinic.

TEN

An hour later Red knocked on the door, then entered Ms. Spencer's room again. He picked up a scarf that was lying on the floor. One whiff of the fragrance lingering on it, and it was as though he were with Sharon again, riding in a horse-drawn carriage the night they got engaged.

But why would Sharon visit Ms. Spencer?

Then he remembered that Bethany wore Fantasy. *Maybe this is hers.* He set it on the chair and walked over to the side of the bed. "How are you feeling?"

"I'm all right." Dawn reached for the remote to turn down the volume on the television.

"I see. Listen, I—" Before he could finish, his cell phone rang. He made a quick apology, excused himself, and stepped outside the room to answer it. Before he even had a chance to speak, he heard her. "Hello? Who is this? Dawn?" The caller was clearly feminine, but he didn't recognize her voice. "This is Dr. Richison. Who's *this?*"

"Oh!" There was a slight pause, then, "This is Bethany Fabrizio. I had a call at home from this number—caller ID said Taylor Hospital."

So much for the anonymity of not leaving a message. At least he was talking with her now. Red leaned against the wall.

"Yeah, it was me. I was going to tell you about Ms. Spencer. She developed an infection, so we've had to keep her another day."

"She mentioned that. I was just up there to see her. I dropped back by my house to get her a pamphlet on postabortion syndrome. Since I may never see her again, I want to be sure she has it."

Bethany's kindness warmed his heart even more. This woman definitely went the extra mile. "That's thoughtful. Was that your scarf I found on the floor?"

Bethany paused. "White silk?"

"That's the one."

"Yep."

"Where are you now?"

"Just getting ready to pull out of my driveway."

"Where's that?"

"Duh. Next to my house."

Red laughed.

"I live on Munger," she finally offered, and Red heard a smile in her voice as well.

"So you live just a few blocks from here?"

"Yep. I get to hear the sirens all night. My roommate and I have a two-bedroom place about six blocks from the hospital."

"You're close to me then. I live over on Swiss Avenue."

"Wow, in one of those mansions?"

"No, no!" Red hoped she wouldn't be disappointed. "Those mansions had small carriage houses for the help, and I sublease one of those. Tell you what. Why don't I meet you at the main entrance to the hospital? That way you won't have to park again. I'll bring your scarf, and I can take the brochure back up to Ms. Spencer for you."

"Well, aren't you thoughtful. But I know you're busy, and I wouldn't want to trouble—"

"Oh, it's no trouble." Absolutely not. After all, it was a chance to see her again. "I'll be right down."

In less than five minutes, Bethany pulled up to the curb at the main door. Red bent down as she lowered the car window. He eyed her Mercedes. "Hello, Ms. Fabrizio. Nice wheels."

"Thanks." She flashed him that heart-jolting smile. "It was a gift from my dad. And please, call me Bethany."

"All right, Bethany. Then you can call me Red."

"Thanks, Red. You certainly went out of your way to help today." She handed him the brochure, and he set her scarf on the seat.

"Guess that makes two of us. Ms. Spencer is lucky to have a friend like you."

Bethany smiled.

He rested his hands on her open window. "Listen, I'd love to see your clinic sometime."

The driver of a car that had pulled in behind Bethany leaned on his horn, clearly impatient.

Bethany grimaced. "Guess I'd better go."

"Maybe we could grab a bite to eat one day and take a look."

She inched her car forward, but called back, "Hey, we need docs anytime. You've got my number."

Red straightened and watched her go, straining his neck for the last glimpse as she passed out of sight. He did indeed have her number, and he had every intention of calling it. Soon.

On Wednesday evening when the patient load slowed down, Red ducked into a call room and pulled Bethany's card out of his pocket. He paced and then reached for the phone. He started to punch in her number, then hung up and put away her card. But after another minute, he took it out again and grabbed the receiver. When her cheery answering machine came on the line, he started to hang up, then paused.

Come on, leave the lady a message. She'll probably know it was you calling anyway. You told her you would—

Just then the machine clicked off, and he heard a woman's voice.

"Hello?"

"Hi, Bethany?"

"No, this is Heather. Would you like to speak to Bethany?"

"Yes, please. This is Dr. Richison...Red Richison."

When Bethany came to the phone, Red said the lines he'd been mentally rehearsing: "Hey, I was wondering if you ever did clinic tours on Sunday afternoons? My on-call schedule's pretty hectic, and other than this Sunday, I don't have a real free day for a week and a half."

Red fidgeted when she didn't respond immediately to the little speech he'd blurted out. But then she spoke.

"Sure. We've been known to accommodate doctors who are willing to volunteer." Her voice sounded warm. "What time were you thinking?"

"Any time after church."

"Great. So you want to make it about one then?"

Red felt his confidence returning, and he slowed down. "Sure. But I figure we'll both be hungry. If you'll give me directions to your place, how about if I pick you up and we can go grab a bite somewhere?"

"Sounds great." She gave him the address before hanging up.

Red sat back and grinned as he heaved a sigh of relief. Then he got up to return to work, sailing out the door as he went.

Sunday afternoon Red walked from the sanctuary across the parking lot. He was lost in thought, feeling some discomfort with the morning's message to "rescue those being led away to death and hold back those staggering toward slaughter."

So many babies had been lost through abortion by his colleagues. Grief cut at him, and he knew he should speak up, taking a bolder stand in defense of the defenseless. But what about his work relationships as a resident? Getting pegged as the antiabortion guy could make his life even tougher than it already was.

He got to his blue convertible MGB parked in the shade of a huge live oak tree, got in, and turned the ignition. Nothing. He tried again. Silence.

After opening the hood, he stared down at the dual carburetor system, then walked to the passenger side and fished around for the screwdriver in the glove compartment. He walked back over to the hood.

"You need help, buddy?"

He glanced up and saw a couple in their car looking at him from across the near-empty lot. "Maybe." Ducking back under the hood, he unscrewed the cap, checked the oil levels in the carbs, and adjusted the choke with a screwdriver. Then he slid back behind the wheel, crossed his fingers, and tried again. The engine cranked, but it wouldn't start.

Great. Just great.

He could tell by the sound that the battery was fading. *Oh ma-a-an!* He played around with the choke adjustment, then he tried the engine once again. Still nothing.

The couple pulled up next to him.

Fearing that the battery might have drained and he would have too little charge left to start the car even if the choke worked, he lowered the top. Then he pulled up the snaps on the carpet behind the front seat, took off the metal cover, and located the battery.

"Guess I need a jump," he said to them.

"Okay." The husband popped his hood, then got out of the car.

Dirty, oily, and frustrated, Red looked at his watch and groaned.

Bethany looked at her watch. *1:30.* And still no sign of Red. She'd tried to occupy her mind by turning on the television, but every few minutes she glanced out the living room window to see if a car had pulled up yet.

The phone rang, and she sprang to answer it.

"Bethany, this is Red."

Finally! "Hi."

"I'm so sorry! My car broke down, and I didn't have my cell phone with me. Thought it was a dead battery, but it wasn't. Anyway, I tinkered with it long enough to get it working again, but now I'm covered in grease. Would you kill me if I asked for a rain check?"

Bummer. Next weekend I'll be out of town. Bethany did her best to hide her disappointment. "No problem. When did you have in mind?"

"Tonight. Could we do dinner instead?"

"Oh, sure!" *Dinner? All right! This is much better than postponing a week or more. It'll be fun and maybe—well, who knows!*

"Terrific. And…hey, you might want to bring a band."

"A *band?*"

"A hair band…to pull your hair back. The little culprit's an MGB convertible."

"Okay, sure." She'd figured Red for the conservative sedan type, which made this new image all the more intriguing.

Red clocked the time from his driveway to Bethany's place. Seven-thirty—he'd made it in under four minutes. The evening was unseasonably comfortable for late July in Texas. He parked under the shade

of a towering tree in her front yard and made his way up the stone walk.
A manicured yard surrounded the bungalow, which boasted a wide
porch and swing. Finding no doorbell, he opened the glass storm door
to knock. He smelled cookies baking. *Chocolate chip!*

He heard footsteps, and then a barefoot young blonde in black
workout shorts and a baseball shirt opened the door.

"Hi, you must be Red." She grinned.

"Yes. Red Richison."

"I'm Heather—Bethany's roommate. She ran next door for a second. I ran out of eggs for the second batch. Come on in. She should be
right back." She gestured for him to come into the living room, and
then she made her way back to the kitchen. "I'm making cookies," she
called out. "And I never plan ahead. But our neighbor next door is a
great cook who loves to help us."

Red surveyed the décor. Antiques, Victorian lamps, Monet prints
on the wall, a plush carpet… It looked homey and comfortable. "Nice
place. So what do you do, Heather?"

She peeked around the corner. "I'm a botanist. I work up at the
arboretum."

"That would explain the nice yard."

"Thanks." She smiled, then ducked back inside the kitchen.

Just then Bethany appeared wearing a nautical navy blue-and-white
shirt with matching shorts and brown sandals. She was holding three
eggs.

Red held the door open since her hands were clearly occupied. "Hi,
Bethany." He noticed she already had her hair tied back. She'd obviously
spent some effort on her appearance in preparation for their time
together. *She's awesome, but that fragrance…*

"Great car." She motioned toward the MGB.

"That's my baby. Love it when it's running smoothly, but it spends
too much time with my *friends* at the mechanics. And there aren't many
who can work on the classic British roadsters."

She laughed. "I like it. Looks fun."

"Yeah, it is, when it's running. The rev of the engine, the sound of
that muffler. Truly a sports car. But when they fail you in the hot Texas
sun…"

"That must've tested your character." Bethany took the eggs to the kitchen and then reappeared.

"Again, I'm so sorry I left you stranded for lunch, but I knew by the time I got cleaned up—"

Bethany waved it off. "Hey, no need to apologize, Red. This works great. So where are we going to eat?"

"I figured with a name like Fabrizio, I'd be crazy to try to choose a good Italian place. But do you like Chinese? The Snow Pea is good."

"Terrific." She turned toward the kitchen. "Be back in a few hours, Heather."

Red chimed in. "I have to be at work tomorrow morning at seven, so I promise not to keep her out too late."

Heather poked her head around the corner again. "Well, it's a good thing, son." She shook a wooden spoon at him.

Bethany looked at Heather, curtsied, then laughed. "Nice to meet you, Red," Heather said.

"You, too." When Red turned to leave, out of the corner of his eye he caught her reflection in the mirror: She was giving Bethany a thumbs-up. He suppressed a smile.

He walked her out to his car. "I sure like your place."

"Thanks. You should see what Heather's done with the backyard. I love to hang out in the hammock back there."

"How did you two meet?"

"At church."

"Where do you go?"

"Park Cities Chapel. You should go with us sometime. We have a great singles group."

"I'd love to go." He smiled, and she smiled back. He opened her door, and she slid in. As they drove to the restaurant, they didn't try to talk. The noise with the top down and the purr of the motor were too loud for conversation, so he tuned the radio dial to top forty tunes. He glanced over at Bethany, admiring her profile.

Had it really been nearly a year since he'd had a woman sitting next to him like this, the wind blowing through her hair? At least that.

Well then—he smiled—*it's about time...*

The restaurant manager spoke barely discernible English. "For two?"

Red nodded.

"Smoke or no-smoke?"

"Non." He looked at Bethany. "I mean, I assume you don't…"

"Right."

The manager guided them to a secluded booth.

"So tell me about yourself," Bethany said once they were settled. "Red has to be a nickname."

"Yeah, my real name's Julien." He made a face that showed what he thought of it.

"Is it a family name?"

Red shook his head. "My mother loves French, so she gave me a French name. But when I got to school, the kids called me *Julie N* and teased me about being a girl. My teacher had mercy and nicknamed me *Red* for my hair. The name just stuck. Now most of my friends don't even know my real name, and that suits me just fine, by the way."

Bethany smiled.

"As for the rest, well, I'm on call every third night, I love golf, and medicine is my life. What else would you like to know?"

"You're a second-year resident, right?"

"Yeah. Last year I did a rotating internship. I covered medical wards, general surgery, ER, various clinics—a really broad experience." He shook his head, remembering. "I was tired all the time, like a walking zombie. But I saw a ton of exciting stuff, got to know the people, and learned my way around the hospital. Which is a good thing. As a second-year now, they expect me to know what I'm doing and to actually take care of some people."

Bethany bit her lip. "If you don't mind my asking, aren't you older than most of the second years?"

"Uh-huh. I'm thirty-two. Spent about five years working in a biotech lab before deciding I wanted to go back to med school."

"So you did college, worked, then four years of med school, and now you're in your second year of residency?"

"Right. Took me a long time to decide what I wanted to be when I grew up!"

Bethany chuckled. "And you have a Southern accent. Are you a native Texan?"

Red leaned back and crossed his arms. "Guilty. Texan, born and bred, from Garland. A whopping twenty-five minutes from here."

The waitress brought the platters of food to their table, and they scooped generous helpings onto their plates.

Red paused. "Would you mind if we prayed?"

"That'd be great."

Bethany's sincere tone—and her beautiful smile—were all the encouragement Red needed. He took her hand and gave thanks for the food and the opportunities that lay ahead for them. When he had finished, Bethany beamed up at him.

"How did you become a believer?" she asked.

"Came to faith at a camp down in Marble Falls when I was eight. My folks got converted later. So I spent my summers down in the hill country, first as a camper and later on work crew. And I've pretty much tried to keep my commitment to the Lord since then. I hit a rough spot one year in college where I had a few too many brewskis with my friends on a regular basis. But I put that behind me. It was a long time ago."

"How are you liking your second year as a resident?"

"I'm loving it. There's one doc who has sort of emerged as my mentor—Dr. Dalmuth Kedar. He's the head of Maternal-Fetal Medicine. We call it MFM, for short. Anyway, he's brilliant, and he seems to have taken me under his wing. It's quite an honor."

"What made you decide to do ob-gyn?"

Red smiled and leaned back. "All through med school I saw myself as a cardiologist. But in med school they hook you up with practicing docs; it's called it *preceptorship*. I got paired with a family practice doctor for two weeks in a little town near here. This guy was sort of a salty old ex-Navy doc. After hanging out with him, I was hooked."

"How did he change your mind?"

"While we scrubbed for deliveries, Doc Hollingsworth would sing and recite limericks. The women he saw through childbirth would bake him cookies, and always just the way he liked them." Red raised his eyebrows and took on a mock serious tone. "How could you beat that?"

"So you do it for the cookies?"

Red laughed. "Well, sure!" He liked the way Bethany's eyes danced when she teased. "When he let me deliver my first baby, I was as excited as the expectant parents. I can't describe the feeling of telling them they had a boy. I told them, 'He's the most beautiful baby I've ever seen.'" Red grinned. "Doc said that *every* time he delivered a baby, and I've kinda picked it up. After that delivery he told me to sit and sew up the episiotomy; it had torn and extended a little. When I couldn't figure out what went where, he laughed his head off and had to show me what the finished product was supposed to look like. After all that, I was pretty much hooked. With my sports background, I like to win, and OB has mostly positive outcomes with happy parents. The obstetrics unit is usually a happy part of the hospital. Sure, there are those terrible moments. But overall it's a great specialty."

Bethany nodded. "That sounds great." She fell silent for a moment and pressed her lips together. "I hate to do this, but if you don't mind…"

Red had the feeling she was mustering the nerve to ask something. "Yes?" He encouraged her with a nod.

"I was wondering. Could I ask you a couple of OB questions? I have some concerns about Dawn Spencer's treatment over at VIP."

VIP? What did she know about VIP? Well, whatever she knew, he could certainly share some concerns of his own.

ELEVEN

Red straightened his shoulders, delighted that Bethany would look to him for medical expertise. Still, anything that involved VIP couldn't be good. "I'd be glad to answer your questions if I can. What would you like to know?"

"Can you tell me the usual protocol for RU-486?"

"Sure. The process involves a series of pills that induce chemical abortion. The patient needs several clinic visits for cervical exams, so it's not true that they can just pop one pill and it's over like most people think. The first pill, mefipristone, depletes the uterine lining. It prevents progesterone from working, and as that occurs the blood supply to the developing embryo is shut off, and the baby dies. Two days later the patient usually returns to the doctor's office to receive the second pill, a prostaglandin, which induces labor and causes the delivery. You with me so far?"

She seemed to be following him. "Uh-huh."

"After that, the patient usually feels nauseated. Then the cramps and bleeding start. It takes some hours for the entire process. One awful part about the whole thing is that many women don't expect to see a tiny, intact baby lying in the toilet when they're finished delivering. Women using RU-486 have to take the medication when they're between seven and ten weeks of pregnancy, and by then the baby has formed. It's quite recognizable, though tiny, of course."

Bethany winced. Red lowered his chin and studied her face for an honest response. "You sure you want to discuss this over dinner?"

"You're almost finished, right?"

He nodded.

"Okay, then go ahead. I need to know."

"All right. The patient usually goes back for a third visit, during which the doctor examines her to be sure the abortion has gone to completion. About 5 to 10 percent of women still require surgical procedures to complete the process."

Bethany seemed lost in thought when she nodded. "Oh, I see."

"What?"

"Well, it's just that Dawn said they gave her one prescription and told her she might need a surgical procedure after that. It sounded a little strange."

Red leaned his arms on the table. "My hunch is that she forgot a few steps in between. That happens a lot when a patient is upset, as so many of these young women are. She might have misheard or misunderstood. Or maybe she just didn't take the prostaglandin."

Bethany seemed unconvinced. "Once the patient finishes aborting, in terms of her body, is it pretty much all systems normal?"

"Actually, no. Sometimes the bleeding can last up to a month. We see more infections with RU-486 than with surgical abortions. Some patients have sleep disturbances, and there's some concern about impairing future fertility. In a few cases we also see hemorrhaging, but that's fairly uncommon."

The waitress brought the bill with two fortune cookies, and Bethany took one. She broke it open and pulled out the slip of paper. "You will meet someone who will help you," she read.

"Well, how about that?" Red opened his fortune and grinned. "Here's mine: 'You will meet a woman who is beautiful in every way.'"

"It doesn't say that!" She tried to snatch it.

Red pulled it away, then relented. "You're right. I made it up."

"That's okay. I made mine up too." Her smile was both teasing and warm. "Ready to go?"

He grew serious. "Yeah, but just one more thing about what we were talking about. I'd be the last doc to defend the VIP clinic, but here's my hunch…"

Bethany leaned closer as he went on.

"It's July, right? And all the new residents start in July. The new chief resident is still staffing the place with the new folks. So perhaps we're seeing the results of just plain inexperience."

Bethany shrugged. "Maybe. But it seems like I hear these stories year-round. And I can't help wondering…"

"What?" Red prompted.

Her gaze was somber. "Shouldn't someone try to stop them?"

Red agreed, but he had no idea how.

Bethany had given clinic tours a hundred times but never alone with a nice-looking single doctor who had just bought her dinner. She realized her hand was shaking as she fumbled for her card key. She led Red down the walk to the empty building, then stood under the awning that identified in bold letters WOMEN'S CHOICE CLINIC as she unlocked the door. They heard the beeping of the alarm threatening to blast. She groped along the wall and flicked on the light, then entered and motioned for Red to follow as she went to silence the nagging box.

"Nice place."

"You seem surprised." Bethany glanced over at Red as she disarmed the squawking cube.

"I guess I expected it to be more, I dunno, austere." He surveyed the reception area with its wallpapered borders, paintings, flower arrangements, oversize love seats, and Queen Anne end tables.

Bethany followed his gaze. "We have some generous donors. Someone gave us that sofa; somebody else donated fabric and did the reupholstering for us. Now it looks like new. Somebody else donated all the artwork."

"Cool."

Bethany shifted her weight from one leg to the other. She was not yet comfortable enough with Red to know how to fill the silence, so she opted for action and motioned toward the hall. "C'mon. Let me show you around."

Red followed.

"This is where our volunteers talk to clients." She pointed to a conference room partitioned into three semiprivate areas. They continued down the hall lined with pictures of babies and mothers—unspoken success stories. Then Bethany pointed to another door.

"In there we have the ultrasound machine. One of the local doctors donated it and provided training in how to use it. Since then, we've seen an enormous increase in the number of abortion-minded women decid-ing to carry their babies to term."

"Really? And you attribute that to…?"

Bethany cocked her head. "Maybe it's harder to believe that a baby is just the product of conception once you've seen a beating heart."

"Makes sense. Mind if I see the machine?"

Bethany opened the door and led him in.

He looked it over and whistled. "Great sono."

"Feel free to come by and help us use it sometime."

He looked her in the eyes. "Definitely. I'll be back."

She certainly hoped so. She gave him a faint smile, wanting to seem calm rather than too eager to see him again.

Further down the hall, Bethany showed him the room where the center stored donations of used maternity clothes, baby furniture, and canned goods. The place smelled like pine, from the floor solution, mixed with fresh paint. "Some contractors from a local church just helped us finish out this area," she told him.

Stopping at the next door, Bethany slipped a key into the lock and turned the knob. "This is my office." A wood table with an antique lamp sat centered in a mauve and green room. A couch and two chairs and an Impressionist oil painting of a mother with her child added a touch of class. One corner of the room, near a large window that over-looked the street, boasted a lush ficus tree.

Red surveyed the photos on the walls and credenza. "Are you into sailing?"

She nodded. "I'm from the West Coast, near Seattle, in Bremerton, Washington. So I spent most of my summers on a boat of some sort, though it's cold enough that you have to wear a wet suit. I miss the beauty, especially the Olympic Mountains—snow-covered peaks, even in August."

"What's this?" Red was focused on a photo of teenage Bethany in midair doing a back flip.

"Gymnastics was my life, until the beginning of my senior year of high school."

He looked at her. "You must have been really good! So what hap-pened your senior year?"

She had hoped he wouldn't ask, at least not yet.

"Long story."

Before he could press, she gestured for him to look across the hall, closing her door behind her. Next she led him into the boardroom, where she opened the small refrigerator in the corner and took out two bottles of Evian.

"Want one?"

"Sure."

Pulling out one of the massive chairs, she motioned for Red to join her.

"How long have you been the director here?" He sat down next to her.

"Two years. Before that I volunteered two nights a week while I was gainfully employed in human resources. I worked for a financial services corporation."

"What made you decide to make the big leap from business to a not-for-profit? Did you sense some sort of call from God?"

Red's words sounded almost flippant, but his open expression told Bethany he was truly interested in her answer.

"M'm-h'm." She often shared her story in public, but she had hoped to establish more of a relationship with Red before going into the details of her past. She opened her mouth, then hesitated.

Red leaned toward her to touch her forearm as it rested on the table. "I'm sorry. If you'd rather talk about something else…"

He has good eyes. Kind, brown eyes. "No, Red, it's okay. It's not like it's some deep, dark secret. I share about it sometimes in public, so I may as well tell you now." Bethany took a deep breath.

"Okay, but you don't have to. Really. I mean it."

"Thanks. I know. But still…" Bethany thought a minute, then launched in. "As is often the case with people who work with crisis pregnancy patients, my involvement with abortion is, unfortunately, personal."

She breathed a sigh of relief when she saw that her words had no visible effect on Red. He continued to look at her, his eyes understanding, his expression gracious.

"I was seventeen, just starting my senior year." Bethany glanced down at the floor and fixed her eyes on a spot in the carpet. She lowered her voice. "As I said, I grew up outside of Seattle. I'm the middle child of three girls. Dad was a deacon in the same church where he'd grown up, and Mom played the piano. A lot of people back then told me I was the model of a good Christian girl." She gave a humorless smile and met Red's gaze. "You know the deal—captain of the gymnastics team, officer in the youth group."

Red nodded.

"In the middle of my sophomore year, I started going out with the soccer team goalie. Even though he didn't share our beliefs, he really cared for me. He started coming to youth group with me, and we hung out a lot. But one weekend when my parents were out of town... Well, you know how it is. And he had a car, so there were lots of other opportunities after that...and, well, I got pregnant."

"He made you get an abortion?"

Bethany shook her head. Sadly, it was more complicated than that. "Actually, no. My boyfriend was decent and willing to do right by me. But when we went to my parents and told them we needed to get married, my dad flipped. It was then that I realized something far more devastating than finding out that I was pregnant. For my deacon father, it was more important to save face than to save my baby's life."

"Ouch."

Bethany nodded.

"So what did you do?"

"I got an abortion, just like Dad said."

"I'm sorry."

Bethany rubbed her eyes. "Yeah, well, it got worse. Mom agreed with him, so I got no support there. And I had no idea it would affect me like it did. No one warned me about the depression. The people at the clinic told me it was not a baby and not to refer to it as one. But I was upset that I'd killed my child, and I went nuts inside as I considered my father's two-faced religion. My relationship with my boyfriend unraveled, probably because I directed most of my rage at him. I knew he would take it—at least, I thought he would. But we drifted apart that year. So I came down here to go to school at SMU, and he stayed at

Seattle Pacific. The whole thing broke his heart, but then out of nowhere I heard he'd gotten married."

Red opened his mouth, but hesitated before speaking. "That's tough. And your parents? Is your relationship with them better now?"

Her answer was barely audible. "No."

"I'm sorry."

"Yeah, it's a long story, and this is getting depressing. Sorry."

"If it's your life, I'm interested." Red scooted closer.

"Thanks. Okay. Well, my dad's a bankruptcy lawyer, so he was thrilled when I decided at age fifteen to follow in his footsteps. When I announced I'd been accepted at SMU, he bought me the Mercedes."

"I didn't figure you bought it on clinic earnings." Red smiled.

"Not hardly."

"But you didn't go to law school, right?"

"Right."

"Uh-oh! And he didn't make you give back the car?"

"Actually, I offered, but that only made him more angry."

"Ouch."

Bethany nodded. "I got down to SMU, and my first year I acted out. I was devastated at my parents' hypocrisy. So I went through a party-hearty stage. Then I went home on break, and my mom found, uh, pills in my purse. Not a pretty sight."

"How'd you get it together?"

"I had a great roomie. She was this big, boisterous woman with a David Letterman gap in her front teeth. Not much to look at, but a heart of gold. She saw the way I was living—a promiscuous lifestyle and drinking a lot on the weekends. She never preached at me. She would just shake her head and sing songs like, 'Looking for Love in All the Wrong Places.' Because I was from out of town, her family let me stay with them at their house in South Dallas over breaks from school when I didn't go home.

"One day she thought I was out, but I was just doing my hair in the bathroom. She got down on her knees by her bed and started pouring out her heart to God over me, saying 'Jesus, Jesus, Jesus. She's my friend, you've got to help her.' She was rocking back and forth, pleading."

Bethany felt her voice begin to tremble, so she cleared her throat to help gain her composure. "I had never felt so loved in my life. I just stood in the doorway weeping as I watched her. She was embarrassed when I finally let her know I was there. But she told me, 'Girl, you need life. Real life.' She talked to me about the Lord. I told her I wasn't ready to make any decisions—I'd been active at church growing up, but had never embraced the faith for myself. So I agreed to go to church with her. And boy, was *that* an experience."

"How so?"

"This was no steepled chapel or strip-mall white church filled with spiritually impotent people. This was a multicultural group that met in a one-room place with paint chipping on the outside and a couple of broken windows. I drove us there in my Mercedes, all dressed up for the occasion. But as I sat there, I listened to former dope addicts singing praise songs and watched reformed hookers take communion, tears streaming down their faces. After the three-hour service, they had a big spread on the lawn. We ate casseroles and chocolate cake and visited all afternoon. I had a great time, so I went back two more times."

Red seemed quite interested, so she kept going.

"During my third visit, they had a special service for people to share their hearts and tell their stories. I don't know why, but I told it all."

"Did your roommate know about the abortion before that?"

Bethany shook her head and stared at her water bottle. "No way. That was the whole point, right? To save face? So nobody knew but my parents and my boyfriend. And when I finally let it out, well, the preacher came over and laid his hands on my head and said, 'Somebody has to pay.'" She glanced up at Red and saw that he seemed puzzled.

"Yeah. I was surprised, too. I expected him to say I was forgiven or something comforting. But he repeated it. 'Sister, somebody has to pay.' The look on my face must have told him I wasn't getting it. So he said, 'When somebody does wrong, and abortion's wrong, somebody's got to pay. Who's gonna pay? You or Jesus?'"

"Wow," Red whispered.

Bethany was silent for a long time. Finally she spoke. "I grew up with cultural Christianity, but that day I came face to face with the real meaning of grace. At that moment I genuinely trusted that Jesus died

for me, for my sins. And I realized he offered me forgiveness. I hadn't
imagined that God could forgive me, perhaps because I couldn't begin
to forgive myself—or my parents. My life began to change at that
moment. I was really free from a weight I couldn't even identify. Still,
that doesn't mean it got better for me with my family."

"What do you mean? Why would your family be unhappy about
your faith?"

"Well, Red, for starters my parents were incensed to hear me say I'd
found Christ when they insisted they'd raised me to know about Him
all my life. But the other killer was that I started volunteering at the center. I wanted to help women who were facing the decisions I'd faced—
I wanted them to have the choice I didn't get to have. My roomie used
to work here, so I found out about it from her."

"So you told your parents you'd gone public?"

"Eventually, yeah. And that meant my sisters learned about it, so
then they were hacked at my parents. My sisters saw right through their
justifications, so it was a mess. When I graduated from college, I passed
the LCAT to get into law school, but I decided instead to take the HR
job I'd heard about from a friend. I wanted to work for justice, but
instead of going through the courts, I decided to help people at their
point of need. I volunteered a couple of nights a week at the clinic and
started doing some speaking."

Red shook his head. "Oh boy, I'll bet your parents were thrilled
about that."

"Yeah, well, if Dad was hot about the fact that I'd gotten pregnant,
he was a blazing forest fire when he found out I'd gone public. And add
that to his being crushed when I disappointed him in the law thing. To
this day, my relationship with them is rocky. It's been years, but it's
still…" She buried her face in her hands.

"So all that is what drives you to reach out?"

She nodded, suddenly afraid to take her hands away and look at
him. What was she *thinking* to reveal so much about herself? And now
what was he thinking?

The warmth of his hand on her forearm gave her the confidence to
find out. Her eyes met his gaze, and she saw understanding. And something more.

"Bethany, what you told me tonight...it's beautiful."

A shiver of pleasure ran up her spine. "I'm glad you see it that way."

"You bet I see it that way. And thank you for being so honest with me. I'm honored by your trust." He smiled at her. "Oh, and by the way, sometime when you've got a decade, I'll tell you some of the mistakes I've made."

Warmed as much by his words as his manner, Bethany reached over and gave his hand a squeeze. "Thanks."

She felt sure Red meant what he'd said, both about her past and about his own life. And if that was true, didn't it mean they'd be spending more time together?

That was just fine with her.

TWELVE

Bethany dropped the miniblinds and hopped up on the bed where Heather sat cross-legged, munching on buttered popcorn.

"You were gone so long I figured either you were having a great time or he'd killed you." Heather had a wicked gleam in her eye.

Bethany laughed. "We weren't gone *that* long."

"Five hours for a clinic tour? Puh-*lease*. Hate to tell you, but that qualifies as a date."

"We had the best time. He said he's planning to come to the clinic on his day off next week and give us a few hours of his time. And he *also* said if there's a cool evening next week, maybe we should take his convertible out to the lake."

"Ooh!" Heather's eyebrows danced.

"Only bad thing is, he's so *tall.*"

"Bethany, a guy who's five-foot-six would be tall to you. So what was it like to go out with a doctor?"

"It wasn't really a date."

"Yeah, yeah. You know, Bethany, if you snag this guy, maybe there's hope for you and your old man after all."

Bethany sensed this was a setup, but she was curious enough to take the bait. "How so?"

"Why, the only thing better than being an attorney is being with a doctor."

"Heather!" Bethany gave her a fake slug. "You're so bad!"

Heather and Bethany sat sipping iced tea in their backyard. After a sweltering August day, the evening air still hung thick.

"I'm guessing you haven't heard anything more from Red, or you'd have told me," Heather said.

"No, but I didn't expect to. He works—"

"Hey? Anybody home?"

The women turned to see Teresa Murdock standing at the side gate. Bethany called out, "Hey! Come on in."

Teresa opened the gate and let herself into the backyard.

Heather smiled at her friend as she approached. "Can I get you some iced tea?"

"Sure. Thanks."

Heather headed inside while Teresa pulled up a padded deck chair, sat down, and handed Bethany a satchel.

"Whatcha got?"

"Just some papers for you to sign." As chair of WCC's board, and legal representative for the not-for-profit organization, Teresa devoted much of her time to clinic business. "Should be pretty self-explanatory, so I'll just leave it with you. I have a big case coming up next week, so I thought I'd better get some of this stuff done before that hits."

Heather reappeared with tea and cookies.

"What's the latest?" Bethany was referring to clinic business, but Teresa apparently had something else on her mind.

"The doctor—Dr. Dalmuth Kedar—he's been seeing me pretty regularly, keeping a close watch." Teresa patted her stomach. "I just found out his wife is Yvonne Cobb-Kedar, you know, that woman on channel eight?"

"Kedar?" Bethany asked.

"Yes, Yvonne Kedar."

"No, I mean the doctor."

"Oh. Dalmuth Kedar."

"He wouldn't by any chance be the head of Maternal-Fetal Medicine, would he?"

Teresa gave Bethany a surprised look. "Yes! Do you know him?"

"No, but I'm pretty sure Red said Dr. Kedar was his mentor."

Teresa's brows furrowed. "Who's Red?"

"Red Richison, Bethany's new love interest," Heather jumped in.

"*Love* interest?" Teresa's eyes grew wide and a smile played at her lips. "Tell me more!"

"Heather!" Bethany shook her head. "I give him a tour of the clinic, and the next thing you know, Heather's planning the wedding."

"I am not!" Heather looked wounded, and Bethany shot her a look. "I'm only planning the engagement."

Bethany crossed her arms. "See what I mean?"

"You know what?" Teresa had a funny look. "I think I met him…Red, I mean. I believe he helped with my case."

Bethany nodded. "Makes sense. He said Dr. Kedar was giving him some exposure to tough cases. How've you been feeling?"

"Ugh. A lot of morning sickness, but I'm so thankful to still be pregnant. As my husband says, 'Every barf a blessing.'"

Heather shook her head. "I'm amazed that your success story hasn't been all over the news."

"No way. Docs abhor publicity over experimental stuff like this. Dr. Kedar asked us to avoid any public splash until the twins are born. He's already taken some flak from his colleagues for not following the standard procedures, but it's hard to argue with his results. Besides, what can they say? He *is* the chief of OB."

Red had just released a patient when he stepped into the hall to see chief OB resident Dorie Chambers surrounded by a group of first- and second-year residents. She'd just announced their night-call schedules. The young doctors stood there, lodging a series of complaints, when Dr. Chambers silenced them by ceremoniously drawing a pen from her white jacket pocket and holding it before their eyes. She tilted it. "Ladies and gentlemen, picture, if you will, a hill."

They nodded.

"Do you know what rolls downhill?"

Just then a patient scooted past her, aided by a walker, so Dorie edited her words. "Um…*stuff* rolls downhill, ladies and gentleman."

She smiled, and they murmured.

"Yes, it all falls to the lowly first-year resident—lousy call schedule, bad patients, assisting bad-tempered surgeons, running blood to the lab. You name it, you get to do it. But from now on, whenever I hear such complaints, you may expect to see my slanted pen to remind you of the force of gravity. You are at the bottom of the hill, and it will all roll down to you."

At this little speech, two young doctors walked away, and Red overheard them as they passed.

"Gee, *that* was encouraging."

"Hey, at least she's better than the last chief—what a jerk. Last I heard he was asked to rule the universe, but he said that was beneath him."

Red turned to get back to business when Dorie spotted him and motioned him over. He complied and waited for the crowd to clear.

"I need to talk with you," she said.

"What about?"

"I have a business proposition, but I've got to run down to ER. Walk with me."

"Okay." As usual, Red had to trot to keep up with her.

"I heard you helped Dr. Kedar with an experimental ectopic procedure."

"True. It was amazing."

"Yeah, precisely the kind of heroics that make insurance companies and legal people nervous."

Red's mouth fell open. "But he saved two babies' lives!"

Dorie shrugged. "Perhaps. But perhaps not. It's too early to tell, isn't it?"

"Maybe, but they'd definitely be dead by now if he hadn't intervened."

"Yes, but it's also possible that he merely delayed the inevitable."

Red couldn't imagine why a chief resident would reprimand him for a procedure initiated by the chief of OB. "So am I in some kind of trouble here?"

"Not at all. You're doing good work and you're making powerful friends. In fact, how would you like to do some work for me? Some moonlighting."

Red hoped this wasn't about VIP. "What did you have in mind?"

"I'm prepared to offer you what I've offered some of the other residents. Sixty thousand dollars a year to do elective abortions over at VIP.

You only work three nights a week. Good money for decent hours, and I'll help arrange your call schedule here so you have no conflicts. We've got an opening over there right now."

Dr. Ophion's clinic? "No thanks. You should probably know that I'm against elective abortion."

Red expected Dorie to have a negative reaction, but his words didn't appear to faze her. "Oh, I see. Well, I respect your views, even if I do consider them shortsighted."

"Besides, I've seen some stuff coming out of VIP—the abortions, certainly, but other things, too—that concerns me."

"What kind of things?"

"I treated an incomplete—an RU-486 case—from there just last week."

Dorie dismissed his concerns with a wave. "They happen. You know the stats."

Red fixed his eyes on her, determined to respect her position as chief resident. One thing was sure, he couldn't say what he thought: *Sure, accidents happen, but it's always* something *over there.* He studied her silently. How much did she know about Ophion?

She tucked her Palm handheld into her pocket. "I do appreciate your concern, really. I want us to give women the best care we can. So if you ever hear of problems with VIP, get me the specifics, and I'll check into it."

Red stood in line in the Adolphus Hotel hallway, admiring the opulence of its old-world charm. Before him a long line of current and former residents waited their turns at a snack table loaded down with a broad range of fruits, cheeses, and desserts.

The Texas Gynecologic Association had invited them to three days of meetings, and so far he had spent all day Thursday and now much of Friday in workshops. Because the theme this year was high-risk obstetrics, Dr. Kedar was one of the few in-town experts to speak. He had done a fine job first thing Thursday with a plenary session, but Red noticed that both in his lecture and in the tough questions that followed, he'd steered wide of any mention of treatment for ectopic pregnancy.

After the presentation, physicians had surrounded Dr. Kedar. But now, at the afternoon break, Red spotted him by himself, holding a plate, looking for the best place to sit. Red left his place in line and walked over to him. "Great job, Doctor. I'm proud to know you."

"Hello, Red." Dr. Kedar made a slight bow. "Good to see you here."

"You, too. How are the ectopic twins doing?"

Dr. Kedar looked around and lowered his voice. "About all I can say at this point is that Mrs. Murdock's is certainly the most *monitored* pregnancy of my career."

"No doubt." Red took his cue to change the subject. "Listen, while we're talking about controversial topics, may I ask you about something?"

"Certainly."

"I need to know…are there any protocols using RU-486 that don't require prostaglandin therapy to initiate labor?"

Dr. Kedar paused, then shook his head. "No. The early European work demonstrated that using RU-486 alone would terminate the pregnancy, but the bleeding was unpredictable, sometimes even dramatically prolonged. Without the prostaglandin to start contractions, bleeding would start, but there was no telling when it would stop. Without it, they saw significantly more complications with hemorrhage and infection. Why do you ask?"

Red pursed his lips. "It's just a hunch, but it seems the VIP clinic may be offering the RU-486 without completing the therapy. I saw cases that made me wonder the last two times I had weekend call."

Dr. Kedar appeared to consider these words and then shook his head. "It would make no sense for them to do that. After all, VIP does not need more bad outcomes. I would be more inclined to think the patients misunderstood or simply failed to return for required follow-up."

"I suppose so. But I know of several patients—"

A physician unfamiliar to Red approached with outstretched hand. "Dr. Kedar! Congratulations on a most stimulating lecture!" Dr. Kedar turned to greet him, and Red recognized it was time to duck out of the conversation.

"Hey, Bethany!"

She looked up from her desk, and her eyes met Red's as he stood leaning in her office doorway. The pleasure on her face when she saw him filled him with delight.

"Red!" She jumped up. "Great to see you. Come on in." She gestured toward her couch and joined him in an adjacent chair. "I was so glad to hear you'd called."

"Well, I got caught up on my sleep this morning and I had a few extra hours. So I called, and Margaret told me—"

"We can *always* use your kind of help down here. We didn't have a physician volunteer to do sonos this afternoon, and we have a patient coming in who needs one. You're a godsend. Did you meet the staff?"

Red shook his head.

"C'mon, I'll introduce you."

He followed her to the boardroom, where several women, two in lab coats, were eating a Domino's pizza.

"Hey, you guys, we've got a new doc volunteer!" Bethany announced.

Standing in the doorway next to Bethany, Red couldn't help but feel conscious of his towering height next to her small frame. Bethany went around the group introducing each person by name and giving her job functions. She ended with Diana, a social worker who specialized in postabortion stress syndrome.

Red made a quick wave. "Hi, y'all. Sorry, but you'll probably have to tell me your names again a few times."

Bethany turned to him. "And don't feel outnumbered, just because you're the only guy and the only doctor."

"Pretty much goes with the specialty"—he shrugged—"but it's not all bad."

"Come on in," Diana said.

Red and Bethany joined them at the table, and the women spent the next fifteen minutes peppering Red with questions. It didn't take long for him to learn that half had had abortions.

When the staff finished eating, they gathered their things and headed out. "You'll be with me this afternoon," one of the nurses told

Red. "We have about an hour until we see a patient, but we may get a walk-in before that."

"She's in charge of the sono machine," Bethany explained.

Red nodded. "Thanks." Then he turned to Diana, who was still seated. "You said you're the postabortion counselor, right?"

"Yes."

"I've seen some research that tries to downplay the aftereffects of abortion, discounting the existence of postabortion syndrome."

"Yes, well, I can tell you both personally and professionally that it's real."

"I would think so."

"In my late twenties, when I was single, I had a liaison at work and ended up pregnant. I never told the father; I just went and got an abortion. I felt okay about my decision for about a decade. But today I'm married with two teenagers, and about eight years ago, it all hit— depression, anger, anxiety, feelings of worthlessness, guilt. I started having dreams about what my child would have grown to be. I'd gone back to school to enter social work, and I ended up concentrating most of my research on postabortion stress syndrome."

"So what do you tell patients?"

"I always start with forgiveness. My personal favorite is the story about Jesus telling the woman caught in adultery, 'Neither do I condemn you; go and sin no more.'"

"Do you tell them about your past?"

"Actually, no. They rarely ask about me. I'm just some middle-aged woman they don't even know. But *I* know about it, and when the questions about guilt and God come up, I've never met a patient who objected to unconditional forgiveness." She held up her index finger. "Not one."

Red nodded. "Do you ever talk to patients from the VIP clinic down the street?"

"Sure, all the time. VIP is the busiest clinic in town, so of course we see a large number of clients from there, and boy, could I tell you some stories."

Red raised his eyebrows. "Really? What kind of stories?"

"Ever heard of a doc named Ophion?"

"Sure. He's the director over there."

"Yes. In fact, the saddest case I've ever seen is one the Big Doc himself was involved in." She shook her head. "It was pretty hush-hush in the news, but the patient told me all about it. She's nineteen years old and has Crohn's disease—you know, inflammatory bowel."

"Uh-oh. Don't tell me he—"

"Yeah, Ophion didn't read her patient information sheet carefully enough, and he missed it. He never should have done a surgical procedure like that at the clinic without better evaluation. When he did her D and C abortion, he not only perforated her uterus, but he also pulled out part of the intestine."

Red cringed.

"She's hoping to get her colostomy reversed in the next year. And her case cost Ophion in a big way; they got him on gross negligence. The settlement was $2.5 million, which ran half a million over policy. So he's paying out of pocket for punitive damages—pain and suffering not covered by his insurance."

As Red listened, a few pieces of the puzzle fell into place. *No wonder he's cooking the books.* Diana's story had definitely stirred Red's curiosity.

What *else* was Ophion up to?

THIRTEEN

When the end of the day finally came, Red plopped down on the couch in Bethany's office.

She smiled at him. "So how did it go?"

"Great." He looked at his watch. *5:30.* "What's your evening look like?"

Bethany's smile captivated him. "I'm free. What's up?"

"I thought maybe we could do the tandem bike thing over at the lake."

Her eyes lit up. "I've never done that!"

"Let's both go home to change, and I'll pick you up for dinner in about an hour."

"You want to bike on a full stomach?"

"I was planning to do the scenic ride, not the Tour-de-France."

"Works for me."

Red grew serious. "After we eat, I've got some stuff I want to run by you."

The evening sun cast a golden glow over White Rock Lake, making each ripple sparkle. Red and Bethany had dismounted their bike and seated themselves on the grass at the edge of the lake, where they sat talking as they watched the sailboats glide by.

"Even speaking in vague generalities, you sound as though you've got good reason to think something's fishy over at VIP. So what are you going to do?" Bethany asked.

"I'm not sure I can do much."

"What?" She sat straight up. "How can you say that?"

Red continued staring out at the boats. He shook his head, then looked over at her. Her eyes questioned, and he knew he had to explain. "Something happened at the hospital awhile back. I'm not real comfortable talking about it."

She looked away, but not before he saw her hurt expression.

He opened his mouth, but no words came out. After playing with a blade of grass for a few minutes, he tried again. "It was last year, my first year of residency." He glanced up at her, then back at his knees. His voice quivering, he finally choked out the words. "I let a nurse put a preemie...in formalin."

Bethany reached over and touched his hand. He'd expected her to be shocked, but her eyes were filled with compassion. He stared back at the water.

"May I ask, what's formalin?"

"It's the stuff we use to embalm. It's not exactly anesthetic."

"How did it happen?"

Red told her the details.

"Would the baby have died anyway?"

He nodded. "I couldn't resuscitate her, so I just wanted it to be over. And ultimately, it didn't change anything but me." Finally the words he'd been trying to form spilled out. "I should've carried her to the nursery—just let them keep her warm. I should've told the mother I was mistaken and the baby was alive. She wouldn't have survived more than fifteen or twenty minutes, but it would've been better to let her die naturally. To hasten that child's death was just wrong. I knew it the moment I nodded, but I didn't do anything more. I just sat there. Or maybe I could've just held her and let her die in the comfort of someone's arms." He rubbed his chin. "Unfortunately, when you're an inexperienced resident, you avoid making waves with the nurses, especially this one. She chews up residents for fun. Besides, if somebody's got experience, and that nurse did... Still, that doesn't make *my* part any better."

"I'm sorry, but I'm grateful you told me."

Red watched a sailboat floating by. "I was engaged at the time, and my fiancée, Sharon, broke our engagement the next day. The timing was hard to ignore. For a long time, I was convinced God was punishing me."

"Had you told your fiancée about the baby?"

Red shook his head. "No, and something Diana said today made me realize maybe I haven't given forgiveness much thought for myself."

Bethany looked him straight in the eyes. "You *are* forgiven."

"I'm starting to believe that."

Red's cell phone rang, jolting them from the conversation. He answered it. It was a nurse from the hospital.

"Dr. Richison, I know this is your day off, but Dr. Kedar is asking for you if you're available. That ectopic you helped him with—looks like it's gone. He's got to do an emergency D and C."

Red jumped up. "Be right there." He turned back to Bethany, holding his hand out to help her up. "I'm sorry! I'm needed in surgery—a D and C for a twin tubal pregnancy."

Bethany gasped, and Red saw the horror on her face.

"It's Teresa Murdock, isn't it?"

Red met Dr. Kedar at the scrub sink and read the concern on his face.

"The patient is bleeding and cramping, Red."

"No warning? Just like that?"

Dr. Kedar shook his head. "I cannot say it is totally unexpected. Several days ago, we learned she had lost the first twin, but we were still hopeful. Yet when I did her sonogram in my office this afternoon, we found no heartbeat."

Red spoke in a hushed tone. "I'm sorry, both for the loss of two lives and for the disappointment you must feel."

"Thank you." Dr. Kedar blinked hard.

"How is Mrs. Murdock?" He eyed Dr. Kedar, wondering how he'd broken the news.

"It was difficult, but she seemed relieved when I told her that the deaths did not appear to be related to a problem with her tube. For some reason that was important to her." Dr. Kedar took a deep breath and moved on to the information Red needed. "I did a sono of the pelvis, checking for free fluid, which might signify her uterus had ruptured, but it looked good. She is bleeding though, and we need to do a

D and C immediately to empty the uterus, get it to clamp down, and prevent any new problems."

Red crossed his arms. "Are you concerned about perforating the uterus or possibly reopening the incision on the back wall?"

Dr. Kedar nodded. "Both. With this procedure we have increased risk of pushing the suction curette through the old incision or, at the opposite extreme, of not being aggressive enough to remove all the tissue, which would put her at greater risk for infection and hemorrhage."

"What can I do to help?"

Dr. Kedar gestured toward the scrub sink window, through which Red could see the surgical staff. "I have them prepping her for a dual approach—both abdominal and vaginal. We will start by putting in the laparoscope and visualizing the pelvis to get a good look at the back wall of the uterus and the site of the fallopian tube transplantation. Then we will hook up the scope to the television camera, and I will leave you in the abdominal field to direct the camera so I can watch."

Red smiled, putting it all together. "So you'll not only feel it, but you'll also be able to see anything that looks worrisome."

"Correct. Ready?"

Red nodded.

They finished the scrub, entered the room, and then gowned and gloved. Once they had made the necessary incisions and attached the television camera, they could see a panoramic view of the pelvis. Everyone watched the screen. The back wall of the uterus was a strange sight, with a tube diving into the uterus, looking like someone standing with his hand in his back pocket.

Dr. Kedar glanced over at Red. "You stay here and keep the camera on that spot on the back wall. Once I get started, the uterus will move around a bit, so stay with me."

Red hoped he wouldn't shake too much. "Got it."

As Red held the instruments, Dr. Kedar selected his tools from the back table and began the suction procedure. As Dr. Kedar had warned, the uterus moved around like a bobber on a windy day at the lake. Red felt a pounding in his chest, but Dr. Kedar quickly completed the procedure and then sounded the depth of the uterus to make sure all was as it should be. When he was finished, he asked Red to close the abdominal incisions.

Red heaved a sigh of relief.

Afterward, they walked with Teresa, who was still unconscious, as the anesthesiologist wheeled her into recovery.

Red looked over at Dr. Kedar. "I'm glad it went well in there, but it's sure too bad we didn't have a successful outcome overall."

Dr. Kedar nodded and gave him a sad smile. "But the good news is that the failure was not due to the procedure. So I am hopeful that in the future, in rare cases, the procedure will be a viable option. Still, so many factors would have to be perfect."

At 7:15 the next evening, Red wheeled his blue MGB into Bethany's driveway and jumped out. He walked up the steps to the porch and found only the outer glass door closed. After knocking gently, he listened for footsteps, but none came. Seeing smoke rising from behind the house and the smell of dinner coming from the backyard, he walked around and found Bethany barbecuing chicken.

"It's a little hot for that, isn't it?"

She turned to him, and her eyes lit up. "Hey, Red! Come on in." She gestured toward the meat in front of her. "Heather got this started and realized she needed more sauce, so she left me tending it while she made a run for the store."

"The Plan-Ahead Queen strikes again, eh?"

Bethany smirked as she wiped sweat from her forehead. Red saw that perspiration had soaked the back of her oversize T-shirt as well.

He walked over to her. "Need any help?"

She shook her head, and motioned to the lawn chair in the shade. "Have a seat. I talked with Teresa about an hour ago. She told me one of the twins had gotten smaller, while the other was bigger."

Red nodded.

She sighed. "I was starting to think it really might work. So the second twin was actually dead when they did her last sono?"

Red nodded again. "I stopped in to see her just awhile ago. When

I told her I was headed here, she said I could discuss the case with you. It was a pretty dangerous procedure. Her uterus could have ruptured."

"It's so sad. She and John have tried for so long. I'd like to go up and see her tonight."

"She took a sleeping pill right before I left."

Bethany nodded. "Maybe in the morning then. You working?"

"Yeah. Seven-to-seven shift."

Heather appeared with a jar of sauce and waved at him. "Hey, Red! Care to join us for dinner? I put enough on for an army."

"I see that." He eyed the seven or eight chicken breasts on the grill. "And you've got a deal. I'm famished!"

Heather spread the sauce. "Y'all want to eat outside?"

"No way!" Bethany wiped her face again. "It's seven hundred degrees out here."

Red shook his head. "No, Bethany, It's only six hundred. Really, you shouldn't exaggerate."

"Okay, you wimps." Heather eyed Bethany's soaked shirt. "Look at it this way, I saved you from having to go work out tonight."

"Thanks a lot," Bethany said. "In fact, if you'll excuse me, I'm going to go change."

As Bethany ducked inside, Heather turned to Red. They chatted for a few minutes, and then he helped her carry in the platter full of food. After grabbing some plates and utensils, they set the table in the breakfast nook that overlooked the backyard. Red heard the blow dryer, and moments later Bethany reappeared in denim shorts and another T-shirt, her hair pulled up off her neck in a black hair band.

As soon as Heather had finished her chicken, she excused herself, saying she needed to do some work. Red and Bethany exchanged glances and smiled. They continued with light conversation, enjoying the food and the company until dusk fell. Then Red helped clear the table and began to run hot water in the sink, while Bethany put away the leftovers.

"Whatcha got going tonight?" Red rinsed barbecue sauce from the plates.

She looked over at him and smiled. "Nothing really."

"Want to take a drive over to the lake? " He glanced outside at the trees. "Looks like there's a bit of a breeze now, so it should be more comfortable. Maybe down to five hundred degrees?"

Bethany laughed.

They finished cleaning up the kitchen and, minutes later, were buzzing by the mansions on Swiss Avenue. Red pointed to a carriage house behind an enormous red brick estate and raised his voice above the road noise. "That's my place."

They cruised up Garland Road and turned onto the drive that circled the lake. Joggers and bikers dotted the shoreline as Red drove around and pulled into a parking place under the shade of a live oak, facing the water.

He turned off the motor and looked over at Bethany. She wore a peaceful expression as she watched the ducks playing in front of them. *I love her dark eyes and those long lashes.*

Finally she glanced over at him. "It's beautiful here."

Red nodded, then motioned for them to get out. They stretched out on the grass, leaning back on their elbows as they enjoyed the scene.

Red inhaled deeply. "You smell nice."

"Thanks." A tinge of red touched Bethany's cheeks. "It's just my shampoo, not my usual perfume."

"Yes, I know...Fantasy."

Bethany sat up and smiled. "Hey, you noticed."

"Yeah." Red spoke the word more harshly than he intended, and Bethany tipped her head.

"Something wrong?"

Red worked to find the most tactful words. "No, it's just...it reminds me of..."

"Oh. I see." Bethany turned back to the water.

They fell silent, and Red hoped he hadn't ruined the mood. After a time, she glanced at him. "It was a nasty breakup, huh?"

Red nodded. "And you're definitely more beautiful than she is."

Bethany cracked up. "Why, thank you!"

Red grew serious. "I mean it, and it's not just your beautiful eyes. I mean in every way."

"Thank you, Red," she whispered, casting a bashful glance to the ground.

Seeing the effect he had on her sent a thrill surging through him. He wanted to reach over and hold her hand, but he knew the time wasn't right. Not yet. He'd started to tell her about Sharon; he needed to finish that.

"Sharon didn't like the long hours I was working. She felt neglected and didn't think she could handle being married to a doctor. But there was a lot more to it than that. She was bipolar, but on meds she did fine. Unfortunately, her counselor told her meds were wrong, that they were a crutch to keep her from really dealing with her issues. So she went off them, and when she did, she totally changed. First she broke off the engagement. Then a few months later, I called to wish her a happy birthday, and..."

"And?"

"A guy answered the phone. Said it was good I called because she wouldn't be at that number for long."

"She was getting married?"

"Worse. She was moving in with him. Turns out that's *really* why she ended our engagement. She pinned the breakup on me, like it was my work that split us up, but she'd started seeing her therapist behind my back."

"Her *therapist?* Why would her therapist be more attracted to her when she was *off* her meds?"

"At the beginning of being off her meds, she was manic, a real charmer. Supercharged. I've heard that they split up whenever she's depressed and get back together when she's manic." Red looked at Bethany and shook his head. "Anyway, here I was, her fiancé, and we'd never slept together. As Christians we chose to wait. So finding out that she was sleeping with him... Well, I was pretty shocked. I mean, things got carried away a few times after we got engaged, but we were totally committed to wait until the right time. I'd had concern about her mental condition, but medication really had her balanced. She was delightful."

Red wanted to change the subject, but he couldn't think of a smooth transition, so he kept going. "She lives about forty-five minutes from here. Anyway, she wore the same perfume you do."

Bethany winced.

"Look, don't worry about it. It's really a lovely fragrance."

"But when I wear it, you think of her?"

"I wouldn't have put it quite that way."

Bethany looked at him, smiled, and then tilted her head to one side. "Then I have an idea. I'd say I'm in need of a new signature fragrance. How would you like to go shopping with me?"

Red stared at her. Was she serious? "I wouldn't ask you to do…to give up something so personal."

Bethany flashed him a heart-stopping smile. "You didn't ask. I offered."

Red fought to suppress a grin. From what he knew of Bethany, he was sure she wouldn't make such an offer if he didn't matter to her. But was his broken heart healed enough to care for someone again?

"Red, I appreciate your saying I don't have to change anything." Bethany fixed her gaze out at the water, and another smile played at her full mouth. "But I like the idea of marking the beginning of a new relationship with a new fragrance." She angled a look at him.

Red reached over and took her hand in both of his.

After several minutes Bethany spoke again. "Have you given any more thought to what we can do about VIP? Maybe by working—you and I together—we can shut it down."

Red froze, then stared at her. He'd been resisting for weeks the prompting that told him to speak out on behalf of the helpless. "I'm only a second-year resident, Bethany. I need to lay low, to establish more credibility before I alienate my peers."

Bethany bit her lip, then nodded. "I think I understand. It's just that all those innocent human lives…"

"I know. But Dr. Ophion saw what I did. With that baby. He came into the room while the baby was still alive and in the formalin. It was *his* patient. If I take him on, he could sabotage my residency."

Regan tiptoed into Teresa's hospital room and found her resting.

She leaned over her friend and whispered. "Teresa, are you awake?"

Teresa opened her eyes, then struggled to sit up when she recognized her friend.

"How do you feel?"

"Okay." She motioned for Regan to have a seat next to the bed, then pressed the control to adjust it so she could sit up.

"Are you in any pain?"

"No. Your brother has taken excellent care of me. I'm just really sad—mostly feeling lots of guilt."

"Guilt? But, Teresa, it's not like any of this was in your control."

"Uh, yeah, Regan, in a way it is. This really is my fault."

"How can you say that?"

Teresa blinked back the tears that glistened in her eyes. "I've never told you what caused my infertility, have I?"

"No."

Teresa drew a deep breath. "I used to be a lot different. In my past I had three abortions. Two of those pregnancies were conceived with married men."

Regan stared. *But you're so religious!*

"I'll spare you the sordid details, but suffice it to say I used to fight for sexual freedom and the right to choose abortion. I drank and slept around to my heart's content, but my personal freedom consisted of servitude to substances. In the middle of all that, I ended up getting pregnant by someone whose name I hardly knew. I wish I could say I agonized over my abortion, but it was based on expedience and fear."

Regan could hardly believe her ears. Teresa had always been so pro-life. In their IVF class she had been outspoken against freezing embryos, and she even volunteered for a pro-life clinic.

But Teresa wasn't finished. "I had two more abortions after that. One pregnancy was after a one-night stand, but the other was in the course of a long-term romance. In each case, I viewed the pregnancy as a prison sentence."

Regan blinked. "But you seem so different now."

"Yes, I am. About a year before I met my husband, I started to attend Mass. I had to get a grip on my drinking problem, and my twelve-step program emphasized my need for a higher power. But the Church's opposition to abortion...well, I couldn't see how any educated, progressive woman could deprive herself or anyone else of the right to make choices over her own body."

"What changed your mind?"

Teresa leaned her head back against her pillow. "I realized that the big debate over viability and legal definitions of murder weren't at the heart of the matter. Bottom line, scraping or sucking out whatever you decide to label the living creature in a woman's uterus is an act of violence, an act of power by the strong over the weak. The women's movement, of which I'm still a wholehearted supporter, has focused on *men's* exploitation. But with abortion, even in the worst-case scenario, a guy walks away. It's the *woman* who destroys a human life. How can we cry out against male violence when we resort to such abuse ourselves? And violence to an infinitely more helpless creature?"

"But Teresa! You're so antiabortion now that you were even willing to die if it meant your baby's heart could beat for a few more weeks. How pro-life is that? You risked losing three lives instead of two."

Teresa sighed. "I confess, I sometimes get so rigid that I'm more antiabortion than I am pro-life. It's just that so many people justify abortion on compassionate grounds, saying they don't want to bring a child into the world because there wouldn't be 'enough to go around.' But in my case there was plenty to go around—more than most of the world will ever enjoy. So while I *said* there wouldn't be enough for my child, I *meant* not enough for me."

"So you think you're being punished for how you used to think? Is that why you feel guilty?"

"Not punished. My conversion has definitely helped me see that God forgives when we repent. But I'm facing the consequences of my choices and actions. My tubes are shot because I got a sexually transmitted disease, and that's why the babies got caught in bad tubes."

She closed her eyes, and a tear traveled down her cheek. "So you see, it is my fault. If I had lived differently, we wouldn't be infertile."

FOURTEEN

The next morning Bethany visited Teresa. Afterward she found Red leaning against a wall, waiting for her. At first he didn't see her emerge from Teresa's room, so she sized him up, admiring the way he looked in his blue scrubs.

Great red hair, muscular, terrific smile. Definitely a keeper.

When he turned his head and noticed her, his eyes lit up. He immediately walked over to where she was, and she caught a whiff of his aftershave.

M'm, I didn't remember that he wore any. "I see you got my page."

"Yeah, thanks. I was assisting Dr. Kedar, but we got done in time. Glad I could break away." He guided her toward an empty waiting area. "Are you doing okay?"

"Yeah. Teresa's having a rough go of it though. We talked about showing ourselves the same grace God shows us."

"This I understand." Taking adjacent seats, they turned toward each other. "You look great, Bethany. I'm glad you're here. How'd you sleep?"

"Pretty well."

"Not me." He smiled. "I couldn't stop thinking about—"

Suddenly Bethany realized they weren't alone; she looked up to see a woman in a lab coat standing there.

The woman nodded to Red. "I hate to interrupt, but I need your help."

Red jumped up and motioned to Bethany. "Uh, Dr. Chambers, this is Bethany Fabrizio, my, uh, my friend."

Bethany noticed he was blushing. She stood and extended her hand to the doctor.

"Bethany, this is Dr. Dorie Chambers, the chief OB resident."

"My pleasure," Bethany said.

"Nice to meet you, too." The doctor turned back to Red. "We need you down in the clinic." She looked at Bethany with a twinkle in her eyes, then back to Red. "But no need to rush. Take another five or ten minutes."

Red nodded. "Okay. Be right there."

Dr. Chambers departed, and Bethany looked up at Red. "I guess I have to let you go."

"When can I see you again? There's a new movie showing at the Galleria theater that might be fun. And I'm off day after tomorrow—dinner and a movie?"

Bethany couldn't stop the slow smile that spread over her face. "And don't we have some shopping to do?"

Red breathed in the warm midmorning air as he made his way over to the hospital clinic. Today was a screening day for new patients in early pregnancy. Those who met the right criteria qualified for enrollment in the hospital clinic service, through which they'd receive all the benefits of a Taylor Hospital delivery.

Though the staff attending physicians were available for consultation, the resident physicians served as the primary caregivers for clinic patients. The patients paid less than half of what they'd pay to see a private doctor—an attractive option for those with no insurance or limited financial resources. Ordinarily, the clinic accepted new patients on the basis of case interest or the limits of the clinic budget, but it was early in the fiscal year, and accepting a number of cases meant giving the residents maximum experience.

Scanning through the file on his first patient, Red acquainted himself with the information on the thirty-two-year-old mother of two. *Ten weeks pregnant. Husband laid off. No insurance.*

Shelley Brennan had heard about the clinic from her private physician, who told her he would act as a consultant if needed. Red knew the story well: The private docs didn't want to do charity cases if they could help it. The clinic served as a good in-between option in these cases, but Red didn't expect any input from her previous doctor.

He entered the exam room to find a woman with curly dark hair and big blue eyes. Taking her history, he determined that she was accustomed to quality medical care. When the nurse joined him in the room, he asked the patient to lie down and lift her left arm.

"My breasts are already swollen and tender," she told him.

Red nodded. "Do you do breast self-exams?"

"Sometimes but not regularly."

Red began the exam gently, palpating the breast, beginning out in the underarm area and working in concentric circles to cover the breast. Her glandular tissue was dense, which wasn't unusual in pregnancy, but it did make the exam more difficult.

He could feel several small nodes in the armpit, but nothing remarkable. Then he reached the area just above the nipple. The rather consistent lumpiness was interrupted by a hard edge. Red worked to keep his expression from betraying his concern. "Does this area hurt?"

She shook her head and chuckled. "No more than anywhere else."

Red covered the area again. He had never encountered anything quite like it.

He checked Mrs. Brennan's other breast, which was negative, as were the abdominal and pelvic exams. After doing a pap smear, Red took the OB pelvic measurements, though Mrs. Brennan had already delivered an eight-pound baby vaginally.

"Let's see if we can hear this little one with the Doppler."

Red's patient broke into a grin. "Oh! I'd love to hear the baby's heart! We have two girls, and we're hoping for a boy."

He took the Doppler from the nurse, smeared a little gel on the patient's lower abdomen, and in a matter of seconds found the rapid *whoosh, whoosh, whoosh* of the baby's heart. He smiled. "There it is."

"Wonderful!" Mrs. Brennan wiped a tear. "We've been wanting another child. My husband's unemployed, but we're sure he'll find something soon, so it'll be okay…"

Red wiped the gel off her stomach and helped her back to a seated position.

"Well, Mrs. Brennan, you are going to have a baby."

She returned his good-natured manner. "No kidding!"

Red sat on the stainless-steel stool and began to fill out the chart. As he was making a note of his findings on the breast exam, he hesitated, then looked back to the patient. "Things are looking very good, but there was a small area on the breast." He had her complete attention. "I notice in your family history that you didn't mention any problems with breast disease."

"That's right. What did you find? Is it bad? Is it cancer?"

Red tried to soothe her. "Hold on there. It's just an area I'd like our chief resident, Dr. Dorie Chambers, to examine. She has years more experience, and we just want to be sure when it comes to your health."

"Okay." Mrs. Brennan relaxed her shoulders, but the color had drained from her face.

"If you'll wait here, Dr. Chambers is in the clinic today. I'll go find her." Red excused himself and went to the nurses' station, where he found Dorie quizzing the med students over obstetrical diagnoses. He waited for her to finish.

"Yes, Dr. Richison, what have you got?" As was usual for residents, she retained a degree of formality in front of patients and med students.

Red leaned against the counter. "It's probably nothing. But I have a patient in room four. While doing her breast exam, I found one area I thought was suspicious. I wondered if you could reexamine her and give me your opinion."

"Absolutely." She rose from the chair. The med students looked hopeful, clearly anticipating an invitation to participate. "Please wait here," she told them, and several faces fell. Red held back a smile; how well he remembered those days.

"This may be delicate," Dorie told them. "But if the patient is amenable, I will invite one of you back to examine her as well."

Dorie glanced through the chart, then followed Red back to the room. He knew not to say where he'd found the questionable site to keep from biasing her.

Dorie extended her hand to the patient, who took it. "I'm Dr. Chambers." She then repeated the same examination. She took more notice of the nodes in the armpit than Red had done, and she carefully moved around the breast. She, too, stopped in the area that concerned Red. Then she moved on. She examined the other side as well.

"All right, Mrs. Brennan, you can sit up."

"What did you find?"

"Dr. Richison has done a careful exam and has found a small mass in your left breast, just above the nipple."

The patient seemed to hang on every word.

Dorie continued. "I agree fully, so we'll need to do a little more investigating."

"Is it cancer?"

Dorie, who now stood beside the patient, touched the woman's arm. "It's much too early to know that. Most of these things in pregnancy just represent the enormous increase in the hormones. Rarely do we find anything more worrisome than that. But we need to be sure. Did you breastfeed your other children?"

"Yes, for nine months on the first, and six months on the second."

"Good. Very good." Dorie gave the patient a reassuring smile. "We'll need to arrange a mammogram, and perhaps a breast sonogram as well." She turned to Red. "Make a note on the request that the patient is pregnant and will need shielding. And also tell them the location of the questionable area." She returned her attention to the patient and laid a gentle hand on her knee. "It was a pleasure to meet you. We'll take good care of you."

"Thank you," Mrs. Brennan whispered.

Red gave the woman's back a light pat. "You may re-dress, and I'll be back in a few minutes with the lab forms and the mammogram request."

Once outside the door and out of hearing range, Dorie turned to Red. "Good catch. It's not easy to find anything in an early pregnant patient; you did well."

"You think it's anything?"

"Yeah, I think it's something. She will be a complex teaching case. I think she has some nodal involvement. They felt a bit too prominent in that armpit."

"I noticed that, but I've never yet seen a breast cancer in pregnancy."

"If I'm right, it doesn't look too good for her. We'll have to do a biopsy and special hormone studies. Then, depending on the type of tumor, probably remove it, take some nodes…chest wall radiation and chemo."

"What about the baby? Can't this wait until after it's born?"

Dorie looked back to him and assumed her most professional tone. "Her survival will be directly proportional to the type of tumor, how far it has spread, and how quickly we can begin the therapy. Most of these are stimulated by pregnancy hormones and grow rapidly. Of course, it will be the patient's decision, but if we are correct, continuing the pregnancy will shorten her life span, probably dramatically."

"How dramatically?"

"Perhaps from years down to months."

Red shook his head.

"Best case, we abort her and move to surgery and chemo. Occasionally we just go ahead with the chemo and let the pregnancy miscarry. H'm, no, at ten weeks, she'd need a D and C anyway, probably. It's best to abort the pregnancy and then turn our full attention to the mother's survival. You can run it by Dr. Kedar once you get the mammogram and biopsy reports back, but that's what I'd recommend."

"That's awful. She really wants to have this baby."

Dorie responded, not unkindly, but emphasizing what was at stake. "Yes, but she already has two children at home who need their mother."

At six o'clock Bethany approached the steps of the carriage house that led to Red's upstairs apartment. As she fought the butterflies in her stomach, she reminded herself that she had no reason to feel nervous. She'd simply wanted to avoid the August heat in an unair-conditioned car. So she'd left a message on Red's machine telling him that she'd be happy to drive, and now she was there to pick him up.

Red opened the door to his apartment, and the smell of eucalyptus greeted her.

"Come on in. I cleaned up for you."

Bethany chuckled. The dishes drying on a rack proved he was telling the truth. As she entered, she saw a nice one-bedroom apartment with picture windows that made the open kitchen and living areas even more inviting. The windows were dressed with expensive-looking drapes in tans and beiges, and the rattan furniture gave the room a summer feel. In the center of the solid wood dining table was a large dried eucalyptus arrangement.

Bethany raised a brow. "Are you into decorating?"

Red grew quiet. "No, uh, no, not me."

Ah...Sharon. Clearly Red's ex-fiancée was responsible for the look. Bethany nodded and changed the subject by commenting on his eclectic music collection. Red seemed relieved as she went on to notice his golf memorabilia and his shelves full of medical books. When he had finished showing her around, she worked to break the awkwardness she knew she'd created.

"I like it." Spotting a cluster of athletic photos on one of the bookshelves, she gave him a cheeky grin. "You're certainly lookin' good there. College golf?"

He shook his head. "No, it's way more recent than that. I got dragged against my will into doing some studio shots."

"They're great. I'd love to have a copy of this one."

"I've got an extra or two in one of the photo albums here." He pulled an album off the shelf and began to flip pages. A five-by-seven photo tucked inside the front cover dropped to the floor, and Bethany eyed it as Red bent to pick it up. It was upside-down to her, but she could see that it was a modeling pose of a well-built woman with waist-length blond hair. Red shoved it back into the book and turned pages until he found the shot of himself that matched the one Bethany liked.

"Sorry about all that." Red stared straight ahead as they cruised the freeway toward the Galleria.

"About what?" Bethany asked.

Red sighed. "Let's just say you're not the only one who's ready to make a new start."

Bethany reached over and squeezed his knee. "Thanks, Red. But please don't worry about it. Besides..."

He looked over at her.

She shot him a smile and turned her eyes back to the road. "I didn't realize just what a great compliment you were giving me when you said I was more beautiful."

Red relaxed. "Oh, easily…in *every* possible way."

Overcoming the earlier tension of the evening drew Red and Bethany together. He walked close to her, often placing a hand on the small of her back as they walked, and she enjoyed his strength and tenderness.

When they'd finished eating and stood outside the restaurant, Red looked up and down the mall. "Honestly, I'm not sure where to begin."

"No problem. Saks Fifth Avenue has great shoes and a terrific assortment of perfumes."

"Shoes?" The dismay on his face almost made her laugh. "Are we shopping for shoes?"

Bethany shook her head. "Relax. I just gauge the quality of a store by its shoe department. My friends sometimes refer to my closet as Imelda's Place, as in Imelda Marcos. Even if I have a bad-hair day, my feet should look great."

Red looked down at the new black leather heels she was wearing. "I'll have to pay better attention."

"Yes, you will!"

They both laughed and headed for Saks.

When they got to the first perfume counter, Bethany spread her hands at the possibilities before them. "First find some names you like. Opium sounds illegal, and too many women already wear Obsession. Who wants a signature that's like everyone else's?"

Red seemed to be suppressing a smile.

"What do *you* think?"

"Well, obviously Fantasy is out. My Sin is theologically unsound. Wind Song is what my mother wears. White Linen and White Shoulders and all the Chanels have too many memory associations."

Bethany stared at him. "How many girlfriends have you *had?*"

Red raised his palms. "Hey, I'm in my thirties, and I've spent a decade and a half trying to find you!"

Bethany cast him a sideways glance. "Oh, smooth. *Very* nice save."

Bethany turned her car onto Swiss Avenue, sorry that the night was coming to an end. "That was a fun movie and so sweet of you to buy my perfume. It was quite an extravagant gift."

"If you're willing to change your signature fragrance, it's the least I can do."

"Whisper...I love the name." She looked over at him and saw a tender smile that sent her pulse racing.

When they pulled into his driveway moments later, Red came around to open Bethany's door. He reached for her hand and helped her out, then drew her into an embrace. "M'm, you smell so great," he whispered in her ear. "Good night." He kissed her cheek, and then helped her back into her car. She waited as he walked up the steps, watching as he turned to wave again before going inside.

Bethany fell back into her Mercedes seat and let out a slow, drawn-out sigh.

Red had spent the morning in the lab with Dr. Kedar. Now it was lunchtime, and when he went to the break room at the clinic, he found a group of first- and second-year residents helping themselves to free food. One of the drug reps had made a short presentation, then offered plastic foam dishes full of enough Caesar salad and lasagna to feed a crowd. Now, as they ate, the woman was joining in the doctors' banter, even egging it on.

"Is it true what the medicine residents tell me? That they're the smart ones?" she asked.

The crowd responded with "Ooh!" and "Whoa!" Then everyone laughed.

A medicine resident volunteered, "And surgeons are ex-jocks that love to operate."

Another chimed in, "'A chance to cut is a chance to cure,' the surgeon's mantra."

By now everyone had joined in the competition.

"Aw, you medicine guys just can't make a decision." It was a surgeon this time. "You just sit around thinking all the time, 'Maybe this drug, maybe that one.' Make a call! Operate!"

"And the pediatricians?" Enjoying what she'd started, Beverly, the rep, had a wicked grin.

"They're all fixated in childhood. They can't carry on an adult conversation, they like to talk baby talk, and they wear ugly ties."

"Ouch!" One of the pediatric residents made a playful wince.

"And the psychiatrists?"

"*Everyone* knows that one," Red said. "They all need therapy individually *and* in groups."

A psychiatric resident turned the tables on him. "What about the OB guys?"

"Oh no!" Red ducked and covered his head. "Here it comes."

"Yeah, they all think they're ladies' men."

Red grabbed his heart as though he'd been shot.

Someone called out, "Actually, being a doc is the only way these guys get to be near any women."

"Do any of the OBs here work at the VIP clinic?" Beverly looked around the room. "I'm taking lunch over there next week."

At this most of the residents, not being OBs, returned to private conversations and eating. Having failed to receive any response, Beverly turned to Red, as he was the only one who'd been singled out as an OB. "Do *you* work at VIP?"

He shook his head. "Some of the residents do. But I don't get it."

"What do you mean?"

Red thought a minute. "Fighting for the lives of mothers and infants, delivering babies at the hospital, and then aborting them on the side at the clinic." He shrugged. "Just doesn't make sense to me."

Beverly leaned closer. "Then since you're not on the VIP payroll, would you mind answering a couple of questions for me? Because I have a hunch there's some shady dealing going on over there."

FIFTEEN

Red raised his eyebrows at the woman's words and looked around. "I'll hang around to help you clean up after lunch."

Half an hour later, when everyone had cleared out, he shut the door. As they gathered the trash, Beverly began. "My sister had a little problem with VIP. Actually, she's married—got married two years ago—and she's only twenty-two. Her husband's still in college, and she's been putting him through by working long hours doing hair and nails at a salon. She was on the pill, and they had one year to go before graduation."

Red nodded as he dumped some trash into the large bag she was holding.

"Anyway, my sister had an acne problem, so she took Minocin, the tetracycline derivative. As I'm sure you know, that medication diminishes the effects of the pill."

"Uh-oh."

Beverly grimaced. "Yeah, she got pregnant. It was *terrible* timing. She went to VIP and asked for the abortion pill. She thought it would be a one-time, easy deal and it would all be over."

Red pursed his lips—this story was becoming all too familiar.

"They gave her *a* prescription and told her which pharmacy to go to for a price reduction." She slanted a look at him. "Emphasis on *a,* as in a singular prescription."

Just like with Dawn. "Interesting."

"After that, she found out her insurance would cover obstetrical care and delivery, so she reconsidered. She thought maybe they could handle having a baby." She sighed. "But after talking it through, she decided it was best to go through with the abortion. She came and showed me the script her doctor gave for the RU-486. She wanted to know if my company carried it, hoping she could get samples for free. Well, my company *does* make the prostaglandin agonist that accompanies the RU-486 pill. When I saw the prescription for RU-486, I asked her for the accompanying prescription. But she said she only had the one prescription and some samples. Figuring VIP was giving away samples of the prostaglandin, I asked to see them." She smiled. "Never hurts to know the competition. But when she showed me the envelope with instructions, it was Anaprox DS!"

Red straightened at that, staring at the woman. "A prostaglandin *inhibitor?*"

"Exactly. Why would they have given her that?"

He couldn't believe it. "Anaprox? Are you sure?"

Beverly nodded.

"What did you do?"

"I got her to call VIP, and they told her to come in and get the prescription she needed. But since I had samples, she didn't bother."

"Maybe somebody got the wrong stuff out of their samples cabinet." Red was unconvinced, even as he said it.

"Possible. But since I used to work at the pharmacy where VIP sends patients, I got a former coworker to run records on all the RU-486 patients from VIP. It was surprisingly easy. Since the special price was the result of an agreement between VIP and the pharmacy, they tracked everything."

Red secured the garbage bag by tying the top in a knot. "What did you find out? That the docs at VIP weren't prescribing the prostaglandin?"

She shook her head. "It wasn't that simple. A lot of their patients got it, but usually the prescriptions that Ophion *himself* wrote were not accompanied by a script for the prostaglandin."

Red stopped short. "Ophion was misprescribing the meds?"

"So it would seem."

He slapped the table. "Then you've got him!"

She shook her head. "I don't have *diddly*. If Ophion gives samples, there's no record of what he's dispensed, so there's no way to trace whether he's been giving patients the wrong stuff. Besides, what he's doing isn't illegal. It just means a higher risk for complications."

And more complications mean more procedures, which mean more money.

"I just don't get it. It makes no sense," Beverly continued. "What possible reason could Ophion have for drawing out the process of aborting? It can't be money—"

"Why not?"

"The patients with incomplete abortions need D and Cs, and the residents handle those, not Ophion. It's not like he could personally pocket anything."

Red thought about that for a minute. "Maybe so, but the residents are salaried, and Ophion makes a percentage of every case."

Beverly's eyes lit with understanding. "So the more cases—"

"The more profits." *That does it! We've got to go after this guy!*

Bethany was in her office doing paperwork when Teresa called.

"How are you feeling?" Bethany asked.

"I need you to pray for us. We have to make a big decision. One of my partners from the firm called this morning to tell us that a birth mother who is eight-and-a-half-months pregnant wants to connect with an adoptive couple."

"Teresa!"

"Wait, Bethany." Teresa burst into tears. "It's so soon. I don't think I'm...*we're* ready. We're still so heartbroken over our loss, and I just don't know if I have the emotional reserves right now to begin the home-study process. But everyone will tell us we were crazy to pass up the opportunity."

"I won't. Not if it's not right for you."

It took Teresa a minute to compose herself. "Thanks, Bethany. It seems like when people hear I lost the twins they always say, 'Well, you can always adopt.'"

"I'm sorry. I know it's not that simple."

"I think I need to grieve our infertility before any other options will look appealing."

"Very understandable. What's the situation with this child?"

"A young woman who already has one baby came in looking for an attorney to handle a private adoption. She said she was suspicious of agencies but she can't handle another child. She told my partner that the one she already has is sick a lot. One time when she ran out of formula, she even took some canned tomato soup, diluted it with water, and put it in her baby's bottle. So handling two kids doesn't exactly sound like the wisest option for her."

"Oh, wow, no! So do you feel responsible to help?"

"No, it's not that. We have a long list of potential adoptive parents. But I can't help but wonder…I mean, if I don't take this chance, will I get another one?"

Bethany fell silent. It was a fair question. Opportunities like the one that had come to Teresa and John didn't happen often. Even so, she felt what Teresa needed right now was her support, not her opinion.

After a moment, Teresa sighed. "Thanks, you've helped a lot."

Bethany gave a small laugh. "I have?"

"Yeah. It helps to know I have at least two friends, you and Regan, who won't tell me I was crazy to let this one go. But the time just doesn't feel right."

"I'll support you in whatever you decide, Teresa. And I'll definitely pray with you about this."

Red dropped by Bethany's place unannounced on his way home. When she answered the door, she had red, puffy eyes.

"Red, I'm so glad it's you." She opened the screen and motioned him inside.

"Are you okay?"

She shook her head and sniffed, then motioned to the love seat in the living room. When she started to head for the chair across the room, Red gripped her hand and pulled her over to sit next to him. He didn't let go once she was seated.

Bethany's words came in halting bursts. "It-it's my dad. He had a heart attack last night." She closed her eyes for a moment, and when she opened them, he saw a mixture of grief and anger in those dark depths. "But my mom didn't bother to tell me until late this afternoon, and then she left a message on my machine instead of calling me at work. I found it when I got home."

Red clenched his free hand into a fist. *How could someone be so callous?* "Is he…?"

"He's stabilized, and they think he's going to be okay. But they're talking about double bypass surgery, so I'll probably fly to Seattle, not that I'm needed or even wanted there." At this, she started to cry again.

Red wrapped his arm around her and pulled her close. "Maybe your mom got caught up with all the medical stuff—doctors, hospitals, admission. I imagine she's in pretty major shock herself."

Bethany settled into his arms and seemed to be considering his words. But then she buried her face against him, sobbing. "I'm so afraid he'll die before he forgives me."

A noise drew Red's attention to the back door. Heather stood there, concern on her features. Apparently she'd started to come in the back door, but now she nodded at Red and turned around to stay outside.

Red wanted to tell Bethany that there was nothing to forgive, but he knew better, so he kissed the top of her head and held her close. Eventually she seemed to calm down some and got up to get a tissue.

"I'm sorry to hit you with all this, Red."

"Why?"

She shrugged. "I'm usually a pretty strong person."

Red nodded. After all, she was both pretty and strong. He patted the seat next to him, coaxing her to sit back down. She came and sat, but not close.

"You're not hitting me with anything. Besides, I'd cry too if my dad had a heart attack, especially if the relationship was as strained as yours is with your father."

She gave him a faint smile. "Thanks. And I'm guessing you had a reason for dropping by."

It'll wait. "Actually, I'm looking at the reason, okay?"

She nodded and gave him the faint smile again. "I'm glad you came."

Red was glad too. While it hurt to see her in pain, it brought him great satisfaction to be the one she had turned to. In fact, being her comforter was a role he could get used to.

On Saturday morning Bethany sat at her desk, daydreaming. She had rearranged her work schedule so she and Red could be together all day Tuesday, and she found herself wondering how they might spend the time. The buzzing intercom interrupted her thoughts.

"Yes?"

"We have a patient to see you." It was Margaret. "She's been to VIP and has some questions."

Bethany's heart sank. In staff parlance, *been to VIP* meant more than a counseling visit—it meant the woman had had an abortion. "Okay. Send her in."

Bethany rose and opened the door.

Margaret escorted the patient into the office and introduced the two women to each other, and then she handed the chart to Bethany. "I had her fill out an information form."

"Thanks, Margaret." Bethany turned to the patient. "Please, have a seat on the sofa." She waited until the woman was settled, then leaned back in her chair. "Now, how can we help you?"

The pale woman looked out the window as she spoke. "I had a D and C over at the Center for Reproductive Choice, but I still feel pregnant. You know, kind of queasy, tired, tender breasts."

Bethany thumbed through the woman's chart and noted she was nineteen with only one pregnancy listed. *She's articulate, looks collegiate.* "Okay, let me see here. Your chart lists your last period as a little more than three months ago, right?"

The patient picked at a button on the couch. "Yes."

"And you're married?"

"Right. We got married a little less than two months ago when we found out I was six weeks' pregnant. We decided we couldn't hurt our baby, and we really love each other, so we went ahead and got married."

"I see. But then you decided to have an abortion?"

The patient looked up. "Oh no! When the people from the clinic called to check on me, I told them we'd gotten married and were keeping the baby. And they offered to do a free sonogram, so I went back to see how the baby was doing."

"I see. And what did they tell you?"

"They said the pregnancy was abnormal, that the baby had died, and that I needed to have an operation, a D and C. The doctor said they could do it that day, and that it would take care of everything."

"Do you know which doctor you saw?"

"I saw two. One was pretty young—he did the sono. I remember he had a ponytail. Then he went and got the head guy, Dr. Ophion. He said he'd charge me only what the insurance company would pay."

Bethany nodded. "So they did the first pregnancy test and recommended an abortion, but you refused?"

"Right. I wanted the initial test, and when they said it was positive, I waited to talk it over with my boyfriend. At first I thought we might have to abort the baby." She looked away for a moment. "But I just couldn't."

"And your D and C was…let's see…nine days ago?"

"Right."

"Are you still bleeding?"

"Not really, but I still wake up every morning feeling awful. And I'm so tender I can't even put on my bra. I called the clinic, and they said it takes a few days for those symptoms to subside after the operation. Something about hormones…"

"That's right. But it usually only takes a day or two. This sounds too long." What in the world was going on? This was confusing. "We have a doctor here today. Let's have him do a sonogram and see if we can figure it out."

"Okay."

Bethany walked the patient to the sono room, introduced her to the physician volunteer, and told him the situation.

The doctor looked at the woman. "I'll bet we can figure this out. Are you bleeding at all?"

She shook her head. "I spotted up until a couple days ago, but there's nothing now except a little cramping."

"All right. If you would just undress from the waist down and cover yourself with this sheet, Ms. Fabrizio and I will step outside and be back in a minute to take a look with the sono."

When they stepped outside, Bethany turned to the doctor. "What do you suppose…?"

He shrugged. "Hard to say. Let's wait for the sono before we venture any guesses."

Minutes later, they returned to the exam room. Bethany sat in the corner and watched the wall-mounted television connected to the sonogram machine as the doctor typed the patient's name into the computer. He then prepared the vaginal transducer.

"All right," he said with a reassuring smile, "this part of the sonogram machine goes into the vagina. It's painless, and you can't hear the sound waves, but it will project a picture that you can see on the television behind me while I look here at the monitor. Okay?"

"Yes, Doctor. I've had sonos before, though never an internal one."

"This is more accurate in complicated cases such as yours."

The doctor began to scan. After a minute he spoke, and his words contradicted his soothing voice. "I'm afraid we have a bit of a problem. Do you see this little black circle here?"

Bethany saw the imaged pregnancy sac and felt her mouth drop open. *She's still pregnant!*

"Yes…?" The patient's voice quivered.

"And this"—the doctor pointed—"this is the heart beating."

Understanding dawned in the woman's eyes, and she looked stunned. *"What?* I'm still pregnant? But what about the D and C?"

"Yes, you are pregnant. Unfortunately, the pregnancy is not in the uterus, but out in the tube—on the right side. I'm so sorry. Let me get some numbers here, and then we can talk."

Bethany watched as he took the measurements, and her eyes widened as she realized what she was seeing. The woman was about seven weeks along, with an active fetal heartbeat. Bethany frowned. *But she's supposed to be twelve or thirteen weeks!* If this woman was married less than two months ago, there was no way she had been six weeks pregnant when she went to VIP the first time. Clearly, she wasn't pregnant at all when she got married. Then, when she did get pregnant, it was in the tube.

Bethany gripped the arms of the chair and gritted her teeth. "Excuse me." She went to her office to call Red, and her hands shook as she punched in his beeper number. She paced the floor while she waited for his return call. Fortunately, he didn't leave her waiting for long. When the phone rang, she picked it up halfway through the first ring.

"Red! We're sending a woman over to the ER, and we need you to get a good history regarding the dates."

"What? What's happening?"

She could hardly believe what she was saying. "I think…Red, I think somebody at VIP performed an abortion on an empty uterus!"

SIXTEEN

Shortly after 8:30 that night, Red followed Bethany into her backyard, where she had set the table.

He licked his lips when he saw the spread. "Linguini? Looks great. You didn't eat yet?"

She shook her head. "I figured if, as you said, you searched for a decade and a half for me, I could wait an hour or two for you."

He laughed. "Thanks. I'm famished. It *was* a long day. Where's Heather?"

"Her boyfriend's in town for the weekend, so they went out."

Red raised his eyebrows. "Is this a significant other?"

Bethany took her seat. "Heather's hoping he's *the one*."

"Sounds serious." Red sat down and watched as Bethany dished out the food. The mournful sax in the background was mellowing his mood. "Any word on your dad?"

"Yeah. I talked with Mom late last night. It looks like the heart attack was minor, so they'll let me know on the bypass surgery—maybe early October. Talking with her went better than I thought it would. I guess you were right about Mom being overwhelmed. Thanks."

He smiled at the relief he heard in her voice. "I'm glad."

Red said the blessing, and when he had finished, he looked into Bethany's eyes. "You know what I loved today?"

"What?"

"How we worked together."

She tilted her head and looked at him, brows furrowed.

"You saw a woman who had been tooled around, recognized that she needed help, and you called me. If you'll forgive me the dramatics, together we may have saved a woman's life today."

Bethany rested her arms on the edge of the table and leaned closer. "We always see people come and go at the clinic, with the life of a baby at stake, but it's not often that the *mother* is in danger. I sure appreciated your being on at the hospital so I knew she was going to get good care."

"We make a great team." He winked.

"I agree," she whispered.

"There's something wonderful about having a purpose that goes beyond our individual selves, don't you think? And I love that you've made a tragedy in your own life into a means of ministering grace to a lot of hurting people."

"Thank you." Bethany gazed at him for a moment, a sweet smile on her face. "So how did it go in the ER, anyway?"

"She was still groggy when I left. The surgical team got her in around four this afternoon for an emergency laparoscopy. I just hope she and her husband can make a go of it, despite their rough start. They probably haven't yet figured out that they weren't even pregnant when they got married. The husband was furious enough. He asked me how he could nail those suckers for not finding the ectopic. We called in Dr. Kedar to assist with the laparoscopy. I tried to bring him up to speed on the case, but he was in a bit of a hurry to get back to his own patients. But he did listen. And I'm taking notes, starting to keep a file on all the disaster drills from VIP."

"It does seem like the level of incompetence at VIP has reached an all-time high."

"I'm beginning to think it's more than incompetence." He filled her in on his conversation with the sales rep.

Bethany's eyes widened as she listened. "How low can they get? That sounds like what happened to Dawn!" She set her jaw. "What are you going to do?"

He met her gaze. "Even if I lose my job, this has got to stop. I've made up my mind to talk with Dorie Chambers. She's the chief OB resident you met in the waiting room the other day, and she does all the scheduling for residents over at VIP."

"What can she do?"

"I talked to her once already, and she didn't seem too interested in pursuing it. But that was before this situation. Now we've got more to go on. She's got a strong sense of justice about women getting messed with, so I think if I can convince her there's something more here than my personal bias against abortion, she'll take it seriously. And she has access to all the records. Still, I wish I had something rock solid, some legally sound information."

At Bethany's curious look, he shrugged. "Let's face it, doctors make mistakes, but proving intentional misconduct is trickier."

Several hours later, as they sat talking on the front porch swing, Red glanced at his watch. It was getting late.

"Red, do you think it's ever okay to lie, like if someone's convinced it's for a good purpose?"

He turned back to Bethany. "Well, *there's* an odd question."

She didn't laugh as he'd expected. Instead, she remained silent.

Red thought it over. "I don't know. In some ethical systems, it's considered okay to lie for a higher purpose, like saving a life."

"How about in *your* ethical system?"

"I don't know. I can't say I've thought much about it. But I'm not planning on telling Dorie any lies."

"I see. Okay, thanks."

"You planning on telling *me* lies, Bethany? Because I can name a few I'd love to hear."

"Like what?"

"Like…like that I'm the most handsome, buff dude you've ever laid eyes on?"

"Ah, but then I wouldn't be lying." She looked into his eyes.

"And have *I* mentioned that you have the most perfect lips I've ever seen?"

When those lips formed a tender smile, he leaned down and kissed her gently. He looked at her for another moment before speaking again. "I was right. They're just perfect."

As Red drove home that night, he was humming a love song and planning how he could make Tuesday an extra special day together. But when he pulled into his driveway, his heart skipped a beat. Sharon's car was in his driveway.

What's she *doing here?*

He parked and glanced inside her car, but she wasn't there. Then he looked up at his apartment and saw the lights on. When he got to the door, he knocked, but there was no answer. "Sharon, Are you in there?" The only sound was the CD player blaring out what used to be their song.

Taking out his key, he hesitated, not sure he wanted to know what he'd find. He cracked the door and peeked in to find Sharon stretched out, sound asleep, on the couch. He had to admit she looked sweet lying there surrounded in blond hair. She was wearing shorts and a knit tank top, all clearly designed to accentuate her marvelous figure.

If there was one thing Sharon knew how to do, it was get a man's attention.

Red drew a deep breath, then moved to touch her shoulder. "Sharon, what in the world are you doing here?"

She let out a little yelp and shot straight up.

Red stood staring at her.

"Red, you scared me to death!"

"I scared you?"

At his tone, she began to cry. "I knew I shouldn't have come here."

This is nuts. Shaking his head, Red sat in the chair beside the couch and lowered his voice a few notches. "Why did you come?"

Sharon turned to plant her bare feet on the floor. She was wearing the ankle bracelet he had given her during his last year of med school. "I came because…because I'm a fool!"

Red shrugged, thinking he couldn't argue with that. He rose to turn off the music.

"No one else understands me like you do, Red."

He didn't reply; he just moved to sit down on the couch. "No, Sharon, I can't say I ever understood you. Not really."

"But nobody has ever treated me like you." She gave him a puppy-eyed look.

"What about that guy you're living with?"

She wrinkled up her nose. "It's over with us."

Again? Red had trouble conjuring up any sympathy. "Ah, I see. Well, I guess I sort of know how you feel."

"That's just it, Red. I realized what I'd done to you, and I'm here to tell you how sorry I am."

"Thanks. Duly noted."

Clearly, she hadn't expected the terse response. She looked away.

"When did all this happen?"

"This morning."

Red kept himself from rolling his eyes. "Uh-huh. So where are you planning to live now?"

"That's just it, Red. I have no place to go."

"What about your parents?"

"They disowned me when I moved in with Chad the last time."

"Well, it's over with him now." Red still couldn't bring himself to say Chad's name. "I imagine your parents won't let you live on the street. Why don't you try to patch things up with them?"

"I'd rather patch things up with you." She reached out and put her hand on his knee. "You're the only person I could ever really love."

He placed his hand over hers, and she smiled. But when he took hold of her hand and removed it from his knee, the smile faded into a pout. Red sat thinking while she waited for his response. Finally, he stretched out his palm.

A huge grin crossed her face, and she reached out to hold his hand. But he shook his head. "The key. I want the key. Sharon, you can't stay here. I'm sorry for what happened to you, but you'll have to find someone else to help you."

Her mouth gaped open.

He continued to hold out his hand until she dug in her purse and pulled out a key. She all but slapped it in his hand and looked away. "That's it, Red? That's all you're going to say? Not even 'Let's go out once for old times' sake?'"

All the affection he once felt had turned to pity. "No."

"Red, I know I hurt you badly, but I never expected you to be this cold."

He couldn't help it—he chuckled. "Cold? Me? Sharon, *you* broke our engagement, blamed it on me, then moved in with some guy you'd been seeing behind my back. Now you show up a year later in my apartment, looking for a place to stay? Did it ever occur to you that I might find someone else?"

Sharon glared at him. "That's it? You've got another girlfriend?"

He nodded and watched as the warmth in her eyes turned to rage.

"I see." Her voice sliced like ice as she stood, then marched out the door.

Red watched her go, expecting to feel a tinge of sadness, but was instead relieved to be free of the pain that had kept him awake for so many nights. He shuddered to think that he might actually have married Sharon. Then his thoughts turned to Bethany, who was coming to mean more to him every day.

"Okay, Red. I'll look into it."

Dorie's somber expression told him she meant what she said. "These are some serious allegations, and I appreciate your bringing all this to my attention. It's a little touchy since we're talking about investigating my boss, but I'll try. Still, to be frank, I wish you'd been more honest with me."

Red was taken aback. "What do you mean?"

"I mean, you told me when I offered you the job that you were antiabortion, but yesterday I ran the test myself on your girlfriend."

"The test?"

"Her positive pregnancy test."

Red was too stunned to speak.

"So you have to admit it looks a bit like a double standard."

"Did you say *my* girlfriend?"

"Sure. You introduced me to her, remember? Bethany Fabrizio, right? Don't worry. I don't think anyone you know at VIP will make the connection. And I do appreciate your concern that we have high standards there, though your pharmacy rep friend seems to have bent a few rules in the process of snooping around."

Red wasn't taking in what she was saying. He was still trying to absorb her earlier comments. "Bethany…was at VIP yesterday?"

"C'mon Red, it's nothing to be ashamed of. It happens to lots of people."

"I'm *serious*."

Dorie stopped cold. "You didn't know?"

"What did she tell you?"

She shook her head. "She didn't see me. I just saw her coming in and figured you'd appreciate it if I discreetly handled it for you. When the rabbit died, so to speak, I saw that she was taken straight to Ophion. Right to the boss. I figured you might appreciate—"

"She told you she was *pregnant?*"

"No, Red. We told *her.* But please don't worry; nobody else knows. As I said, I ran the test on her myself."

SEVENTEEN

Red stared at Dorie. It couldn't be true…it just couldn't.

"She can't be pregnant, Dorie."

"Sorry, Red. These things happen. And with all that's happening in your life right now, I appreciate your coming in to cover for a sick resident when you were supposed to have the day off today—especially on a twenty-four-hour shift. Why don't you go ahead and take off Thursday morning if you want to go with Bethany? You know, give her some moral support."

He rubbed his suddenly aching temples. "Thursday?"

"She's scheduled for her D and C then. And rest assured, I'll check into what you said about the samples, but my hunch is that there's just some misunderstanding."

Red stood there, feeling like a gutted salmon in the mouth of a bear.

Dorie's pager went off. "Hang on." She looked down to read it. "Whoa, it's Damon calling from VIP with a stat."

Red, still too shocked to move, watched as Dorie walked over to call Damon from the nearest phone. Seconds later she strode off down the hall. "Come on, Red! We've got an emergency on—"

Red's beeper sounded.

"I'll bet that's ER calling you. They're going to need us. Let's go." She picked up her pace.

Red looked down at his pager and read the number. "You're right. It's ER. What's up?" He jogged to catch up with her.

"Damon called. They had what was supposed to be a twelve-week elective abortion, but it turned out to be a hydatidiform mole. One of the second-year guys must have missed it on the sono. Unfortunately, the blood scared him, so he stopped what he was doing."

"Oh no!" A second-year resident should've known how to handle a molar pregnancy—an unusual complication that behaves like a tumor of the placental tissue. Certainly an ob-gyn resident should know that once you start evacuating the tissue, you can't stop. "He should've kept going!"

"Right. All he had to do was keep the fluids going with the Pitocin to contract the uterus. Once he got everything out, the uterus would've contracted and the patient would've stopped bleeding, but he panicked. His first mistake was a bad diagnosis. His second was to stop the operation once he'd begun. With one of those deals, you should never, *ever* stop."

"Surely Damon knew what to do."

Dorie shook her head. "Unfortunately the resident had the nurse call 911 without even checking with Damon. They had one IV with Pitocin going, but our resident didn't know what to do. Damon probably would've finished the D and C, upped the Pit, and then sent the patient to the hospital for follow-up. But he was on a different case. First he heard of it was the sirens." Her jaw line tensed. "*Not* the kind of advertising we like at the clinic. The first time I did one of those, I thought I'd hit the aorta. It's sure not a procedure you want to do at a clinic."

She gave Red a nervous glance. "They never should've gotten into a mole over there. We've got the sono equipment. This shouldn't have happened—but even when it did, we should've handled it better."

"But it did happen, Dorie. Stuff like this is always happening. I'm telling you, a shortcut here, an error in judgment there… And you're the resident administrator…"

Dorie raised her palms, appearing to surrender, but as she did, she and Red rounded the corner to the ER. The urgency of the case at hand redirected their focus.

The ER patient, having just been moved into an exam room, was still bleeding profusely and lay connected to two IVs. The EMTs had hung a second liter.

"I want double Pitocin in each bag," Dorie ordered. "Type and cross for six units of blood, CBC, chemistry, and a quantitative HCG." She went to the phone and called the OR. "I have an emergency. Partial abortion of a molar pregnancy."

Red took a brief interview history from the young woman, whose eyes were wild with fright.

"Am I going to die?"

He made his voice as soothing as he could. "It's going to be all right."

She reached out a trembling hand and grabbed his wrist. "What's happening to me? Why is all this blood gushing out?"

Red loosened the viselike grip on his arm, then took the patient's hand and held it as he spoke. "You have a pregnancy complication. Actually it's very rare. But something didn't go right in the growth of your pregnancy."

"The guys in the ambulance said it had a high-dated form…"

Red furrowed his brow, then realized what she meant. "Ah, a hydatidiform. Yes, it's called a hydatidiform mole. That just means it's grape-like and, instead of placenta and baby, your uterus was filled with little cysts formed by the placental tissue. We need to get your uterus emptied with a D and C."

"But that's what they were doing when this *happened*. That's what caused all the bleeding!"

Red hesitated, taking care not to cast blame. "Yes, but we have better anesthesia here at the hospital and more sophisticated equipment. We can handle it here, even replace blood if necessary."

"Oh no!" Her voice grew louder. "I don't want blood! I *can't* have it. I'm a Jehovah's Witness!"

Red shot a glance over to Dorie, who turned her eyes to the heavens. She stepped over and put a gentle hand on the patient's upper arm. "All right. We will do everything we can without giving you blood. We have some artificial products that can make a huge difference, but let me be perfectly clear about what you want. You do not want blood under *any* circumstances?"

"Right."

"Even if it means you might die?"

"Yes, no blood." This time the patient spoke faintly. "I won't sign for any blood."

Dorie softened. "All right then." She turned to the nurse. "Please bring in the forms for her to sign, the ones saying that she refuses blood and blood products."

Red squeezed the patient's hand.

"Okay, we'll certainly respect your wishes." Dorie turned to the nurse. "The OR said they could take us now. Call the blood bank, and have them send the hemospan straight upstairs."

The nurse nodded and went to the phone.

"C'mon, Red," Dorie said. "Let's move her ourselves. Time is of the essence."

The patient's eyes revealed her terror as she looked up at Dorie. "You'll be doing my surgery?"

"Dr. Richison and I will be with you all the way through to recovery. You're losing a lot of blood, but your pulse and pressure are good. We'll get you fixed up right away."

Once in the OR, the anesthesiologist soothed the patient. "I'm going to put some medicine through your IV that will put you to sleep. Count backward from five to one," he told her as he injected it. She made it to three before she was sound asleep. Looking to Red, the anesthesiologist nodded. "We're ready."

Dorie and Red had both scrubbed in, but Dorie said she wanted Red to gain experience with the procedure, so he performed it under her supervision.

After a few moments, the anesthesiologist looked at him. "I'd really like to give the patient some blood. She's pretty shocky."

Red shook his head. "Got to stick with the artificial products. Patients' rights, ya know."

Dorie nodded, indicating her support.

"She'll be as anemic as rip," the anesthesiologist argued.

"No doubt."

In the span of only a few minutes, Red suctioned the mole out. As soon as he had done so, the uterus clamped down and stopped bleeding.

Dorie nodded. "It still amazes me that the uterus knows to shut off the flow when emptied." Red didn't say anything, and Dorie studied him. "You *do* know this could have happened to any new doc, Red. Our resident never should have gotten into it, but he's still inexperienced."

Red still said nothing.

"But you're right. We've got to tighten things up."

Red had spent a sleepless night, but he had made some decisions. There had to be a misunderstanding. He would tell Dorie he was taking Thursday off, as she'd suggested, and wait for Bethany at VIP.

When he got to the hospital, Damon passed him in the hall. "It had to be you waltzing in as the hero yesterday, didn't it, Richison?"

Red ignored the remark. If there was one thing he didn't need right now, it was a confrontation with Sir Damon.

That afternoon Red rubbed bleary eyes as he stared at Mrs. Brennan's chart. He was just outside the exam room door, preparing to talk with her, reading her biopsy report. When he read the results, his heart sank. *Oh no! The lump on her breast is cancerous.* An attached note from the breast surgeon said that the nodes looked suspicious as well. *I'm going to have to break the news. Give me grace. Give her grace.*

He took a deep breath and knocked.

"Come in."

He entered and smiled at her. After shutting the door, he sat on the stool and rolled it closer.

"I know it's bad, Doc. Everyone said to wait until the results were final before they'd even talk about it."

Red looked at her watery eyes. He pressed his lips together and nodded. "I'm sorry."

Mrs. Brennan turned her head away and stared off into space. Then she looked back at him. "I've been doing some research on the Internet, and I know pregnancy hormones can make some cancers spread a lot faster."

"Yes."

"Is mine one of them?"

"It's too early to know that yet. We don't have the hormone studies back. We do have the pathology report saying it's malignant, but it'll be another week or two before we know the details of the tumor's hormone responsiveness."

"What are my options?"

Red scooted a little closer so he could speak quietly and still be heard. "We have a pretty complete arsenal—several surgical options, a number of radiation protocols, and some chemotherapy regimens. Unfortunately, they're all much less effective with an ongoing pregnancy. We could wait, letting the baby reach maturity. But to be frank, your best chance of survival is to terminate the pregnancy and then follow with surgery and chemotherapy. We'd need to do very aggressive treatment since you are so young."

Mrs. Brennan gasped, then burst into tears.

"I'm not saying I recommend that you—"

She held up a trembling hand. "I know. You have to give me all the facts."

"Yes."

"And I *want* the facts. I really do. It's just that they're so hard. Abortion…it's hard to even say the word. Do you do abortions, Doctor?"

Red shook his head.

"Good. I mean, I don't know what I'm going to do, but I want a doctor who recommends abortion only as a last resort."

"Then I'm your man."

"My husband is still unemployed…"

"I'm so sorry."

"At the moment that doesn't seem all that important… I guess life and death have a way of making those concerns seem minor. My husband and kids need me."

"While it complicates things that you're young enough to still have small children at home, your age does work in your favor, medically speaking. It should help you handle the aggressive chemo treatment."

She sniffed. "Does this happen a lot? I've never had any pregnant friends diagnosed with cancer."

"It's rare, but it happens."

"It's awful." She began to cry again. "We love children. We wanted another child. We've never favored abortion, and we still don't. But I never dreamed I'd be in a situation like this. Are you sure there are no other options?"

"If you choose not to terminate the pregnancy, we could withhold treatment and try only the surgical option until the baby has matured.

Or we could just wait and watch. But even if we induce labor early, we've still got at least a five-month wait. Meanwhile, you could be at enormous risk because, as you said, pregnancy hormones can speed up the spread of the cancer. It would be a race between the baby and the disease. I don't know any other way to say this, but in trying to save the baby, we could lose both of you."

"What would *you* do?"

Tough question. And he didn't have an answer for her. "I'll support whatever you decide."

"That's not what I asked."

Red took a deep breath. "I might wait until I had the hormone studies to make a final decision, but speaking personally, I think this is one of those cases—and I'm a pro-life doctor—it's one of those times when I think abortion may be the best of bad choices. In a possible choice between one life—yours—or none, we have to consider that you have small children who need their mother. But as I said, I'll support you in whatever you decide."

Thursday morning at 10:45 Red sat in the heat, parked across the street from the VIP clinic. He punched in Bethany's office number and asked for her, but Margaret told him that she was out for the rest of the day. Dorie had said Bethany's appointment was at 11:00, and he wondered if she'd show. *It's 10:58 and no sign of her. Good!*

He watched as male escorts helped women past lines of peaceful protestors who were picketing. Someone was blasting a cassette of a baby crying, while nearby a cluster of people knelt in prayer. A priest was saying the rosary.

Amazing. He'd had no idea it would be like this. It felt like a spiritual war zone.

Red's mind wandered back to Bethany, stewing over all the possibilities. *Could Dorie be lying?* No, that wasn't her style. Besides, she had no reason to deceive him. Surely she'd just gotten the wrong person.

When he saw Bethany's Mercedes pull into the clinic lot, his heart sank. He stared as she got out and walked across the lot. Then he bolted out of his car and ran to intercept her before she got to the door.

When she spotted him, she stopped cold.

"You can't go in there!" he called out.

"Red, what are you doing here?" She looked around.

One of the clinic escorts jogged up and blocked Red from coming closer. Red stopped, and his voice trembled. "Bethany! Don't *do* it. You can't go in there!"

The escort turned and grabbed Bethany by the arm. "Come on, you don't have to listen to this guy; I'll take care of everything." He pulled her away. Bethany looked back at Red.

"We'll talk later, but I have an appointment."

He couldn't believe what he was hearing. "What are you *doing?* You can't go in there!"

"Red, later. Please! Please leave."

Red stood, holding out his hands, pleading without words like a child lost in the airport as he watched her go inside. *I can't believe this!*

He shuffled back to his car and sat staring at the building. Burned again. He'd thought they were building something special together, and now…

He had never felt so confused. Who had she been with? He closed his eyes and massaged his forehead. *I must be the biggest jerk in town. I loved her.*

The last time she'd gone down this path, she'd done it to save her father's reputation. But this time?

This time she's doing it to save her own.

EIGHTEEN

Red had been at work for two hours that afternoon when his pager went off. He glanced down and found a hospital number he didn't recognize. When he called back, he learned that he was being summoned to Lexie Winters's office.

What did the head of the hospital's legal department want with him?

Fifteen minutes later, he sat fidgeting outside Lexie's door. After a short wait, he heard her door open and stood to see an African-American woman who looked to be in her late forties.

"Thanks for coming, Dr. Richison. Please come in." She made a broad, sweeping gesture that seemed well suited to the flair of her fashionable turquoise suit.

She was the epitome of high class, complete with white-gold jewelry; straight, chin-length hair; a smile an orthodontist would covet; and a richly decorated office.

"Please sit down. Would you like something to drink?"

He shook his head. "No, thanks."

She took her place behind her desk and put on a pair of reading glasses. "You are probably wondering why I've asked to speak with you."

"Yes, you could say that."

"Do you remember assisting Dr. Kedar with a hysterectomy case on a teenager who came from VIP?"

Red nodded.

"We have received an intent to sue letter from this patient's attorney, with a request for records of the hospitalization."

Red slumped in his chair, fixing his eyes on his shoes and trying to call to mind the details. "She's suing the hospital?"

Lexie smiled. "Oh yes, Dr. Richison. And the physicians who perforated her uterus, and the VIP clinic, and Dr. Kedar—and you."

He jerked upright. *"Me?* Me personally?"

Lexie nodded.

"But I didn't do anything wrong! All I did was help to save her!"

Again Lexie nodded. "It's part of doing business in a hospital, Dr. Richison. No doubt you know that in your chosen specialty, you can count on getting sued for malpractice at least two, maybe three times in your career on average. And the attorney we're dealing with—well, he's the nasty, shyster type. I know him well from past dealings. Everyone gets sued, every name on the chart, every institution involved. They're looking for the deep pockets, where they can exact their pound of flesh. In these cases they don't care who pays, as long as someone somewhere writes a big check. But I'll give you the best representation I can. You'll do fine. You were a resident training under an experienced physician."

"Dr. Kedar warned me this might happen." He felt a tightening in his shoulders.

"You've discussed this case with him?"

"At the time it happened, sure."

"But not since then?"

"Not in detail, no."

"All right, good. From now on, please discuss it with no one."

"I also spoke briefly to Dr. Damon back when it happened," Red confessed.

Lexie nodded. "Okay. Dr. Damon will receive his own notification. And his involvement does put the hospital in an awkward situation. It makes it harder for us to defend our position because it will mean pointing more of the responsibility toward him. In fact, the VIP clinic attorneys, not those from the hospital, will represent him. The hospital's legal department doesn't actually condone moonlighting. In fact, we discourage it. So please, if you are moonlighting or inclined to do so, now would be a good time to quit."

"No problem. Does Dr. Kedar know he's being sued?"

"Yes, he just left."

"He's going to take a lot of heat, isn't he?"

"Perhaps. But he's an old pro. He took it in stride." She smiled. "As I said, it's all part of the business of being in medicine."

Red spent another sleepless night. Bethany had left a message asking him to call, but he didn't feel like talking.

In the morning he rubbed his eyes and stood checking the L and D board during a lull in the activity, noting the status of each patient. His pager went off, and he looked down to see the number of the lab. He had paged Dr. Kedar, who was returning his call. He walked over to the nearest wall phone and punched in the four digits.

"Hello, Dr. Kedar. It's Red. Thank you for calling me back, sir… Yes, I need some advice on a high-risk patient. She's chronic hypertensive, middle trimester… Sure I can bring down the chart. You're in the lab, right? Okay, thanks."

Red hung up and looked at the administrative assistant. "I'll be in the lab. Page me if you need me." He grabbed the file and took the elevator down. When he arrived, he found Dr. Kedar tinkering with the machine—but the pig was gone. *Oh no!* "What happened?"

Dr. Kedar finally looked at him. "I had a fetal pig on my support platform, as you saw. He made it to about fifty-five hours, and he was actually gaining a little weight. The blood pressure and oxygenation were going beautifully, as was the nutrition."

"Sounds encouraging."

"But the dialyzing arm of the machine really was inadequate. I was unable to balance the electrolytes and chemistry precisely. I tried a new approach, but there were some worrisome trends."

Red waited.

Dr. Kedar sighed and stared at the tank. "Then I got a call telling me that specimen 104 was spiraling downward. The problem seems to have involved the vascular pressure. If I keep the pump low enough to circulate the blood through the dialysis arm, it has too little pressure when returning to the fetal pig. Over time, and not too long a time, they get hypotensive, resulting in cardiac failure and death."

Red had drawn some sketches of possible machinery, but when the pig studies seemed to be progressing well, he hadn't pursued it. "Let me think about this…"

Dr. Kedar nodded. "Progress occurs in small steps." Then he looked up at Red and stretched out his hand. "Now, let me have a look at that chart."

He glanced down to study it, then looked back up at Red through the upper lenses of his bifocals. "By the way, about that news you got from Lexie Winters…"

Red's stomach clenched. "Yes?"

"You will be fine, all right? No worries." He turned his attention back to the chart, signaling to Red that the discussion on that topic was closed.

On the following Monday, Dorie picked up a salad and made her way through the lunch line in the doctors' café. She spotted Denny Damon's ponytail. He was sitting alone, reading a newspaper.

She sighed. *This is probably as good a time as any to bring it up.* She walked over to him. "Mind if I join you?"

"Sure." He stood and gestured for her to sit.

They both took their seats and chatted about the current caseload for a few minutes. Then Dorie grew serious. "Damon, there's something I've been meaning to ask you about."

"Shoot." He leaned back on two legs of his chair.

"It's a case that happened at VIP. A perforated uterus."

Damon banged the chair as he brought it back down on all fours. Then he held up his palms. "Sorry, no can do."

"Excuse me?"

"Legal counsel has advised me… Look, ask me about anything else, but not about that case."

"Legal counsel?" She narrowed her eyes. "*What* legal counsel? Lexie Winters?"

"Nope. Skip Avers."

"Skip? He's the counsel for VIP…"

"Yes, indeedy." Damon's grin was pure arrogance. "And I'll tell you what, I'll bet if you ask Dr. Ophion, Dr. Kedar, and Red Richison, they'll all tell you they can't talk about the case either."

"Red's the one who mentioned it." As soon as she said it, Dorie regretted the words. "I'm just doing some checking to put his mind at ease."

Damon's eyes flashed. "Yeah? Well, you tell Dr. Richison that he's not supposed to be discussing this case with *anyone*." He lowered his voice. "If he talked to you about it, and especially about my involvement, he's an overzealous, undertrained loser who doesn't have the edge to be a great doctor."

"Damon, would you settle down?" As Dorie said the words, it dawned on her why he was so upset. She'd been asking about a patient case, but he thought she was prying into a *legal* case—a case for which Damon was probably the primary doctor responsible.

On Saturday morning Bethany sat across the desk from a woman Margaret had ushered into her office. She had long, blond hair and beautiful lashes. "How did you know to find me here, Sharon? Did Red tell you where I work?"

"Heavens no. Red doesn't know I even know who you are, let alone where you work. I mean, he told me all sorts of things about you, but he didn't mention your occupation. No, I used to hang out at the hospital with him sometimes last year when we were engaged. I got to know the residents there, and one of them told me recently that y'all had been seeing each other and how I could find you."

"Well, how can I help you?" Bethany eyed the tight shirt, the short skirt, and the French manicure. Though she didn't like to admit it, she could see, from a strictly male-female point of view, what Red had seen in this woman.

"I'm here to tell you what Red is too kind to say."

"Really? And what's that?"

"We're back together."

The force of her words hit like a tsunami. It took a few moments, but Bethany finally managed a response. "I see."

"Yes. He's too soft-hearted to say so"— Sharon studied her manicure—"but we're very close again. *Very* close."

Bethany didn't respond.

"I, uh, thought you might want to know, because if you're anything like me, well, I thought you'd rather know the truth instead of wondering. Anyway, we're starting to make plans again, Red and me."

Bethany swallowed hard.

"I was up at his place recently, in fact, and—"

Bethany held up her hands. "You know, I think I have all the details I need. Don't you?"

Sharon bit her lip. "I'm sorry. I've hurt you, haven't I? And really, I came to spare you, Bethany. I can see what he saw in you, and I'm sure you're a really sweet person. I *really* wish you the best. With your looks, I can't imagine you'll have any trouble finding some guy who'll take great care of you. Red is *so* married to his work. Anyway, I just have this feeling that you'll find someone very nice, and soon."

Oh puh-lease. "Thanks." Bethany forced a smile, and rose to show her the way out.

Sharon stood too. "Just one more thing."

"What's that?"

"Let's keep this just between us girls, shall we? Red would be upset if he knew I'd come to see you and you were hurt."

As soon as Sharon had left, Bethany closed her door and got a good cry out of her system. Then she spent the next hour staring out her window. *He thinks I messed around, so he went back to her.* The fragrance of Fantasy lingered in the room, and a whiff of it nauseated her.

She cringed at a realization. Red was on the books to volunteer at the clinic at the end of next week. Maybe she should leave a message asking him not to come. No, despite their personal differences, there were some things bigger than their relationship that he needed to know.

Our outreach to women takes first place over heart matters. I'll just have to be big enough to handle it.

Red lay staring at his ceiling fan, unable to go back to sleep.

It had been a week since he'd seen Bethany on her way to get a D and C, and the days had dragged by since then. He'd just awakened from a dream about being at the lake with her—and the reality of their separation sent a fresh jolt through him. *I really need to talk to her, to get some closure on this—but how?*

The phone rang.

Red squinted to read the digital display. *It's 8:33. My sleep patterns are so messed up.*

He picked up the receiver. "Hello?"

"Red, it's Sharon."

He could tell she'd been crying. "Are you okay?"

"No!" she wailed.

"What's happened? Where are you?"

"I'm sitting outside your apartment in my car."

Red got up and pulled back the shades. Sure enough, her car was there.

"Can I come in?"

Red thought a minute. The last thing he needed right now was a tête-à-tête with Sharon. "No, but I'll come out. We can sit on the steps and talk."

"Okay." She sniffled.

He was still wearing his hospital blues—he'd fallen asleep in them. He ran his fingers through his hair and popped a stick of gum in his mouth to cover the garlic he'd had for dinner. Then he opened the door and met Sharon at the bottom of the steps. She threw her arms around him and burst into tears.

When she settled down, he motioned for them to sit on the stairs. "What happened?"

"You! You're what happened! I'm a wreck because of *you!*"

Red could only stare at her.

"You practically threw me out of here. How could you be so cruel, after all we've shared?"

"But—"

"Red, I'm not sure I can live without you."

"Don't say that."

"I mean it! I'm not sure I *want* to live. You have to take me back. You *have* to! I just don't know what I might do if you don't."

Sharon's pain was clear, and it saddened him, but the pressure she was trying to put on him only repelled him. After being with someone like Bethany, a woman who had a purpose even larger than his love, Sharon's instability held less appeal than ever. *But Bethany...*

"Red, tell me you'll give us one more chance."

He struggled to focus on what he knew was best. "Sharon, please don't do this."

"Why not? I could make you happy, Red. *So* happy. I promise I could."

He sat very still. *Lord, what do I do? I sure don't want to encourage her, but how can I convince her to leave without making things worse?*

She leaned her head on his shoulder, then turned her mouth up and started kissing his neck.

Red swallowed hard. His pain over Bethany and his fatigue threatened to slow his reactions and weaken his resolve, but he shook his head and gripped her arms, putting her away from him. "Sharon, please stop. What's happened to you?" *She must still be off her meds.*

"It's that *Bethany* isn't it?" She stood, her face twisted. "*Isn't* it?" Tears streamed down her face.

He blinked. "I-you… How did you know her name?"

She ignored the question. "It's her, isn't it? How could you forget the magic we had? That girl could *never* come close to measuring up to what we've shared."

"Sharon, *please* stop."

"Oh, so…so now you're defending her? Well, you tell her she'd better back off!" With that, Sharon turned around, flipped her hair behind her, and headed to her car.

Red sat there until his heart rate settled down, then he went back inside and sat on his couch. He stared into the dark, trying to calm his frayed nerves. His thoughts drifted from Sharon back to Bethany until he thought he'd go mad.

Utterly miserable, he decided to read for a while to try to take his mind off his problems. After flipping on the light, he found his Bible on the bookshelf. He opened to the bookmark in the gospel of Matthew and began.

"If your brother sins against you, go and show him his fault, just between the two of you. If he listens to you, you have won your brother over." He read it again. And again.

Well, God couldn't be any clearer than that, he thought with a twist of his lips. *Okay, Lord, I can take a hint. I'll call Bethany tomorrow.*

NINETEEN

Heather tossed a pillow at Bethany, who lay on her bed, channel-surfing.

"Bethany, you sure seem mopey lately."

She continued staring at the flickering television screen. "Do I?"

"You still haven't worked it out with Red, have you?"

Bethany sighed, then rolled over and propped herself up on her elbows. "I drove over there tonight, but when I got there, he was sitting on his front stops with his ex-fiancée."

"Wow. So are you going to call and try to talk to him?"

"No way I'm calling him. If he wants to talk, he can call me."

"You're kidding, right?"

Bethany glared at her, and Heather held up her hands. "Sorry I asked. Want to go shopping? I hear Penney's is having a sale on shoes."

"No, thanks."

Heather's eyes widened. "You don't want to go shopping? Man, this *is* serious."

The next evening after work, Red punched in Bethany's number.

Heather answered, sounding both surprised and pleased that he had phoned. "Hey, Red. Bethany's at the health club right now. Want to leave a message?"

"Sure. Please tell her I called. And if you would, tell her I'll be up at her clinic next Thursday afternoon and I'd like to take her out for a bite to eat after we get finished."

"Great, but that's almost a week away. Where you been lately, man? She's been pretty out of sorts since you disappeared."

Red was a little taken aback by Heather's forthrightness. "Uh, yeah, I'm sorry about that. So what have you been up to?" He knew it was a cop-out, but he wasn't ready to talk yet with anyone but Bethany.

"Just working and planning a wedding."

He blinked. "A *wedding?*"

"Yes! Come spring, Bethany is going to have to find a new roommate."

"That's big news. I wish you the best."

"Yeah, well, you turkey. Here I am all in love and happy, and Bethany's so miserable that she doesn't even want to go shopping with me. I'm telling you. Men! When you don't have one, you're miserable, but when you get one, you can make everyone *around* you miserable."

"People could say the same about women."

"Guilty." Heather chuckled. "I know Bethany will be glad you called, but you need to come around more often. You're not the only man in her world, you know."

Don't I know it.

"And from what I hear, she's not the only woman in yours."

"What?"

"You were her *favorite* there for a while, of course, but you shouldn't leave her alone so much."

"Wait, back up a sec. What do you mean, you heard she's not the only woman in my world?"

There was a long silence. "All right, I'm an idiot. But I have to say that when that blond bombshell showed up at Bethany's office, it wasn't pretty. Not that she believed her, but then she saw you with her last night—"

"Do you mean Sharon? *Sharon* went to her office? And Bethany saw us last night?" Red groaned. "Heather, trust me. I'm *not* seeing Sharon."

"You're not? Okay, well, I'm really stepping in it here. I had no intention of being a mediator, so I'm going to stop talking now. But all I can say is, you and Bethany definitely need to talk instead of just avoiding each other. I'm really glad you called."

After Red hung up, he wasn't sure he felt better, but he knew he'd done the right thing. That had to count for something. Sharon had a lot of nerve visiting Bethany, but why would Bethany care anyway? He fell back on the bed and pulled the pillow up to his face.

Women!

Heather was in the living room watching a video when Bethany returned from working out.

"Red called."

At Heather's casual remark, Bethany stopped and stared. "And?"

"He said to remind you that he's going to be at the clinic next Thursday."

"I'm glad he remembers."

"You thought he'd forget?"

Bethany shrugged. "Or cancel, maybe."

Heather shook her head. "You two definitely need to talk. That's all I can say."

"Not everything is resolved by talking, Heather."

"But *nothing* is resolved by silence, Bethany. Besides, he wants to take you to dinner."

She narrowed her eyes. "Did he say that?"

"No, I'm making it up."

Bethany glared, and Heather tossed the remote on the couch.

"Bethany, ease up! Of course I'm not making it up. I wouldn't joke about something like that. It's really what he said. He told me he's working an afternoon shift up at Women's Choice and to tell you that afterward he'd like to take you out."

"H'm, interesting." A tiny smile appeared in the corner of Bethany's mouth.

"And ..." Heather tried to entice her with more.

"Yes?"

"He claims he's not back with Blondie."

"Yeah, right." Bethany grabbed her workout bag and headed for her room. *Yeah, right. He certainly appeared to be with her on the porch last night.*

Dawn shuffled up the walk to the door of the Women's Choice Clinic. When she pulled open the door, she inhaled the aroma of freshly brewed coffee.

She walked in, stood at the reception desk, and stared down at the Formica desktop. Then she whispered, "They told me I could come back."

"You've been here before?"

Dawn nodded and handed the receptionist Bethany's business card. "I have an appointment. My name is Dawn Spencer. She told me she could help if it got bad." She looked up.

The receptionist nodded and went to get Bethany. Minutes later Dawn sat across from her, weeping, hoping their time together could help rid her of the shame she felt. "I know you tried to tell me not to do it, but I didn't know it would be like this. And now Brad don't love me no more. He says he's tired of my always saying I'm sorry, and then like a fool I tell him I'm sorry for saying I'm sorry too much."

Bethany reached for the box of tissues she kept handy and handed them to Dawn. "Oh, Dawn…life can be so hard."

And this is way harder than I ever thought it would be. "I keep looking at them pictures you gave me, and I think how awful the whole thing was and I…I…wish…" She burst into tears.

Bethany rested her hand on Dawn's knee. "Remember when you called, I said I had someone I thought you should talk to."

Dawn wiped her nose with the back of her hand and nodded. Maybe talking about it more would help.

"With your permission, I filled her in on what happened, and she said she would love to meet you. Her name's Diana. Let me introduce you to her, okay?"

Dawn shrugged. What could it hurt? "Can she give me drugs to help me sleep better?"

Bethany shook her head. "But she can tell you how to find peace." She stood, ushered Dawn back to an office, and introduced the woman behind the desk. "This is Diana, and she's the kind of person you can talk to in a time of crisis."

Diana came around from behind the desk and sat in a chair, motioning for Dawn to sit facing her. Then Bethany excused herself. Dawn watched her as she left, wishing she'd stay. It felt awkward to be alone with this stranger.

"So how are you feeling now?" Diana asked.

"I don't have no more cramps. The bleeding is almost gone too. I'm all right, I guess. But I'm tired a lot and not sleeping good. I wake up early thinking about…it…and I can't go back to sleep."

"What about your appetite?"

Dawn shook her head. "Nothing much tastes good."

Diana looked at her, and the kindness Dawn saw in her eyes broke down her walls of insecurity.

When Diana spoke, her tone was gentle. "It sounds as though the physical healing is progressing pretty normally. But how are you? You sound pretty unhappy, maybe even depressed?"

Dawn bit her lip, and a tear streamed down her face. "*Yeah,* I'm unhappy. Nobody loves me now. And I *killed* it!" Suddenly her crying erupted into sobs of grief.

Diana rose and wrapped her arms around Dawn, pulling her into a comforting embrace. "I've been where you sit, girl. You just cry all you need to."

In that moment, for the first time since her abortion, Dawn felt secure.

An hour later Diana folded her hands and studied the young girl in front of her. Dawn's eyes were red and puffy, and Diana's heart broke for her. "Now that we've talked about your emotions, may I ask you a few questions about your medical treatment?"

"Sure, why?"

Diana licked her lips and chose her words carefully. "We've seen a few…difficulties…from the VIP clinic. We're just trying to make sure that they're treating people the way they're supposed to."

Dawn cursed. "Do you think they messed up with me, because I'll bet—"

Diana halted the angry flow of words. "I certainly wouldn't say that, but tell me, what exactly did they tell you? What did they recommend?"

Dawn told Diana all that she'd told Bethany, and Diana struggled to keep her anger with VIP from showing.

"Do you happen to have any more of the second medicine, the cramp medicine that they gave you?"

Dawn shook her head. "Naw. I took it all when I got scared. But it only got worse."

I'll bet it did. Unfortunately, that means we have no evidence.

———————

"Teresa, I feel like you're pulling away from me."

At Regan's words, Teresa gripped the phone. Regan couldn't possibly understand what watching that growing belly did to Teresa. She stared down at the checks she'd been writing when the phone rang, absently writing her name on one as she spoke. "Sorry. I guess it's too hard to be around anybody who's pregnant right now. Especially because you and I conceived within a week of each other. As I see your expanding waistline, it's such a shocking reminder of where I would be, what I might look like." She tore the check from the checkbook and started writing the next one out.

"I wish you didn't feel that way."

"Please try not to take it personally, Regan. I'm like this with *everyone* who's pregnant."

"But you just said it's especially bad with me."

Teresa rubbed tired eyes. "Again, I'm sorry. I don't want to hurt anybody. Especially not you—you've been such a support through all this. But I admit—I'm having a hard time. I seem to be hurting everyone right now. I don't know what I feel. I don't know what I want."

"Loss does that to you. But you *know* pregnancy after infertility is really scary. With every twitch or pain you freeze, terrified that it's the beginning of the end. Maybe we could just talk by phone?"

"Maybe…"

Teresa didn't want to seem petty—and she certainly didn't want to hurt her friend—but being with Regan triggered her grief, and she had all the pain she could handle right now.

Red winced when he read the hormone studies in Mrs. Brennan's chart. He breathed a quick prayer and opened the exam room door to meet her.

"Good morning, Dr. Richison." Her eyes didn't meet his.

He shook her hand, then sat on the stool and rolled it closer. "How are you?"

"The surgery wasn't too bad, though the news about the cancer being in the nodes devastated us." She broke down.

"I'm sorry." Red looked at the chart. "You had a lumpectomy with lymph node excision, right?"

"Right." She sniffled. "But I didn't go ahead with the abortion, if that's what you're wondering. I know it was risky to wait, Doctor, but I just couldn't do it without knowing what the hormone studies said." Her eyes looked hopeful. "You've got them, right?"

"Yes."

"And?"

Red shook his head. Before he could speak, she burst into tears again.

"I was afraid of that. I *knew* it—" Her voice choked with tears. "I just didn't want to believe it. I guess I don't have any choice now, but my baby…my poor baby… We both would probably die otherwise…"

Red noted her avoidance of the word *abortion,* even though he could tell that's what she meant. "We do have a lot of options if that's the route you choose to take."

She looked up at him.

"There are some chemotherapy regimens. But yes, they're all much less effective with an ongoing pregnancy. As I told you before, I'm not saying I recommend…well, I'll support whatever you decide."

"What would *you* do, Doctor? I mean, if it was your own wife."

Red glanced back at the hormonal studies and thought hard. "I imagine I'd choose to try to keep my wife and the mother of my children over the very probable risk of losing both wife and child."

"I just keep thinking about that verse that says there's no greater love than to lay down your life for someone else. Am I selfish if I don't?"

Red crossed his legs and set her chart against his knee. "You're an amazing woman, Mrs. Brennan. Actually, I've thought about that too."

"You have? So are you saying you think I should die for the sake of the baby?"

"No." Red leaned back in his chair and thought for a minute. "No, I'm just saying I've thought of that verse. In this case the baby probably wouldn't live, so you'd be sacrificing both your lives. But I'll ask the Lord to give you His peace about a good decision, one that will be right for you and for your husband and kids."

She looked down at her hands. "My husband said…he says if it comes down to one life or the other…" She sniffled and wiped a tear.

"Well, he says he wants to hang on to the one he already knows and loves."

When Bethany got ready for work on Thursday, she took extra care with her appearance. She stood for a long time looking at her bottles of perfume, wondering which one to wear... *What message would it send?* In the end she opted for neither Fantasy nor Whisper.

The morning hours crawled, and after eating an early lunch alone in her office, she left her door open so she could be sure to see when Red came in.

A little after noon, she sat watching for his MGB. When she saw it pass by her window, her pulse quickened. *He's so early.* He wasn't due for another hour. Since most of the staff was gone to lunch, they'd be pretty much alone. The image of Sharon and Red together floated through her mind.

I can't believe he went back to her.

She clenched her jaw. *And he assumed I was sleeping around...* She tried to shake away the hurt that dug at her. *They deserve each other, since he obviously didn't trust me.*

A few minutes later, she heard Margaret directing him back to her office. She breathed deeply and kept her eyes glued to her paperwork.

"Hello, Bethany."

Looking up, she saw his familiar face and muscular build framed by the doorway. She stood and motioned for him to sit on the couch, and forced her voice to remain steady. "Hi, Red. Please come in."

"You got a few minutes?"

"Sure."

He entered and took a seat. "It's been a long time—too long. And I'm sorry for that."

She bit her lower lip. *I refuse to cry.*

"I thought if I came early, maybe we could talk some before I get to work."

She nodded. "Was there something you wanted to say?"

"Bethany, may I ask you a question?"

"Sure." *It's always better to ask questions than to make assumptions!*

"Is it true what Heather told me, that Sharon came here to see you?"

"Uh-huh." *We have a colossal misunderstanding, and all he wants to talk about is his girlfriend?*

"What did she say to you?"

"I think you could venture a pretty accurate guess." Before he could deny it, she went on. "Is it true? Not that it's any of my business."

"Not if she said anything remotely related to my having a relationship with her."

Bethany turned and stared at him. "So you're not back together?" Her voice sounded more hopeful than she wanted it to.

"Is that what she told you?"

Bethany nodded. "I didn't really believe her, not at first. Then I drove over to your place to try to talk to you the other night, and I saw you sitting outside together. I have to say that it looked pretty intense. Not that it matters."

Red shook his head. "It matters because regardless of what's happened to you, I want you to know I was being honest with you about her. Remember when I told you she was a little, uh…"

"Unstable?"

"Yeah. Well, she came to my apartment, but I didn't let her in. And she left mad when I wouldn't get back together with her."

"Okay. Well, thanks for clearing that up. Do you feel better now?"

Red stared at her. "You can be so cold."

"*I'm* cold?"

"What? You think *I'm* cold? You betray me, and *I'm* cold?"

Bethany stared at him. "I did nothing of the sort! You think I betrayed you when I did it *for you!*"

Red's mouth dropped open, and he glared at Bethany. What was she talking about? "Did *what* for me? You're with somebody else and you did it for *me?* Well, if that doesn't take the cake. That is so…"

She crossed her arms, and from the look she gave him, he half expected to get frostbite. "You said you needed evidence against the clinic. The one thing you needed was facts, solid evidence. So I got some for you."

Red's eyes widened and he froze. "What?"

Bethany squinted at him and lowered her voice. "Red, I'm not pregnant. I used a pregnant friend's urine."

"What?" *She wasn't pregnant? Then...* Red sank back into the couch.

"I went up to VIP with the urine. They gave me a test, and I used my friend's specimen. They told me I was pregnant, and I didn't argue. I wanted to see what they'd advise me to do about it. I thought if I told you in advance you'd try to talk me out of it."

He tried to respond once, twice, then finally managed, "What did they do?" He leaned forward. "Surely they didn't just schedule you for an abortion with only a urine test!"

"I asked if they ever used RU-486, and that was all it took to be ushered into Ophion's office. We talked first about possible approaches. He offered to do a sono without charge beyond what my insurance would pay. I agreed to that, so he did one. But he wouldn't let me see the screen. I'll bet they never risk letting patients see the heartbeat, but certainly in my case, he wasn't going to let me see the screen because he wasn't seeing anything!"

"Did he tell you it was too early to tell?"

Bethany shook her head. "No, Red. He tried to talk me into having a surgical abortion! He asked me how far along I thought I was, and I said it had been at least six weeks since I'd had relations."

Red stared at her. *Only six weeks?*

She must have read his thoughts on his face. "It's been *years* but at *least* six weeks."

Red fell back against the cushion, groaned, and covered his face. "Oh, Bethany..."

"Anyway, he asked if the relationship related to the pregnancy was permanent, and I told him it wasn't. So he gave me two options: the D and C or the RU-486. But his main sales pitch was for the D and C. He was prepared to do one that day, but I told him I needed a few more days to think about it. I wanted to see if he'd do another sono and still go through with it. So I set up an appointment for a follow-up. Then that same afternoon I went and had a blood pregnancy test."

"Why? If you knew you weren't pregnant—"

"So I could later prove that Ophion wasn't seeing anything on the screen."

Red shook his head and smiled. He knew Bethany was smart, but he'd never imagined she would cook up something like this. She was amazing. As for Ophion... "I can't believe he would do an abortion without the ultrasound showing anything. That's *so* wrong."

"I'm convinced that man would do anything to generate a client. Anyway, we have some decent evidence now." She looked Red straight in the eyes. "But what we don't have is mutual trust."

Again Red covered his eyes with his hand and hung his head. Then he looked back at her. "Bethany, I am so sorry."

"How did you know I would be there that day anyway?"

"I heard from one of the residents that works at VIP. She told me you had a positive pregnancy test and that you were scheduled to have an abortion."

"And you *believed* her?"

"I didn't *want* to believe it! But she also told me you had a D and C scheduled. So I drove up there, thinking, *hoping* she was wrong. Bethany, really, what was I to think?"

"It never crossed your mind to think I might be getting *evidence?*"

"I'm sorry, Bethany. Maybe if I hadn't been burned before... but it looked like you were upset to see me."

"I was! I thought you'd blow my cover."

Red shook his head. "Oh, man, I should've given you the benefit of the doubt, but the only logical option was that there was some other guy."

"Well, there wasn't."

"I'm so sorry. How could I be such a jerk?"

"It didn't get any better when Sharon showed up."

He looked into her eyes. "So you thought I went back to her when things didn't work out with you."

"Of course."

"Bethany, how can you make plans with someone when you're in love with someone else?"

She shook her head and her eyes clouded over. "You can't. Not if you're honest."

He leaned forward to wipe her tears with his thumb. "I am sorrier than I can say. Please, please say you'll forgive me?"

She looked at her lap and nodded.

"C'mere." He stood and drew her into an embrace, resting his head on hers and then kissing the top of her head. "I'm so sorry."

They stood that way for several minutes. Finally Bethany broke away to wipe her eyes and nose with a tissue. "Do you want to hear what else I found out?"

Red nodded. "What happened when you went back?"

"The day you and I had our little confrontation at the clinic?"

Red winced. "Yeah."

"He did another sono and was all ready to do a D and C when I told him I just couldn't go through with it. So he told me he'd write me a prescription for RU-486, but he got paged, and one of the residents took over."

"Bummer. So close. Still, Bethany, you're gutsy."

"Not my usual style, playing undercover agent. If I had it to do over, I'd try to find a different way to get the evidence. But I'd seen too many injured women coming here from that place."

"Ophion's going to pay. I can't believe he would operate with nothing more than a urine test."

"Illegal, huh?"

"Certainly not medically indicated. He'd have to claim some kind of error. This is bad medicine, maybe fraud. And who knows what else."

But Red knew one thing for certain: He and Bethany were going to find out.

TWENTY

Dorie was the last person left at VIP at the end of the evening shift. Exiting the women's rest room, she made her way back to her office. When she reached the samples cabinet, she stopped. She'd made investigating a low priority because surely Red's concerns were unfounded. But now she looked at the large wooden doors.

Now she wondered.

She opened the cabinet and sorted through boxes of medications, looking for prostaglandin. The section where they stored painkillers was locked, but in the unlocked part, she found Phenergan for nausea, Lomotil for diarrhea, some birth control pills, and Ergotrate—a medicine that makes the uterus contract. She also found several types of prostaglandin inhibitors.

But not one sample of prostaglandin.

Maybe we ran out.

She returned to her office and sat at her desk, thinking. There was one thing she could do.

I hate to lie, but I have to protect our women. She picked up the phone and called the all-night pharmacy that offered VIP patients a discount on RU-486. She was put through to a Dr. Ng, the night pharmacist. Since he could give the information she needed only to a medical doctor, she banked on his recognizing her name. She'd certainly prescribed enough pain medications following abortions. When he came on the line, she introduced herself as the clinic's administrative resident.

"How can I help you, Dr. Chambers?" he asked.

"We really appreciate your pharmacy working with us on the RU-486 prescriptions. And I'm calling because we've had some concern about several of our RU-486 patients. I've been compiling the statistics on our procedures, and I was wondering if you could provide me with a list of the patients that we've sent you."

"I'd be happy to help. What exactly do you need?"

"A few of the patients have not come back for follow-up care. I imagine some may have decided not to have abortions. Others probably did fine and just skipped the return visit. But if you can tell us which patients actually have had their prescriptions for RU-486 filled, we could check them against our records of patients who haven't returned so we can contact those still needing follow-up appointments."

"Ah, very good. I can run you a printout."

"Great. And it would also help if you can get me the numbers on Misoprostol, the prostaglandin you've been sending to us. I can't find the drug rep's card, so I'm assuming we get our samples from you at a discount."

"No, Doctor, we carry the medication and dispense it by individual prescription only. I have no record of sending any to the clinic itself."

Dorie's shoulders drooped. "I see."

"We track the referrals from VIP to make sure our partnership continues to be profitable," he said. "So I'll get you a list of patients for whom we've dispensed either RU-486 or the prostaglandin—in most cases, both."

"That would be wonderful, but I wouldn't want you to go to any trouble."

"No trouble. These are computer reports; we can do them in five minutes. Besides, it's a slow night here. What's your fax number?"

Dorie gave him the number and asked him to put her name on the cover sheet.

"I can probably have it ready tonight. Is there any other data you need?"

Dorie hesitated. "Does your database also include whether the patient paid or whether it was an insurance pay?"

"Sure. Would you like that information, as well?"

"That would be great."

During her lunch break at the VIP clinic two days later, Dorie stared at the spreadsheet of data she was compiling. She had been studying a printout of seventy-eight names, and what she read made her cringe.

She called the pharmacy during the day and asked to speak to Earlene, a pharmacist she knew. After Dorie sat on hold for a few minutes, Earlene came on the line. The women exchanged pleasantries, and then Dorie got straight to the point.

"Earlene, I have a printout from your pharmacy that lists some of our patients who got their RU-486 prescriptions filled there, but they didn't get the prostaglandin with it. Do you happen to know anything that might help me understand why?"

"Sure. I've seen a bunch of those come through in the past six months or so. I've even asked a few of the women to make sure they got an accompanying prescription."

"What did they say?"

"Simple explanation, really. They didn't need the prescription because they got free samples."

"Earlene, did you happen to see the samples?"

"No. Why?"

"I'm just running a little quality control here, okay?"

"I read you…"

"Thanks. I'd appreciate it if you'd ask to see the samples next time it happens. And if you can, see if they'll tell you which doc they talked to."

"Sure. But it doesn't happen with all of the RU-486 patients, Dorie. Only some of them. In fact, I can tell you that Dr. Ophion's the only one who does it. *And* I've noticed it's usually the more affluent women, not the down-and-outers. So I figured he's just scoring points with the lookers."

Of course! That explains it. A grin crossed Dorie's face. "Earlene, you're brilliant. Knowing Ophion, I'll bet you're absolutely right." More than likely he'd given most of those patients the right samples. The rep's sister was probably just an isolated accident. Or maybe one of the nurses dispensed the wrong medication by mistake. That had to be it.

Because the alternative was too appalling to even consider.

"Hello, Red, it's me."

Red winced at the sound of Sharon's voice at the other end of the phone. "Sharon, it's after eleven o'clock."

"That never used to bother you."

He sat up in bed and didn't bother to argue. It was pointless to reason with Sharon when she was lonely, and if she was calling this late she had to be lonely.

"I was wondering when your next day off is?"

Red sighed. "Why?"

"Because I was thinking of putting together a picnic for us."

He noticed that her speech sounded slurred. "No, Sharon. Where are you?"

"Staying with Mother and Daddy."

"So they took you back? Good."

"Yes, all is forgiven. And they're dying to see you again, sweetie."

Irritation flooded him. "Why didn't you just ask one of the other residents for my schedule? They seem to know everything else about me, like where you could find my girlfriend."

There was a long silence. Finally Sharon whined, "I *told* her not to mention it to you. I only did it because I love you, Red. You have to believe me!"

"Sharon, I'm sorry for your pain. Really I am. But—"

"Then why do you keep *hurting* me?"

"You're not the only one who's been hurt in this."

"You're right, Red. I'm sorry. I'm such a failure. All I do is mess up the lives of the people I love most."

After Red hung up, he made a mental note to get an unlisted number. But Sharon's words haunted him. She had done enough to mess up his life, and he was determined that she'd done all the damage she was going to do.

The following night Red ran himself ragged while, as usual, Damon slept in a nearby call room.

Around one o'clock, one of the hospital's clinic patients came to the ER with first-trimester bleeding. Red had several patients in labor, but when it seemed he could safely get away, he ran down to the ER to evaluate the patient. She'd had a miscarriage and needed a D and C right away. Red cringed. He wasn't supposed to leave the L and D area uncovered, which meant calling Damon to do the D and C.

Red did the workup, ordered all the labs, arranged for the surgery, soothed the patient, and got her on the schedule. Then he made the call.

Damon answered. "Yeah?"

"Dr. Richison here."

"What is it? Something you can't handle? This better be good."

"Actually, it's pretty straightforward. Got an incomplete at ten weeks with robust bleeding, decidual tissue at the cervix. Inevitable. Got her labbed and headed to the OR. They'll be calling you when they're ready."

"Can't you handle *anything?* We used to do a paracervical block in the ER and do a D and C right there."

"I have some labor cases progressing, and Dr. Chambers said we weren't to do those anymore under local—"

"Soft! You new guys are all weak, and, Richison, you're the worst of the bunch. You know, whether or not you *approve,* I've got other responsibilities. I can't be getting up to cover you all night."

I've already gone the extra mile for you, buddy. If you weren't working two jobs, you wouldn't have to sleep through your nights on call. But I'm going to do everything I can to see that your other job gets eliminated. "I've already done the workup. Her name is Mrs. Ramirez. They'll call you from—"

Click.

Forty-five minutes later Red looked up from writing in a patient's chart. As a bedraggled Dr. Damon came through L and D on his way back from surgery, he shot a disgusted glance at the board and then glared at Red. *He's probably here only to make sure I'm sufficiently busy.*

"Case went fine," Damon said. "*You* can make rounds on her in the morning and send her home." Without awaiting a response, Damon headed back to the call room.

Shortly after lunch on Tuesday, a few days later, Dorie found an empty hospital call room. She returned Earlene's call and waited for her friend to take another line so she could talk in private.

"Okay, Dorie. I've got one for you. One of Dr. Ophion's patients came in yesterday with a prescription for RU-486. But when I asked if the doctor had given her a prescription for the prostaglandin, she said he had given her some samples instead. So I asked if she had them with her."

Dorie's hand gripped the phone. "Did she?"

"Yes. And it was Anaprox DS—a prostaglandin *inhibitor.*"

The ramifications hit like an earthquake. "Earlene!"

"I know! And it gets worse. I asked what the doctor had told her, and she said she was to take the first prescription and then after a few days take the sample. He'd warned her there was always a chance that she'd have to have the surgical procedure, too, but if that happened, she shouldn't worry, because her insurance would cover it. When she told him her insurance didn't cover abortion, he said it would cover complications."

Dorie leaned back in the chair. This changed everything. What was she going to do? She loved the added income and responsibility that VIP afforded her, but...

If she exposed Ophion, she risked it all. She'd lose her job at VIP, and who knew how it might affect her reputation in the community. She'd hoped to join a practice here in Dallas after residency. Still, women's lives were at stake.

That evening when Dorie got to her office at VIP, she waited for a lull in the action, then, having accessed the clinic's main medical records file, she pulled up the names of all the patients who had received prescriptions. She made sure no one was watching, and e-mailed the information to her home account.

After that, she called in one of the clinic's nurses and handed her a handwritten list of names with instructions to pull their files. Later she called in a different nurse and gave her another set of files to pull.

Once she had all the files she needed, she created a spreadsheet.

On Thursday night Damon stepped into Dorie's empty office to leave her a list of his preferred dates to work at VIP. With the holidays approaching, he wanted some time off to take one of the nurses out of town. When his pen ran out of ink, he opened Dorie's desk drawer to find another one, but he stopped when he saw a file marked VIP.

I'll bet that's the holiday call schedule I need. He pulled it out and opened it.

He hesitated. This wasn't a call schedule. The pages looked like photocopies from VIP files. Stapled to one VIP record was a private lab report with a note that said "Dorie, Here's a copy of the test I told you about. Red."

He doesn't even work at VIP. What the...

Damon moved to the door to make sure no one was coming, then went back and flipped through the pages. Red's information was stapled to a VIP record on someone named Bethany Fabrizio, who had a positive urine pregnancy test and sonogram. But attached to Red's note was a test result from a private physician's office. Damon stared at the results.

Negative-beta HCG; less than five—on the same date! Not pregnant? Damon's heart pounded. That scheming Richison was planning to nail VIP; Damon was sure of it. Why else would he be giving Dorie this kind of information?

His eyes narrowing, Damon looked at the file again. He'd have to find out who this Bethany Fabrizio was and if she was helping Richison.

And then he'd find out how to stop them.

Dr. Ophion's secretary had called to set up a meeting ASAP between Dorie and her boss. Dorie's only available time had been early in the morning before the clinic opened. Now she parked in her usual place and found that Dr. Ophion's was the only other vehicle there.

Does he know something or is he just reviewing my progress? She knew she'd have to wait to tell him what she thought of his grandiose scheme for *helping* women. She didn't have it all put together yet, but she knew enough to conclude he needed to clean up his act.

She grabbed her briefcase, punched in the security code at the back door, and entered. Finding the place deserted, though the lights were on, she made her way down to Dr. Ophion's corner office. She found the doctor, dressed in his usual expensive clothes, sitting at his desk reading some papers.

"Good morning, Dr. Ophion."

He looked up and greeted her more formally than usual. "Dr. Chambers." Without smiling, he gestured for her to take a seat.

As before, Dorie sank into the leather couch behind a glass-topped coffee table, and Dr. Ophion took the wing chair opposite her.

He folded his hands and looked down at them, then looked back up at her. "Dr. Chambers, do you know a Dr. Ng at the pharmacy where we refer patients?"

Dorie felt a wave of apprehension and shook her head. "I don't know him personally."

"But you've spoken with him, haven't you?"

She nodded.

"He called here late yesterday afternoon, before I left for the day. He said he'd left out some names of patients you need for a report you're doing."

Dorie swallowed.

He snarled at her. "What report might that be, Dr. Chambers?"

"I'm putting together a statistical analysis of the different cases we handle." Even as she said this, she knew this bluff made little sense.

"I see. And since when, Dr. Chambers, do you conduct research on the activities of my clinic? These are unauthorized, unethical, and, in my opinion, actionable." Clearly, this last word was a threat. "Fortunately for you, I don't plan to pursue a legal remedy."

"Yes sir."

"Dr. Chambers, after I received the call from Dr. Ng, I went back in the fax memory and was able to make a copy of what he sent you. It was a list of patients who've had prescriptions filled at that pharmacy, with a cover letter to your attention. So no doubt, you know what's coming next." He rose and motioned for her to follow. Together they went to her office. "You may take only your personal effects. No charts, no records, no faxes. The entry codes will be changed. Your office lock will be changed. You are dismissed, and I want you gone before the staff gets here. If I hear that you have discussed this with anyone, I will reconsider my decision not to sue. Am I clear?"

Dorie hadn't been caught red-handed at anything since the third grade, and she loathed the humiliation. She vowed to turn the tables.

Someday it'll be him cowering—I promise.

"He *fired* you?"

Red stared at Dorie, wondering how she could seem so calm. She just sat there eating her sandwich, as though nothing monumental had happened. He looked around the doctors' café to make sure no one was listening. "Amazing."

Dorie shrugged. "Not really. I mean, it makes sense. The guy's an octopus; he's got his tentacles in everything at that clinic. And the minute he suspects someone's onto him, he's going to make sure they're in no position to do damage."

"I'm sorry, Dorie. I got you in a heap of trouble."

Dorie finished chewing and held up a finger, indicating that she wanted to speak when she finished. "Are you kidding? You apologize for helping me to stop a bottom dweller like that? Don't waste your breath. Besides, it's not over yet."

"What do you mean? Didn't he threaten to sue you?"

Dorie smiled. "That patronizing chauvinist. He's not going to get away with exploiting women patients—or doctors! He's going down."

"But how can you get any more evidence from the outside?"

"First of all, I don't think he realizes how much I know. He may think I was just checking on his prescription habits in general, not specifically RU-486 patients. I noticed he was prescribing a lot of painkillers. I have a copy at home of the pharmacy printout. I also e-mailed myself some of the clinic records. And I've got photocopies of more than seventy charts."

Red sat slack-jawed, staring at her. "You got copies of *charts?* Did you find anything in the records?"

"Nothing yet. I haven't had time to study them in detail, but the fact that Ophion fired me confirms he's got something to hide. So it's just a matter of time before I dig it out and expose it." Her brows lifted. "It would appear your hunch about medication fraud is right on target." With that, Dorie told him about her conversation with Earlene.

"That certainly fits with what we've seen."

She hesitated, then leaned back in her chair. "I've got a question for you, Red."

"What's that?"

"How close are you to Dr. Kedar, in case I find something?"

He looked at her with furrowed brows, thinking what an odd question this was. Dr. Kedar? What did he have to do with this? "What do you mean?"

"I mean, we're just a couple of residents. We need somebody with some serious clout to take this on. Otherwise Legal probably won't touch it. I doubt this issue has huge financial ramifications for the hospital, so we need someone who can apply some political pressure. Are you close enough to Dr. Kedar that you'd feel comfortable pressing a chief of staff to get involved if I can uncover something solid?"

It was a good question. Red chewed his food, thinking, and then nodded. "I'll do whatever it takes to help us put VIP out of commission."

Denny Damon parked his car in the reserved parking space that bore his name. As he did, he noticed that someone had already painted over Dorie's name. He allowed himself a slow, pleased smile.

I'll bet Ophion's planning to give me her job. I'm certainly the most likely candidate. He imagined giving himself more convenient hours and lording it over the other residents as he made their moonlighting schedules.

It was going to be great.

Once inside, Mary Sue greeted him. "I'll let Dr. Ophion know you're here."

A half-minute later, Dr. Ophion strode down the hall. A full head taller than Damon, Ophion smiled down at him. "Good morning! Please, come back to my office." He led the way.

"Sit down." As Damon did so, Ophion picked up a contract that was lying on the table between them. He studied Damon carefully. "I suppose you've heard that Dr. Chambers is no longer with us."

"Yes."

"She just couldn't handle the administrative details. I doubt it will come as a surprise to you that I'm offering you her job."

Damon grinned. "Thank you, Doctor. Glad to know you're not holding the lawsuit against me."

Ophion waved that off. "You did fine. It was the overly zealous Dr. Kedar who messed that up. No fault of yours."

"Thank you, Dr. Ophion. But I should probably tell you that one of our residents, Dr. Richison, helped him, and ever since then he's had somewhat of an attitude about VIP."

This, too, Dr. Ophion waved off as though Red were as insignificant as the carpet he walked on. "Yes, I know Dr. Richison."

Damon continued. "And, uh, I have reason to believe he and Dr. Chambers might have been trying to gather evidence against the clinic relating to the case."

"Oh, really?" Dr. Ophion stared.

Damon nodded. "He sent Dr. Chambers some test results that contradicted—"

Dr. Ophion held up his hand. "With the deposition coming up, perhaps it would be best if you didn't tell me the details until afterward. You understand?"

"Ah, yes I do."

"I've taken care of Dr. Chambers. I was aware that she had overstepped the boundaries of her responsibility. I don't expect any further trouble from her. As for Dr. Richison's involvement"—Dr. Ophion leaned back in his chair and studied Damon over tented fingers— "might that be something you can take care of?"

A twisted smile crossed Damon's face. He relished the opportunity to endear himself to Dr. Ophion while going after the resident he most detested. "Yes, I think so."

"If not, I may have a way to handle him."

"No, I can take care of it for you." It would be his pleasure.

TWENTY-ONE

Red looked down at his vibrating pager and saw his own home phone number light up. *That's strange.* He went to the nearest phone and punched in his number.

Sharon answered in her most seductive voice. "Hello, Red?"

"Sharon! What are you *doing* there? How'd you get in?" He set his jaw.

"Nice to hear *your* voice too."

Red sighed.

"I thought you had Tuesday off. I came by to see you, and you weren't here."

"Sharon, get out of my apartment and cut this out."

"I'm not going to let you go without a fight. Admit it, Red. At least you're flattered."

He groaned. "How did you get in?"

"I broke a window."

The mental image of his scared-to-break-a-fingernail ex wielding a ladder made Red smile, despite his annoyance. "Sure, Sharon."

"It's a no-brainer. I had a copy of the key made long ago. I kept one in my wallet and one on my key chain."

"I'd like to have them back, along with any other copies you might have. Feel free to mail them to me at the hospital." *Guess I'll be changing the locks, too.*

"You used to like it when I showed up unannounced, Red."

"That was then; this is now."

"So when am I going to see you again?"

"You're not. We have nothing to talk about, Sharon. Don't call me again. Listen, is someone regulating your meds now? It would appear you need to be reevaluated."

"What? There's nothing wrong with me. Boy, you have a lot of nerve!" *Click.*

On his way home that evening, Red picked up Bethany so they could go cycling before dark. He mentioned Sharon's call, but they didn't dwell on it. They had more important things to discuss. As he drove to his place, he filled her in on his conversation with Dorie.

"Bethany, can you start keeping a record of patients who come to your clinic after having problems with Ophion?"

"I've already started a file."

"Good." He pulled into his driveway. "Come on up for a sec. I'll change, and then we can go, but it's too hot for you to sit out here."

"Okay." Bethany followed him up the stairs.

When Red opened the door, they both stared. Chairs lay overturned, videos and books were strewn across the floor, contents of files had been dumped out, and fire extinguisher foam had been sprayed all over the walls. All the pictures on one shelf—including Bethany's—had been thrown on the floor and lay in broken glass. And in the foam on one of the walls were the words "Back off."

Bethany was aghast. "Red! Who would do something like this?"

"Sharon."

"Sharon?"

Red nodded. "When she called, she didn't sound like she was thinking of doing anything like this though. But then, I wasn't exactly cordial. I'm sorry, Bethany."

"Why are you apologizing? You haven't done anything wrong."

"I don't know. I just try to imagine how I would feel if I were you. But don't worry, I'll get the locks changed tomorrow."

"She's really out there, isn't she?"

Red sighed. "Her condition can be managed. Too bad if she won't do anything about it."

"Do you think she's dangerous?" Bethany opened her hand toward the mess. "This looks pretty angry."

Red shook his head. "Disturbed, but not dangerous. Like I said, I'm so sorry…"

She straightened her shoulders. "If you think I'm worried that she'll steal you from me, guess again." Bethany wrapped her arms around him and kissed his cheek, then rested her head on his chest. "I would imagine hers is not the kind of behavior that would rekindle the old flames."

Red laughed. "Uh, no! If it did, there is still *plenty* of foam left in that fire extinguisher over there to douse me with."

"Come on. I'll help you clean off the walls."

"No. I'll do it when I get back. Let's go to the lake. I refuse to let Sharon wreck our plans for the evening."

Red sat across from Lexie Winters and watched as she pulled some papers out of a folder. "We're at the interrogatory stage," she told him.

"What does that mean?"

"You answer some questions in writing, and we notarize them. It carries the same weight as testimony under oath. The opposing side's lawyer needs some background information."

"What kind of background information?"

"Nothing difficult. Where you got your training, any corporate connections, that sort of thing. It's pretty straightforward. They're looking for conflicts of interest or places where your pockets might be deeper than they thought."

Red laughed. "No risk there!"

"Ever published any articles?"

"No."

"Has a hospital or medical board ever brought disciplinary action against you?"

Red shook his head.

"Ever had your license revoked?"

His heart was pounding. "I haven't had it long enough for that, but…" *This is it, but even if it costs me my job, we have to stop what's happening at VIP.*

Lexie looked up at him with furrowed brows. "'But,' Dr. Richison?"

"Dr. Ophion. He might have something on me."

Red leaned into the doorway of the chief resident's office and found Dorie with her laptop open and charts spread out in front of her. "You wanted to talk to me?"

Dorie looked up, and then gestured toward the chair that faced her desk.

Red took the seat, scooting it closer so he could speak in lowered tones. "How are you?"

"All right, I guess. I'm still pretty angry with Ophion, but I'm finding some satisfaction in knowing he probably won't get away with what he's done." She sighed. "I was up to see Lexie Winters today."

"Me, too. You're not part of that lawsuit, are you?"

"I told you, Ophion said he's not planning to sue me."

"I meant the DeVeer case. Never mind. What's up?"

"I told Lexie about my dismissal and the information I was gathering," Dorie said.

"What did she say?"

Dorie shrugged. "She told me to get independent counsel and gave me the name of somebody. I don't have a case yet, so there's not much she can say. But I'm working to rectify that." Dorie looked back at the charts.

"Found anything?"

"I've opened the files I e-mailed myself. But it also occurred to me that Ophion knew about the pharmacy printouts I requested, so I'm guessing whatever made him scared enough to fire me is in there. That's where I'm focusing most of my attention. I'm looking for all the RU-486 patients who ended up getting D and Cs. That's where I need your help. I need you to spend some time over in ER and hospital clinic records. Start with the files on patients who had incomplete abortions who came here as walk-ins or with private docs. Then get me a list of all those patients who used RU-486. From there we'll have to narrow it down to the ones that started out at VIP. I'm just looking for connections, something out of the ordinary to validate my suspicions."

"I'll see what I can do."

"Thanks. That should cover it for now."

Red rose and started to leave, but when he got to the doorway, Dorie stopped him. "Hey, Red? Listen, ever since you told me what happened, I've felt especially bad about what I caused between you and your girlfriend."

"How could you have known?"

She grimaced. "If I'd respected patient confidentiality, it wouldn't have mattered whether or not I knew, would it? Sometimes when we're trying to help, we make things worse."

"So true."

Dorie looked down at her desk. "I'd like to talk with her myself, if you wouldn't mind arranging it."

"Bethany? You want to talk to Bethany?"

"If she's willing to speak to me."

Red wasn't sure he wanted to open that chapter again, and he couldn't imagine Bethany being enthusiastic about the idea. Still, maybe, on the spiritual plane, Bethany talking with a pro-choice doctor could have more of an impact than either of them could imagine.

A few hours later, down in the basement near the lab, Red pushed open the door to Medical Records. He stood at the window and rang for assistance, noticing the seemingly endless racks of Manila charts.

A young woman came and slid open the glass.

"Yes? May I help you, Doctor?"

Red nodded. "I'm Dr. Richison. I called a little while ago and asked for all the charts from the past year coded for RU-486 that are listed under the ob-gyn department."

"Yes, we have those right here."

"Thank you. And I also have a list of patient names. Would you mind pulling any of these that we have?" He handed her a list with sixty-four names.

The woman looked at the list of names, then back up at Red. "When do you need these?"

"As soon as possible, please. In fact, I'll review them here at the station while you pull them, if that's all right."

She gave Red a face.

"I don't know how many on the list were patients here at the hospital, but I'm trying to cross-check."

She plopped down, set aside her cup of coffee, and tossed the list on the desk.

Red picked up the stacks of charts she had already pulled, hauled them to a carrel, and began to study them. As he did, he could hear her muttering.

"Like I've got nothing better to do. We're supposed to have twenty-four-hours notice on lists of more than ten patients. Who does he think he is? He's only a resident…" Then he heard her fingers clicking away at her keyboard.

After about ten minutes, she leaned her head around to talk to him. "Lucky for me, the recent stuff hasn't been converted to microfiche, so it won't take as long as I thought. I've found twelve, but you already *have* ten of them."

"Do you know, were they ob-gyn cases, those two I don't have?"

"Hang on." She went to check on the computer and then came back. "No. One was a motor vehicle accident, and the other was pneumonia."

"Thanks. Then no, I don't need them. If you'd just print me a list of the ten that overlap, that should do it."

Two hours later Red leaned on the two back legs of his chair and stroked his chin. In his stack were all the patients who had started out as Dr. Ophion's patients at the VIP clinic but who had ended up at Taylor Hospital needing emergency D and Cs. Of the fourteen hospital cases requiring D and Cs after RU-486 in the past year, ten had been Dr. Ophion's patients.

Red stood and asked the records assistant to keep the files handy for another week, then made his way out the door, lost in thought. Sure, a number of doctors were using RU-486, but only one had had an inordinate number of complications.

The wily Dr. Ophion.

Bethany stood waiting for Red at the entrance to the Dallas Museum of Art, and as he approached, she couldn't help but smile. Just the sight of him did her heart good.

Once they got inside and began to walk from painting to painting, Bethany grew serious. "I'm probably going to fly home in two weeks."

Red looked at her. "Is everything okay?"

She shrugged. "I guess so. They've scheduled Dad's surgery, and I want to be there. Not that I'm needed or anything. I just feel like I should go. I'll probably stay for about a week."

He reached for her hand. "It'll kill me; I'll pine away."

"I'll call you every day," she said. "My cell phone has unlimited minutes."

"Good, 'cause I'll need lots of minutes." Red took both her hands in his. Now was as good a time as any to tell her. "Listen, I made a decision…"

She looked up at him. "About what?"

"I talked to the hospital's legal counsel, and I told her everything Ophion had on me."

Bethany stared, wide-eyed. "You told her? Red! What happened? Did they fire you?"

Red pursed his lips and shook his head. "Not at all. Lots of folks use formalin, but nobody talks about it. It's like a conspiracy of silence. It wouldn't have played well before a jury or the medical board if they got surprised with the information. And the hospital probably would've let me go just for the PR problems—you know, to protect itself and its reputation. But still, Lexie told me that baby had no legal status. So while it's a troubling moral issue, it's not a significant legal issue. Ophion can't impeach my testimony with it."

"Wow."

"Yeah, I had mixed emotions when I heard that."

"But, Red!" Bethany stared at him, then gave him a hug. "Telling her really took guts. I'm proud of you."

He smiled at her. "Gee, if I'd known it would evoke this kind of reaction, I'd have fessed up a long time ago!"

Bethany laughed. "What about Sharon? Have you heard from her?"

"She hasn't returned any of my calls. Why would she go on a rampage in my apartment to make you back off, but then not answer my calls?"

"There's no logic in it."

"Good point. Logic has never been her strong suit. But before we move on to that, I have to tell you, I've been digging up some evidence on my own."

Bethany straightened. "What?"

"I've been digging around in the records, and I've found some odd coincidences."

She raised her eyebrows.

"For one thing, a high percentage of the VIP-related incomplete abortions happened between Saturday evenings and Monday mornings, probably because VIP is closed on Sundays."

"So the overflow went to the hospital instead of the clinic. That makes sense."

"It does, doesn't it? You figure a certain percentage fell when the clinic wasn't open, so the ER and hospital clinic got the overflow. No doubt the actual number of complications is significantly higher, considering that the other six days a week, Dr. Ophion can cover his own problems at VIP."

Bethany seethed. "That snake. Just think of all the pain and suffering he's caused."

"Oh! Speaking of pain and suffering, there's something else I forgot to tell you. Dorie wants to meet you."

Bethany's brow wrinkled. "Why would that fall in the pain-and-suffering category?"

"I was referring to the pain our misunderstanding caused."

She nodded. "Ah. Well, I already met her, and I wouldn't have much to say."

"I think she wants to apologize. You willing?"

Bethany thought hard. "Can't she just write me a note? It could be awkward."

"Bethany, though I know you'd never do it, you could sue her for the breach of patient confidentiality. She probably won't sleep well until she's sure you're not going to." Red studied her, not wanting to pressure her, but hoping she'd agree. "Besides, maybe you could be a good influence on her—you know, spiritually speaking."

"Oh, all right."

Red spotted Dorie waiting for them. In the balmy late-September breeze, she sat alone at a picnic table under a pergola at the Landry Fitness Center watching runners circle the outdoor track. Looking up, she saw Red and Bethany walking toward her, and she stood to meet them.

Bethany squeezed Red's palm as they approached.

"Dorie, you remember my girlfriend, Bethany Fabrizio?"

Dorie extended her hand to Bethany. "Yes, of course."

"Hello, Dr. Chambers." Bethany hoped Dorie hadn't noticed the tension in her voice.

"Please call me Dorie." She gestured to the table in the shade.

After Red and Bethany were seated, Dorie led the conversation. "I may as well cut to the chase." She looked at Bethany. "I owe you an apology. I spoke out of turn, and I'm really sorry."

"It's okay. I know you were just trying to help."

Dorie looked her straight in the eyes. "You sure?"

Bethany nodded.

Dorie heaved a sigh of relief. "To be honest, I didn't really appreciate your covert action, coming to the clinic under false pretenses. But I can see why you did it. The very thought of Ophion doing what he did to you, and apparently to a lot of other women—"

"Undercover is not exactly my usual way of operating," Bethany said.

Dorie sighed. "Yeah, I get that. And I'm guessing Red told you about how I got myself dismissed with an investigation of my own." Dorie flashed her a nervous smile.

"I'm sorry that happened. You took a pretty big risk to help," Bethany said.

"Clearly, Ophion's nervous about something. If he wasn't afraid I'd find something incriminating, I imagine he would've just given me a slap on the wrist. But I think I've figured out what he had going."

Red leaned closer. "Creative prescribing of meds, right?"

Dorie shook her head. "More than that." She looked at Bethany. "My hunch is that your insurance would have covered complications of RU-486. Am I right?"

Bethany nodded.

"Did Ophion mention your insurance when he talked to you?"

"Yes."

"I'm betting he not only knew you had insurance, but he also wanted to get a sense of whether you were willing to use it. Sometimes patients won't, for fear of someone finding out."

"So you think this might be an insurance scam?" Red asked.

"Uh-huh."

Red pressed his hands together. "Dorie! I know of a hospital case where Ophion lied about the age of the fetus to get a bigger payment. He even told me so at the time. I can pull the chart, and it'll show where he crossed out the age and changed it. Just one patient wouldn't prove much, but if we can establish a pattern."

This time when Bethany squeezed his hand, he felt her affirmation.

Dorie raised her eyebrows. "It's hard to say if that one record would tell much, but at this point, a line of evidence that supports our hypothesis can only help."

After lunch with Bethany in the doctors' lounge on Saturday afternoon, Red headed down to the lab to work on his microsurgical technique. A little over an hour later, he completed the incision on a rabbit's skin, then carefully entered its abdominal cavity. He used moist sponges to pack away the intestines and elevated the two-horned uterus into the operative field.

Amazing that this small animal's uterus is roughly the diameter of the human fallopian tube.

His plan was to cut one of the two uterine horns in half. He hoped to sew the two halves back together as if sewing two ends of a fallopian tube. This mimicked the procedure needed to restore fertility for women that have had their tubes cut and tied. Making such fine movements pressed him to the limits of dexterity, because it involved stitching with a needle so small he needed a microscope to see it well and a suture that was finer than human hair.

He had blocked out two hours for the procedure. When he was about halfway through, he was thoroughly frustrated with his own clumsiness.

Dr. Kedar came down to check on his fetal pig. "Hello, Red. How are you?" He came over to get a close look.

"Pretty well, though knot tying, particularly on the backside, is giving me some trouble."

"No problem. Let me check on this specimen, and then I can give you a hand."

Dr. Kedar checked on the pig and then directed his attention to the table where Red was working. "May I have a pair of gloves, eight and a half?" he asked the tech.

The assistant went for the gloves as Dr. Kedar pulled off his lab coat and stood in his scrubs. He reached for the gloves and motioned for the tech to move his stool so he could sit on the opposite side of the table from Red.

"How long have you been working on this?" he asked Red.

"Maybe ninety minutes. I've just about got the first side done." The procedure was taking longer than he'd thought.

"May I?" Dr. Kedar asked, picking up the scissors.

Red hesitated. He had other plans for the day, and he knew his own skill, or lack thereof, but he never contradicted an attending. "Of course."

Dr. Kedar picked up the opposite uterine horn and snipped it cleanly in half.

Red gulped. *Another whole side? I'll be here all day.*

"Watch. This is how I do it, and you may find this helpful." Dr. Kedar picked up the tiny needle and placed the first perfect stitch. Then he tied three perfect knots without a single slip, and then placed a second stitch at the opposite side.

Red stared. "You've done this before, eh?"

"Yes. A time or two…" Instead of cutting the stitches, Dr. Kedar held them with a small hemostat on each end. "Now I have control at 12:00 and 6:00. Using these as guides, I can rotate the tube and place the stitches easily." He demonstrated by placing a few more stitches on each side, and then looked to Red with a smile. "Good technique is important, but sometimes a little experience can go a long way."

Red began to stitch in a similar way, though not as smoothly as Dr.

Kedar, but still quite well and much improved. Dr. Kedar irrigated the field, tied the suture, and cut it. "Perfect." They had finished in less than thirty minutes.

As they cleaned up afterward, Red joked. "Will you *always* scrub with me?"

"You are a good surgeon; you can train your *own* assistants."

"So how's Mr. Pig today?"

Dr. Kedar glanced sideways toward the lab technician.

"Why are you looking at *me?*" The tech made a face. "Are you suggesting *I'm* Mr. Pig?"

Dr. Kedar's smile was his only acknowledgment of the humor. "An update, please."

"Chemistries are looking good, pressure acceptable, slight abnormality in sodium and potassium," the tech said. "I'm working on the dialysis arm to correct it."

Red removed his gloves. "I've been wondering about the last pig we lost. Dr. Kedar, what kind of pressure should there be on the return to the fetal pig?"

"Perhaps a third more. But if I increase the pump pressure, the dialysis doesn't balance. Then the specimens go into overload and die."

"May I make a suggestion?"

Dr. Kedar stared through the top of his bifocals. "Certainly!"

"I've studied your diagram and the specs on the machinery." Red reached into his lab coat pocket and pulled out Dr. Kedar's diagram. It showed the blood going from the pig, through the heart-lung pump, then into the dialysis machine, and back to the pig. Red began to draw his own sketch.

Dr Kedar folded his arms. "I have already tried to put the pump downstream and have the blood dialyze first, but—"

Red shook his head. "But you lose all the pressure to the pump; it backs up and kills the specimen."

"Correct." He smiled at Red. "You *do* understand!"

"Yes. But if we put them in parallel, that is, we circulate blood through the pump and the dialyzer at the same time, we split the flow straight from the fetal pig."

"Like Christmas lights that stay on when one goes out!" The lab tech stood looking over their shoulders. "They're connected in parallel rather than in a series."

"Yes," Red said.

Dr. Kedar studied Red's diagram. "That will allow the lesser pressure to the dialyzer while getting flow to the pump. We would need to increase the volume in the tubing, but we could figure that. Yet this pump... I am not sure it could make the fine continuous adjustments to sweep along the current with the dialyzed blood. And it would take longer to dialyze..."

"Exactly right. We need a more efficient pump with greater sensitivity and immediate response."

"Yes. But where to find such a pump?" Kedar looked him.

"Back when I worked at Biomedtech, we were working on an artificial pump that's much like the new, self-contained heart we keep hearing about in the news."

Dr. Kedar's brows lifted. "You worked on that?"

"Not directly. I worked mostly on the prototypes that preceded it. But we had some working models with more the range we are looking for here. With the computer program and readings you've already obtained, I'm confident I can work out the parameters that might give this a fighting chance."

Dr. Kedar clasped his hands together. "Machines in parallel, and a more efficient, rapid-response pump? That is genius! When can we get one?"

Later that day Red sat in Medical Records poring over the evidence. Dorie had given him a copy of Dr. Ophion's call-and-off schedule, so Red made a chart of the days of the week. Then he blocked out what days and times the RU-486–related cases took place.

Several hours later, he had compelling evidence supporting his theory that if Dr. Ophion's patients got into trouble during the day, they probably went back to VIP and saw Ophion himself. But if patients had problems at night or on a weeknight when he was in town, Dr. Ophion came in to the ER and did the D and C. Red clenched his teeth when he noticed that, in each case, Dr. Ophion had profited by charging insurance the full rate.

All of the pathology reports said, "normal products of conception, decidual tissue." Red had to admit that the records were clean, but the number of cases seemed inordinately high. At first he was puzzled that he didn't find alterations on the gestational ages of the abortions. But then he realized that if the baby's ages were listed as being much later, the pathology would show fetal parts. He felt a slow burn rising up the back of his neck.

Ophion was smooth in covering his tracks. *He certainly knows how to work the system.* But each day the evidence was mounting. Red pictured Dr. Ophion in orange overalls behind bars, and the image made him chuckle aloud.

Even covered tracks are no match for bloodhounds.

TWENTY-TWO

Bethany picked up Red and drove him over to her place on Sunday evening. "How was church this morning?" he asked.

Bethany pouted, then smiled. "Great, other than the fact that you had to work."

"Actually, I had to sleep. Got off work at seven this morning after pulling an all-nighter. Ugh. But someday I hope we can go together on a regular basis."

"I'd like that."

He leaned over and kissed her cheek. Then he reached to turn on the radio but stopped when his hand touched the dial. He looked at Bethany. "I did have an interesting message on my machine while I was at work."

"Yeah?"

Red nodded. "Sharon's mom called."

Bethany glanced over at him and raised her eyebrows.

"She said Sharon asked her to call and let me know she was back with Chad."

Bethany smirked. "Sharon didn't want to talk to you herself? Ha! I can't imagine why not. So she had her *mother* call you? I don't suppose she said anything about trashing your place."

"No."

"Pathetic. So how's the other investigation going?"

Red shook his head. "Slowly. Insurance fraud is tough to pin down. How could I prove those babies were smaller than he said? My word against his." He shook his head. "Ophion is a slippery one."

"Even slippery ones can get caught," Bethany said, and Red nodded, hoping she was right.

———

On Monday morning Regan made her way out through the doctors' waiting area full of women, most of whom were pregnant. Though now she was one of them, Regan still felt like an impostor. During her months of infertility treatment, she had always hated the sight of an expanding belly, and now she herself had one. At sixteen weeks, she was just starting to let herself believe that she and Phil might actually have a baby in another five months.

In the parking garage below her OB's office, as she walked to her car, she passed under the PATIENT ONLY sign and smiled at the irony. She felt anything *but* patient about this baby's arrival.

When she got to her car, she opened the door and moved the driver's seat back so she could get in. Then she moved it forward again once she was situated. She pulled the seat belt around her middle section and punched in Phil's number on her cell phone, but she got a message saying he was on the line. Not wanting to leave her news on voice mail, she hung up and pulled out of the lot. She wound her way around through the hospital complex and out to the main street.

After about ten minutes, once she'd made it out to Central Expressway, she tried again to reach her husband.

Phil answered this time.

"I have news!"

"Yeah? What did the doctor say?"

"It's probably a girl, though they weren't *totally* sure. But, oh, Phil, wouldn't that be fabulous?"

"Yes!" Phil had three sisters and often said he wanted a little girl of his own.

"Though I probably need to wait a bit before buying pink paint because—"

Regan let out a yelp, slammed on the brakes, dropped the phone, and steered slightly to the right toward the shoulder, but she was too late. Her car bashed into the pickup truck that had screeched to a halt in front of her. A moment later someone hit her from behind.

Regan sat in a daze for a moment. Hearing her husband's voice yelling to her through the phone brought her back. Fortunately, it was a minor crash, as traffic had been inching along to begin with. Regan found the phone on her floorboard and put it to her ear.

"Regan! Are you okay? Are you there? Regan!"

"Yes, I think so. I'll call you back." After getting out, she surveyed the damage. She'd barely scratched the pickup, but her own left headlight was knocked out. Her back bumper also had a lot of scratches, but that was the extent of the damage to her vehicle.

As the drivers exchanged insurance information, passersby honked and traffic stacked up. A few drivers made gestures and called out rude remarks about Regan's nationality as they inched around the wreck. After a few minutes, the other two drivers got back in their cars and took off. Regan pulled over to the shoulder and called Phil back.

"Regan! Honey, are you okay?"

"Yes." She gasped. "I'm okay, but it *scared* me."

"Thank God! Are you sure you're okay?"

She calmed herself down. "Pretty sure."

"Call the doctor."

"But I'm fine."

"Regan, you know how they always say you can walk away from an accident feeling fine, but then you find out later that you're really hurt?"

"You're scaring me."

"I'm not trying to scare you, baby. I just want to make sure you're okay."

When she phoned the doctor, his nurse relayed the message to him, and he said he wanted Regan to go to L and D observation. So she drove to the hospital. When she arrived, she gave her name to the charge nurse and grinned sheepishly.

"We've been expecting you," the nurse said.

"I'm fine, really. It was just a little fender bender."

"Your doctor got tied up at the office, so he requested the chief resident. He also mentioned that your brother might like to know you're here. Would you like for me to page Dr. Kedar for you?"

Regan started to object, but then changed her mind. "Yeah, actually that would be nice." She fought the tears that surfaced in response to this kindness.

"Okay. Let me take care of *you* first." As the nurse led her back to the observation area, she explained that the usual L and D nurses staffed it, but it was less busy and thus quieter. Here patients were observed but not admitted. The nurse showed Regan an area with three-walled cubicles, each of which had a television and a monitor behind a thick curtain. The nurse handed her a gown, then departed.

Before long another nurse came in and hooked up Regan to the monitors with a belt holding them in place, one monitor to check her heart rate and the other monitor for contractions. Both women smiled when they heard the heart rate.

"You've got a robust 160 beats per minute going there, Mom. And no uterine activity, no contractions."

Regan took a deep breath. "It really wasn't a severe crash. I wasn't too worried."

"They'll probably want to watch you for a few hours, so make yourself comfortable."

Regan did so, stretching out and forcing herself to relax. Then she heard her brother's voice.

"Dalmuth!" She stretched out her arms as he entered.

He came over and wrapped her in a hug. Then without a word, he looked up through his bifocals to scan the data on the monitors in front of him.

"Everything looks great," the nurse told him. "No cramping, no vag bleeding, normal heart rate."

"Thank you so much."

"Guess you can go back to the office. Sorry to have messed up your day," Regan said.

He gave her a kind smile. "No trouble. We want to take extra good care of you." Then he pointed to her stomach. "And you, too."

An hour later the baby's heart rate had increased from 160 to 170. The change was hardly significant, but the nurse asked the attending physician for a bit more time to observe her.

Dalmuth returned and found Regan on the phone to Phil. He looked at the chart while she talked. Then he motioned for the nurse to join him outside the cubicle. "Why has she been changed from two-hour to twenty-four-hour observation?"

"I noticed a subtle elevation in the fetal heart rate." She gave him the numbers.

"I appreciate your sharp observation, and I agree with your assessment. I will return in about forty-five minutes." He ducked back inside the curtain to the room where his sister sat fidgeting. "I need to get back to the office, but we are going to keep you overnight."

Regan stared at him. "What? Why?"

He tilted his head. "There is a minor elevation—very minor—in your baby's heart rate. And we would rather be too conservative."

"What causes that?"

"It could be nothing." *But then again, the baby's life could be in danger.*

About two and a half hours after Regan's arrival, Dalmuth returned to find the baby's heart rate steady but still slightly elevated. Phil, who was sitting in the corner, looked up when he arrived.

"Is the baby going to be okay?" Regan's eyes pleaded with him. "Why do I have to stay overnight?"

Dalmuth laid a strong hand on her arm. "Everything looks good. We just need to proceed with caution. Besides, you get only two options for staying here. You either get the two-hour observation fee or the twenty-four-hour room rate. Since you have bought the whole twenty-four hours, we might as well watch the baby for the whole time." He smiled. "Uncle Dalmuth cannot be too careful."

The nurse came in to take the vital signs, and no one spoke while she waited for the pulse rate. Then she wrapped the blood pressure cuff around Regan's arm and took the reading. "Everything looks pretty good. And no contractions." She readjusted the belt with a cheerful smile.

"Ouch!" Regan winced.

Everyone looked at her.

"It's kind of tender where the belt is. It feels a little too tight…probably pushing on the bruise I got from the steering wheel."

"May I take a look at it?" Dalmuth wasn't the doctor in charge, but as chief of OB, he ranked above most of the physicians in the hospital. He knew his sister wouldn't mind, and he would feel better knowing what was happening.

"Okay," Regan said.

He pressed a bit here and there. Her uterus was still soft, which was a good sign. It seemed tender only at the bruise site. *Good. But car accidents can cause placental problems. I hope the baby's heart rate returns to baseline soon.* "I think it is okay, so I am going to meet Yvonne for dinner now, but I will come back afterward."

"Anybody home?"

They all looked up to see Regan's ob-gyn dressed in a business suit. He poked his head through the curtain, which he then pulled back and entered.

"Oh, Dr. Wallace!" Regan greeted him. "I hardly recognized you in street clothes. I'm glad you're here! Hey, you know my brother, Dr. Dalmuth Kedar. And my husband, Phil."

Dr. Wallace shook hands with the men. Then he turned his attention back to Regan. "Dr. Chambers called me and told me everything was stable and that you were in good hands. But I thought I'd drop in on my way to the opera with my wife. She should be here in a minute."

"Your wife's coming here?"

"No, sorry. I meant Dr. Chambers. Speak of the devil..."

Dorie walked in through the double doors. The doctors reviewed what had happened and assured Regan that they'd do everything they could to help. Then everyone left except Dalmuth, who closed the curtain again. While Phil had gone to use the rest room, Dalmuth scooted a chair up close to Regan's side. He laid his hand on her arm and squeezed it. "I know you are afraid, and I am sorry."

At this, Regan teared up. "Dal, you know how important this pregnancy is to us. It seems so unfair that you and Yvonne have no children, and for so long it looked like we were unable to have them. This may be our only chance, not just for us but for you, too, in a way."

He nodded.

"Remember when we were little how you and I were the only ones in the family who wanted girls? Everyone else said they wanted boys."

"Yes," he whispered.

"Well, today Dr. Wallace said this is probably a girl." She touched her stomach and looked at him with glistening eyes.

He squeezed her arm.

"Dalmuth, all my life with so many brothers and sisters, I never dreamed any of us would grow up childless. If anything, I thought we'd have more than we could manage. But life sure didn't turn out like we thought it would, did it?"

He shook his head.

"And now I have a chance to have that dream child. Please, please," she pleaded. "Don't let anything happen to this baby!"

In the middle of the night, Regan called for a bedpan. Less than a minute later she called out, "Nurse! There's blood on the tissue!" It wasn't much, but it was bright red.

The nurse came from her station. "I'll get the resident in charge of L and D."

Phil held Regan's hand while they waited. Within moments, the resident arrived and introduced herself. "I'm Dr. Ellen Tsai. I understand you're having some light spotting."

Regan nodded.

The doctor checked Regan's vital signs. "Car accident, huh?"

"It was just a little mishap, really."

"Well, your pulse and blood pressure are normal—that's good. And the fetal monitor tracing shows nothing dramatic. The baby's heartbeat is good, though a wee bit high. I'd like to do a sonogram, okay?"

"Fine, whatever we need to do," Regan told her.

The nurse looked at the doctor. "I'll get the sono machine from L and D."

"Thanks." Dr. Tsai removed Regan's monitoring belt, and as she did, she looked at the bruise. Then she touched it gently. "Is this tender?"

"Uh-huh. A little."

"It doesn't look too severe."

When the nurse came in with the machine, Dr. Tsai took the sono gel and squeezed a dollop of the goo on Regan's abdomen. Then she flipped the switch and the machine fired up. She slid the transducer across Regan's abdomen. "You say you're about sixteen weeks?"

"Right."

She smiled. "Your baby looks good, and very active! Heart beating rapidly, good amniotic fluid. Anterior placenta…yep, anterior placenta." She looked at Regan. "Your placenta lies on the front wall of the uterus, right under where the steering wheel hit. It's possible that's where the bleeding's coming from." She scanned the uterus for a few more minutes. Then she looked up. "There's a small dark shadow under the placenta. I'm not sure, but it could be a small abruption."

Regan waited for the doctor to explain what that meant.

"It's a small separation between the placenta and the uterus where it attaches, a collection of blood. It's probably leaking out and responsible for the blood you saw. The placenta is not low down, not by the cervix, so I'm confident I could safely examine you vaginally if we start seeing contractions." She thought aloud. "Actually, we don't need to check the cervix if we're sure that's where the blood is coming from. But I'm going to call Dr. Chambers, okay?"

Regan nodded.

After Dr. Tsai departed, Phil moved close to reassure his wife. "It's okay, honey. It all sounds pretty good, really."

About fifteen minutes later, Dr. Tsai reappeared with Dr. Chambers. *Her scrubs are so wrinkled—I'll bet she was sleeping in them.* Regan noticed that Dr. Chambers's green eyes were bleary and her uncombed, sandy-blond hair was pulled up off her shoulders in a silver hair clip. Touching Regan on the shoulder, Dr. Chambers gestured toward the sono machine. "All right with you if I take a look?"

Regan nodded. "I'm getting kind of scared. First the heart rate went up, and I had to stay overnight. Now I've got some bleeding. What does this all mean?"

Dr. Chambers sat down and took the transducer in her right hand. She repeated what Dr. Tsai had done, taking care at each step to tell Regan what she saw. When she had finished, she scooted away from the machine and looked at Phil, then back at Regan. "So far the bleeding is minimal. The uterus is still soft, so I concur with everything Dr. Tsai found. Sometimes blood inside the uterus may make it tender or cause it to contract. But the baby looks good, so we'll continue with bed rest and monitors. I'll talk to Dr. Wallace when he calls in; I took the liberty of phoning him already. And I'll be here for the rest of the night too, so page me if you need me."

"What if the bleeding continues?" Phil was wide-eyed.

"Some bleeding and a few contractions are to be expected in situations such as this. But we have to do all we can to keep labor from starting because the baby is way too immature to survive."

Later when Regan was alone again, she buried her face in the pillow and dissolved into tears. She wanted to stop crying all the time, but the hormones of pregnancy—along with all the complications—made that nearly impossible. She took a deep breath and forced herself to settle down. Then she rubbed her stomach and whispered to her child, "I'm so sorry, little one. Now please—behave!"

TWENTY-THREE

Red opened the door to the records room. He slipped inside and found Dorie sitting at one of the carrels.

"Thanks for agreeing to meet me on such short notice, Red."

"No problem. You're the one who's been up all night." He leaned against the stall, resting his arm on top of it. "I heard about Dr. Kedar's sister."

"Yeah." She leaned toward him and lowered her voice. "I wanted to tell you what I found."

Red raised his eyebrows.

"I checked out all the pharmacy's RU-486 patients that ended up having D and Cs at VIP, and they were all *insurance-to-be-filed* cases. Then I compared the same list with the one you put together of patients who'd had D and Cs here at the hospital. Sure enough, every one of the Taylor patients had insurance. So it looks like those who got the right scripts from Ophion—prescriptions that included the necessary prostaglandins—were all indigent folks, or at least patients without insurance coverage. So he was targeting patients with coverage for complications of abortion. This is no simple scheme."

Red seethed. "So how do we prove it?"

Dorie leaned back. "That's another story. It'll be tough to prove. But there's no doubt in my mind that he's guilty."

"We *have* to find a way."

The next morning Dalmuth arrived early. He scooted the chair over next to Regan's bed and took her hand.

She turned her head away. "Dal, it's all my fault this happened. The accident was my fault."

Dalmuth said nothing.

She turned and looked at him. "It *was.*"

"You can't blame yourself for this."

She smiled and shook her head. "I've always loved that about you—you never add baggage when I'm on a guilt trip."

Dalmuth smiled. "Let me go have a look at Dr. Chambers's sono pictures." He patted her arm and stepped outside the curtain.

He found Dorie and studied the pictures. Then he went down to the lab and tried to tie up some loose ends, but he couldn't concentrate. *None of the last few cases of second-trimester abruptions have had happy endings. And this one's my sister's child! God, if You're there…*

Fifteen minutes later he returned to Regan's room and found the curtain open.

"What did you find?"

"I agree with Dr. Chambers that the pictures suggest a small abruption. But it is quite tiny, and if it remains this size rather than expanding, I am optimistic that your pregnancy will progress uneventfully."

Dalmuth felt the knot in his stomach relax when Regan leaned back into her pillow and smiled. Maybe he had been convincing enough to gain her at least a few hours' peace. But it was going to take many days of such convincing before his sister had even the remote possibility of a happy outcome.

Red pulled Bethany's car into the driveway at the Mansion on Turtle Creek and glanced at her. He'd told her he had plans for her birthday dinner, but he hadn't mentioned where he was taking her. He hoped she liked it. "Ever been here?"

Bethany beamed. "Never. But it's been at the top of my list for a long time."

He reached behind the seat for the gift-wrapped box he'd brought. Then he got out and handed the keys to the valet.

"You don't need a receipt for my Mercedes?" she asked under her breath.

Red smiled and shook his head. "No, here they just *remember.* You look fabulous, by the way. That black number is awesome. But the matching shoes,"—he pressed his thumbs against his index fingers like a conductor ending a concerto—"they make the outfit."

She pointed at him. "Hey! You're catching on, aren't you?"

"I've been in training."

Once they were seated and made their menu selections, Red took her hands. "It was wonderful to finally get to go to church with you this morning."

"I appreciated your arranging your schedule so we could spend all day together."

He leaned forward. "I'll tell you a little secret. Dorie makes the schedule, and she was very willing to oblige, not that I want her to feel guilty for our misunderstanding. But I can't say I minded her eagerness to make it up to you. Besides, she was pretty happy with some work I did for her on the case."

"Are you going to tell me about it?"

"First things first." Red nodded to the waiter, who had come to take their orders. When they were finished, he lifted the box from the padded bench and set it on the table.

Bethany fingered the ribbon, her eyes shining. "Now?"

"Yes. There's another box coming, but this is the more entertaining of the two." He hoped she wouldn't think it was cheesy.

She gave him a sideways glance. Then she peeled off the paper to find a medium-size white box. Inside was a small photo album. "Thanks, Red. I'll fill it with pictures of us."

Red grinned. "Keep going. It's already full."

She opened it to the first page and found a photo of Red as a baby. "You were adorable!" The next was his toothless, first-grade shot. They laughed at another of him in third grade, looking like a raccoon with two black eyes. Bethany seemed enchanted. There was one shot each for junior high, high school, and college. When she flipped to the next page, she found Red standing under a sign for "Bethany Road."

"You drove all the way up to Allen, Texas, for this?"

He winked. "I guess all roads lead to Bethany."

She laughed aloud when she saw that the next shots were of Red standing in front of a Bethany School, a Bethany Florist, a Bethany Retirement Home, and a Bethany Christian Church. Next he was at the entrance to Bethany College and in front of the Chamber of Commerce in Bethany, Oklahoma. "You drove all the way up *there?*"

Red grinned. "Okay, not the last two. It's amazing what you can do with Photoshop."

The last page had a note tucked inside instead of a photo. When Bethany looked at Red, he coaxed her with a nod. She pulled it out and opened the crisp cotton paper, then read aloud: "Everywhere I go, I take you with me in my heart. I love you. Red." She wiped away a tear. "That is so sweet."

"No, it's totally silly, but I'm glad you like it."

Red refused to talk business all through dinner, but by the time the waiter brought dessert, Bethany raised her eyebrows. "Are you going to tell me or not?"

Red nodded. "Sure. Little by little we're piecing it together. I've spent hours in the records lately."

"Find anything?"

"Maybe. When I compiled the records on patients who started out at VIP that came to Taylor with incomplete abortions, I found that the number is completely out of proportion to the usual number of complications with RU-486. So I'm starting to keep track of new patients we see that fit the scenario, those coming from VIP with incomplete abortions following RU-486. And I'm scouring the records for anything else I can find. It's painfully slow, but it's all I know to do right now. And we have to do *something* to try to stop him."

After dinner he took her back to her place, where they spent a few hours with Heather and several friends. After everyone else went home, Red and Bethany sat on the porch swing. Red told Bethany, "There's something else I want to give you on this most fine September 30, darlin'." He walked over to one of the potted plants on the porch and reached behind it. Then he returned with a wrapped shoebox.

Bethany smiled as she opened the wrapping, taking care not to rip the paper. "A shoebox from Saks Fifth Avenue? Such discriminating taste!" She opened the box, and her eyes grew wide. She pulled out one of the wine-colored shoes. "They're the ones I was panting over the night we shopped for perfume!" She reached over to hug Red.

Her exuberant response was all the thanks he needed. "Shall we see if they fit our fairy princess?"

"Okay." She giggled as she handed Red the shoe she was holding, and he slipped it on her foot.

"Just perfect," he said.

"Like this day, Red."

The very words he wanted to hear. "Glad you're pleased. I hoped you would be. Happy birthday, Bethany." He pulled her close and looked into her eyes. "And speaking of perfect, you've got the most perfect lips." Then he kissed her until he knew he'd better go.

Red stood outside the lab door and gave it a couple of gentle kicks.

In seconds the lab tech opened it.

"Sorry. As you can see, my hands are full." Red entered carrying what looked like a tackle box.

Dr. Kedar stared. "I know you play golf, but are you a fisherman as well?"

Is that the first attempt at humor I've ever heard from him? "No, it's the prototype pump I told you about."

Dr. Kedar stood up and came to look.

"My friend at the lab said they'd be happy for us to try it out on loan. They have some smaller, more advanced models they're using in the replacement heart studies."

Dr. Kedar clasped his hands together. "Wonderful! May we take a look?"

"Of course!" Red gestured for him to move back, along with the tech, so he had room to open it.

"Will you look at that." Dr. Kedar shook his head.

The tech grinned at Red. After tracing the connection adapters with his fingers, he jumped up, went to a drawer, and pulled out Red's sketch. Then dashing about the lab, he collected equipment and began to assemble the new configuration.

For the next few hours, the three men ran practice tests with saline in the pumps and tubing, checking pressures and connections as they went.

"Wonderful! Red, it is just as you predicted!" Dr. Kedar turned to the tech. "Prepare a pig for me. I want to see this thing in action!"

"Ready for a sponge bath, Mrs. Hartwell?"

Regan looked up at the nurse and nodded. "I'll sure be glad when I can go home and use my own shower again. After nine days without it, I have a new appreciation—"

"What's wrong?" The nurse smiled, her eyes twinkling. "You don't like the room service here?"

"No, though I do like the soft diet better than the liquid diet they had me on."

"You didn't care for raspberry Jell-O three times a day? Fussy, fussy. We have to torture all our prisoners here at the penitentiary. How'd your walk go yesterday?"

"Great. The doctor hasn't said anything about going home, but I'm getting more hopeful. If only the baby's heart rate would slow down…"

Dr. Wallace entered on his morning rounds. "Good morning, Regan. How are you today? No signs of bleeding?"

Regan shook her head.

He checked the fetal heartbeat. Glancing in her direction, he smiled, and then focused back on the machine.

"What?" She didn't even try to keep the hope from her voice.

"The baby's heart rate has finally returned to normal."

Regan beamed and raised a victorious fist. "Yes! So when do I get to go home?"

He raised a cautious hand. "Let's see how it goes today. If you'd like to go down to the ground floor, maybe sit and visit in the courtyard, that would be okay."

After he left, the nurse finished preparing for her sponge bath, and Regan got up and headed into the bathroom. She screamed when she saw red. "Nurse! There's blood!"

"How much?" the nurse called in to her.

"Not a lot. But still…"

In minutes a team of physicians arrived. Dr. Chambers laid a hand on Regan's abdomen. "It's contracted. We need to restart an IV, stat, and push fluids. Half normal saline, two hundred cc bolus." Another doctor helped her adjust the bed. "I want you to lie flat on your left side instead of sitting up."

Regan complied.

Dr. Chambers kept a hand on Regan's abdomen, waiting for it to relax. The nurse wheeled in the sono machine, and Regan pulled the gown away from her stomach so Dr. Chambers could cover it with gel. Taking the controls, Dr. Chambers focused on the screen.

"It looks as though the abruption has enlarged a bit, but not significantly. How much bleeding did you say there was?"

"Just traces."

"Okay, looks like you've got blood irritating the uterus, so your baby's heart rate's decreasing in response to that persistent contraction in there."

A tear rolled down Regan's cheek and landed in her ear.

"Let me go call Dr. Wallace," Dr. Chambers said.

Regan's eyes pleaded with her. "Could you please also call Dr. Kedar?"

Fifteen minutes passed, though it felt more like an hour to Regan.

Dr. Wallace hurried into the room. He shook his head as Dr. Chambers gave him the vital information, then he turned to Regan.

"The situation isn't too bad yet, but we have to get the uterus to relax so the blood flow to the baby will improve. The contracting uterus is driving down the fetal heart rate. Hopefully, the fluids will work. If not, I'll need to try a medication to relax the uterus, but it may cause the bleeding to increase. This is a delicate situation."

She suppressed a sob, then pulled herself together to ask questions. "You're trying to keep me from going into labor, right?" He nodded. "It's too early for this child to have any chance at all?" She bit her lip.

He nodded again. "We'll need to get you strapped back on the fetal monitor."

Dalmuth appeared in the doorway, and Dr. Wallace filled him in on Regan's status. The two men conferred and agreed on a small dose of subcutaneous terbutaline.

The nurse left and then returned with a syringe. She gave Regan the shot and reapplied the monitoring belts. The two doctors watched the monitor to see if the medication was going to help.

Dr. Wallace smiled. "The heart rate's returning to normal. That's a good sign. We'll keep a close watch here and watch the bleeding, as well."

Two hours later the nurse checked the fetal monitor again. "Looks good. The baby's heart rate is not only back to normal, it's actually elevated a bit."

"Oh no! Elevated?"

"No, it's okay," the nurse assured her. "The medicine will do that."

Regan lay back into her pillow and sighed. "Our little girl is so far from being big enough to survive. How will we ever make it two more months?"

"Red, can you imagine? He is still alive!" Dr. Kedar squatted down eye level with the pig in the tank. "After eight days. And no sign of distress."

"So does that mean it's time?"

Dr. Kedar nodded. "It is nothing short of astounding. I was going to leave you to dissect him, but I do not know if I could wait to know."

The three men worked together to disconnect the fetal pig. Then, with the assistance of the tech, the two doctors did a careful dissection, postmortem exam to see if the pig had met all the developmental milestones. When they had finished, Dr. Kedar looked Red in the eye.

"Outstanding work, Doctor. Simply outstanding."

Red hadn't felt so proud since his dad cheered for his first home run.

Dr. Kedar turned to the tech. "If you would, please get this tank cleaned up for another specimen. I want us to start again soon. We have to find out how long a specimen can survive."

Thoughts of the potential for success made Red's pulse quicken. And to think that he, a mere second-year resident, got to be a key player in such an experiment. If they could hone this technology…what possibilities for saving tiny babies! Who knew how far back they could push the age of viability for early preemies?

TWENTY-FOUR

"Regan, are you asleep or just resting?"

At the whispered question, Regan opened her eyes to see Teresa standing by her bed, holding flowers.

"Hi!" Regan reached for the button to raise herself to a sitting position. "Have a seat."

"I don't want to bother you if you're trying to rest."

"I wasn't sleeping. Thank you so much for coming."

Teresa set the flowers on the table and sat by the bed. "How are you?"

"I was just thinking...thinking too hard. The only thing I do is think." She turned her head to the flowers. "Thanks for the chrysanthemums. They're beautiful."

"You're welcome. What are you thinking about?"

Regan saw compassion in her friend's eyes. "Give you three guesses."

"The baby, the baby, and the baby."

"Right."

"Scary, isn't it?" Teresa squeezed her hand. "You just crossed the seventeen-week mark, right?"

Regan nodded. "Seventeen and a half, a minimum of six weeks from the earliest possible chance of viability. They say one medicine may make the bleeding worse, which may make the contractions worse, which may compromise the baby." She closed her eyes. "It seems like nothing makes everything better. If we have consensus on one thing it's this: Six weeks is a long time to wait." She looked at Teresa, fighting the tears that seemed ready to fall at any moment. "Even if I make it that long, which seems like an eternity, we're talking about a dangerously premature baby."

Teresa's sad eyes expressed her compassion. "I'm sorry you have to go through this." She got up, reached for a Kleenex, and wiped her friend's tears.

"And I'm sorry you lost the twins, Teresa. It means a lot to me that you're here. I know it's hard."

"Thanks," she whispered.

Regan shook her head. "So much at stake. All those years of trying. Then a successful IVF cycle and thrilled family members. Then *boom*. I'm talking on the cell phone in traffic, not paying attention. What a *stupid*, idiotic mistake. I'm not sure my body will hold out another *hour*, let alone six or seven weeks!"

"Regan, you can't blame yourself for this."

"Sure I can. Because I could have prevented it."

"I know that feeling! And there's no pit so deep that guilt can't drive it deeper, right?"

"Yeah, I guess you know what that feels like. I appreciate your thinking about *me* when you have so much of your own pain to work through." Regan gripped her friend's hand.

Tears welled up in Teresa's eyes, and she nodded. "You're not alone, Regan. You are *not* alone."

Suddenly pain shot through Regan's abdomen, and she grabbed at it and groaned.

Teresa's eyes grew wide. "You okay?"

Regan nodded. "It wasn't all that painful. Physically, that is."

Teresa shook her head. "But we're not taking any chances here, are we?" She pressed the call button.

When Red returned from the lab, Dorie motioned him into her office.

Her expression warned him before her words. "Bad news."

"What's up?"

"We've had a setback."

He sat down.

"An incomplete came in while you were down in the lab, and she started out at VIP with Ophion."

"Is she in bad shape?"

Dorie shook her head. "Not that kind of bad news. The trouble is, she doesn't fit the neat little scenario I had all figured out. She got RU-486 and she did have insurance."

"But that *does* fit. What about the prostaglandin?"

Dorie nodded. "That's just it. I asked to see her sample if she had it, and she said she didn't get any samples. She had a prescription for the prostaglandin in her purse."

"What do you think?"

"I think either my theory was wrong"—she met Red's gaze—"or Ophion got nervous, and he's changed his game plan."

Dalmuth dropped in to see Regan shortly after seven that evening and went straight to the fetal monitor.

After several seconds Regan studied him. "What are you thinking?"

"Let me go call Dr. Wallace. I'll be back in a few minutes."

He departed, and she gripped the sides of the bed. Was the baby's heartbeat still too fast? Too slow now? It seemed that every recommendation the doctors made complicated something else. She tried to look at the fetal monitor, but couldn't turn her body far enough with the straps on. All she could do was lie back and listen to the *beep, beep, beep* of the baby's heartbeat, hoping it was stable.

A few minutes later Dalmuth returned. "Dr. Wallace is on another case, but he has agreed with my suggestion to up the terbutaline. We have to try to stop the contractions, though it increases your risk of bleeding. Anything we try is going to carry some risk." Dalmuth sat down in the corner of the room, sighed, and bit his lip.

"Yeah, I sort of figured that out." Weary from the lack of good sleep, the liquid diet, and the emotional ups and downs, Regan spoke with resignation. "Do whatever you think is best."

At 5:30 the following afternoon, Dalmuth arrived. He looked at the monitor, then at Regan and Phil, who had arrived earlier.

"It feels like I'm contracting again. I just don't want to believe it." She stared at the foot of the bed.

"Has Dr. Wallace been by?"

She shook her head. "He's due anytime."

Dalmuth took the seat in the corner again, and the three sat watching Yvonne on the evening news report. During a commercial break, Dr. Wallace came in. He greeted everyone and then read the fetal monitor. Dalmuth got up and assessed the data as he did.

"I was hoping you would get here soon," Dalmuth said.

Dr. Wallace turned to him. "What do you think?"

"What is it?" Regan looked from one doctor to the other. "What's wrong?"

Hearing this, Phil turned his attention from the television and joined his wife in looking to the doctors for a response.

Dr. Wallace glanced at Dalmuth and then focused his attention on Regan. "The meds we're giving you don't appear to be helping as much as we'd hoped."

Regan sank back into the pillow.

He continued. "The fetal heart rate is doing all right, but the uterine pressure is increasing. It looks like you're starting to break through with contractions again, and we don't want to up the dosage any more. It's too risky with the bleeding, but there's a heart medicine we can try that's seen some success in stopping preterm labor."

"Okay." Regan's voice was faint and full of resignation.

Dr. Wallace motioned for Dalmuth to join him in the hall. "I'm concerned that we're just delaying the inevitable. We're weeks from viability, and I don't see any way we can keep her from going into labor that long."

"I know." Dalmuth stared at the floor. Then he looked back at Dr. Wallace. "But we have to try. Even if it were not my niece, you know I would do all in my power to try...it is a human life..."

Red sat with his feet propped up on the coffee table in the doctors' lounge.

"I hate good-byes."

"Me, too, Bethany. Thanks for bringing me lunch so I could see you one last time. It's gonna be a long week. I'll miss you. How are you feeling about the trip in general?"

"Nervous."

"About the medical side or the relational?"

She furrowed her brows. "Both."

"You're going to give me a daily update, right?"

"Okay, as long as you remember that it's two hours earlier on the West Coast."

Red smiled. "All right. I'll call you when I get to work. That should make it right about 4:30 A.M. your time. You'll just be getting to bed."

Bethany laughed.

"Hey, I like those shoes on you."

"Thanks. They were given to me by the most *extraordinary* man."

"Well, certainly by a man who's going to miss you plenty. Your flight leaves early in the morning, right?"

"Yeah. And I'm guessing we'll practically live at the hospital for a few days while Dad recovers. But I'll be staying with my sister who's an attorney, and I'm planning to ask her if she has any advice on helping us bring down VIP."

Red sighed. "Let's hope she has some creative ideas, because it looks like, despite all our efforts, Ophion's winning this war."

The phone had been ringing all morning. Sitting in her office at the law firm, Teresa wasn't getting much done. When the phone rang again, she heaved an annoyed sigh. "Hello?"

"Mrs. Murdock?" The voice sounded young, timid, and almost British.

"Yes."

"You're an attorney, right?"

"Yes."

"Very good. You don't know me, but I got a list of attorneys and agencies from the Women's Choice Clinic. They said you might be able to help me. See, uh, I'm pregnant. With twins. I thought the doctor could just flush them, implant them in someone else, but—"

"No—"

"Right. They told me that's impossible. See, I'm not married. And I don't want to abort them. But still, I'm from Belarus, studying international business on a four-year scholarship, and there is no way I could manage with children right now. So I was thinking about adoption. But I don't begin to know the laws in Texas or how to find adoptive parents."

Teresa gulped. She and John had started considering adoption lately, thinking perhaps they should begin to explore the option.

Thursday night Dorie Chambers hung up the phone after talking with Dr. Wallace. His words still rang in her ears, and she didn't quite know what to make of them. *All this latest effort is a flaming waste of time. Nothing's going to work anyway with an abruption. You essentially never win.* She made her way to Regan's room, where she found the patient with her husband and Dr. Tsai.

"I just spoke with Dr. Wallace," she told Regan. "He's tied up, but he has agreed to have your brother do another sonogram, so Dr. Kedar will be here in a minute."

A nurse wheeled in the sono machine and prepared it and Regan in anticipation of Dr. Kedar's arrival.

"Regan!" Dalmuth's face appeared in her doorway.

Tears blinded her. She wiped them and said nothing but shook her head.

Her brother's eyes were kind. He took his place on the stool in front of the machine and patted her arm. Then he squeezed the gel onto her stomach and scanned with the probe. After long moments spent staring at the screen, he cleaned off the transducer and scooted back to face his sister. "We definitely have an abruption of the placenta. It is not more than 10 percent, but it is still enough to cause the uterus to contract. The baby measures normal for the dates, but, of course, she is very, very small. We need to go ahead and try the alternative medication." He turned and gave the orders to the nurse.

Regan nodded. Then she winced.

He stared at her face. "Are you in pain?"

"That was a contraction." She burst into tears.

Dorie stepped into the hallway to get a drink, and Dr. Tsai, the resident, followed her. "What do you think, Dr. Chambers?"

"About what?"

Dr. Tsai pointed to Regan's room. "The whole thing."

"I think it's pretty sad."

"Do you think they need to give up?"

Dorie shrugged. "Nothing's going to work." She doubted they'd be trying these senseless heroics if the patient were not the chief's sister. "As they say, it's hard to be objective when you're related to the patient—a perfect example of why you shouldn't treat family. She's going to deliver, and I doubt the baby will even survive labor."

Regan gripped her husband's hand, looking to her brother for some bit of hope. "Am I going to have this baby tonight?"

Dalmuth nodded. "The nifedipine is not working…"

Regan moaned through her sobs.

Dalmuth, sitting in the chair in the corner of the room, closed his eyes while Phil did his best to comfort her.

"Dalmuth!" his sister cried. "Isn't there something you can do?"

He shook his head.

"Not *anything*?" She was oblivious to the pain her words were inflicting.

"We do not have anything yet for babies this size." Dalmuth went to take her hand. "Their lungs are too immature. Not one of the vital organs is mature enough. We are at least six weeks from viability. I am so sorry."

"Is there nothing?" Phil pleaded. "Nothing we can try? Another drug? A C-section? Whatever it takes."

Regan added, "Maybe you could try a new procedure, like you did for Teresa Murdock?" Her slurred speech betrayed the painkiller that now coursed through her veins.

Dalmuth grimaced.

"But those babies…well, but at least you *tried*," Phil argued. "You're the creative genius. There must be *something* you can do."

Dalmuth answered him only with a long silence. Then he took a deep breath, followed by a sigh. "There is *nothing* we can do. Medical science has not advanced to this point yet. Yes, in the lab I have been trying to come up with some ideas for micropreemie babies, but we are just not there yet."

"You've been trying something?" Phil pressed. "What are you doing?"

"I have been working on some techniques to try to give these little ones a chance, to buy time so they can develop enough—"

Regan's hand rubbed her stomach in response to another contraction.

Dalmuth noticed and exchanged glances with Phil.

"Dal, we've got nothing here. What are you doing in the lab?" Phil's voice trembled.

He opened his mouth to protest, but Phil continued.

"You know our baby means everything to us, and we probably won't have another chance. At the moment, this baby has *no* chance."

Regan looked at her brother, the tears in her eyes begging for a word of hope.

"You know I would do anything for you, and for this baby," Dalmuth insisted. "But what I have is not yet ready. It is not even *close* to ready."

"What is it? *What* isn't close to ready?" Regan pressed him for more.

"Something I have been working on. But it is still at the conceptual stage."

They both stared, so he continued.

"Picture a combination heart-lung-dialysis machine for tiny babies. That is what I am looking for—trying to design. But I have only begun to experiment with it."

"It? You already have one?"

"Yes. I have been working with fetal pigs." He punctuated each word with staccato emphasis. "But it is just not ready to try on a human. It would be irresponsible."

"Bro, what choices do we have?" Phil argued. " If this labor continues, this baby is gonna be born, isn't it? My daughter, *your* niece. She's coming, isn't she?"

"Probably." Dalmuth looked at the floor.

"And she can't possibly survive using the current equipment in the hospital, right?"

"Correct." Dalmuth continued to look down, blinking back the tear forming in the corner of his eye.

"So what have we got to lose?"

"Look, Phil…Regan." He looked back and forth at them. "I do not think it is right to get your hopes up falsely. That would just drag out the pain, and it is already profound. Even if the baby survives for days or weeks, which was the *best* scenario we have had with the pigs, that still won't be enough. Not even close."

"That's more than we have now. Right now we've got zero hope."

Dalmuth shook his head. "We have no guarantee she will even survive labor and delivery, or what kind of shape she will be in if she does. We probably need to just accept—"

"It's your niece. Our *baby.*"

The grief and desperation in his sister's eyes cut Dalmuth to the quick. "Yes…"

"*We* want to do everything we can. Don't *you?*"

Phil's biting words stung. "Yes, of course."

"And everything *you* can do might be enough. You are the most creative…" Phil looked away, his voice cracking again. He sighed, then turned back to Dalmuth, no longer trying to fight his tears. "Just give us a shot, would you? What do you have to lose?"

Dalmuth put his head in his hands. As a scientist, he knew this was madness, but as a brother and soon-to-be-uncle, his heart was leading him. "Let me think on this." He looked up and pointed to the monitors. "Perhaps all this will settle down."

"We all hope so," Phil agreed. "But if not, tell me you'll help us. That you'll do all you can."

Dalmuth was silent for a long time before answering. "I will. Will you excuse me?" He hung his head as he rode the elevator to the basement. He walked to his lab, punched in the security code, and flipped on the lights. The sound of his steps reverberated off the tile flooring as he walked over to his experimental station. The lab tech had cleaned the tank, as directed. Dalmuth pulled up a stainless-steel stool and sat next to the contraption. Staring at it, he thought for a long time.

God, if You are there, how can You be good if You allow so much pain? But then again, if You are not even there, why am I so sure that You are supposed to be good?

His thoughts returned to the science at hand. He got up and tinkered with the controls. Then he scratched out some calculations on a prescription pad. He caught himself staring at the cabinets in front of him. *I am certifiably insane.*

Some hours later he made his bed in a hospital call room. He was awakened at 2:15 Friday morning by a ringing phone.

"Doctor, you're needed in Labor and Delivery."

He swallowed hard. "What is it?"

The new nurse answered matter-of-factly. "The patient's labor has broken through the meds. She's gonna go."

She must not know it's my sister. He was dead silent.

"She's dilated three to four centimeters. It'll probably be another centimeter or two before the baby can fit through. It's headfirst."

Before proceeding to L and D, Dr. Kedar made another soulful walk to the lab. He turned on his equipment and fine-tuned it. Then he refilled the tank, adjusting the warmer so the fluid temperature would be 99.4 degrees, the intra-abdominal temperature of the human womb.

Regan reached out both arms to greet him when he arrived. "I'm in labor," she said through her sobs. "The baby's coming!"

He returned her embrace, then stood back, nodding and blinking.

"But the bleeding hasn't increased noticeably."

The voice was Dorie's, and Dalmuth turned to hear her assessment. "The baby's heart has remained strong throughout." She gestured toward Regan. "We've given her an epidural so she won't have any significant pain, and if she has any trouble after delivery, we'll have an anesthetic."

Phil spoke up. "I told them to be careful with this delivery, that you have an idea, a research idea that may help…"

On the spot now, Dalmuth caught Dorie's eyes, then Dr.

Wallace's—each of them looking as though he had sold his relatives real estate on Mars.

"You *can't* mean the fetal pig tank—" Dorie stopped herself. "Sir…"

"I know, the odds are against us, but—"

"But it never worked well with fetal pigs."

"Yes, but we have a new setup with a special pump that has already shown some promise. Besides, they refused to take no for an answer. So I have turned it on, warming up the solution, and will establish the support system immediately after birth."

They thought he was crazy; their stares told him that quite clearly. But now, his decision made, Dalmuth didn't care. He had to try.

And maybe, if God was real, this crazy idea would work.

TWENTY-FIVE

After several moments of stiff silence, Dr. Wallace gestured toward the door. "Let's step outside, shall we?"

Dalmuth and Dorie followed him out into the hall. Dalmuth spotted Red at the desk and motioned for him to join them.

Dr. Wallace glared at Dalmuth. "Look, I know you're the chief of OB staff and the MFM department head, so with all due respect—are you nuts? This is a seventeen-weeker! There's no way this baby has a chance. It's cruel. Didn't you learn *anything* from that ectopic experiment you did?"

Dorie raised her eyebrows and nodded her agreement.

He didn't blame them. He would probably say the same if he were in their shoes. "I know, it is a long shot. In fact, it is longer than a long shot. But for the mental health of my family, and even for my own peace of mind, I have to give it a try. I have to know we did everything we could."

"Give *what* a shot?" Dr. Wallace was clearly disgusted. "With all your heroics of late, are you *trying* to get brought up for review? This baby probably won't even survive birth, certainly not with an intact neurological system. And there's no way I'm gonna section this kid for fetal distress, so don't even ask me."

"I would not ask that of you, but if we get a fairly nontraumatic delivery, I have a setup down in my lab, a kind of artificial placenta, if you will. And it is the only chance we have. I know, not *much* of a chance. But if we try and fail, we can all live with that. I really think we should give it a try, if you could just help to deliver this baby alive."

Dr. Wallace grabbed his temples as though he had a raging headache. When he spoke, he emphasized each word. "Don't you think, maybe, perhaps, because it's your sister in labor that your judgment may be a wee bit clouded, sir? It's unauthorized, unprecedented, and—I'm certain—uninsured from a liability standpoint. You're talking about a human experiment here."

"Yes, but that is precisely the point, Dr. Wallace." Dalmuth's voice was steady. "It is a *human* experiment. She is a human—tiny, living, and my niece."

Red jumped in to defend him. "I've seen the lab setup, and I think it could work."

All eyes turned to him.

Then Dr. Wallace looked back at Dalmuth. "You're the chief. *You* get the signatures." He held up his palms. "Get the legal department. Get everything signed. I don't want to be part of this grandiose experiment. I'll give your sister the best care I can. I'll try to deliver this baby with all due respect. But it's just too immature, *Doctor.*" He made the title sound like a four-letter word. "You know she can't survive."

"Anything you need set up in the lab?" Red asked.

Dalmuth was grateful for the support. He took out a prescription pad and wrote. "Here is the number—page the lab tech. Tell him to set up for a micro case, probably within the hour." He ripped off the sheet and handed it to Red. "Can you go down and assist?"

"No problem."

He looked Red in the eyes. "Thank you. I'm grateful, Doctor."

As Dalmuth turned to go back into the labor room, he overheard Dr. Wallace berating Red. "This is nonsense! The man thinks he's a superstar. What are you, one of his groupies?"

Dr. Wallace and Dr. Chambers followed Dalmuth back into the room to check on Regan.

"It is all set," Dalmuth told his sister. "We should be ready to go in an hour or so." Catching a glimpse of the monitor screen, he noted that the fetal heartbeat was still acceptable, although slight decelerations suggested that the head had started its passage through the birth canal.

Dr. Wallace did a quick vaginal exam. "She's about six centimeters, which is complete for a baby this size. We can start pushing anytime."

Regan, comfortable with the aid of the epidural, fixed her gaze on Dalmuth. "Should we push now?"

He looked at Dr. Wallace. "Can we slow it a bit, not push just yet? Give me a little time to get things ready?"

Dr. Wallace's lip curled, and he shook his head. "It's time." He turned to Regan. "But do it gently. See if we can ease this baby out." Then he glanced over at the nurse. "Just two series of pushes per contraction. Only about six seconds per push. And watch the monitor for any problems. Call and open a delivery room; we won't deliver here in the room. We'll go back so we have the lights and all the equipment that Dr. Kedar might need."

Dalmuth exhaled his relief. "Thank you. The only unusual thing is, please do not cut the umbilical cord. Just leave it attached to the placenta after delivery. We will cross-clamp it with an atraumatic clamp. But I need all the cord and all the blood that is in the placenta."

Dr. Wallace shook his head and left the room muttering.

In his absence, Regan began to push. The infant seemed to handle it well, and forty-five minutes later, its arrival was imminent. The staff moved Regan to the delivery room. Dalmuth had a warmed, mobile transport unit standing by ready with oxygen. Red stationed himself at the elevator door, ready to rush the baby to the lab.

In accordance with Dalmuth's instructions, Regan lay on the delivery table, prepped and draped, a precaution taken to reduce the risk of bacterial contamination.

Having been notified that the baby was ready for delivery, Dr. Wallace returned. "Gently push," he told Regan. "I'm going to cut an episiotomy to lessen the pressure to the baby's head. It's quite delicate, and we don't want any intracranial bleeding."

Wonderful! At least he's willing to try.

Shortly after Dr. Wallace made the cut, the purplish, bruised head appeared at the vaginal opening. The membranes had remained intact, so the baby was being born *en caul,* with the water sac still in place. As the head emerged, Dr. Wallace ruptured the sac and a distinct, pungent smell filled the room.

"No meconium staining; too early for that," Wallace noted. Then he maneuvered the tiny shoulders and hips out through the vagina, holding the baby in the palm of his hand.

Dalmuth surprised himself by getting so choked up he was speechless. He'd seen thousands of babies, yet... *She's so tiny and beautiful. My niece...*

The pale-skinned, dusky gray infant let out a soft squeak— her version of a cry. Her thin, bloodstained skin looked transparent. She seemed disproportionate, with her hairless head being much larger than the rest of her body. Dalmuth leaned over his sister's legs to put an oxygen mask to the child's little face.

"Are you going to intubate?" Dr. Wallace wasn't even trying to hide his skepticism.

"I'm afraid they don't even make a tube small enough, but we are all right—until the placenta separates, that is. Then we have to move." Even as Dalmuth said this, a gush of fluid and blood signaled that the placenta had completed its separation. The process that had begun with the small corner that abrupted in the accident was now complete.

Dalmuth's heart pounded. *We've got to transport her ASAP!* While Dr. Wallace covered the placenta in warm, wet, sterile sponges, Dalmuth wrapped the baby in a warm blanket. Then he rushed to place her, with placenta still attached, into the transport incubator. Spiriting the 'child away even before Regan could get a good look at her, Dalmuth wheeled the mobile unit down the hallway to Red and the waiting elevator.

"Is everything ready?" Dalmuth barked.

"Everything I could think of!" Red punched Door Close and stared at the tiny marvel before him on the cart. "Wow."

I wish this elevator would go faster!

They rode to the basement and then sped the unit—baby and all— to the awaiting lab.

Red sat using the loupes, special glasses that magnified the visual field, while Dr. Kedar peered into the microscope. *Got to hurry!* He heard Dorie come tearing in the door.

"Unbelievable!" Her hushed exclamation echoed in the silent room.

Neither of the two doctors bothered to acknowledge her arrival. Dr. Kedar was too busy threading the tiny catheters into the baby's umbilical cord—two arterial lines, one bigger vein—while Red was deftly tying knots that would stabilize the plastic catheters in the baby's blood vessels.

The infant was breathing the oxygen provided, but retracting already. Her lungs couldn't handle the chore of oxygenation.

"There!" Dr. Kedar looked up. "Red, I need you to tie down these vascular lines with this nonabsorbable suture so they do not slip. I have to get the blood from the placenta to prime the machine. Volume will be critical."

"Got it." Red took over, and Dr. Kedar moved to a new task. "How'd you learn to do this part, anyway? Did you practice on the pigs?" Red asked.

"H'm?"

Red looked at Dr. Kedar's busy hands as he spoke. "How'd you figure out how far to thread each catheter?"

"I have been working on human fetuses. I have an arrangement with the VIP clinic for their second-trimester abortions."

Red froze. Then, conscious that he had stopped what he was doing, he worked to regain his focus. *This isn't the time or place to get into this.*

"I've been studying the anatomy and blood supply on these little ones for a while," Dr. Kedar continued. "Though I can only use those from the partial-birth abortions. The other specimens from VIP are too traumatized."

He sounded so matter-of-fact. Red blinked fast, took a deep breath, and shifted his weight to keep from losing his balance. *Keep it together. Focus on this baby.*

No one spoke for several minutes, then Dr. Kedar glanced at him. "Red, are you okay there? How are you coming along?"

Having just finished the task, he took another deep breath. "I'm done here. Now what?"

"All right. Without contaminating yourself, I need you to pick up the baby with all the attached lines and bring her over here." He pointed. "Put her on the gel pad in the center of the tank."

The apparatus looked just like a ten-gallon fish aquarium, only about half the height. The doctors had attached three small plastic tubes to the baby's umbilical cord, and Red filled them with saline. These were capped off with three-way valves, while Dr. Kedar prepared to connect them to his machine. Dorie joined in and assisted in moving the other ends of the tubes, while Red cradled the fragile wonder in his hands.

"First, we will connect her to the heart-lung machine," Dr. Kedar spoke in rapid fire. "We have to get the oxygen problem solved, then connect her to the dialysis arm of the apparatus with our new setup."

Once the heart-lung pump was filled with the blood from the placenta and cord, Dr. Kedar made a special connection with the catheters in the baby's umbilical arteries and vein. Then he hooked up both arterial lines to one port, and the venous catheter to the other. After that, he flushed the lines on the side of the machine to be sure no air remained. The smallest bubble of air entering the baby would lodge in her tiny heart and instantly kill her. Next, Dr. Kedar unclamped the catheters, allowing the blood from the baby to reach the machine. Her tiny heart provided the initial propulsion.

Red watched Dr. Kedar punch in a few numbers, taking measurements on the baby's blood pressure. Then he dialed up the pressure from the machine. In seconds a green light lit up, indicating equilibration.

Amazing!

"There we go! We are on the pump now!" Dr. Kedar grinned.

The baby's dusky blue color began to change. Within two minutes, she grew more and more pink. All three physicians hovered over the tank and marveled.

"Okay, we can dial it back a bit now," Dr. Kedar told Red. "She needs less oxygen at this stage." He punched a new code into the computer.

Oh no! "Her respirations are slowing. Is that okay?" Red asked.

Dr. Kedar nodded. "She does not need to breathe for herself. She is getting all the oxygen she needs from the machine. You can take the mask off her face now, and we will submerge her."

Dorie stared at them, open-mouthed. "We'll do *what?*"

"We are recreating the womb. Her thin skin cannot handle being dried out. You will notice she lacks the usual vernix." He was right; she lacked the usual cheeselike covering that full-term babies have at birth. "Watch."

Red reached down to remove the mask. "But what about the IV?"

"We will leave it for now. I will take it out once she has stabilized." With that he turned a valve, and the tank filled with warm saline. He glanced down at the thermostat and smiled. "Just right. And we can cut the bright lights now."

Dorie walked over to hit the Off switch.

As the warm water solution covered the baby, she continued to breathe. Her lungs filled with the carefully calibrated sterile saline, and she relaxed.

Dr. Kedar smiled. "Warm, secure, oxygen."

"This is unbelievable!" Dorie was mesmerized.

"No lie," Red agreed. Suddenly he had to sit down. He grew still as he stared at the seventeen-week-old baby he had just placed in a tank of fluid. In the dimly lit room, he watched as the breathing infant lived under the fluid. *It's just like before, only this time...* His throat constricted, and he struggled not to cry. *This time, I've helped to preserve a life rather than take one.* He closed his eyes. *This is Your doing, Lord.*

Dr. Kedar stared into the face of his niece. "This is the easy part, getting her started. But the balance is so delicate. She is so fragile. Anything that goes wrong—" He bit his lower lip.

Dorie stared down at the tiny form. "What do you figure she weighs, Dr. Kedar?"

He looked up at her. "Probably about three hundred grams."

Dorie converted the calculation. "About a half a pound."

"I imagine you wonder what her chances are." Dr. Kedar looked at Dorie through the top of his bifocals.

"True."

"I know it has never been done," he defended himself. "And honestly, the chances are slim, very slim, like one in forever. A million different complications could spell disaster. But I still had to do it."

"I understand. Really."

"What is happening upstairs?"

"It was pretty touching. Your sister's husband was nearly blubbering, saying the usual good stuff, 'Did you see our baby?' and 'She's so beautiful, though I got only a glimpse of her.' Dr. Wallace wasn't saying much. He was finishing up the stitching when I left. I hung around to help with the delivery, but once I wrote the orders, I had to come down and see what was—"

A knock interrupted her, and she rose to open the door.

"Hello, Phil." Dr. Kedar's mood was subdued as he greeted his brother-in-law. He motioned for Dorie to let him into the secured area. So Phil walked in, carrying a video camera slung around his back by a strap. He went straight to his child and gazed, open-mouthed, at the sight of her. Her eyes closed, she lay on the gel pad completely submerged in temperature-controlled fluid and connected to a miniature heart-lung machine. He drew close to her and leaned over the tank.

"Hello, little sweetie. I'm your daddy. You're so tiny," he cooed. He looked up at Dr. Kedar. "I've never seen anything like it. She's not much bigger than a doll." He returned his gaze to his daughter. "And lucky for you, you look just like your mama." He continued to dote on her. Then he looked up at Dr. Kedar again. "I guess I can't touch her, right?"

"Sorry."

"That's okay." Phil spoke to the baby again. "Your Uncle Dalmuth is a genius. Did you know that? A sheer genius."

Red saw Dr. Kedar grimace, but Phil didn't notice.

"Isn't she fantastic?" Phil asked no one in particular.

"The most beautiful baby I've ever seen," Red said. And he meant it.

Several hours later Dorie had returned to work, and Dalmuth and Phil decided they'd better go back up and give Regan a full report, complete with video footage. Red volunteered to stay behind and keep an eye on the baby. Now, in the dimly lit room, he sat staring at the tank. After a few minutes, he stood up and rested his hands on its frame, watching the tiny marvel make subtle movements.

Even if she lives only a little while, heavenly Father, thank You. You're so full of grace, the giver of second chances. He wiped a tear, then another. "Father, let her live," he begged aloud. "Please let her live."

He heard a noise behind him and turned to see Dr. Kedar standing in the doorway wiping the moisture from his own eyes.

TWENTY-SIX

Throughout the rest of the night Dalmuth made adjustments to the tank as necessary. As he sat alone in the quiet room, he mentally replayed the night's events. As expected, Regan had seemed more alarmed than happy when she first viewed the video of her tiny child, whom she and Phil named Christina. In his experience, no one was ever quite prepared for how fragile micropreemies look.

O God, whom Red calls Father, I know this is crazy, but if You are out there, please let this baby live.

By midmorning when Christina had stabilized, Dalmuth called Red and asked him to come keep an eye on the tank for about fifteen minutes. Then he took the elevator up to the Neonatal Intensive Care Unit, referred to as "Nick U" by the staff. Scoping out the NICU isolation room, which generally was reserved for infectious babies, he tried to anticipate everything he'd need to move his niece upstairs. *Electrical outlets—we have lots of machinery. And we will need plenty of room. Hopefully we will also have a little privacy.*

As quickly as possible he returned to the lab.

Red seemed to study his face as he came in. "How's it looking up there? Think it'll work?"

Dalmuth nodded. "When I designed the unit, it never crossed my mind that we might have to move it up to where the nurses are. But with the help of a few interim battery systems, I think it will be all right."

After Red left, Dalmuth kept one eye on Christina while he made numerous phone calls, the last one to his sister. "We have a transfer scheduled for noon today," he told her. "We are planning to bring little Christina up from the basement to the NICU isolation room, where she can have constant supervision. The room is separate from, but connected to the unit so the expert nurses, the monitors, and the nursing station will all be accessible to her."

Dalmuth knew the odds were stacked against them, but he still hoped the extra care would be enough to help Christina survive. Getting her stabilized in the tank was a step—a small one, but still a step.

At least she was still alive.

On Friday morning Bethany landed in Seattle and stepped off the plane. Reaching the inside gate at the terminal, she looked around. Would her mother be the one to meet her? She spotted her sister, Rosemary, pushing her way to the front of the crowd. Seconds later, Bethany was engulfed in a bear hug.

"It's so great to see you!" Rosemary stood back to look at her. "I hope you brought warm clothes. We've got a high of fifty-three here today."

"I came prepared." Bethany smiled. "Man, it's great to see you."

"Welcome home, Bethany, I'm *so* glad you came."

The genuineness of Rosemary's words brought relief.

"Dad's scheduled to go under the knife in about four hours, so we'll have to book it back to Bremerton to get you settled in at my place before we join everyone at the hospital. Did you check any bags?"

"Are you kidding? This is me you're talking about."

"Oh yeah, you'd take a trunk to a slumber party."

Bethany laughed. "You look terrific, Rosemary. How's life at the firm?"

"It's all right, though I sometimes wonder if the point of litigation is to bring the truth to light or to manipulate it. But maybe that's because some of my colleagues lack even a rudimentary moral compass. Still, the money's good. How about you? Still at the clinic?"

Bethany nodded.

"I'm sure Mom will be just *thrilled* to hear that."

On Friday at midday, Phil stood filming the procession to move the baby, providing commentary as the tape rolled. "Talk about your Main Street Electrical Parade."

Regan, who sat in a wheelchair, added her own perspective. "We are at about nine hours here, and our little fighter is still holding her own."

With the help of the maintenance department, Dalmuth had rigged a special transport battery. Now numerous wires fed into the pack. Another doctor handled the heart-lung machine, and a nurse was supervising the transfer of dialysis equipment. Several medical students had volunteered to hold elevator doors, both in the basement and on the floor where the baby was going.

As the group passed, everyone stopped to watch, first amazed by the cluster of workers and then astounded as they caught sight of Christina.

Several of the new parents with children in NICU murmured about how big their own babies now looked in comparison.

Dalmuth hovered around the equipment, paying meticulous attention to the most minute details. He was handling the stress the only way he knew—by reverting from uncle to doctor mode. If anything was going to go wrong, it would not be because of any failure on his part.

Bethany followed Rosemary into the hospital sitting area where her sister, Hollie, and her mother sat waiting.

Hollie rose to give the first hug. As Bethany embraced her, she noticed that her mother hesitated, then stood.

When it was her mother's turn, she barely touched Bethany's shoulders as she put her cheek against Bethany's and kissed the air. Her voice was as cool as her embrace.

"Hello, dear." She turned to Rosemary and frowned. "You're late."

"We are?" Rosemary looked at her watch.

"They took your father in early… He's already gone to surgery."

Bethany took a seat and settled in for a long afternoon.

After hours spent thumbing through magazines in mostly awkward silence, Bethany and her family finally received news. The doctor came out to say her father had made it through surgery, then he ushered them into the recovery room. Although her dad was still asleep, Bethany was taken aback by the monitors everywhere, the tube in his mouth, and his lack of facial color and muscle tone. A nurse explained the monitors and then gave them a number to call in case they had questions.

Bethany had plenty of questions, but none any nurse could answer.

O Lord, I need Your help! Please bring us all back together somehow—and take good care of Dad. Bethany jumped when she heard a ringing in her purse. She fumbled around, found the phone, and answered it.

"Hello, beautiful!"

"Red! I didn't think I'd get to talk to you until tonight."

"I'm waiting for an OR to open up and wanted to hear your voice. Been thinking about you. How's it going?"

"Pretty well." She walked out to the hallway for a little privacy.

"How's the climate?"

"It's sunny, but in the fifties—"

His tone was playfully chastising. "You know that's not what I meant."

"Ah. Sorry." She chuckled, not at all penitent. "I got a somewhat icy reception with Mom, but I'm hoping it's only because she's so worried about Dad. Rosemary picked me up, and things seem better than ever with her, so at least my time at her place should be fine."

"What about your other sister?"

"Hollie's hard to read. Maybe the stress with Dad...too soon to tell."

"Did you get to talk to your father before he went under?"

"No. They ended up running ahead of schedule, so Rosemary and I got here right after he'd gone into surgery."

"Bummer. Well, I'm praying you'll witness some miracles, because I've seen a few here since you left."

At midnight the two sisters pulled into Rosemary's driveway. Bethany rubbed her eyes and yawned.

"You must be exhausted," Rosemary said. "It's 2 A.M. your time."

"Yeah, I'm craving a soft pillow right about now."

"I hope you won't lose any sleep over how Mom acted."

"She's stressed. I know that." Bethany tried to comfort herself.

"That little air-kiss thing she did when you got here was sort of interesting."

"You noticed."

"Of course I noticed."

They got out of the car and entered the house through the side door.

"How'd you feel about seeing Dad?" Rosemary asked.

"It was better than with Mom—probably because he was virtually unconscious."

On Saturday afternoon Bethany sat reading another magazine while her father slept. The phone in her purse rang, and she rushed to grab it before it woke him. It was Red.

"How's my favorite girl?"

"So far so good. Dad's still pretty grogged out. Mom and my sisters just went down to the cafeteria, so we're here alone."

"What are the docs saying?"

"Dad's still in a lot of pain, but the surgery was successful. Now we're trying to ward off infection and all the awful stuff that can happen after bypass surgery."

"How's it going with your family?"

Her father stirred and groaned.

"Better hold off on comment right now, Red. How's Regan's baby?"

"Didn't we skip something?" The tender humor in Red's voice warmed Bethany. "You know, the good stuff…about how you miss me and wish I were there. It's sad when I have to beg."

She chuckled. "Sorry! I definitely wish you were here. And I miss you."

"Good. Okay. *Now* I can tell you about the baby. She's still stable. I can't stop staring at her. It's just so amazing. Keep praying, because the time between days two and three is critical. "

"I will," she whispered.

"Bethany, are you okay? You sure your dad's all right?"

"Yes, I just don't want to wake him. His doctor said the surgery was fairly routine, but one particular area was difficult. They're watching him closely at this stage."

Apparently the next few days would be critical for both of their patients.

At two o'clock on Sunday morning Dalmuth headed to a call room to catch a few hours of sleep. It seemed mere seconds later when the phone jarred him awake with only one ring. He grabbed the receiver, glancing at the clock.

Five o'clock. Well, at least I got a few hours of sleep.

"Doctor?" Dalmuth came fully awake at the alarm in the nurse's voice. "All the machines are working, but the baby seems to be going downhill."

"I'll be right there."

He dashed to NICU and found Christina looking unchanged. But when he checked the labs, he saw that the nurse had made a correct assessment. Christina's blood pressure was low, her blood count was lower, and her need for oxygen was increasing. Not a good sign.

He dialed up the oxygen level and transfused a bit more blood through her umbilical catheter. Then he called for the ultrasound machine. Minutes later, his heart pounded as he sat finishing up an underwater sono on the tiny child. *Sure enough. An intracranial bleed...grade two, though the grading system cannot really apply to babies at this size.* His heart sank.

There was nothing he could do to save her.

He took a tiny sample of Christina's blood from the machine and ordered it stat for clotting studies. Sitting by the baby, whose eyes were yet unopened, he waited what seemed like an hour, but a glance at his watch when he received the report told him it had taken only twenty minutes. He studied the lab values and frowned. *Bad news.* One of her clotting factors looked particularly low. A sense of doom enveloped him.

"I need some cryoprecipitate," he told the nurse.

When she brought it, he calculated the dosage for weight and transfused it. Even if this worked and the bleed didn't progress, how much damage was inevitable? How would he tell Regan? He rested his head in his hands, ran his fingers through his hair, and let out a deep sigh. As much as he hated to admit it, it looked like the beginning of the end.

One complication follows another.

Bethany sat in her father's room staring at a magazine as she prayed. At midmorning, everyone else had left to run errands, but she'd stayed behind so he wouldn't be alone when he awoke.

She looked up when her father stirred. He opened his eyes and surveyed the room. Then he smiled and reached out for her hand. Bethany
tried not to let her shock show—her father rarely touched anyone with
more than a handshake.

Her father moistened his lips and managed a smile. "Hi."

She squeezed his hand. "How do you feel?"

He ignored the question. "Thank you for coming all the way out
here, Bethy, just for me."

She waved it off.

"It took courage."

Bethany was grateful for his kind words, but they still struck her as
an odd thing for a father to tell his daughter at a time like this.

"How's your mother been?"

"She's worried about you."

"I meant to you. How's she been treating you?"

Bethany wished she could give a more encouraging answer. "Oh.
About the same as usual."

"I see. Sorry."

She noticed the moisture that formed in his eyes.

"She blames all this on you, you know. It's not really fair."

"What?" Bethany sat straight up. "She blames it on *me?*"

Her father nodded. "All the stress. It's bad for my heart."

Bethany stared, slack-jawed.

He squeezed her hand. "I'm not saying I agree. I just thought it
might help you understand your mother."

"And you? What do you think?"

He looked at the blank television screen, then back at her. "It's
always good to try to keep the peace."

"But—"

"I've done a lot of soul searching through all this. I was too angry
back then. I said things I shouldn't have said, but that was a long time
ago, right?"

She bit her lip and nodded. "Thanks, Dad." She knew that was as
close as he would get to an apology. And as they sat together, she realized something.

During every conversation she'd had with her father for the past five years, Bethany's mother had been in the room, always there intercepting, interpreting, controlling.

For the first time, she'd had her father all to herself. Was he just trying to pass off the responsibility for their fractured relationship? Or had she seen his real heart for a change? And if so, did he ever stand up for her?

Red jogged down to Records to get a copy of the file on the latest RU-486 patient, despite the fact that she didn't seem to fit the profile of Ophion's targeted patients.

The assistant brought him the stack of charts he'd kept in the reserved stack, along with the new one. Red thumbed through it and read the resident's notes, followed by Dr. Ophion's comments. A slow smile crossed his face as he realized something he had not noticed before: In each of the cases he had reviewed, Dr. Ophion himself, rather than the resident, had dictated the file notes. The only indication of a resident's involvement was with this new chart and also the chart that Red himself had completed—the one Dr. Ophion had altered. Red remembered that he had delivered the footling breech before Dr. Ophion arrived.

Red noticed another difference as well. This new file was missing a notation that had appeared on all the others: "Instructed to call Dr. Ophion if problems develop."

Four hours after Dr. Kedar rushed to Christina's room, he watched with astonishment as her blood pressure improved and her blood count remained stable. When he did another sonogram at 11:15, the bleed had not enlarged as he'd so feared it would. So he sat back, only a little more optimistic, and began to hope again.

All night Tuesday Bethany tossed about. By four o'clock she lay wide awake staring at the walls. *It's six o'clock in Dallas. Red should be getting ready for work right about now.* She turned on the lamp by the futon bed and reached for her purse to get her phone. Then she punched in his number; he answered on the first ring. "Red, it's me."

"Hey, babe. You're up early. You okay?"

"No." She propped herself up with a pillow.

"I've got all the time you need."

The gentleness in his tone made her cry. She filled him in on the conversation with her dad. "Maybe I should be happy to know he does care about me and even seems to get it, but part of me feels betrayed that he hasn't stood up to Mom on my behalf."

"I'm sorry. What about Rosemary?"

"She's been warm, but I think she's torn between wanting to please Mom and wanting to have a relationship with me. I love my family, Red, and it hurts. I'll keep working at it with them, but I've also got to keep building my own separate life and future apart from them."

"Yes, and I'm not going anywhere—at least, not without you, if I can help it."

She smiled, grateful that he always seemed to know the right thing to say. "Thanks."

"When are you comin' home to me? Nothing's fun with you gone."

She plucked at the fringe on the bedspread. "Probably Friday."

"Two days. It'll seem like a year. I'll try to work the schedule so I can meet your flight."

"You're awesome. So how's the baby?"

"She's a fighter. I'm amazed she's made it five days so far. We've had a few scary moments, but she's holding her own."

"I'm a little surprised it hasn't been on the news."

"Me, too. Media people keep calling, but we all just say 'no comment.' A little information is bound to leak out, but Dalmuth has begged the staff not to talk to anyone, not until the time is right."

As he talked, a sense of security in this relationship replaced the loneliness she felt. By the time they hung up, her apprehension about interacting with her mother had faded. She prayed for grace with new resolve.

TWENTY-SEVEN

When Red got to work Wednesday, he passed Dorie in the hallway. A second later he heard, "Hey, Red. I'm glad you're here. I need to talk to you."

He turned back around to face her. "Yeah? I've been needing to talk to you, too. What's the latest on Ms. Brennan?"

Dorie shook her head. "She did have a therapeutic abortion at the same time as her mastectomy and lymph node dissection. Everything went well, no complications."

Red stared at the floor, saddened by the news.

"Listen, meet me in the residents' call room, all right?"

"Okay."

"Someone we know is in it pretty deep." She gave him a knowing grin.

A few minutes later, Red entered the call room. "What's up?"

Dorie couldn't seem to stand still as she talked. "I think I've finally got Ophion, that lying dog. That last incomplete must have been a legitimate exception, completely unintended. I think we've got him on medical malpractice. He gives the wrong regimen of RU-486 to insured patients, hoping some will need operations. He doesn't have to do the surgeries himself, as long as the clinic makes a profit. When patients with insurance have bad outcomes, he turns a thirty-dollar case into a four-hundred-dollar profit. Even if their insurance doesn't cover abortion, it covers the complications, so—"

"Sure, but—"

She waved her hands at him. "Don't interrupt me when I'm on a rant! I've been sifting through the charts, and he left a flawless paper trail. Every one of the charts on the D and C patients who received RU-486 said the patient also received a prescription for the prostaglandin. And there was no way we could know exactly what prescriptions the patients got simply by comparing hospital and VIP records. But once I compared the pharmacy's records from the patients we'd culled out, I found it. It's unbelievable! It's his coding system. This is the killer."

"What've you got?"

Dorie lowered her voice almost to a whisper. "All of Ophion's files on patients who ended up needing D and Cs had a little starlike mark in the upper right-hand corner. That is, all but that one case, which was probably legitimate. And guess what…"

"What?"

"*None* of the patients with good outcomes had a star."

"Maybe he put the star *after* they had the D and C."

She shook her head. "I wondered that too. But it can't be. There were some he wouldn't have known about because we did them here at the hospital when he was gone. All his insured patients that you saw here who showed up with complications from a VIP abortion had this special mark. And everybody who got the legitimate regimen, according to pharmacy records, didn't have anything out of the ordinary. I'm guessing he's such a stickler for tracking things that he wanted some idea about how much this special treatment netted him. The records match the scenario perfectly. So Ophion had to have targeted these patients. The man looks like a patient advocate, but he's a bottom-dwelling scum sucker."

Red filled Dorie in on all that he had found.

"Dorie, how are we going to bring him *down?*"

"Unfortunately, I've already worn out my welcome with Lexie. And I'm afraid we need the strength of the hospital's legal department behind this if it's going to fly."

Red was incensed. "Why wouldn't they want to take this on?"

"The hospital views it as a clinic problem that I need to address by hiring my own counsel. A private clinic terminating an employee who happens to also work for the hospital is not their problem. Besides, Lexie may think I have a personal vendetta since he fired me."

"Is the information that Bethany got of any help?"

She shrugged. "It'll be somewhat useful, but it would be Ophion's word against hers, and they could accuse her of having a personal agenda against abortion. By itself it's not strong enough to bring charges."

Red saw the door opening as he heard a knock. It was Damon.

"Oh. Excuse me."

"We'll be finished in a minute," Dorie told him.

He shut the door.

"Think he heard anything?" Red asked.

"Probably. But don't worry about it."

Red nodded. Maybe he was getting paranoid, but he didn't like the look he'd seen in Damon's eyes. Even if he did hear something, why should *he* care? It was Ophion they were going after, not him.

Red opened his locker in the doctors' lounge and scrounged around in his shaving bag until he found his contact case and solution. He walked over to the sink and took out his contacts so he could let the shower water hit him in the face with full force. Looking at his reflection in the mirror, he groaned and told himself he looked better blurry.

He left his locker open as he stripped off his scrubs, grabbed a towel, and headed for the shower. Turning his face up toward the warm water, he let the jet spray pelt him. After two days on his feet nearly around the clock, he was counting the hours until he could see a bed.

He heard the door creak, but didn't think anything of it. Doctors frequently came in and out of the doctors' locker room. When he had finished, he pulled on fresh scrubs, put his contacts back in, and returned to work.

Dr. Ellen Tsai was new to the GYN service rotation, but even she knew better than to disturb Dr. Damon without good reason. She only hoped he thought it was good enough.

"I'm sorry to bother you Dr. Damon," she told him. "It's just that one of the clinic patients came in for treatment for her cervical cancer—she's had surgery and radiation therapy—and I had to admit her. Now she's got a high fever and shaking, with chills."

Damon looked skeptical, but Ellen hurried on. "I took the history in the ER, and what concerned me most was that I got some neurological signs."

He looked down his nose at her. "Like what?"

"She's got a stiff neck, some nausea, vomiting. She's unsure about whether it's related to her therapy or just a bad flu bug, and I didn't know either. But I'm telling you, the woman looks really sick."

Ellen breathed easier when Damon seemed to show some genuine interest in the case. "All right, let's go see her."

Ellen accompanied him to the patient's room. She watched as he did an exam, focusing on the neurological signs. When he tried to move the patient's neck, she cried out in pain.

"Nuchal rigidity?" Ellen asked.

Dr. Damon nodded.

The patient whimpered. "The lights in here are killing my eyes."

"Okay, we'll dim them for you here in a minute," Ellen said.

"I just need to look in them first," Dr. Damon told the patient. He performed a fundoscopic exam, and told Ellen his conclusion. "No papilledema."

She looked at the woman, then back at Dr. Damon. "Since her optic disc isn't swollen, are you going to do a spinal tap?"

Dr. Damon nodded.

"Please...the lights..."

Ellen patted the woman's arm. "I'll dim them as soon as we're finished, Mrs. Stewart."

"I think this is worse than the flu. It's pretty toxic looking." Dr. Damon straightened and looked at Ellen. "It's probably some type of meningitis—bacterial or viral—and unrelated to her GYN problem."

"Should we get a consult with an infectious disease specialist?" Ellen asked.

"Yeah. But we can start some lab work now and do the spinal tap."

Ellen was eager for the experience. "I did one as a med student, but this will be my first lumbar puncture as a resident."

Dr. Damon shook his head. "Sorry. The patient's too sick to risk it. I'll handle it."

"Okay." Ellen gave a little sigh, then fetched the tray and called the nurse. She and Damon positioned the patient on her left side and instructed her to curl up so her knees touched her chest and her head was bowed under. While Ellen helped to hold her in place, the patient let out a groan.

"Okay, Mrs. Stewart, you're doing great," Dr. Damon assured her. "First we need to wash off your back with an antiseptic solution. All you have to do is lie still—*very* still. Dr. Tsai and the nurse here will help. I'll tell you everything we're doing and let you know as soon as we know something."

"Thank you, Doctor."

He scrubbed her back and put on sterile gloves. Then he reached over and opened the wrapping on a plastic tray and reached inside for a sterile sponge stick wrapped in a plastic covered towel. Using concentric circles, he cleaned off the patient's skin. He did the same using the second sponge on the tray, and then a third. Next he opened the sterile drape, a plastic-covered paper with a hole in the center that looked like a sheet with a circle cut out of the middle. The drape covered the patient's back, and Ellen observed as Dr. Damon placed the hole over the washed area. Touching the drape with his gloved hand, he found the patient's hipbone, then followed an imaginary horizontal line over to the spine, using his thumb to mark the right spot.

"I find the right space," he told Ellen, "and then it's just like doing the epidural, except you use a tiny needle, and you don't stop at the dura." He pointed to the fibrous structure surrounding the spinal cord and containing the fluid. "You pop through it to get the spinal fluid. Give yourself a couple more months, and you'll be able to do these in your sleep."

Turning back to the patient, he soothed with his voice. "All right, Mrs. Stewart, now you're going to feel some pressure. It's just my thumb finding the perfect spot to do this test. Now I'm wiping off the sterile soap and I'm going to numb the skin up. This feels like a little sting—a little twinge—and I'll need you to hold *very* still."

The patient held her breath.

"There now," Dr. Damon continued. "Let's give that a moment to take effect."

The patient exhaled.

"I'll put a little more of the numbing medicine a bit deeper. Hopefully all you'll feel from now on is pressure from my pushing. Are you okay?"

She nodded, sobbing softly, then moaning. "My head hurts."

"Okay." Dr. Damon took the spinal needle, which was equipped with a stylet, or a little metal shaft going down the middle of the needle. He slid the needle in, then pulled out the stylet and advanced it.

The patient flinched.

"Hold still!" Dr. Damon's tone was sharp, and the woman froze.

Ellen watched as a cloudy spinal fluid spilled out into the vial.

"Great! Got it!" Dr. Damon hooked a manometer to the needle, giving him the pressure reading for the cerebrospinal fluid.

"It's only slightly elevated," Ellen noted.

Dr. Damon nodded and began to collect the fluid for examination and culture. He removed the plastic tubes from the tray and, one at a time, filled and capped each one.

"Dr. Tsai, would you please record the pressure and the fluid clarity?"

"Certainly." Switching places with the nurse, she went across the room to write in the chart.

Dr. Damon got a closing pressure reading. "Still the same," he called over to her.

She looked up and saw four vials full of the fluid before recording the reading. Dr. Damon pulled out the needle and held pressure on the site.

"Okay, Mrs. Stewart, everything went great. Now you'll feel a little pressure here." He put a dressing on the patient's back and turned to the resident. "Dr. Tsai, would you get her cleaned up while I mark the tubes?"

"Sure." She helped the nurse clean the soap off the patient's back and get her comfortable again. Then she turned to help Damon and hesitated. *That's odd. Only three tubes for the lab. I could swear there were four.*

"Okay, Dr. Tsai. Fill out the requisition forms and run these stat to the lab."

"Yes, Doctor." She dimmed the lights and reached for the specimens. As Dr. Damon stretched out his hand to give them to her, she saw the extra tube in his scrub shirt pocket.

She couldn't imagine what he would need the other vial for—

research perhaps? But she didn't have much time to wonder. She had to get to the lab.

Red's stomach growled. One more patient and then he could grab some lunch. He reached for the chart and was glad to see he'd be talking with Mrs. Brennan.

He studied her test results, then tapped on the door before entering. "Good morning, Mrs. Brennan. How are you doing on the Adriamycin and Cytoxan?" Red asked. She had come in for a follow-up appointment.

"The antinausea medicine's helping, but I still feel queasy. I've also got a lot of mouth ulcers." Despite her complaints, she sounded optimistic. "I'm pretty tired, but I still have all my hair, so that's encouraging. And I'm doing lots of arm stretches to keep the scarring from limiting me."

Red nodded. "Good. How are you holding up?"

"I've got a great bunch of doctors. And my husband and family have been wonderful. Did I tell you my husband found temporary work?"

Red smiled. "I'm glad to hear it." He took out a form and started to write orders.

"But about the other…"

Red looked up.

"The, uh, the baby…" Her eyes brimmed with tears as she said the word *baby*.

"Yes…," Red whispered.

"That part was really hard. I'm not sure I'll ever get over that."

He took her hand. "You don't *have* to get over that."

"Thank you, Doctor. You've been so kind. I appreciate your saying so. Not many people know about it, but a few who do have told me these feelings will pass. I know they meant to encourage me, but they don't seem to understand that I never want to forget."

Red folded his hands and bowed his head. Then he looked back up at her. "Before you leave, let me give you the card of someone who might be able to help you."

"Thank you, Doctor. As for the cancer, I'm a fighter. And I'm feeling pretty good, optimistic that I'm going to lick this thing."

He reached out and squeezed her hand again. "I'm glad to hear it. And your chances are quite good. There will be some rough days ahead, but down the road, I believe you will have lots to be hopeful about." He finished writing the orders, then looked back at her. "I'm so sorry for all you're going through." He handed her the paperwork. "We need to make sure your white blood count looks okay, so please take this with you down to the lab. I'll call you myself as soon as we know something."

Bethany searched the crowd for Red as she walked into the baggage claim area at Dallas–Fort Worth International Airport. She spotted him holding a bouquet, a broad smile on his face. He wrapped her in a long hug and then gave her a kiss. "Welcome home. Seems like forever since you left."

She held his gaze. "You've never looked better, Red." She kissed him again.

He handed her the bouquet, and she held it to her nose. "Thank you. They smell marvelous."

"So do you."

Red took her carry-on, and they waited for the baggage to arrive. "I've got so much to tell you, Bethany. So much I wanted to share with you all week. But first I want to hear about the rest of your trip."

"Dad's healing nicely, and I had a great time with Rosemary."

"Did you talk to her about VIP?"

"I sure did. She said it would be tough to get Ophion unless someone sued him again for malpractice. And she warned me to be *very* careful. I think the whole situation scared her."

"No doubt. And your mom and your other sister? How'd it go with them?"

"The climate never warmed up there."

"I'm sorry." He took her hand and held it as they waited.

"It hurts, but it's pretty much out of my control. I gave it my best shot, and I'll keep trying. What's new here?"

"Dr. Kedar gave me their symphony tickets for tomorrow night, since he pretty much lives at the hospital with Christina. Are you free?"

"Sure!"

"Great. And I had an interesting conversation with Sharon."

Bethany's eyes grew wide. "When the cat's away, the mouse will play."

Red stopped and gave her a wounded look.

"I meant *her*, Red. Not *you!*"

"Oh. Sorry. Guess I'm a little touchy."

Bethany squeezed his hand. "I trust you. Don't worry. What did she have to say for herself?"

"When I confronted her about trashing my apartment, she seemed shocked and insisted she didn't do it."

"Yeah, right."

"I know you'll probably think I'm naive, but I believe her."

Bethany stared. "Really?" If Sharon didn't do it…then who did?

Red shrugged. "She's not that good of an actress. She got really upset about it. In fact, it seemed to frighten her."

"Then why would someone want to trash your apartment and tell you to back off?" As soon as she'd said it, Bethany gasped. "Someone at VIP?"

He nodded, his expression somber. "Maybe."

Alarm swept Bethany, and she tightened her grip on his hand. If someone from VIP was willing to ransack Red's apartment, what else might they be willing to do? "Red, please be careful!"

TWENTY-EIGHT

Bethany headed into the office for a few hours on Saturday morning. She was halfway through the mound of mail when the return address on an envelope caught her attention.

The Center for Reproductive Choice?

She opened it and found the medical notes on her urine test. Only now instead of positive, her record from VIP read *negative.* She whipped the envelope over and stared at it. Her name was typed, and the letter included no correspondence.

Her heart pounded, and she reached for the phone to call Red. *Somebody changed the record!* But how had they found out? And how much did they know?

Red arrived at Bethany's on Saturday night at 7:30 sharp. They talked about the letter all the way to the Meyerson Symphony Center.

"Do you suppose Dorie told someone?"

Red shook his head. "Unlikely. Besides, why would she blow open her own investigation?"

"It all makes no sense."

"Agreed."

As they entered the symphony hall, Bethany suggested they quit talking about it and not let it ruin their evening. When the orchestra started warming up, she rested her arm on Red's. Throughout the first half of the concert they indicated their appreciation of the music with occasional squeezes of the hand. At intermission they went to the bar and got a Coke. Then they stood by the windows, enjoying the tiny white lights that twinkled in the trees outside the music hall.

Red looked down at Bethany, hoping his eyes communicated the tenderness he felt. "It's so wonderful to be able to give you my undivided attention without any outside demands."

Bethany smiled. "No, what's wonderful is being the recipient of your attention."

When the concert ended, it was close to ten o'clock. They walked hand in hand through the parking garage back to her car.

Bethany leaned against Red as they walked. "You must be tired after working all day."

He shook his head. "There's something energizing about being with a beautiful woman. Especially when you happen to love her."

She smiled at him.

"Besides, it's only eight o'clock West Coast time, right? So the night is young."

They drove up to North Park Mall for a late dinner, and they got to talking about dumb things they had done. Red had Bethany laughing until she cried and begged him to stop talking so she could breathe again.

"Want to know the *dumbest* thing I ever did?" Red grinned.

"Sure."

He grew serious. "The dumbest thing I ever did was not getting all the facts before I jumped to conclusions about you."

Bethany held his gaze. "I said I forgave you, and I meant it. Honestly. So please forgive yourself and let it go."

He took her hand and squeezed it.

She cocked her head. "So how about if I tell you one of the stupidest things I ever did?"

"Okay."

"I was sitting in algebra class, and this new girl was sitting in front of me. So this guy, Mike, hands me this note and tells me to give it to her for him. And like a sucker, I do what he tells me."

"What's wrong with that?"

"She opens it and then gets up and leaves. And the next thing I know, I'm being summoned to the principal's office. Apparently the note said, 'Your dress is ugly. From Bethany.'"

Red tried to suppress a smile. "How cruel!"

"It was pretty tough to convince them that I didn't write it or even know what it said."

"How did you get out of it?"

"Mike was so amused with himself that he started bragging about what he'd done, so eventually I was exonerated."

The waiter came with the bill, and Red laid his credit card in the folder. Then he looked at his watch. "It's 11:30. Shall we go in a minute?"

"Yeah, it's late and you have to work tomorrow."

"No problem. I'm probably good for at least another hour. I'd ask you back to my place for a bit, but I'm not sure how smart it would be to take you there alone, especially when it's so late and you look so beautiful."

Bethany smiled. "Thanks. Heather's at our place, so why don't you come over for a bit. I really hate for this night to end."

"Okay. Your place it is."

When they reached Bethany's, it was almost midnight and all the lights were off, but Heather's car was in the driveway. Bethany peered at the house. "She must have just gone to bed."

"I won't stay long."

They stepped inside, but when Bethany reached for the light switch, Red stopped her, then moved her hand and placed it against his chest. He pulled her close, wrapping one arm around her waist and another behind her head. He stroked her hair, looping it behind her ears as he looked in her eyes.

"I want to spend the rest of my life with you. One week apart was enough to tell me I don't want to live without you." He kissed her, gently at first, but then with abandon.

He could feel her holding back, trying not to let herself go, but he also read the signs—the elevated pulse and the slight change in her breathing pattern. The realization that she was experiencing more pleasure than she was letting on shot a jolt of passion through Red. He kissed her mouth, neck, and ears, then her forehead and her cheek and her nose before returning to her lips.

At first she hesitated, but after a moment she seemed to let down her defenses and began to respond with increasing eagerness. As hard as it was, Red forced himself to pull back. Bethany breathed a sigh against his lips, then kissed his cheek and rested her head against his chest.

"Let's go sit down on the couch," she said, flicking on the hall light.

"All right."

"Can I get you anything to drink?"

Red shook his head. "I'm drinking exactly what I want right now."

"Thanks, that's really sweet." She gave him a dreamy look. "But I'm dying of thirst." She took him by the hand and tiptoed through the house. In the living room, Red sat on the couch. Bethany let go and went into the kitchen. From where he sat, he saw the light from the refrigerator reflecting off the wall and then heard its door shut. He heard her rustling a piece of paper and wished she'd hurry back.

"Red…" He jumped slightly when she spoke aloud.

"What?"

She returned to the living room and sat next to him. "Heather's not here."

"What do you mean? Where is she? Her car's here."

"She left a note saying she went to an eleven o'clock movie. A friend picked her up."

Red's heart pounded. They were alone. All he wanted to do was pull Bethany into his arms, but he knew better. The way she affected him, he couldn't take that kind of chance. So he settled for taking her hand and drawing her down onto the couch beside him.

"I should go."

She met his gaze, and he could tell she understood what he wasn't saying.

"I know." She leaned forward, letting her forehead rest on his chest. "I hate for you to leave, but I know it's best."

Red stroked her hair. "This could go really far, really fast, couldn't it?"

She pursed her lips, closed her eyes, and nodded.

"And we don't really want that."

"No, not in the best parts of who we are. At least not yet."

"Something about vows, right?"

"Yes."

Red nodded and sat up straight. He moved so they sat with knees touching, took both of her hands, and looked her in the eyes. "Bethany,

I'd be lying if I said I wasn't crazy about you. You're an exciting, passionate woman, and I'd love to stay, but…"

She nodded. "There's too much at stake." Her lips trembled as she gave him a smile. "It would certainly make it easier if you didn't have a two-thousand-volt kiss!"

Red laughed and drew her close. "I'm glad you think so." He rested his cheek against her head. "We need to talk about the future, don't we?"

She didn't answer, but seemed to be holding her breath.

"I commit to you right now that we will wait. And we'll get it right, with a lot of divine help, that is."

"I commit the same to you."

He kissed the cheek where a tear had fallen. "Why are you crying?"

"Because I recognize love when I see it."

Red nodded. "It's definitely love. I'd better go."

When he reached the door, he took her face in his hands and left her with the gentlest of kisses.

He drove home with the top down, hoping the cold October night wind would cool him down as it blew through his hair. He felt as if he were floating, filled with the thrill of being in love and the depth of connection he felt for Bethany. *I can't wait to get some time to think and make plans. I have so many hopes and dreams for us.*

On Sunday afternoon Bethany went straight to the hospital after church. She was really looking forward to seeing Red again.

The assistant at the main desk in L and D paged Red for her, and about three minutes later he appeared. His eyes lit up when he spotted her. He slipped his arm around her waist and gave her a quick kiss.

"Hello, beautiful." He spoke in a low voice. "I couldn't wait to see you." He walked her back to the doctors' lounge, and they sat on the couch. "You look terrific. And I had a wonderful time last night."

"Me, too. Thanks again for the symphony, for dinner. It was all lovely. Please express my thanks to Dr. Kedar for the tickets."

"Hey, want to thank him yourself? He's here all the time these days—probably in NICU right now. You could see the baby, too."

Bethany jumped at the chance. "I'd *love* to."

Red extended his hand to help her off the couch. He pulled her up into a hug, and then guided her out the door.

They made their way to the neonatal unit, and Bethany gowned at the entrance.

"It's too early and too risky to take you inside, but you can look through the window."

At first Bethany was disappointed at Red's words, but she realized he was right. The baby's safety was most important.

Red glanced toward the glass, and then walked Bethany over to it. "Looks like Dr. Kedar isn't here, after all. But you can still see the baby."

Bethany gasped when she saw the submerged child. "She's under water!"

"Yeah, just like in the womb—the ultimate waterbed."

She stared. "I've never seen anything like it."

"Nor has anyone outside of this hospital," Red said.

She looked up at him with admiration. "And *you* helped to save her life."

Red glanced down at his pager. "Hang on…" He walked over to the phone and made a call. After hanging up, he turned to Bethany. "Dorie's on her way up. I told her about the letter, and she said she had something to tell us."

When Dorie arrived, the three of them ducked into a small conference room.

"What's up?" Red asked.

Dorie sat and pointed for them to have a seat as well. "We've had an interesting development. When I was doing morning rounds on Monday, we had a patient come in with an incomplete abortion. She was from VIP. She'd had a D and C in the night, and the resident involved was one of my guys from over there. He was leaving, and I needed the patient's information to get her discharged when appropriate. So I asked him to have VIP fax over the patient's file, which he did. The patient was—surprise, surprise—well insured. And she got the doc on call for OB cases, Dr. Kedar."

"Did you tell him what you know about Ophion?"

Dorie shook her head. "He was the attending on call, but the resident did the procedure, so Dr. Kedar didn't really have any involvement.

Anyway, the file said the patient got a prescription for RU-486 from Ophion. And I understand Ophion has cut a new deal with a different pharmacy, so I called the new place to verify what she got. The pharmacist there said her prescription was only for the RU-486. And—"

Bethany and Red leaned forward. "And?"

Dorie's smile was triumphant. "Ophion's little star was right there on the chart."

Red slapped the table. "This has gone on long enough! This will keep happening unless we do something *fast*. We need a solid case, someone with evidence who's willing to testify against Ophion."

"There was Dawn," Bethany said.

Red shook his head. "She didn't keep any samples, so we have no evidence, only testimony. They'd eat her up in the courtroom."

"What about the D and C with the missed ectopic? VIP told her she was pregnant when she wasn't," Bethany asked.

"We've got testimony, but no evidence. And about the best we could hope for there would be negligence in missing the ectopic."

Dorie shook her head. "Not good enough."

"I guess anything *I* had from going to VIP is gone now," Bethany said.

Again, Dorie shook her head. "How they found out is still a mystery to me. Honestly."

"And the molar pregnancy patient?" Red asked.

Dorie said, "That had nothing to do with this. It was an inexperienced resident. That stuff happens."

"What about the latest patient?" Bethany asked.

Red smiled. "What about this latest patient's *attending doctor?*"

When they were done meeting, Bethany went to the rest room. While she was washing her hands, Dorie came in.

Bethany looked under the stall doors to be sure they were alone. "Hey, listen, before you leave…did Red mention to you that someone trashed his apartment? I'm afraid it might have been related to VIP."

Dorie looked alarmed. "No, when?"

Bethany filled her in on the details. "Maybe I'm making too much of it. I know people get their houses broken into every day. But they left a message to back off, and that seems a bit more personal, don't you think?"

"Yes, I do. But you say his ex-girlfriend was giving him some trouble? Maybe she went on a rampage and felt bad about it later. She used to hang around up here—I met her a few times. And from what I've heard about her in the past year, she was fully capable of trashing Red's apartment when she didn't get her way."

"That was my initial thought too, but she denies doing it. And Red believes her."

"Sorry, Bethany. But from my experience, men can be gullible, especially where a pretty face is concerned."

Dorie left to go back to work, and Bethany stared after her. She didn't know whether or not to hope Dorie was right—either way the ramifications were unsettling.

Dr. Damon had spent a quiet night in the call room. Now, at 5:40 A.M., while Red dozed in a room across the hall, Damon was awake.

He went out to the administrative secretary's desk. "Hey, sorry to bother you, but I left my locker key in the pocket of my scrubs again yesterday and then tossed them in the laundry. Could I borrow the master for a minute?"

"Sure. No problem." She handed him the key with a smile.

Damon carried his briefcase to the doctors' lounge and opened his locker. He removed the vial of Mrs. Stewart's spinal fluid, which he'd hidden in a pair of shoes, took it back to his room, and shut the door. When he found that the lid on the Opti-Cleanse bottle he'd bought to match the one in Red's locker could not be unscrewed, he cursed and went to the supply room. Afterward, making sure no one saw him, he returned to his room and shut the door.

Minutes later, he went back to the locker room and opened Red's locker with the master key, replaced Red's contact solution with the bottle he had contaminated, and shut the door. He stashed Red's bottle of contact solution and the vial back in his own locker. Then he scrubbed his hands.

After checking once again to see that no one was around, Damon returned the key to the assistant and strode down to check the L and D board to make sure no OB happenings would throw off his plans.

All was quiet. Damon saw from the board that Red had requested a six o'clock wake-up call. Checking his watch, Damon calculated that he had about a fifteen-minute wait, so he returned to his room.

At six sharp Damon heard Red's phone ringing. Through the doors he could hear Red answer, then head out minutes later.

After a few minutes, Damon entered the locker room. He found Red shaving. "Quiet night, eh?"

Red grunted. "Yeah."

Damon brushed his teeth and started to shave.

When Red finished brushing his teeth, Damon watched as he squirted solution into his contact case, then popped out his contacts and put them in the fluid. After locking all his sundries in his locker, Red made his way to the shower.

Damon turned to smile at his reflection in the mirror. *I am a genius!*

TWENTY-NINE

Red turned down the temperature of the water, allowing the cool vapor to spray in his face. Showers often gave him another two or three hours' worth of new energy, and he could feel a second wind rejuvenating him. After pulling an all-nighter, he was glad at the prospect of a more relaxed schedule for the day ahead.

He took his time drying off. Then, after slipping the damp towel around his waist, he headed back to his locker. He put on new blues, then took his contact case and Dopp Kit back to one of the sinks. He popped his contacts into his eyes, put his supplies back into the locker, and headed to the hospital wards to make rounds.

At lunchtime he went down to the doctors' dining hall to meet Dr. Kedar. When he arrived, Red spotted his friend already seated, so he went over to him.

Dr. Kedar handed Red his dining card. "Go load up your tray and put it on this."

Red had learned not to argue. "Thanks." He returned to the line, got a sandwich with chips, and made his way back to the quiet corner where Dr. Kedar had saved him a seat.

"How's your niece this morning?" Red asked.

"It was an uneventful night. What about you? Did you get any sleep? You seem like you are in another world."

Red rubbed his eyes. "I've got a lot on my mind." Dr. Kedar waited for him to elaborate.

"There's some medical stuff I've seen that's troubling me—troubling events over at VIP."

"Are you still worried about the perforated uterus case?"

"Actually, that's the least of my worries."

"Really?" Dr. Kedar set down his fork and stared at Red. "The *least* of your worries?"

"Well, yes. First there **was** the perforated uterus, then there was the patient with the hemorrhage—the mole. Not to mention Ophion's suit with the small bowel that pulled through, and—"

Dr. Kedar studied him for a moment. "You think that is a lot for one clinic?"

"I know any clinic with high volumes is going to have its share of complications, but—"

"Right, Red. It is a numbers game. Odds. The odds of all that happening, well, you see it more in a place where they do a high number of cases. And VIP does the highest volume in the city."

He nodded. "I know, but it's Ophion, more than anything. He's—"

"Other than the bowel, his main involvement is hiring the residents. Some of our best, right?"

Red blinked, then blinked again. "Yes, but it's the RU-486 cases, too." Red hesitated. Should he say any more? Taking a breath, he went on. "I believe Dr. Ophion is engaging in some unethical activities."

"Yes, I know you think abortion is wrong."

Red shook his head. "While to me that is the worst part, those are not the unethical activities I meant. I was referring to 'creative charting' to get more insurance money."

"Creative charting?"

Red nodded. "He's faking test results—one I know about for sure, and several I suspect." Red clenched his jaw. "He'll *lie* to get insured women to the OR, all the while claiming to be helping them. And—"

Dr. Kedar was staring at him now. "These are serious charges. Do you have any hard evidence?"

Red opened his mouth, but Dr. Kedar continued. "And what would you like to see happen, Red? Dr. Ophion is already involved in a multitude of legal actions, but he is well insured and well represented. Surely you do not see any financial gain in this for yourself?"

Red shook his head. "Of course not."

"So what are you going for here?"

Red focused intently on Dr. Kedar and leaned forward. "I'd love to shut the place down."

Dr. Kedar's eyes grew wide. "Oh my."

"Short of that, I'd like to stop Ophion from breaking the law and using RU-486 to generate more surgeries and endangering patients' lives just so he can make a buck."

Dr. Kedar leaned back. "The whole point of RU-486 is to give women the option of aborting at home without a surgical procedure. How would RU-486 generate *more* surgeries? How could that possibly benefit the clinic? I understand they have an arrangement for patients to procure the drugs almost at cost. That is most generous, in my estimation."

"Dr. Kedar, they aren't *giving* it correctly! Ophion's giving the RU-486 to patients, but he's only selectively prescribing the prostaglandin. In fact, the *un*insured or those without financial resources get the correct dosage of medications. The women with good insurance, those whose companies will pay, get RU-486 and a prostaglandin *inhibitor*."

Clearly Dr. Kedar was stunned. "No, that could not be correct! That would significantly increase the complication rate, to withhold the prostaglandin on the proper schedule—"

"Right! Dr. Ophion artificially causes abortion complications—partial miscarriages. Then he brings the patients back in for surgical abortions. He gets the best of both worlds. He culls out those who can't or won't pay, gives them the right prescriptions, and lets the pharmacy worry about payment. But for the patients with means, he arranges for complications." Red stopped for a moment and rubbed his eyes.

Why on earth are my contacts bothering me so much?

Dr. Kedar took on a serious tone. "I am concerned about you, Dr. Richison. That is a criminal allegation. It goes beyond medical malpractice, certainly to fraud, perhaps even to some type of assault. You are not talking negligence here. You are accusing Dr. Ophion, a skilled and experienced colleague, of criminal conduct."

"I know. Don't you see? That's why Dorie got fired. She was—"

Dr. Kedar shook his head. "Fired? When?"

"About a month ago. They fired her. And do you know why? Because she uncovered some of this illegal activity. Dr. Kedar, I wouldn't even waste your time telling you about all of this, but frankly, as a resident I don't have the clout to bring justice here. And when Dorie talked to Lexie Winters, she got the brush-off."

"VIP *fired* her? Dr. Chambers is an excellent physician."

"Yes. And now they've involved *you*."

"No." Dr. Kedar pressed a finger to his lips. "What do you mean? Do you mean the DeVeer case?"

Red shook his head. "Do you remember signing for a D and C here last Sunday night? For an incomplete abortion?"

"Vaguely."

"Well, it was one of VIP's patients, who slipped through Ophion's ever-expanding crack. He didn't give her the prostaglandin, she had complications, VIP was closed on the weekend, and *you* had to take care of it. I put together a list of cases you've had to sign off on, from the DeVeer case to this one, and it's not a short list."

Dr. Kedar leaned toward Red and emphasized each word. "So once again I have been made party to another possible malpractice case from the VIP clinic?"

Red saw fire in his eyes. "Yes."

"I was so focused on Christina that another incomplete from VIP did not even register. I just staffed the case." Dr. Kedar looked around, then stroked his chin. "Okay, Red, get me everything you have—*everything*—on this RU-486 situation."

He pulled a pen out of his pocket and took a clean napkin out of the dispenser, then made notes as Red unfolded the evidence again, beginning with Dr. Ophion's altering of dates for Medicaid records and ending with the latest patient mishap.

"Have there been any patient complaints?"

"Not to my knowledge. That's part of the problem. How would the average patient know she got the wrong follow-up medication? Most women take RU-486 because they've heard it's easy."

Dr. Kedar nodded. "We would need a solid, airtight case. If we could prove everything you have just said, Dr. Ophion would probably lose his medical license. He would also be exposed in the malpractice cases currently open. He might even serve time if we have a woman or two who got the wrong prescription with the RU-486 and had to endure an unnecessary surgery, especially one with complications."

"We have all the names that Dr. Chambers found, *all* of whom had good insurance coverage for complications of abortion. But to our knowledge, not one of them knows what Ophion did to them, so why would they come forward?"

"Let me think on it. Have Dorie get me copies of what evidence she has, all right?"

"Great."

Dr. Kedar paused, then studied Red. "You are rubbing your eyes a lot, Red. Perhaps you should go home and get some sleep."

"My eyes *do* feel irritated. I've probably been up too many hours to be wearing contacts. Thanks again for lunch and for listening. I know you have a lot of other concerns right now."

Dr. Kedar waved his words off. A few minutes later Red was back at his locker. He removed his contacts and put them in the case. Then he slid on an old pair of glasses. He threw the supplies in his backpack and went to leave a note for Dorie. Then he headed home.

After sleeping for four hours, he awoke—and grimaced. The irritation in his eyes was even worse. He called Bethany and asked if she had any evening plans.

"I was hoping to see you."

"Miss Fabrizio, your wish has been granted. But I don't have a lot of energy."

"I'll bet you're exhausted."

"My eyes have been bothering me some, and I'm pretty tired. How about something tame, like a movie?"

"It's a date."

Red arrived at her place an hour later carrying a pizza box and a video.

Bethany greeted him at the door. "I didn't know you wore glasses. Did you lose a contact?" She looked closer, and concern filled her face. "Your eyes are red."

"They are?" He walked over to the living room mirror and leaned close to get a good look at his eyes. They looked as bad as they felt. "Yeah, you're right. That'll teach me to leave in my contacts for too long."

They sat on the carpet and turned on the television. Yvonne Kedar was on the news, and they watched her while they munched on pepperoni and sausage. Bethany finished first, so she crawled up behind Red on the couch and began to massage his shoulders and neck.

Red closed his eyes. "Ah."

"You like?" She moved her hands higher and massaged his head.

"M'm, yeah. That feels great." He leaned back. After a minute, he reached around and pulled her face down to his. "Let's watch the movie now. I think that would be the most prudent choice, don't you?" He kissed her.

She looked into his eyes. "Yeah, good point."

"I'll plan to leave right after the movie's over; I've got to be back at work by 6:30 in the morning. But if I can get free tomorrow night, we'll do something special, okay?"

"Sure." Bethany slipped off the couch and sat back next to him on the floor. Red slid his arm around her shoulder and pulled her close to rest his head on hers.

When Red awoke Tuesday morning, his eyes were watering and he had a slight headache. He took some Tylenol and put on his glasses, glad that he was scheduled only for a regular day and wasn't on call.

Dr. Kedar stopped when he saw Red in the hall. "I have been thinking about what you told me. When can you get me whatever evidence Dr. Chambers has?"

"I left her a note to get in touch with you."

Dr. Kedar looked more closely at him. "Are your eyes still bothering you?"

Red nodded, noticing that even the fluorescent lighting of the hospital corridor seemed painfully bright. "I'm wondering if it's a corneal abrasion."

"Which eye?" Dr. Kedar leaned toward him to get a better look.

"Both."

Dr. Kedar furrowed his brows. "In *both* eyes?"

Red shrugged.

"You had better get it checked out. It could be something else."

"Ugh. Okay. How's your niece?"

"Still stable."

"Good. I'll stop in and see her before I head out."

By the end of the day, Red's head was pounding. He checked the L and D board, and it looked quiet, so he went and found Dorie. "I think I may be coming down with something, and Tylenol hasn't helped."

"Let's get you cleared to go on home then," she said.

"That would be great if it's okay."

She nodded. "Your eyes look mighty red. Are you all right?"

"It's probably nothing. Did you get my note about Dr. Kedar?"

Dorie smiled. "I'm trying not to get my hopes up, but I sure appreciate your going out on a limb to ask him.

"He did think I was crazy at first."

"I'll get the records copied today."

Bethany looked up to see Dawn Spencer following Diana down the hall. When Dawn saw Bethany, she gave her a shy smile and stopped at her door.

"Hey!"

"Hi! How's it going, Dawn?"

"Pretty good." She leaned in and lowered her voice. "Diana and me have been talking about forgiveness. You were right about her. Thanks."

Bethany smiled. "I'm really glad."

"Well, good to see ya." Dawn headed off down the hall.

"You, too!" Bethany called after her. As she sat there ruminating on Dawn's progress, Margaret appeared in the doorway with a new client.

"Bethany, this is Shelley Brennan."

Bethany stood, shook the patient's hand, and gestured for her to come in and sit down. She noticed Shelley was older and better dressed than most of their clients, and she had very thin hair.

"Bethany, I'm here at the recommendation of my doctor. He's been really wonderful. I'm sure you know him, Dr. Red Richison. He speaks so highly of you."

"Thank you. I think pretty highly of him too. How can I help you?"

"I had an abortion, but it's not what you probably think…" Shelley's eyes clouded over.

Bethany reached out and touched her knee.

"I have breast cancer. It looks like I'm responding well to chemo, but…but…we really wanted that *baby*." She burst into tears. After a minute, she pulled it together. "I probably would have, uh, wouldn't have made it…"

"I see."

"And I just thought, maybe…well…it might help to talk and cry and pray with someone who…who understands what I just went through and believes every life is important to God."

When Red got outside, his hands flew up to cover his eyes, but the bright October sunlight seared through. He unlocked his glove compartment and took out the dark prescription glasses that he never used. All the way home, he squinted and cupped a hand above his eyebrows to shield his eyes from the sun's scorching brightness.

Climbing the steps to his apartment took every ounce of energy. Once inside, he left the lights off, shut all the miniblinds, and closed the curtains. He hated to call Bethany, but he knew he was in no shape to go anywhere with her.

He called her cell phone, and when she answered, he could tell she was in her car. "Where are you?"

"Headed home and then to see you."

"Oh, Beth—" Red's heart sank.

"What is it?"

"I sure hate to disappoint you, but I'm not feeling too hot. Maybe I picked up a bug somewhere. And my eyes are killing me."

"Bummer for both of us! Anything I can do? Bring you dinner?"

"No, I just need to sleep. I hate to let you down."

"Don't you worry about that. You just take care of yourself, okay? And call me when you feel better."

Within minutes Red fell asleep, but when he awoke in the middle of the night, his eyes were in agony and his chills shook the bed. When he moved to sit up, the horrible pounding in his head made him catch his breath and hold still until the sharp pain settled into a dull one. He tried to call out to his parents, then realized he was not at his parents' house.

Why would I think I was there? Strange. I haven't even lived there for years.

He realized through the haze of pain that he was holding his neck. A vague sensation turned into a clear realization: He was disoriented.

Something was wrong. Seriously wrong.

Alarm ripped through him, and he groped for his phone and called Bethany.

She answered with a groggy voice, then realized it was him. "Red! Are you all right?"

He groaned.

"What's happening?"

"I can barely move… head and neck… like someone's hitting me with a sledgehammer."

"I'll be right there."

He hung up, then punched in the speed dial number for ER. The doctor on call listened to his symptoms, and then told him to come in right away.

Five minutes later, he heard a key in the lock. He let out a yelp and covered his eyes when the light came on.

"Turn it off!"

"Red!" Bethany's alarm was clear in her voice. "What's the matter?" She flicked off the light.

The pain was so intense he thought he would pass out. "It…hurts my eyes."

"I can't see where I'm going. Can I turn on the light in the bath-room?"

Red moaned. "Uh-huh."

He heard her grope her way down the hall, then turn on the bathroom light. Through slitted eyes he watched as she cracked the door open enough to see her way around his apartment. "Will that work?"

Red groaned, "Yeah." He closed his eyes, and when he opened them again, she was standing over him. He felt a cool hand on his forehead.

"Red, you're burning up!"

"Can you drive me to the ER?"

"Of course."

He started to sit up, but a jolt of pain tore his breath—and a cry of agony—from him.

"Red!" Bethany stared at him.

He lay back down, whimpering, his hands squeezing his temples.

"Red, this is scary."

"Oh, man. It's like somebody poured lighter fluid in my head and lit a match."

"Let me get you a cool cloth."

Red held up a hand. "I already called Dr. Packard in ER. He said to come in *now;* they've seen a couple cases of meningitis lately."

Red almost hoped that was what was happening. At least then he'd know what he was dealing with. Whatever it was, he needed some answers—and some help—right away.

THIRTY

Bethany did her best to hold Red up as they staggered into the ER. She fought back her terror as he leaned on her slight shoulders and moaned about the pain that made every step hurt. Thankfully, a cluster of nurses met them, one with a wheelchair. They helped Red into it and rolled him to a room with swift efficiency. There they put him on a gurney, and the ER doc, along with the nurse, examined him. Bethany didn't like the expression on the doctor's face. The nurse slid a digital thermometer in Red's ear and seconds later read it.

"It's 104.4 degrees."

Bethany breathed a desperate prayer as the doctor gently placed his hands on Red's cheeks and moved his head from side to side. Red cried out in agony.

"You've got some definite meningeal signs and nuchal rigidity," the doctor told him. Bethany watched as he shone the bright light of the ophthalmoscope into Red's eyes; Red got teary-eyed from the discomfort.

"Good night! Your eyes are not only red, you've got blisters on the cornea. I've never seen anything like it." The doctor turned to the nurse. "We'll need some blood work, and start an IV, Ringer's Lactate at 150 ccs per hour."

She nodded and left the room.

The doctor turned back to Red. "We'll need to do a lumbar puncture to rule out meningitis and see what we're up against. Of course, I'm going to admit you."

Red offered no resistance and lay absolutely still. The physician turned to Bethany. "You'll need to step outside while we do the spinal tap."

She complied and paced as she waited, stopping every few minutes and straining to hear, hoping Red was not in too much pain. When they had finished, the doctor came out and motioned for her to return. Standing by Red's bedside, she listened as the doctor told them the news.

"Looks like viral meningitis from the appearance of the spinal fluid. I'm sending him to the infectious disease ward, and we'll be putting him in isolation. We'll get him hooked up to some monitors—"

Bethany stroked the back of Red's hand. "What kind of monitors?"

"Heart and—"

O God, no... "You're expecting him to have a heart attack?"

The doctor shook his head and held up his hand. "Just being extra cautious. He's sick and will probably get sicker, so we need to watch his pulse and blood pressure, just the usual things." He looked at Red. "Any meningitis on your service?"

Red mumbled, "Not that I know of, but I know the GYN service had a case recently."

"Okay. After we admit you, we'll hydrate you, treat your symptoms, and make sure what you've got isn't bacterial. But I've never seen eye findings like this, so I'll call ophthalmology and get them in for a consult in the morning."

By dawn Red had grown worse. He groaned from the head pain that required strong medication to knock him out. The staff tried to bring down his fever with cooling blankets, and his doctors discussed using medication to drop the temperature as well. Yet when they called in the infectious disease expert who had treated all the meningitis patients, he advised differently. He directed them to hold back on giving more meds until they had the cultures.

Bethany sat slumped in a corner chair, listening to all the reports, her heart pounding. *Father, I'm so frightened.* Had she found Red only to lose him?

He lay as still as a stone. She'd never seen anyone so listless, so lifeless. Images filled her mind—Red laughing, Red cupping her face and kissing her. Every touch, everything they'd shared stirred two thoughts that haunted her: Was Red going to recover?

And was she going to come down with whatever he had?

———————

Dr. Casey Bolton had been an ophthalmologist for ten years, and he thought he'd seen everything. Until now.

He'd received the call about a half-hour ago about a second-year resident, Red Richison, who'd shown up in ER with inexplicable symptoms. Now he walked into Red's room and wakened him so he could have a look at his eyes.

He shone his light, then stared and blinked. He looked again and shook his head. "What the—?"

"What is it?" Tori, the nurse, asked.

He straightened, crossing his arms, and spoke to Red. "Well, Doctor, I'm afraid this looks pretty bad. Both of the corneas"—he still could hardly believe it—"they're covered with tiny blisters. And it's strange. The blisters are in a circular shape." What on earth was going on? "Do you wear contacts?"

The young man nodded, but with careful movements, as though the action caused him great pain. "Uh-huh."

After putting a drop of local anesthetic in Red's eyes, Dr. Bolton took a tiny sterile brush with plastic bristles and cultured each eye separately. "Do you have any family in the area?"

"No," Red answered.

The nurse spoke up. "His girlfriend is out in the waiting area. I'll bet she could help you."

"What does she look like?"

"She's tiny, with dark hair, dark eyes. Wearing jeans and a red T-shirt. Want me to go get her?"

"No, I'll go find her. Why don't you get these specimens off to the lab?" Dr. Bolton walked out in search of a woman who fit that description. Spotting only three people in the waiting area, he had no trouble finding the right one. He introduced himself, and the woman stood up.

"I'm Bethany Fabrizio, Doctor." Her troubled gaze rested on him, as though seeking some sign of encouragement. "Do you know what's wrong with Red?"

He didn't answer. "Do you know if he brought his contacts?"

She shook her head. "He didn't bring anything but his wallet."

"Think you could find a way to go get his contacts for me?"

Bethany looked surprised. "He needs them?"

"Not to wear. We need to examine them."

"Oh! Okay. Sure. I've got his keys in my purse since I drove him here. He lives just about five minutes away. I could be back in fifteen."

"Great. I'll wait."

When she returned, Bethany handed Dr. Bolton the bag with Red's contact case and cleanser.

"I have a hunch Red's contacts were involved, so I want you to wash up now, even though you touched only the case."

Her eyes widened. "Do you think I'm at risk?"

"You do need to be careful when you're around him. And let your physician know at the first sign of any symptoms, such as fever or headache, that sort of thing." He touched her arm and gave her a smile. "But I think you'll be okay."

"Did he get this from one of his patients?"

Dr. Bolton shook his head. "Hard to say. I talked with the infectious disease doctor about the findings, and he told me nobody here with meningitis has had any problems with eye blisters."

"That's strange."

She has no idea just how *strange.*

Dr. Bolton took the contact case, excused himself, and headed down to the viral lab to speak with Dr. Fawdry, the director himself. Dr. Henry Fawdry was responsible for the City of Dallas's forensic work, and he could examine a specimen and maintain a chain of evidence with the best of detectives. He was, however, less meticulous in his attention to personal style. He wore disheveled, outdated clothing; his hair never looked combed; and his cluttered office matched his dress. Still, in his organized chaos, he knew where everything was, and his unbiased sense of justice had earned him the respect of his peers.

Dr. Bolton found Dr. Fawdry immersed in a pile of paperwork. When he explained the situation, Dr. Fawdry gave him a sly grin. He took the contact case, carried it straight to the lab, and requested a thorough examination and culture of both the lenses and their irrigating fluid.

———————

The following afternoon Dr. Bolton received a phone call.

Dr. Fawdry came right to the point. "What's the latest on Dr. Richison?"

"I just came from seeing him. He's heavily sedated, with temps spiking to 105 but only going down to 101 on meds. What have you got?"

"Dr. Richison's viral type exactly matches the type of meningitis identified in Mrs. Stewart."

"Interesting. The eye blister culture matches the virus in his spinal fluid. That means he had to have come in contact with the fluid, and then touched *both* of his eyes—so much so that he thoroughly contaminated them. Was he treating Mrs. Stewart?"

"No. Infectious Disease says his name wasn't on her chart. And the first-year resident caring for Mrs. Stewart just told me there were no notes on her chart from Dr. Richison. I've asked the resident to come down here so I can ask her some questions. Want to join me?"

"Be right there."

Dr. Bolton joined Dr. Fawdry at a small table, and minutes later the resident knocked on the consultation room door. He could see the fear in her eyes as Dr. Fawdry motioned for her to sit down and began to question her.

"Dr. Tsai, are you aware that Dr. Richison has been admitted?"

She nodded. "I know Red and like him. I heard he was in and really sick, but I've been too busy to stop in and see him."

"Dr. Richison has viral meningitis, an unusual herpes variant, just like Mrs. Stewart has."

Dr. Tsai stared wide-eyed. "Whoa."

Whoa, indeed. Dr. Fawdry pursed his lips. "We're assuming he saw the patient and somehow contaminated his eyes—specifically his contacts."

Dr. Tsai shook her head. "But…how? To my knowledge, he's had no contact with her. I've cared for Mrs. Stewart the whole admission, and Red hasn't been involved at all. He's on OB rotation, and this is a GYN case."

Dr. Bolton nodded. "Dr. Richison has an enormous number of corneal blisters, suggesting that the infection began in his eyes. So you have no idea how that could have happened, Dr. Tsai?"

"I haven't a clue. That's scary. I wish I could help you." Her pager went off, and she looked down to see who was calling. "Sorry, Dr. Damon's summoning me."

"That's all right." Dr. Bolton leaned back in his chair. He'd hoped she would be of more help. "We're finished."

She took several steps toward the door but then hesitated. She put her finger to her lips and turned back. Dr. Bolton had the clear impression that she was troubled.

He lowered his chin. "Yes...?"

"Uh, I-I don't know if it makes any difference at all, but since it was my patient, Mrs. Stewart...when we did the LP on her about a week ago, well, we took an extra tube of CSF."

Dr. Fawdry frowned. "Did Dr. Richison do the tap? I thought you said he hadn't seen her."

She shook her head. "No, it's not *that*. It's just... Dr. Damon...he took four tubes and sent me to the lab with three."

Dr. Bolton exchanged glances with his colleague. Dr. Fawdry pressed for more. "What did Dr. Damon do with the other vial?"

A sheen of perspiration now appeared on Dr. Tsai's face. "He put it in his pocket and took it with him. I don't know what happened from there. Maybe he took it to help with some project Dr. Richison's been working on. I've heard Red's been spending a lot of time down with Dr. Kedar in the lab."

Dr. Fawdry cleared his throat. "Do you know if Dr. Damon might have had problems with Dr. Richison? Would he have any reason to—"

Dr. Bolton stared. What was Dr. Fawdry suggesting? "Do you think he *intentionally* contaminated Dr. Richison's contacts with the solution?"

Dr. Fawdry nodded, and Dr. Bolton raised his eyebrows. "Well, it would *fit*. The contact case was loaded with virus, just loaded. But that would be a serious accusation."

Dr. Fawdry's eyes were still glued to Dr. Tsai.

She swallowed hard. "Dr. Damon carries a lot of weight over at the VIP clinic, and I heard Red confront him one time after he perforated a patient's uterus, and, uh..."

"And?" Dr. Fawdry asked.

"This is secondhand information, but the word is that they are both involved in a huge malpractice case involving that incident."

Dr. Fawdry's eyebrows shot up.

"They're sort of in opposite corners," Dr. Tsai continued. "So I've heard there was some bad blood between them."

Dr. Fawdry nodded to dismiss her. "Thank you, Dr. Tsai. And we'd appreciate it if for the moment you didn't mention this conversation to anyone."

Dalmuth had spent several hours in the lab when his stomach reminded him of mealtime. He'd been working on calculations and oxygen concentration so he'd be ready for Christina to make the transition from the tank to breathing on her own. Just as he shut down his computer, his pager went off. He looked down to read the number.

Forensics?

"I guess you heard about Red Richison," Dr. Fawdry told him when he called.

"Yes. It is very troubling. I have not been in to see him, but I am following his progress closely. I had noticed his eyes were red early on, and I should have insisted that he get it checked out immediately. If only—"

"Let me ask you, Doctor. Is there anything you're working on in your lab that might require spinal fluid?"

"No!"

"All right, then, how well do you know Denny Damon?"

The strange questions had certainly piqued his curiosity. "Dr. Damon? Well enough, I guess. We have done the usual number of procedures together. Why?"

"Do you know of any research that Damon's doing in your lab?"

"To my knowledge, Denny Damon has been down here only once or twice in the past six months."

"Thanks, Doctor. What do you know of any animosity that might exist between Red and Damon?"

Dalmuth considered the possibility. "Animosity? Well, they are both being sued in a related case, as am I. But I am not at liberty to talk about it. Lexie Winters can fill you in. Dorie Chambers might also be able to help you. She has a lot of contact with both doctors and would probably know if there has been a problem."

"Yes, since she's the chief OB resident, we just interviewed her."

Knowing Dr. Fawdry could not tell him much, Dalmuth pieced together where the questions led. "Are you...are you thinking Dr. Damon might be involved with Red's problem somehow? I cannot believe that." Yet even as he said it, Dalmuth had his doubts. Damon was a skilled doctor, and Dalmuth had never seen anything to suggest the younger man was capable of sabotage. But the variety of possible motives gave him pause.

"Let's just say we're checking out all the options. But I'd appreciate it if you didn't mention this to anyone until we know more, all right?"

"Of course." As Dalmuth hung up the phone, he shook his head, deeply disturbed that the illness jeopardizing Red's career—if not his life—might have been caused intentionally.

Dr. Fawdry sat in his office sipping a cup of strong coffee and reviewing the evidence with the detective.

"Let's say we develop probable cause here and we get a search warrant for this guy's locker." Detective Armstrong fixed Dr. Fawdry with a steely gaze. "What are you looking for?"

"Maybe a vial. I don't know exactly, but I wouldn't have asked you out here if I didn't have a strong suspicion."

"And your suspicions are usually right; that's why I'm here. But give me something, anything. I don't mind going out on a limb for you, but I've got to have something besides your hunch if we're going to convince a judge to give us a search warrant."

Dr. Fawdry drew closer. "Cory, I think we've got a corrupt doc here, one that, at best, tried to incapacitate another physician."

"And at worst?"

It took a moment for Dr. Fawdry to voice what had been on his mind for some time now. "Maybe tried to kill him. I'm not sure, but it's starting to add up."

"What's this Damon's motive? A woman? Drugs?"

"He's got a few possible motives. But there's nothing glaringly obvious, though he and Dr. Richison apparently don't get along very well."

"Yeah? I don't get along with my mother-in-law, but I haven't tried to kill her…yet."

Dr. Fawdry chuckled. "Dr. Richison had no contact with the patient who had the particular strain of meningitis that he has contracted. We've got a resident who saw Dr. Damon take a vial of contaminated spinal fluid. And when we began to look for anyone who had access to Dr. Richison's contacts, we found a clerk who says Dr. Damon asked for the master key to the lockers about three nights before our good doctor's health went south."

Cory shook his head. "Asking for the master key? That's hardly suspicious. Maybe he lost his locker key."

"Entirely possible. It happens all the time."

"Certainly an interesting scenario though." Cory leaned back. "I can probably make enough of it to get the warrant. Is this Damon guy suspicious at all?"

"I don't think so."

"Good." Cory stroked his chin. "I'd sure hate for him to go to his locker and tamper with my evidence."

Dr. Fawdry smiled. "Don't worry. I can pull him into the pathology department to tie him up for a few hours, but we need that warrant *today*."

THIRTY-ONE

Bethany sat alone in the Neuro ICU waiting room, trying to read a magazine but unable to concentrate.

"How are you?"

She looked up to see Heather standing in front of her.

"I brought you something to eat. I don't want you starving up here."

Bethany got up and hugged her. "Heather, how thoughtful. Thank you."

"How is he?"

"Not great." Bethany set the bag of food on the table and motioned for Heather to join her. She wiped a tear. "They've got him in isolation now, so I'm not allowed in. In fact he's not allowed *any* visitors for fear of triggering seizures." Her voice trailed off, but she regained control. "His parents came up here yesterday, and they told me he was semi-conscious."

Heather wrapped her arms around Bethany and let her cry.

"The hardest part is that I can't get the staff to tell *me* anything since I'm not family."

"Uh, Bethany?"

"What?"

When Heather didn't answer, Bethany looked up to see Dorie standing there in scrubs and a lab coat.

"He's stable," Dorie said in a reassuring tone. "The temperature spikes aren't getting any worse. They're not improving much either, but we're optimistic. He's got youth and strength on his side, and we're looking for a complete recovery."

Bethany was relieved to hear something—anything. She stood, awkwardly at first, and shook Dorie's hand. "Thank you so much. It was kind of you. Dr. Chambers, this is my roommate, Heather."

The women nodded to each other, then they looked back at Bethany. Dorie smiled at her. "Tell you what. I'll wait for you to freshen up, to get the puffiness out of your eyes. And then why don't you follow me?"

Bethany's heart skipped a beat. Was she going to get to see Red?

Heather gave Bethany's shoulder a squeeze. "I'll see you tonight." She stood to leave.

"Thanks." Bethany jumped up to hug her and then rushed off to the bathroom. A minute later, she returned, and Dorie handed her a white lab coat. Bethany took it and slid it on over her clothes.

"Okay. Now follow me. Don't say anything, just do what I do."

Dorie began to give a medical lecture, using words that were far beyond Bethany's understanding, but she nodded and tried to look as if she was grasping the information. Sure enough, they walked past the nurses' station unnoticed.

Standing outside Red's door, Dorie winked at Bethany, then walked her to the scrub sink. At Dorie's direction, Bethany removed the white coat and together they put on gowns and masks. They washed their hands and then entered isolation. A nurse was sitting in the room, doing the charting.

Bethany had resolved to be strong in his presence, but it was harder than she'd expected once she actually saw him. Red had a nasal oxygen tube, wires connecting him to a heart monitor, and an IV hooked to his arm. He lay completely still and had almost no color.

"How's his progress?" Dorie asked.

The nurse rattled off Red's vital signs, and Dorie nodded. Then she turned to Bethany and told her about Red's history and treatment plan. She explained what they were seeing on the monitors and described the status of his IV fluid balance.

Bethany nodded, while struggling to hold it together. She couldn't tell if Red was asleep or in a coma, and she knew better than to ask.

Dorie continued. "When was he last awake?"

"About an hour ago he was somewhat lucid, but he's not all the way back yet. His reflexes are normal, and the temp seems under control. His white count *is* improving, but when we had the ophthalmology consult, they still weren't too optimistic about him regaining his eyesight."

Bethany let out a little gasp. He wouldn't be able to be a doctor, and that would break his heart! She stared at him, wishing to speak to him, longing to touch him. But she could tell from Dorie's body language that she shouldn't.

"Is the latest scan back?" Dorie asked the nurse.

"Not yet."

"Would you mind checking at the station? I'd like to see what neurology had to say."

When the nurse headed out the door, Dorie placed a gentle hand on Bethany's arm. "You've got about two minutes. If you'll whisper to him, I think he'll hear you." She moved back to allow some privacy.

Bethany moved to the bedside, reaching out to touch Red's face. She leaned over him, took a deep breath, and found her most optimistic voice. "I love you, Red. You get better, okay? I'm staying right outside your door until you do." A tear fell onto his sheet.

When she heard Dorie giving a medical description of meningitis and other neurological diseases, she knew the nurse was coming back. She wiped her eyes, stepped back, and assumed the nodding affirmation of a student.

"No new reports are in," the nurse told Dorie.

"Thank you." She motioned for Bethany to follow, and they left the room. Together they walked out of Neuro ICU and headed for the ladies' room. Once inside the door, Bethany hugged Dorie.

"How can I ever thank you? I just *had* to see him. He looks, well… I just *had* to see him."

"I know." Dorie returned the hug. "My gut feeling is that he'll do well, and I'm not just saying that to make you feel better. I know you needed to see him, and I'll bet he needed to hear you."

"But he didn't move. He didn't respond."

"That's okay. Trust me, he knew you were there."

"But what she said about his eyes…?"

Dorie nodded. "I'm sorry. It's too soon to tell." She looked at Bethany, seemingly studying her face. "Now, are *you* okay?"

Bethany nodded. "Yeah, I'll be all right. And thanks for everything."

"You're welcome." With another quick smile, Dorie went on her way. Bethany walked down the hall, taking weary steps. Waiting was hard work, the hardest work she'd ever done. She knew Red was a fighter, but how could he win a battle that was out of his control?

Maybe he can't, but the battle is the Lord's.

Dorie peeked into the isolation room in NICU and found Dr. Kedar sitting with Christina. She moved to stand beside him.

"How is she?"

Dr. Kedar motioned for her to take a seat. "About the same."

"You wanted to see me?"

"Yes. I wanted to let you know I took your copies of all the evidence up to Lexie Winters last Friday."

Dorie's eyebrows shot up. "Yeah?"

"We are convinced you are right."

She detected hesitation in his voice. "But?"

"But we have to be patient. The case has possibilities, but it is all pretty circumstantial evidence at this point. Lexie said she told you to secure your own attorney. The hospital cannot sue him for firing you, but you can. And then you can present the other evidence."

"Yes, but if I go up against Ophion, I need the strength of the *hospital's* legal force behind me. It would be stronger as a corporate case, not a private one."

Dr. Kedar nodded. "I told her that."

"What did she say?"

"She listened. She is a reasonable woman."

"And?"

"I would not expect anything to happen soon. She has many other cases."

Dorie heaved a frustrated sigh and shook her head. "Does somebody have to die here?"

Dr. Kedar looked at her, compassion in his eyes. "I know. It is not right, but probably. If not an injury, then a major lawsuit against the hospital. Those kinds of things have a way of expediting the legal process." He looked over to check his niece, then back at Dorie. "Have you been up to see Red?"

Dorie sighed again. So much for her hopes that there'd been any progress in the case against VIP. "Yes, a few hours ago. He's still semiconscious. It's been a long week, but he's stable. Did Dr. Fawdry call you, by any chance?"

Dr. Kedar nodded.

"Do you know if they found anything when they searched Damon's locker?"

"Nothing. The contact solution they found in his locker came back clear. Only the solution in Red's locker was contaminated."

Dorie stared at him. "Contact solution? In Damon's locker?"

"What is it, Dorie?"

"Dr. Kedar, Damon doesn't *wear* contacts."

Dr. Fawdry looked up from his desk to see a smiling detective, Cory Armstrong, standing in his doorway.

"I've got an arrest warrant from the Assistant U.S. Attorney's office." His grin broadened. "Want to come with me?"

"What? But I thought…" Dr. Fawdry motioned for his friend to come in. "You'd better bring me up to speed. I thought we had nothing."

Cory sat down across from him. "The solution found in Dr. Damon's locker was clear. No meningitis. But we *did* find Dr. Richison's fingerprints on the bottle. My guess is, Dr. Damon switched out the clean solution and replaced it with a contaminated one. Also, we followed up on that other tip from the chief resident and questioned Richison's ex-girlfriend. Her testimony was that she didn't mess up the apartment. We searched there and didn't find any prints, but we got a neighbor who thinks she can place Dr. Damon's car there on the day of the break-in. The records do show it happened on an afternoon when Damon was off and while Richison was on call. But that part's all pretty circumstantial."

Dr. Fawdry shook his head. "Too many holes in that case. Dr. Damon can say he found Red's solution on the counter and put it away to give him later. Even if we get him on breaking and entering, that's a much lesser charge."

The detective smiled. "Precisely. So while the evidence in the locker seemed to confirm we were on the right track, in the end it wasn't much help. Then we found out Dr. Damon doesn't wear contacts, so our guys took a closer look at the contaminated solution. And we found a tiny puncture in the top, where the cover snaps on. Our working hypothesis was that Damon must have injected the fluid all the way through the bottle when he couldn't unscrew the lid—it doesn't really come off—and then he couldn't fit a needle into the top opening. The needle he used was a larger bore. So we emptied the contents of all the syringe receptacles on the L and D floor and—"

"We don't empty those until they're full!"

"Correct. And that did it! We found one 5cc syringe that had a different bore needle than those the L and D nurses generally use. So we studied it and found Dr. Damon's fingerprints *and* traces of the contaminated spinal fluid. There was even a bit of plastic on the needle that matched the contact solution bottle."

Dr. Fawdry slapped his desk. "Hot *dog!*" Now he was grinning. "Let's go wish Dr. Damon a happy Halloween. I wonder how he's going to like his new pinstripe costume?"

Dorie leaned against the wall of the elevator. Morning rounds had gone smoothly for a change. Thank goodness. She could use a break.

She got off the elevator, followed by an intern and two medical students. Turning the corner to approach L and D, she was greeted with signs of the season: cardboard black cats, skeletons suspended from the ceiling, and plastic jack-o'-lanterns at each end of the counter. At the far side of the desk, two giggling nurses were feeding Damon some Halloween candy. *Ah, once again Sir Damon is holding court, wowing his next conquests with charm and wit.*

Disgusted, Dorie turned to quiz her entourage, but before she could speak, the electronic L and D doors burst open. She looked over, as she always did when someone came through, wondering if something would require her immediate attention.

She watched as Dr. Fawdry entered, flanked by a man in a suit and a uniformed officer. The doctor pointed to Damon but remained by the door as the other two approached the desk.

So he really is responsible for what happened to Red! Damon, how could you?

The man in the suit looked at Damon. "May we have a word with you?"

"Of course!" Damon eyed the officer. Then he laughed it off. "I know, it's Halloween; you can't trick me!"

The nurses snickered and retreated to their positions behind the desk.

The officer pulled out a set of handcuffs. "Dr. Damon? Dennis Damon?"

Dorie wondered how Damon could be so cocky. Was he really so self-assured that it didn't occur to him he'd been caught? "That's me. Hey, who put you up to this anyway?"

"Dr. Damon, you have the right to remain silent…"

Damon looked over at one of the nurses, and his laughter grew a bit more nervous. "Did you arrange this? I'm impressed. It almost looks real."

"Dr. Damon." The officer's steely glare showed no sense of humor, and the grin on Damon's face began to slip. "Anything you say can and will be used against you in a court of law…"

Dorie noticed Damon was breaking into a sweat. Maybe he was finally getting it.

The officer cuffed him and escorted him out of L and D. As they left, Dorie heard Damon saying, "Unbelievable! I don't know who set this up, but—"

The door swung shut behind them, cutting off Damon's protest. Dorie stared at the floor, saddened that a doc who had been a friend, and someone with so much potential, would destroy his own life—after ruining someone else's.

That evening Dorie caught Bethany as she was leaving. "Have you got a minute?"

Bethany turned to her with a weary smile. "Sure."

Dorie pointed the way to a waiting area and sat down, motioning for Bethany to join her. "I guess you know that Red's regained full consciousness."

"Yes!"

Bethany's face was practically glowing, and Dorie smiled. She, too, was relieved that Red seemed on the road to recovery. She looked around the empty waiting area. "I thought you might like to know that the Dallas police made an arrest today."

"An arrest?" Bethany cocked her head. "Why?"

"Did Red ever mention a doc named Denny Damon?"

"Sure."

"Did he ever mention there was some tension between them?"

"Uh-huh." Bethany stared, wide-eyed. "Why?"

"Well, it looks like Damon took contaminated spinal fluid from one of the patients and put it in Red's contact solution."

"*What?*" Bethany's face flushed, then grew white as the meaning of Dorie's words penetrated.

Dorie nodded. "I'm sorry."

Tears streamed down Bethany's cheeks. "Someone did this on *purpose?* How could anybody… Dorie, even if Red does make it through this, he might never practice medicine again, never see my face, drive his car… He might be *blind,* all because someone—oh, that is so low!" Bethany's eyes flashed. "This has been the longest two weeks of my life, not knowing if Red was going to make it. Not knowing if he'll see. Knowing how much pain he's suffered. I can't believe anyone would be so cruel as to do this on *purpose.* What could possibly justify…?"

Dorie shook her head. "Bethany, Red doesn't know yet. Dr. Kedar is supposed to tell him soon. I'm so sorry."

Bethany's hand clenched the armrest. "Do you think Damon did it because of the VIP stuff? How much does he know about what we were investigating?"

"It's hard to say. But he must have been afraid of *something.*"

Her eyes burned. "Do you think his arrest will improve our chances of shutting down VIP?"

"Shut it down? Doubtful. I'd hate to see that happen anyway. I only want to make sure abortion is done safely and legally. I want Ophion gone, but it's really a good clinic; we just need to weed out the bad docs. Apparently Damon was one of them." She shook her head. Enough about that. "I also thought you might like to know more about Red's prognosis."

"Yes, I would."

"We've been using antiviral therapy intravenously, and his eyes are showing slight improvement. But the cornea is still scarred and cloudy, so he has limited vision. We'd consider a corneal transplant—as he improves, that might be an option in the future. But there's always concern that the virus could reactivate and cause damage or rejection of the transplant."

Bethany leaned back in her chair. Not only was Red's illness caused intentionally, but he might reject a corneal transplant? And then there was the moral wasteland at VIP… She shook her head. *O Lord, I need Your strength more than ever!*

THIRTY-TWO

Red lay in his hospital room, still on limited isolation status. He was listening to music when he heard a knock and turned over to face the door. "Hello?" He couldn't make out who was there, so he reached over to turn on the bedside light.

"Hi, Red." It was Dr. Kedar. He came to the side of the bed and extended his hand. Red reached out to take it, but didn't quite connect.

Dr. Kedar moved his hand to grasp Red's. "How are you? You gave us quite a scare."

Red nodded. "I don't recommend this deal to anyone."

"How well can you see me?"

Red peered at him, struggling to focus. It was no use. "It's a bit like opening your eyes underwater without goggles. And there's this sort of Swiss cheese pattern. I've got spots where I see better in some places than others. Fortunately, the eye doc told me today that he expects me to regain more of my sight, though he exercised extreme caution when I asked him *how* much."

"No doubt." Dr. Kedar continued to stand by the bed. "Nobody wants to make promises, but I do not want you to worry about anything, Red, least of all your career. I will take care of things, both with the hospital and your rotations. You can work in the lab until you recover; I can use your help with ongoing research."

Who was he kidding? "What could I do with such limited sight?"

"Plenty. You will see. We can get you a screen magnifier for the computer, and some voice recognition software. While you have been so sick, Christina has continued to do well. She has given me near heart failure at least once a week"—there was a smile in his voice—"but if you can believe it, she will pass four weeks tomorrow! I have been getting national inquiries about the setup; apparently our attempts to keep it out of the media have failed."

Dr. Kedar scooted a chair over and sat with him. Red was touched by such an unusual gesture from the chief.

"So I need someone here who understands what we have done who can also deal with the media. You could handle all that for me, Red. I cannot spend all my time talking to other hospitals and reporters. This could be huge for the hospital, for my career, and, more important, for the tiny lives we can save."

Red's heart leapt. Dr. Kedar had always given him more opportunities than he felt he deserved, and this was no exception. "I would enjoy that a lot, but you'll have to catch me up on what happened while I've been on vacation."

Dr. Kedar took a deep breath. "Now, I am afraid I have some bad news. I need to tell you how you got this nasty strain of meningitis."

Red pulled back and shook his head. "You know? How could *anyone* know?"

"Yes, we know. But you are not going to like what I have to tell you."

Red listened in stunned silence as Dr. Kedar unfolded the events leading up to Damon's arrest. When he had finished, Red lay speechless.

"Are you okay?" Dr. Kedar's voice echoed with his concern, and Red fought to speak past the anger that threatened to choke him. "How could even Damon have done this?" He waved his arms as he spoke. "It's devastating—to think someone would do this on *purpose*. Makes me want to... Well, violence comes to mind."

Dr. Kedar patted Red's shoulder, and Red sank back into his pillow. He felt a tear roll down the side of his face. "But why? We didn't begin to get along, but why would he try to hurt me? He could have *killed* me."

"Red, the police are trying to determine why this happened. But I know you as a spiritual man. Your faith will help you though this, though I do not claim to understand it."

Red nodded. Dr. Kedar was right. As much as Red wanted to dwell on his anger, he couldn't deny the fact that God had kept him from the most severe consequences of Damon's actions. "I have no doubt that I'm here today because God protected me"—he swallowed hard—"and He can accomplish whatever He wants. But still, evil is evil. The guy trashed my apartment, broke my stuff, took most of my sight, maybe my career. I don't have to like it—and I don't."

"Good. If you were not angry, I would assume you were in denial," Dr. Kedar said.

"Does Bethany know about this?"

"Yes. Dr. Chambers informed her."

Both men said nothing for a long moment. Finally Dr. Kedar spoke again. "I do have something to tell you that you might be *glad* to know. Do you remember what I mentioned the night Christina was born? About using fetal tissue from VIP."

Red swallowed. "Yes."

"I never said anything more about it, but I did notice how much that upset you, even though you refrained from saying anything. It is the only other time I have seen you so upset. You were moved by the life of my niece and clearly disturbed by the fetal work. And I confess, that night, it felt strange to save a seventeen-week-old baby, while at the same time buying the fetal tissue of babies aborted at her age. Each day as I have watched Christina, I have found it more difficult to convince myself that such a tiny life is just a biological specimen. We keep driving back the age of viability, and it has made it harder to justify using abortive fetal tissue, even though it is for a good cause."

Red nodded, angling a smile at his friend. "And *you* seem to have exploded the age of viability with Christina."

"Yes, Red. So I have made a decision, and I wanted you to be the first to know. I have temporarily cancelled my order for fetal specimens, at least until I can further think through all the ramifications."

Red reached out, took Dr. Kedar's hand, and squeezed it. "I've seen you caring for the micropreemie babies, even when they don't make it. You care for them gently, tenderly, with all the respect due the human beings that they are. It's one of the reasons I regard you so highly. And Christina, nobody—and I mean *nobody*—would've even given her a shot. But you did."

Dr. Kedar's voice cracked as he spoke. "I am just trying to be a good physician and a good uncle. Besides, those babies have been *born*."

"Right. Their place of residence has changed from the womb to your neonatal unit, but as you wondered, how is a seventeen-weeker fundamentally different from your twenty-one-week-old niece? Size, nutritional demands, oxygen demands, that's it. It's all on a continuum. So if we backtrack, when was Christina *not* a human being? And how do we know? Can't we go all the way back to the first cell?"

Dr. Kedar pondered his words. "You have continued to make me think about many things. Science tells us how, but you also talk about the *why*. Medicine is more than technical expertise; there is also a moral element, the what *should* we do or what *ought* we do. If your presupposition is correct—that God exists and that humans are made in God's image—then it is being human that confers dignity, not function or size."

Red marveled at the words coming from Dr. Kedar's mouth. "Yes. That's why I love medicine. It brings me daily to the intersection, the beautiful intersection, of both the why and the how." Red grew solemn again. "I just hope I can still *practice* medicine someday."

A minute after Dr. Kedar left, Red heard the most comforting sound in the world: Bethany's voice.

"Red! You're awake!" She came to his side and enveloped him in a hug, then kissed his forehead. "How are you feeling?"

He pressed his face into her hair, savoring her nearness. "M'm, you smell great. And you look great too."

"Really, can you see me?"

He grinned. "What difference does *that* make?"

She giggled and took his hand. "I see you still have an IV, and they made me gown. They said I could hug you, but can I hold you yet?"

"Absolutely! I thought you'd never ask. In my medical opinion, your holding me is great for my ailment, or for any ailment."

She wrapped him in her arms and rested her head against his.

A moment later he heard her sniffling. "Listen, darlin', I didn't come through all this to give up now. We're gonna be okay."

"But, Red—"

"I know. They aren't sure about the eyesight, but it's getting better." He forced optimism into his tone.

"Can you see anything? Can you see me?"

"I can see some things. It's just kind of spotty. My ophthalmologist has refracted my eyes and is having some lenses made for me. I should have those tomorrow. They'll be ugly as sin—I'll look like a walking magnifying glass—but this is no time for vanity. Besides, at least my brain seems to be working, and my memory's intact. Uh, who are you again?"

Her playful smack on the arm made him laugh.

"Red! Don't even kid about that! You were so sick."

He took her hand. "I know, though I don't remember much of it. Anyway, I'm glad you're here. I've had pretty depressing news. Why would Damon do this to me?"

"It has to have something to do with VIP, and it looks like even if we somehow are able to bring Ophion to justice, the clinic will still go on, just like before. So in the end, what difference have we made for all you've lost here?"

The pain in her voice troubled him, and he squeezed her hand as she continued.

"Have we just helped to provide safer abortions? I don't want women to get hurt, but safer abortions? We put ourselves through all this so women could have safer abortions?"

Red wished he had a good answer, but he'd wondered the same thing. "I don't know, Bethany. But I do know that the Lord has His own purposes—*good* purposes—in all this that are beyond our earthly vision." He reflected on the conversation he'd just had with Dr. Kedar. "Maybe the Lord's plans in this are bigger than one clinic—even a *big* clinic."

The next morning Red adjusted his bed so he could sit up and look at his visitor. "I didn't expect you to drop by again so soon, Dr. Kedar."

"I was on my way to my deposition."

"Nervous?"

"No. I guess I learned a long time ago to do the best I could and take what comes with the job. Anyway, I have what I think you will consider good news."

"I could sure use some!"

"You know we cannot discuss the lawsuit we are both involved in…"

Red nodded. "Right."

"But I *can* tell you that I spoke again with Lexie late yesterday in preparation for today. And after the way the evidence unfolded in Dr. Damon's misconduct, with his committing a crime here on hospital property, she has asked to look at all the records that you and Dorie gave me."

Red could hear the triumph in Dr. Kedar's voice.

"Red, I have a feeling the hospital may actually get involved."

Dalmuth sat on the heavy leather sofa in Lexie Winters's office. It had been nearly three months since he'd received the intent-to-sue documents, and he was ready to get on with it. He and Lexie had reviewed the case from every imaginable angle, working through the possible questions he might face. This sort of exercise used to make his palms sweat, but not now. That was why he paid the huge malpractice insurance premiums—so he could sleep at night.

Lexie walked in and greeted him. "Everyone's here. We're video-taping the testimony, which is normal procedure. Now remember, answer the questions truthfully, but don't elaborate or volunteer information. And don't let Melvin McMann, the other side's attorney, throw you off track. That's his job. He will try to get you to give testimony contradicting what you wrote in the interrogatories."

Dalmuth nodded.

Lexie leaned her elbows on her desk. "Don't get defensive or try to be persuasive. You can't convince the opposing attorney; don't even try. You know you did a good job, so let the facts speak for themselves. If McMann asks anything you don't understand, ask him to rephrase the question. When he finishes asking you anything, pause for a second to give me time to object, if necessary. That will also keep your answers from looking rehearsed. He will ask if we talked about the case, they all ask that. Tell the truth. Of course we did. Any client discusses a case with his attorney. Just tell them that I advised you to answer truthfully, because I did. And remember, whatever you say here is as legally binding as anything you would say in court."

"Yes." Dalmuth rose and took a deep breath, determined to get it over with. *He won't beat me.*

He and Lexie walked together to the legal department's conference room, which had been set up for the deposition. High-backed gray leather swivel chairs surrounded a long mahogany conference table. At one end, a court reporter sat with her keyboard, and at the other the video camera operator was making an adjustment to his equipment.

Lexie introduced Dalmuth to the counsel for VIP, Skip Avers, then to Melvin McMann, the attorney "representing the plaintiff in action No. 77-091498-L, DeVeer vs. Kedar et al." Dalmuth looked him in the eye and shook hands, knowing they probably had about eight hours of questioning ahead. He didn't relish the thought of such a long day. Then he raised his right hand and vowed to "tell the truth, the whole truth, and nothing but the truth."

Mr. McMann opened his files, looked at Dalmuth, and spoke with an air of superiority. "I want to be sure you understand each question as I pose it, Doctor. I will be happy to rephrase anything that you deem unclear."

"Thank you," Dalmuth said flatly. Then, starting with his full name and address, he began to answer questions.

Several days later Lexie Winters listened as Dr. Ophion sat in the same conference room enduring the same routine. Ophion had done his best to shift the blame to the hospital, pointing out that Damon was trained by this hospital and that Dr. Kedar elected to do the hysterectomy at the hospital. In addition, the hospital staff had helped to remove this "poor woman's" uterus. He had gone on to state that perforation was a known complication of abortion, particularly at this patient's stage of pregnancy, and she had knowingly signed a consent form.

Dr. Ophion concluded his attack on Dr. Kedar with biting words. "Many of these cases respond to conservative therapy; you control the bleeding and administer antibiotics. But Dr. Kedar opted for the radical approach. This approach cost this young woman her future, her fertility."

Lexie had anticipated this line of attack. Now at the end of the day, she leaned back and relaxed as Melvin McMann, the plaintiff's attorney, questioned Ophion. Both men were coming across as more pompous and abrasive than usual, and she had to purse her lips together to stifle a grin.

Melvin was working hard to get Ophion to say anything under oath that might pump up the settlement. Knowing Melvin as she did from past experience, she figured he was willing to go to trial because he believed he could convince a jury to sympathize with Ms. DeVeer. Nevertheless, she knew he'd prefer a huge, quick settlement so he could pocket his percentage and move on to the next victim.

As Melvin went through his list of questions, he seemed to enjoy running the show. Dr. Ophion read Dr. Damon's clinic notes from the chart and stated that everything had been done properly—the sono diagnosis, the analgesia, and the surgical procedure. When a complication had arisen, it was Dr. Ophion's professional opinion that Dr. Damon—who was, again, trained by *this* hospital—responded quickly and appropriately. Damon had transferred the patient, in good condition, to the hospital, and that had been the clinic's only involvement. In fact, Dr. Ophion insisted, he himself had been completely uninvolved in this particular case.

Dr. Ophion's attorney, Skip Avers, took a few minutes to get his client to clarify several points. Lexie wanted to roll her eyes when, at this juncture, Ophion puffed up with the arrogance only a white-coated pseudodeity could muster and declared how, as the head of the VIP clinic, he was always getting summoned to these dog-and-pony shows. He went on to express his resentment of the imposition on his time and to declare how the record showed VIP to be a first-class operation.

Finally, when everyone else had passed the witness, it was Lexie's turn. Ophion had made a show of checking his watch every few minutes. Avers had done his best to speed things along, but by now the doctor was drumming his fingers.

Lexie began by getting the rundown on the clinic, including its high volume of cases and the bottom line of its gross receipts. Skip Avers objected, stating this was irrelevant, but Ophion forged ahead, clearly taking the opportunity to boast about the clinic's financial success.

Beginning with a line of routine questioning, Lexie asked Dr. Ophion about the types of procedures VIP performed. Dr. Ophion described the D and C procedure.

"And how many first- and second-trimester abortions do you perform each year?"

Dr. Ophion stated the figures.

"Does your clinic ever do third-trimester abortions?"

Ophion practically sneered. "Of course not. They're illegal in this state."

Lexie nodded. "And are there any other procedures or protocols that you didn't mention?"

"No ma'am. Women's health, abortion services, that's all we do."

"Besides the surgical procedures, are there no other protocols? RU-486? The morning-after pill?"

"Those two are not the same." Dr. Ophion's tone suggested that he considered the question moronic.

Lexie didn't bite. "Your clinic does offer those approaches as well?"

"Yes ma'am."

"I'm sorry. I thought you said you did no other procedures or protocols besides the surgical ones." She turned to the reporter. "Could you please read back the deposition for Dr. Oph—"

"Yes, yes"— he waved his hand—"I meant no other *surgical* procedures. I did say we offer the full range of abortion services."

"Thank you, Doctor. Now could you explain the morning-after pill and how it works?"

As if speaking to a child, Ophion began. "The label 'morning-after pill' is a misnomer, as most women really use a multiple dose of a standard birth control pill, usually taken before pregnancy has occurred, but certainly before the embryo has implanted."

"Thank you. And the RU-486?"

Ophion exhaled a long-suffering sigh. "After pregnancy has been confirmed, we prescribe two medications to induce private abortion. The first, RU-486, is a progesterone blocker that works best only during the first trimester. The ovary produces progesterone after ovulation, and in a pregnant patient, progesterone continues to be produced at a high level to sustain the pregnancy. RU-486 stops the ovary from producing this hormone, causing the implanted embryo to spontaneously abort. After that, the patient comes back so we can confirm that the first medication has worked. Then we have her take the second, which is a prostaglandin. That one makes the uterus expel the products of conception."

"So, Doctor, the RU-486 protocol requires two visits to the clinic and the two different medications that you mentioned"—Lexie glanced down at her notes—"the RU-486, and this other one, the *prostaglandin,* as you called it."

"Yes, that is correct."

Lexie cast a glance toward Melvin, noting that he looked bored. Neither he nor Dr. Ophion seemed to have caught on to where this was going. *Good!*

"Is there any medical reason for using the RU-486 alone? As you've explained it, both medications are required to effect a safe termination of pregnancy, right?"

Ophion nodded. "Yes, that is correct."

Lexie leaned over and opened her briefcase. After removing some papers with a list of names, she handed copies to each of the attorneys. "Dr. Ophion, do you recognize these names as patients that have been treated at your clinic?"

Dr. Ophion and his attorney looked at each other, reached for the documents, and fumbled through the pages.

"I don't recall," Ophion said. "I don't know the patient names; we see thousands every year."

Lexie spoke with a firm steadiness. "These are patients, Dr. Ophion, whom you treated personally with RU-486. And I have documents here, notarized affidavits from patients and the pharmacy, that you repeatedly failed to order or prescribe the prostaglandin that you yourself testified was essential for correctly terminating a pregnancy by this medically accepted protocol."

Skip Avers glared at Lexie. "Object to the form of the question. He turned to Ophion. "You don't have to answer that. It's been a long day. My client needs a break."

I'm sure he does. Lexie maintained a poker face and nodded. "Of course." She watched with satisfaction as Avers and his client hurried out.

Take all the time you need. She leaned back in her chair. *You'll be answering these questions now or later. I've got you now!*

THIRTY-THREE

Lexie glanced at her watch. Avers and Ophion had been gone for fifteen minutes. She was about to go check on them when the door opened and they returned.

Avers took his seat and met Lexie's gaze. "We've been here for eight hours already. Any chance we could finish this up soon?"

Lexie feigned a sympathetic look. "I do have a few more questions for you, Doctor, but I'd be happy to reschedule another day."

Ophion's expression hardened. "No, thanks. We'll proceed, as long as it doesn't take all night."

She inclined her head. "No, no, of course not."

"I've advised my client to restrict his remarks to facts pertinent to the case," Avers insisted.

Lexie nodded. "Of course."

The video operator and the stenographer resumed, and Lexie plunged in. "We're back on the record. We were discussing cases related to RU-486 when we took our break." She brought the papers to the table.

"I object!" Avers turned to Ophion. "Do not answer questions about patients not pertinent to the present lawsuit." He glared at Lexie. "Let's keep this to the case at hand, shall we?"

Lexie nodded. "Yes, of course. I'm merely exploring a possible pattern of substandard medical care"—she smiled—"which *does* relate directly to the present case, and to your client's veracity as a witness."

"I'm not going to let him answer, and a judge will have to decide if these questions are pertinent."

Lexie nodded. "That's fine." *Because now they're part of the permanent record.* She turned back to the witness. "All right, Dr. Ophion, let's return to matters which your counsel considers more pertinent to this case. You mentioned Dr. Damon, who you said, I believe, was trained by this hospital."

"Yes." Ophion's answer dripped with disdain.

"And he is employed at your clinic?"

"He was, until recently."

"Until his recent arrest, isn't that correct, Doctor?"

Ophion shifted in his chair. "Yes."

"And what was his position?"

"He was a GYN chief resident who worked regularly at the clinic."

"I see. And at the time he assumed his current position, he was early in his fourth year of ob-gyn training, correct?"

"Yes, I believe that's right."

"So he would have some experience with the procedures?"

Ophion hesitated. "Yes. He was a competent physician and a skilled operator."

"Did he hold an administrative position at the clinic?"

"Yes."

"And was he compensated for this position?"

"Yes."

"And what would his salary be?"

"I object to the question," Avers said. Ophion looked at him and shrugged, as if to suggest he didn't mind answering, so Avers nodded. "You may answer if you wish."

"He was paid two thousand dollars per month on top of a monthly rate for actual operating."

"How was he appointed to this position of responsibility?"

Ophion sneered. "*I* selected him after terminating his predecessor for cause. My decision was based on his employment history and his absolute competence as a physician."

Lexie paused. "For cause? Terminated for cause? What was the cause of the dismissal?"

"Dr. Chambers, a female resident, couldn't do the job. She was unstable and unable to handle the pressure."

"Is it your testimony, Doctor, that Dr. Chambers's dismissal had no connection to the files I previously showed you regarding patients given RU-486?"

Avers snapped to attention. "I object! Don't answer that, Doctor. As I've said, we'll not address cases other than that of the particular patient involved in this suit."

Lexie nodded. "In your opinion, Dr. Damon was competent and able to handle the pressure—I believe that was your wording?"

"Yes, I think so, though he was not in the position for very long."

"How did he conduct himself in this position?"

"He did an adequate job."

"Thank you, Doctor." Lexie leaned back in her chair, then held up a hand. "Oh, let me ask one further question regarding Dr. Damon."

"Yes?"

"He has made a statement to the police that you encouraged him to *solve a problem* the clinic was having with a certain Dr. Richison, who was also named in this case. Can you confirm or deny this?"

Avers nearly came out his chair on that one. "I object! I object strongly! Don't answer that question!"

"That weasel!" Ophion blurted out. "I had *nothing* to do with that! That moron took it upon himself!"

"Quiet!" Avers shouted. "Don't say another word." He stood, his hands planted on the table. "This deposition is finished!"

The following Monday Red took a cab to the hospital. He pushed back the thick, black-rimmed glasses inching their way down his nose. Would he ever get used to these things? While he had worn corrective lens since childhood, these were cumbersome—besides which, they distorted parts of the visual field. He pressed his temples, trying to relieve the pain from his daily headache. Unfortunately, he could focus only for short periods of time, and that made any significant reading nearly impossible. The process of reviewing to prepare for the deposition, in addition to the prospect of scrutinizing charts in front of the lawyers for the next six to eight hours, was a bit formidable. *I hope I can handle it.* He made his way to Lexie Winters's office and sat in a chair outside her door. He tapped his foot, then stilled it when he realized what he was doing. Okay, so he was nervous. He'd never given a deposition before.

"Hello, Red. How are you?" He felt a hand on his shoulder.

"Dr. Kedar!" Red rose to greet him. "I didn't expect to run into you here. How's Christina?"

"Keep your seat, please." Dr. Kedar took the chair next to Red. "She is doing well. I am working on her oxygen saturation, hoping to transition her out of the tank."

"Yes. I heard on the news that you're hoping to take her out in another three or four weeks."

"Anytime you want to come back, I can use your help. We have hospitals, MFM docs, and the media calling, all wanting to know more."

"You sure you want me on TV right now? I have a face for radio."

Dr. Kedar chuckled. "You look fine, but whatever makes you comfortable."

"Maybe in another week."

"How have you been feeling?"

"It's been a long week at home. I'm bored. My vision is about the same, and I'm itching to get back to work. I seem to be gaining more energy every day. Bethany picks me up and takes me over to her place when she gets off work, but the days are long. Someone needs to prosecute the networks over the pathetic daytime television lineup."

"Good to see you, Red." It was Dorie's voice.

Again, he stood. "Hey, Dorie. I didn't expect you to be here either."

Just then, Lexie opened her door. "I'm pleased you three could make it. Red, how are you? That was quite a scare you gave us."

"Thank you, I'm okay." He hesitated. "Ms. Winters, why is everyone here for my deposition?"

"Because you're not going to have a deposition."

At Lexie's words, Red groaned inwardly. Would they have to reschedule? "Why not?"

"No?" Dr. Kedar asked at the same time.

"No," Lexie said, and Red had the impression she was smiling. "But I wanted to talk to the three of you together." She motioned them into her office.

Dr. Kedar leaned over and spoke in Red's ear. "I am as surprised as you are. I have no idea why I am here."

"Have a seat, everyone," Lexie said.

The three doctors sat, while Lexie leaned up against the edge of her desk. "I wanted to let you know about something that happened with Dr. Ophion last week during his deposition." She looked at Dorie. "The information you put together was invaluable in helping with this case, and with several others."

Dr. Kedar scooted forward in his chair. "What happened?"

Lexie filled them in on the events as they had unfolded. When she mentioned Ophion's reaction to Damon's claim, Red tensed.

"But there's more," she added. "And that's why I wanted you all here today. Dr. Kedar"—she looked over at Red—"and Dr. Richison, you are dropped from the lawsuit."

"Excellent!" Dr. Kedar's relief was clear.

"What do you mean?" Red asked.

"Your *esteemed* colleague had just enough rope to hang himself. He is in, shall we say, a difficult position legally. The plaintiff attorney, having heard the evidence, has also dropped the hospital in this case. He determined that you did nothing actionable and tells me they have a settlement meeting arranged with Dr. Ophion's suddenly eager counsel. There was no malpractice on the part of the hospital. You used your best medical judgment and took an acceptable, safe course of action. The patient recovered well from your procedure and is healthy today because of your care—at least that's how I painted it, and they really had no effective recourse. Because we were able to shatter Ophion's credibility with the RU-486 cases, he doesn't want to have to answer any more questions. He wants to put this all behind him, so he's pushing to get the case settled, whatever it takes."

Red gripped the arms of his chair. "From what you said, it sounds like Ophion knew something about what Damon did to me."

"Yes, it does." Lexie turned to Dorie. "And now the hospital has turned the tables, thanks to your investigation into the facts and the evidence you all supplied. We're going after Dr. Ophion, and we're taking it beyond this case. Our legal staff is working to reevaluate and perhaps shift settlements from us to the clinic on several previous cases. Dr. Ophion seems to be in a generous mood now, which he needs to be if he has any hope of keeping his license. It will take six to twelve months before he'll know for sure if he can continue practicing medicine, and I'm glad to say that's looking unlikely."

The doctors smiled at each other, relieved yet still reserved. Although the news was good, the gravity of the situation made celebration seem almost irreverent.

"So Ophion's problems are just beginning," Lexie continued. "And I know from my connections with the state's attorney that a federal indictment is on the way for insurance fraud and possibly for wanton endangerment. We have medical malpractice here for sure, and the certainty of winning on the punitive, since the malpractice was intentional. All this is to say that I'm certain Dr. Ophion is through. Probably the best he can hope for is having his license suspended for five years."

"What's the worst?" Dr. Kedar asked.

"Time in the penitentiary."

"And the clinic?" Dorie asked. "What do you think will happen there?"

Lexie waved it off. "I doubt all this will hurt the clinic, because technically it will no longer exist. The word in the legal world is that they're trying to sell the whole operation so they can reorganize and reopen under a new name, with Dr. Ophion's partner maintaining a managerial position."

"Will that work?" Dorie asked.

"Probably, depending on whether their interested buyer decides to go for it. They may be closed for a week or two, but I doubt this problem with Dr. Ophion will shut it down altogether.

Red sighed. *So all that effort gets Ophion, but the clinic work goes on.*

Outside Lexie's office, Dr. Kedar put a hand on Red's shoulder. "Would you like to see Christina before you go?"

"Yes, I'd love to, though I don't know how much I could see."

Dr. Kedar guided him down to NICU. Inside Christina's room, Red bent down and peered into the tank. He gasped. "She's grown so much!"

"Yes, she is so amazing." Dr. Kedar leaned over next to him.

They were mesmerized, like children looking at snow falling for the first time. Finally Dr. Kedar broke the silence. "I have been thinking a lot about our conversations, Red. I have been wondering, do you have a formal religious affiliation or training, or are you are just generally a spiritual person?"

Red shrugged. "No formal training. As for affiliation, well, a lot of people say we all worship the same God, but I don't believe that. I think the greatest marvel in history was that the Creator of the universe would make Himself the size of an embryo, complete a full gestation, and be born a human baby."

"Christianity…"

"Yes."

"And you believe in miracles, do you not?"

Red smiled and pointed to Christina. "How about that one, Uncle Doctor?"

"Oh! That reminds me!" Dr. Kedar jumped up. "I have to show you what I had made for her, as a surprise for my sister on the day they take her home." He went over to one of the cabinets and pulled out a T-shirt that would fit a doll. On the front it said, "I'm a Taylor Tot," and on the back, "I'm a graduate of NICU."

Red smiled and moved to clap his friend on the back. "It's wonderful, as is she."

Dr. Kedar glanced back at Christina. "Yes, wonderful."

Fearfully and wonderfully made. Thank You, Lord.

Teresa Murdock had gone to the Women's Choice Clinic on her lunch break to get Bethany's signature on some legal papers. She was headed out when someone called to her from the hallway.

Teresa turned around and saw Diana. "Hey." She smiled.

"How are you?" Diana walked toward her.

"Actually I've been thinking about talking to you."

"Really? I've got a few minutes right now. Is this a good time?"

Teresa shrugged. "Sure, I guess."

Diana motioned toward her office and led the way. When they were seated with knees almost touching, Diana looked at her expectantly.

"We have an opportunity to possibly adopt twins."

A huge grin crossed Diana's face. She learned forward and hugged Teresa. "That's wonderful!" She sat back down and beamed at her friend.

Teresa gave her a half smile and filled in the details. She ended by saying, "Fortunately, we have time to get used to the idea."

"Get used to the idea?" Diana shifted in her chair. "Teresa, you hardly seem excited."

"That's just it. I'm afraid to get excited. Sometimes it seems like hope makes it harder. Then I might have to deal with the disappointment that follows."

"You're afraid it'll fall through?"

Teresa nodded. "Of course. Lots of birth mothers change their minds."

"How can I help?" Diana asked.

Teresa sighed. "We told our families, and they were ecstatic, but I'm afraid to let go and celebrate. So now some of them question whether I really want these babies. And I *do* want them. It's just that sometimes I wonder if I'll *ever* be able to feel unbridled joy again."

Diana gave her a kind smile. "I hear that a lot from people who've been through loss. And it's okay to be reserved about it. But I'll tell you this. Never underestimate the human heart. It has amazing resiliency."

At two o'clock Dalmuth awakened with a start. He sat up, panting, struggling to calm his heart.

He closed his eyes. *That was terrible.* He'd dreamed of Christina, that he'd lost her to kidney failure. The pain of that scene sliced through him, and he lay trying to think of his caseload—of *anything* else—but he couldn't shake the memory.

After trying unsuccessfully for an hour to forget about the dream, he got up, pulled on his scrubs, and drove down to the hospital to check on her. All the way there he muttered, "O God, let her live, please let her live…"

An enormous wave of relief came over him when he stepped into the room and found her alive, with good color and all systems functioning normally. He rolled the stainless-steel stool over next to her and sat, watching in wonder by the light streaming through the cracked door. As the minutes ticked by, he thought more about the conversation he'd had with Red two days earlier.

God, I have been wondering about You for a long time. Is it really true? Did You become a human embryo? That seems impossible.

As he stared at his niece, his mind kept circling from spiritual things back to Christina and then to the mysteries of it all. He thought about the night of her birth, when every colleague but Red told him he was crazy. *But Red believes in miracles, so he supported me. O God, please save her life. And if You are there...*

As Dalmuth watched Christina, her eyelid flickered. His eyes widened. Had he imagined it? Then it happened again. A moment later his tiny, twenty-two-week-old niece opened her eyes for the first time and looked up at him.

Dalmuth gasped. Then he reached down into the tank through the solution and touched her palm with his fingertip. As she continued to hold his gaze, Christina wrapped her tiny hand around his index finger. And Dalmuth wept.

And I believe too.

THIRTY-FOUR

At eleven-thirty Red heard a knock at the door. He walked to it, put his hand on the deadbolt, and then stopped. "Who is it?"

"It's Bethany. I took an early lunch and came to give you a ride. Don't you have an appointment with Dr. Kedar today?"

He opened the door. "Thanks! I was just getting ready to call a cab."

"I know, but it was a great excuse to see you."

"I do wish I could see *you* better." He caught himself. *No whining allowed, Richison.* "Even so, I can tell you are more beautiful than ever."

"And you—*you're* looking fine yourself."

"Right. With the squinty eyes and walking into the furniture. Is that it? You find that irresistible?"

"I knew I'd never be able to keep that a secret." She wrapped him in a hug.

Red put on his jacket, grabbed her hand, and walked with her to her car. Passing by his MGB, he patted it. "One day we'll tour the town again."

At least, I hope so.

Bethany dropped him off at the hospital entrance, and he made his way to the doctors' café. When he arrived, he heard Dr. Kedar's greeting.

"Red, I have already been through the line. I got a sandwich for you. I took a guess that since you usually get ham and cheese, you would be up for it today."

"How thoughtful." Red heaved a sigh of relief that he didn't have to navigate the food court, dodging people and selecting food he could barely see.

Dr. Kedar guided him to a private corner table, and Red took the seat across from him.

"How's Christina today?" he asked. He waited for an answer, but he heard nothing. "Dr. Kedar…?"

"Yes, Red." His friend spoke in a hushed tone.

"Is she all right?"

"Yes. She's wonderful. I will take you up to NICU later." Dr. Kedar cleared his throat. "But before that, we have much to talk about."

He launched into a technical explanation of all that had transpired with the tank and the life-support equipment since Red had been gone. Then he added his opinion about the best approach for dealing with the many media inquiries.

"Red, I want you back on Monday, if you are ready."

Red had sat quietly, taking it all in. Now he asked Dr. Kedar a question. "Since we can grow the early embryos in a dish, and now that you've gotten mechanical support successful back at even seventeen weeks, do you think we'll ever close the gap?"

"You mean totally raise human beings outside the womb?"

"Yes."

"Of course that is always a question. And anything developed for good can be used unethically, so no doubt that will be a matter of concern. I do think someday it could happen. But I am convinced that the optimal way is how God designed it, a marvelous engineering of complexity and beauty."

Red paused. *Did he say God? What in the world…*

"We built the APP so we can help people like Phil and Regan carry a child to term or support their baby until it can survive. With every medical advance, I am more and more convinced that humans have value and dignity from the first cell. And that is what I want you to emphasize when you handle all the calls."

Red stared, a huge smile on his face. "And that's exactly what I *want* to emphasize!"

"I know. That is why you are perfect for this job, despite the fact that you are, no doubt, restless to get back to practicing medicine. I am beginning to think your current limitation has put you right where you are supposed to be, Red."

When they had finished eating, Dr. Kedar took Red up to Christina's isolation unit, but he stopped outside.

"I have a surprise for you, Red."

"What? What is it?"

"I think you will see. If not I will tell you, but I think you will be able to see well enough."

Dr. Kedar opened the door. He kept the lights off and walked Red over to the tank. Red looked around. "Tell me… What is it?"

"How well can you see Christina, Red?"

He leaned down and stared into the solution at the tiny baby inside. "Not great, but I can see that she's still in the tank and—" His breath caught in his throat. "Dr. Kedar! Her eyes are open! She's beautiful!"

Kedar's voice trembled as well. "Yes!"

"That's amazing." He turned to his friend. "When did it happen?"

"Very early this morning. It was awesome, just awesome. And I have a question for you."

"What's that?"

"You say God can use anything, even bad things, for good. Does that include bad dreams?"

Bethany sat on her living room carpet with Red as they munched on a pizza. She reached over and gave his knee a squeeze. "How was your first day back?"

He gave her a thumbs-up. "It's wonderful to be productive again. I spent most of my time returning phone calls, talking to people about Christina's tank. I talked to a few radio stations, but mostly it was MFM physicians interested in building devices similar to what Dr. Kedar built in the lab."

"Red…" Bethany's voice quivered.

"What? What's wrong?"

"We got a referral today at the clinic from Dorie. Did you know Ophion's partner hired her back to work at the newly reorganized VIP?"

"I heard that today, yeah. Bummer."

"Red, the clinic never even closed down! That's so depressing. What about all the *babies?*"

He took her hand, cradling it in his own. "We knew that was a possible outcome, sweetheart. Dorie's a great person—a compassionate, competent physician. Yet when I tried to talk with her about the Lord not long ago, she was completely uninterested."

"So in one sense, we've failed."

Red shook his head. "No, no. I've given this a lot of thought, Bethany. Look at Dr. Kedar. He's so different now. I told you about his spiritual awakening. And think about how the initial change in Teresa Murdock came about. When it comes to these sorts of issues—the really tough heart issues—I think it's good to work through whatever channels we can, including the legal system. But people change from the inside out. They change one heart at a time, so that's where we need to focus our energy. And that's what you do, care for one person at a time at the point of greatest need."

Bethany nodded and rested her head against his arm.

"Oh! And speaking of people needing to change, this afternoon I had the most interesting call of all—from the attorney for VIP."

Bethany swallowed hard. "What did *he* want?"

"He asked for a meeting with me and Damon."

She jerked upright. "What? Are you gonna do it?"

"I'm not sure yet. I went ahead and scheduled it for two weeks from today, on December 2. Normally they wouldn't be so patient about waiting an extra week, but with Thanksgiving coming up… Besides, I wanted to meet with Lexie first, so I made an appointment to get her advice."

"What do you think she'll say?"

He shook his head. "I have no idea."

"Do you *want* to talk to Damon?"

Red leaned back against the couch. Did he? He'd been so angry at first. If he'd seen Damon then, he might well have done the man harm. But now? So much had happened, and so much of it seemed to be God at work.

He sighed. "I think so." Then he nodded. "Yeah, I do."

Lexie sat at the table pressing her fingertips together, looking every inch the legal professional. Red was glad she was on his side.

"Did you have a good Thanksgiving, Red?"

He patted his stomach. "Other than overeating, it was great. And you?"

She smiled "Yes, I could say the same." Her smile faded. "Now you know, as I said when we talked earlier, you don't have to meet with these guys. It's not too late to cancel. Are you sure about this?"

"Yes, I'm certain."

"And you're still sure you don't want to press criminal charges?"

"Yes. Based on what you said though, I reserve the right to change my mind depending on how this meeting goes."

"Based on what I said?"

"When you told me Damon had been fired, you said he'd never find another residency in this country. That pretty much convinced me. I'd like to keep him out of the hospital—and I'm speaking of his career, not his health, of course." Red chuckled.

Lexie smiled. "All right. That's your call."

"And if there's any way, I'd like to know *why* he did it. And I want an apology. Just once, I'd like to see Damon humble."

"Well, Red, you may get your chance today." She left him in the conference room adjoining her office and went to get Damon and his attorney.

Red sat humming a song that had been stuck in his head all day. When the door opened, Lexie was leading two men. The first was in his forties. The other was Damon.

Red stood as Lexie made the introductions. "Dr. Richison, this is Mr. Avers, counsel for VIP and Dr. Damon's attorney."

"Doctor." Avers nodded and extended his hand across the table. Red clasped it and shook it, working to focus his eyes on the man.

Then without an introduction, Damon stepped forward and reached out his hand. "Red."

Did he have to touch him? "Dr. Damon." Red shook it and let go.

They stood in awkward silence, until Lexie broke in. "Please, gentlemen, be seated." As she walked around the table to sit next to Red, she looked across to Avers. "You scheduled the meeting, and we are here, though I've counseled my client against it."

Avers gave a nervous laugh. "Ah! Good! We have agreement already. I counseled my client against it as well." Even he seemed to realize his attempt at humor fell flat.

Red kept his gaze fixed on Damon.

Clearing his throat, Avers started again. "My client asked to meet with you today. He has demonstrated remorse for his actions and has come to communicate those feelings—"

"Oh, is that it?" Lexie didn't even give Damon a chance to speak. "This is about demonstrating remorse so it'll sound better in court?" She turned to Red. "This is a lawyer trick. You don't have to stay here for this." She got up.

Red was still focused on Damon. "No, wait. I'd like to hear what he has to say." *I think I'm entitled to an explanation.*

"It's your choice, Red. I just don't want you to be part of a legal drama played out for a sympathetic jury."

"Thank you. I understand, but I'll stay." Red sat with his hands folded on the huge table. He leaned forward to see better and noticed, almost with amusement, that Damon had cut off his ponytail. An uneasy silence lasted several seconds.

"Red, man…" Damon's voice was low and hoarse. "I didn't mean for it to be so bad."

Red waited, but there didn't appear to be any more coming. He frowned. "Exactly what *did* you mean to happen? You had to know I'd get the virus."

"Yeah, but you know how unpredictable they are, especially diluted with the contact solution. I thought you'd get a headache, maybe even meningitis. But I didn't figure it would localize in your eyes. I-I thought the antibacterial in the solution might make it less potent, too. I didn't want to hurt you. I only meant to scare you. I figured you'd be out of action at the most for a couple of weeks."

Anger choked Red, but he fought it down. *Lord, help me.* "But why? What did I do to *you?*"

Damon ignored the question. "I just wanted to tell you that I didn't mean for it to get so bad, man. No hard feelings, okay?"

Red shook his head. Was this guy for real? No hard feelings? He sat back in his chair. "No, that's not gonna do it for me, Damon. You trashed my apartment, too, right? What were you looking for?"

"Nothing. It was just a warning."

Avers turned to his client. "I think you've said what you needed to say. There's nothing to be gained by dredging up old—"

"Dredging up? We're talking about my *life!*" He looked back at Damon. "Let me lay it out for you: I've decided not to press criminal charges."

Mr. Avers's eyes grew wide, then he smiled. Damon sat motionless.

Red continued. "The hospital and the medical board, well, that's another matter. But I'm dropping the criminal case. So Dr. Damon, I think you can at least muster up the courage to answer a few questions honestly."

Damon stared at Red, and his voice softened. "Yes, I trashed your apartment. It was a message to back off, to leave VIP alone. I've got debts to pay, and you were messing with my livelihood. But you wouldn't let it go. You kept pressing."

"So it was about the clinic?"

Damon's nod was stiff. "Right. Nothing personal."

"Nothing *personal?*" Red ran his fingers through his hair.

Damon shook his head and looked away. "I made a mistake, man. It went too far. I thought you'd get sick, but I figured you were strong, you could weather it."

Red shook his head. He leaned forward and lowered his voice. "You violate my privacy by breaking into my place. Then you wipe out my eyesight, nearly kill me, and take away my livelihood. And it's a mistake, nothing personal? I'm strong, I can weather it?"

"It got out of hand—"

"*I'll* say! So tell me, was this *your* idea, or did Ophion put you up to it?"

Damon froze; Avers snapped to attention and glared at his client. "No way you're answering that! Your career is still on the line, and you're not getting involved in that. Don't say another word."

"Come on, Damon. It's only fair that you answer the question. Was Ophion behind this?"

Without a word Damon, looking straight at Red, gave the slightest of nods. Then he turned to Avers. "Okay, I won't say a word." He turned back to Red. "It was just a business decision."

"Yeah, business for you, maybe." Red sighed and shook his head.

"I'm sorry, Red."

Red took a deep breath. Damon finally sounded sincere. *That's better.*

"You've got to believe me."

Red nodded. "Thank you. I'm angry, Damon. You've caused me a lot of pain—pain that I still endure every day. And though you didn't ask and though it doesn't even feel like it at the moment, I choose to forgive you. Every day, when I want to be bitter, I'm going to make the choice to forgive."

Damon furrowed his brows and stared at Red.

Lexie stood. "I think we're finished here."

THIRTY-FIVE

Red walked into the neonatal nurses' station where Dr. Kedar sat working on charts. "You paged?"

Dr. Kedar smiled at him. "Yes, Red. It seems I have hardly seen you for the past few weeks."

"They don't let me take night call or operate yet, so I staff the clinics and cover the in-house patients pretty much every day. I'm the perpetual house mouse—I put out all the little fires." He grinned. "But hey, I'm not complaining! It's good to be back."

"No doubt. How is the eyesight coming along?"

"Probably 80 percent back, maybe more. And with the Coke bottles here"— he pointed to his glasses—"pretty good visual acuity. Still fuzzy in the peripheral fields, like looking through a straw, but at least the straw's getting bigger in diameter. And it's better than when it was like a sieve."

"Wonderful. And by the way, you did a marvelous job handling the public relations on Christina."

"Thank you. I really enjoyed the opportunity. They treated me like a world-renowned researcher, like you."

Dr. Kedar smiled. "It has been an astounding few weeks, going from having her in the news nightly to where her survival is pretty much accepted. Anyway, I wanted you to help me here. Today is a red-letter day for her."

"Really?" Excitement filled Red. He'd forgotten! "Is this the day?"

"Yes. Today she gets liberated from the tank." Dr. Kedar's grin was wide. "My niece is going to dry dock."

"I'd be thrilled to help! A whopping twenty-seven weeks—"

"Almost twenty-eight." Dr. Kedar beamed.

"Okay, let me make arrangements with L and D. With Christmas coming up this weekend, they're having their staff party this afternoon, but I'd rather be here."

"Great. I will call Regan and let her know so that she and Phil can witness the big event."

Red folded his arms. "You must be pretty confident then."

"Yes, all the physiologic parameters are encouraging, and if Christina cannot tolerate the oxygen mist, I can always submerge her again and let the device take over for another week."

Several hours later Red joined Dr. Kedar at the scrub sink as they prepared to enter Christina's unit. Red nodded to Phil and Regan as they entered, and then he noticed the cameraman and all the equipment.

He angled a look at Dr. Kedar. "More news coverage?"

Dr. Kedar surprised Red when he smiled. "Yes, they will be rolling tape through this whole process. My wife is putting together a story for next month on the sanctity of life. She has been tracking Christina's progress, filming from the early stages."

The sanctity of life... Red smiled. Christina wasn't the only one who'd come a long way.

Dr. Kedar introduced Red to the cameraman, and then continued. "We have documentation of all the major developments—at least the good days."

"So should we watch our conversation?" Red teased.

"No worries. They are not doing sound. They will cut and splice to make an effective documentary. It is for the anniversary of *Roe v. Wade*. You recall that decision was made here in town at the Dallas courthouse, and they acknowledge the date in the news each January. Yvonne will report from the steps outside the building. She wants to do a story, amidst the usual protest marches and rhetoric on both sides, to underscore the inconsistency in the age-of-viability argument. Those who say a baby is not human until it can survive outside the womb now have new information. In a thirty-year timespan, this magical humanity point has shifted from thirty-two weeks to Christina, who has proved viable at seventeen weeks."

It thrilled Red to hear him talk this way. *We didn't get VIP shut down, but we've clearly been a part of something even bigger.* "That should be quite a story." Red pulled on his gloves and awaited instructions.

Dr. Kedar smiled at Regan and Phil, then assessed the scene in front of him. "I have been circulating surfactant in the tank fluid for two weeks now," he told Red.

"To help her lungs handle breathing."

"Right. And I am expecting a smooth transition here. Her lungs should be ready to function on their own. So here is how it should work. I will release this valve"—he pointed to the tank as he spoke—"and I will bring the fluid level down without disturbing Christina. Then we will monitor her blood gases to be sure the oxygen saturation remains stable."

Red nodded. "I'll do my best."

Dr. Kedar handed him a foam wedge. "I will need you to slide this under her so that her head is down. Suction her secretions from the nose and mouth, and hold the oxygen mist over her face as she begins to breathe. If all goes well, I will wean her off the machine and she will be ready for the next stage—life in a normal incubator."

Red smiled and clasped his hands together. "Got it."

The nurse had opened the equipment and now stood ready, prepared to hand the oxygen mask and the suction catheter to Red as needed.

Dr. Kedar looked at Christina. "You are growing up so fast, little one. Soon you will be walking." He glanced over at Red and then motioned to the nurse. "I probably could have done it alone with Devona here, but I thought you would like to have a part."

"I wouldn't have missed it!"

"Besides, I can always use extra skilled hands, and it looks better on camera if we have lots of doctors and nurses."

Red smiled. "Of course, with these special, ultrathick glasses, I look more like the Nutty Professor."

"Perhaps." Dr. Kedar grinned. "But you do make me look better by comparison."

Red laughed. He looked over at the camera and noticed the film was now rolling.

As the fluid level in the tank fell, Christina's face broke the surface and she opened her eyes. Everyone in the room gasped. Red instinctively reached in and began stroking her arm. He noticed her heart rate elevated slightly, evidencing minimal distress, and her breathing motion picked up reflexly. He slid the wedge under her tiny body, now weighing just over two pounds.

After Red suctioned the secretions from Christina's nose and mouth, Devona handed him the oxygen mist. Dr. Kedar's eyes moved back and forth between the readouts on his machines and Christina's tiny form.

"Her color looks good." Red hoped he was reading all the signs correctly.

Dr. Kedar nodded and smiled.

"Great!" Regan sounded thrilled.

Red looked back to see her dabbing her eyes, an expression of joy mixed with fear on her face. *She's been through so much, Lord. Thank You for this miracle.*

He turned back to Christina, cleared the secretions, and noted that her air exchange improved.

"Her respirations seem unlabored." Dr. Kedar gave Red an approving nod. Dr. Kedar had worked diligently to keep conditions in the tank much as they would be in the womb, so Christina's normal color had been slightly grayish blue. Now, with the oxygen mist in her lungs, she began to pink up—first her torso, and then out to her tiny fingers and toes.

Red shook his head. "Amazing."

"She *is* beautiful." Devona looked first at the child and then to the adoring parents, who now stared at their tiny daughter in joyous disbelief.

Dr. Kedar studied his monitors and noted the oxygen saturation rising. "Her lungs are working. Excellent."

The room was so quiet that Red could hear the machines in the next room. Christina breathed on her own for the next fifteen minutes, and finally Dr. Kedar turned down the oxygen coming through the machine hooked to the umbilical cord remnant. Over the course of the next hour, the doctors monitored her, but she handled the transition comfortably.

Dr. Kedar turned to Red, a huge grin on his face. "Uneventful!"

"We *like* uneventful."

"Yes, we do!" Dr. Kedar turned back to begin weaning the baby off the heart-lung part of his invention, which he left as a safety backup, so that it began to function as a glorified IV.

Red continued to keep the baby's nose and mouth clear of secretions, but her respiration was smooth and regular, with no retractions and no evidence on the cardiac monitor of any distress.

Dr. Kedar turned to his sister, and when he spoke, his voice was choked with tears. "Would you like to hold your daughter?"

"I thought you'd never ask!" Regan and Phil stepped closer to the tank.

Dr. Kedar lifted Christina several inches, and Regan slipped her hands under the tiny baby, who was still connected to the machine at her umbilical cord. "Finally, I get to hold you!" She cooed at her child, and the only other sound in the room was an occasional sniffle.

"Now *that* will make some fine footage!" Red glanced over at the camera.

"I have no doubt that Yvonne will edit the last hour down to a few seconds, but it could not have gone more smoothly," Dr. Kedar said. "Now we just wait and watch."

"When do you think you might move her to the regular incubator?"

"At least twenty-four hours. Once I take out the umbilical artery connections, I do *not* want to have to come back."

Regan handed the baby to Phil, who wore a goofy grin as he held her. A few minutes later, he placed her back on the foam. The heat from the overhead warmer kept the tank environment stable, even in the absence of the saline fluid.

The doctors sat back and watched Christina. She was tiny, beautiful and pink, breathing unaided, with her own heart sustaining her. From time to time she would open her eyes, move her lips, or stretch her arms and legs.

Eventually Devona excused herself.

Rob, the cameraman, took down his equipment. "Thanks, Doc. Mrs. Kedar should be pleased."

"Thank you for participating in this miracle. Have you ever seen anything like it?" It was half-question, half-declaration.

Rob shook his head, "Nope. That is one tiny kid."

"Tiny?" Dr. Kedar's smile gave the lie to his indignation. "She is *huge*—more than double her birth weight!"

"Man, I've thrown back bass twice that size," Rob said with a laugh. He pulled off the gown that covered his street clothes, and then he took his equipment and left the unit.

Phil departed as well, to return to work. When Regan went to get a drink, the doctors were left alone with Christina.

Red stared down at the sleeping child. "This is a giant milestone."

"Indeed, medically"—Dr. Kedar looked at Red—"and personally. I must thank you and little Christina for helping me to find the truth. This will be a most special Christmas for me."

Red smiled and leaned forward, crossing his arms on the sidewall of the tank, just above Christina.

"And I want to thank you for recommending Believers' Fellowship," Dr. Kedar continued. "Yvonne and I have been attending for the last few weeks, and I am learning so much. I have also noticed a number of my colleagues are members there. I was a little surprised."

"We have lots of people on staff here who believe."

"So I have discovered. Some of us have met for lunch. It has been helpful to find like-minded professionals who are further down the spiritual pathway to help guide me."

Red grinned, marveling at the words. "Dr. Kedar, you've made my day."

"Well, I have taken up half your day anyway."

Red's pager vibrated, and he looked down at it. "It's Bethany. She's meeting me for lunch in the docs' café."

"You should have seen your eyes light up when you saw that it was Lady Bethany. You two have quite a good thing going."

Red smiled. "Yeah. Let me call her, and then I've got something I'd like to show you."

"All right."

Red stepped out of the room and made the call. Then he went to the scrub area, where he had hung his white coat. He took a small box out of the pocket and then grinned at Dr. Kedar through the window. When he returned, he raised his eyebrows. "Would you like to see my surprise?"

"Certainly."

Red opened a small, white box to reveal a diamond marquis engagement ring.

Kedar's eyes widened. "My, you do have a good thing going! When are you going to ask her? Soon?"

"I wanted to wait until my eyesight was fully recovered, but that's taking longer than I'd like. Still, I wanted it to be special. I was hoping to drive her out to the lake in my MG, back to where we had our first picnic together, but it's been so cold."

"Ah, but the weather is beautiful today. And I had heard you were driving again."

Red pointed to his thick glasses. "Yes, with the aid of these. But I have to work until seven."

"H'm." Dr. Kedar pulled off his gloves and walked with Red toward the door of the NICU. Through the glass, they noticed Bethany approaching.

"I guess the L and D nurse gave away our position," Dr. Kedar said under his breath.

"No, I told her we were up here and that Christina was out of the tank. Is it okay if she takes a look?"

"Certainly. Everyone should get a look at my niece. But, eh…"

"What?"

"Are you not going to put away the box?"

"Oops!" Red tucked it back into his pocket and pushed open the door. "Hi, Bethany." He could feel the heat on his face.

Dr. Kedar took mercy on him and stepped forward. "Hello, Bethany, so nice to see you again. Would you like to have a look at the most beautiful baby in the world?"

"Of course!" Bethany's smile was engaging. "I understand she's passed another milestone."

Dr. Kedar's pride was undeniable. "Of course she has. But what else would you expect from our wonderful little Christina?"

The three walked over to the tank and stood gazing at the baby. Christina lay tipped down to assist with secretions, but she was pink and breathing contentedly.

"I can hardly believe my eyes." Bethany stared at her, clearly enchanted. "She's so much bigger than last time. Her head's the size of a tennis ball!"

"She's huge!" Red exclaimed.

"And beautiful." After a few minutes, Bethany pointed to the umbilical cord still connected to the machine. "When does she get a belly button?"

"I plan to test her tomorrow, and if she passes, I will take it out." Dr. Kedar gave his niece an adoring look. Then he broke his focus. "Well! You two must be off." He looked at Red. "Where are you taking your date? It's a beautiful day; why not go for a drive?"

Red laughed. Dr. Kedar couldn't have set the stage better if he'd tried. "Yeah. Unfortunately, I have to w—"

"I hear the lake is nice."

Red hesitated, and when he saw a twinkling gleam in Dr. Kedar's eyes, he suddenly understood.

"It's one of my favorite places," Bethany said. "There's a special spot where we like to go. But Red has to—"

Dr. Kedar held out his hand to Red. "How about if you give me your pager, and I will cover the house for you until you return. Take your time. I will be in the hospital for the next few hours anyway."

Overwhelmed by the generosity of this gesture, Red grasped Dr. Kedar's hand, then gave him his beeper. "Thanks." They exchanged knowing looks, then Red turned to Bethany. "Maybe we could stop by the store. I'm thinking a picnic."

Blissfully clueless, Bethany took Red's arm and looped her own through it. "That sounds perfect, Red. Just perfect."

Six Months Later

"Dr. Richison, you look downright smart." Dr. Kedar shook Red's hand.

"You're not looking too bad yourself, sir."

"Thanks. I am sorry I could not make the big dinner last night."

"No problem. I understand you had an emergency."

"Yes, but all is well now. We had a patient whose water broke at thirty weeks, but the baby is fine."

Red smiled. "I'm honored that you're here at all."

"I would not have missed it, and the honor is mine. So how is your recovery coming along?"

Dr. Kedar looked into his eyes, and Red felt the wonder that he could see his friend's face almost as clearly as before he'd been ill. *Thanks, Lord.* "Ever since the corneal transplant, I'm seeing better all the time. And I just found out on Thursday that I should be back assisting with major surgeries in another three months."

Dr. Kedar clasped his hands. "I am so happy for you—and for me!"

Red heard the music swell and saw one of his men motion to him that it was time. Dr. Kedar straightened the tie on his tux, and they all lined up and walked out together.

Red smiled at his family, then at Teresa and John, who sat beaming with their newly adopted twins. He spotted Dawn Spencer sitting with the clinic staff. He spotted Dorie with a group of residents. Regan and Phil were in the back with little Christina. Red shook his head. Hard to believe that tiny infant was now eight months old.

Red waited as Bethany's sisters walked by, followed by Heather, who smiled broadly at him, then took her place and turned to watch her best friend.

Red noticed Mrs. Fabrizio dabbing her eyes, and he gave thanks for the healing that had begun between her and Bethany during the weekend when they had flown to Seattle to "meet the family."

The music swelled with the familiar notes, and, finally, there she was.

Red caught his breath as he took in—with nearly perfect vision—the sight of Bethany in the doorway. His dazzling bride on the arm of her father.

He watched, nearly overcome with joy as his wife-to-be—God's precious gift to him—made her stately walk down the aisle. When her father kissed her cheek, Red took her hand in his and didn't let it go during the entire service. It seemed like mere minutes before the minister made his pronouncement and nodded to him that it was time.

Holding her in his gaze, Red pulled back Bethany's veil and took her face tenderly in his hands. "I love you," he whispered. Then he sealed his vows with a kiss.

For information on topics covered in this book:

aspire2.com—The authors' Web site provides information about their publications. In addition, they feature articles (often with links to other sites) on bioethical topics such as abortion recovery, sanctity of life, infertility, pregnancy loss, end-of-life issues, stem cell research, and cloning.

pregnancycenters.org—The Pregnancy Centers Online Web site provides information on how to find a Pregnancy Resource Center near you. It also tells how to get help after abortion.

cbhd.org—The Center for Bioethics and Human Dignity exists to help individuals and organizations address the pressing bio-ethical challenges of our day.

hannah.org—The Hannah's Prayer Web site provides information and support for couples facing infertility, pregnancy loss, and adoption issues.